The Reeds

The Reeds

a novel

Arjun Basu

Copyright © Arjun Basu, 2024

Published by ECW Press
665 Gerrard Street East
Toronto, Ontario, Canada M4M 1Y2
416-694-3348 / info@ecwpress.com

All rights reserved. No part of this publication may be reproduced, stored in a retrieval system, or transmitted in any form by any process — electronic, mechanical, photocopying, recording, or otherwise — without the prior written permission of the copyright owners and ECW Press. The scanning, uploading, and distribution of this book via the internet or via any other means without the permission of the publisher is illegal and punishable by law. This book may not be used for text and data mining, AI training, and similar technologies. Please purchase only authorized electronic editions, and do not participate in or encourage electronic piracy of copyrighted materials. Your support of the author's rights is appreciated.

Cover design: David A. Gee

This is a work of fiction. Names, characters, places, and incidents either are the product of the author's imagination or are used fictitiously, and any resemblance to actual persons, living or dead, business establishments, events, or locales is entirely coincidental.

LIBRARY AND ARCHIVES CANADA CATALOGUING IN PUBLICATION

Title: The Reeds : a novel / Arjun Basu.

Names: Basu, Arjun, 1966- author.

Identifiers: Canadiana (print) 20240357876 | Canadiana (ebook) 20240364635

ISBN 978-1-77041-743-4 (softcover)
ISBN 978-1-77852-293-2 (PDF)
ISBN 978-1-77852-290-1 (ePub)

Subjects: LCGFT: Domestic fiction. | LCGFT: Novels.

Classification: LCC PS8603.A797 R44 2024 | DDC C813/.6—dc23

This book is funded in part by the Government of Canada. *Ce livre est financé en partie par le gouvernement du Canada.* We acknowledge the support of the Canada Council for the Arts. *Nous remercions le Conseil des arts du Canada de son soutien.* We would like to acknowledge the funding support of the Ontario Arts Council (OAC) and the Government of Ontario for their support. We also acknowledge the support of the Government of Ontario through the Ontario Book Publishing Tax Credit, and through Ontario Creates.

Canada Council for the Arts Conseil des arts du Canada

PRINTED AND BOUND IN CANADA

PRINTING: FRIESENS 5 4 3 2 1

Purchase the print edition and receive the ebook free.
For details, go to ecwpress.com/ebook.

In loving memory of Dipak Basu
(1937–2022)

Book One

Need

There is poetry in mini-malls.

— JONATHAN GOLD

Chapter 1

The view evolves. With each new building, with each construction crane, with each new alteration in the dynamic of the cityscape, the river recedes, that great bend of it making its way from the continent to the ocean, the flatlands limping toward the water, the dullness of the thing, changed by economic forces, by an uptick in the city's luck and the realities of the world's migration, it evolves. But the meaning of the view, the *almost* nature of it, the fact that it is almost grand, of what it announces, what it says about him, a view from a closed corner office, from *his* closed corner office, from his base, from where his power emanates, that is unalterable. And there are moments when he feels his corporate power in this view, when he has fully transformed himself into the senior executive, usually as he enters the lobby twenty-six floors below, and this new man, this new power, surges to his loins, and he can imagine pleasuring himself by the floor-to-ceiling windows, spilling his seed softly on the innocent pedestrians below, a mist of his power and import, to prove to himself that he would be capable of marking his might in that way, to be that kind of person — even if below, on the street, he would hate that kind of person — to know what that kind of power would feel like, had he the courage, which he doesn't, he does not have that kind of courage, he never has, everything he has achieved here has been an act, learned; he is not the kind of man who would ever lower his zipper to do what he thinks he'd like to do in such a manner because, in the end, he can't.

For one thing, the windows don't open.

And, more importantly, Roberto Reed is a Family Man. It is what and who he is. Except here.

He returns to his chair and feels the slight give in the spring, the status implied by the sophistication of the technology. The fact that he knows his underlings have inferior chairs.

He likes to think his office chair makes up for the view.

And then the day begins, and the reverie is behind him.

He checks his email. He walks to the door of his office and his assistant, Vachon, is there, already. It's uncanny how she knows before he does, and that is her power, over him, and they both know it. She knows him outside and in, and that is, indeed, one of the sources of her power. "When is my meeting with the new chick?" he asks.

"Fifteen minutes," Vachon says before Reed has finished. "Her name is Lemay."

"Remind me why I'm meeting her."

"You requested a meeting with her, and now you're having one."

Reed grunts. "Is she cute?"

They pause. Reed can only imagine how vile Vachon finds this version of him. She must. Vachon is short and dumpy, and Reed hired her because she was, she is, highly competent and intelligent, but also because she was, is, short and dumpy. He appreciated that she did not feel at all hindered by her appearance and still dressed fashionably. Even elegantly. He knows it's hard to find fashionable things for bodies that are not. He knows that she feels underappreciated, taken for granted, his oxygen.

He hates that he has succeeded in this place while thinking like this.

He also knows the woman with whom he is having a meeting is not only cute but bright as well. He hired her. He knows that Vachon knows this. She knows everything. She knows how he likes his coffee and when. She knows that he prefers to be alone except when he doesn't. She knows the important dates and times and names that he has forgotten. She intuits if he will forget something or if he will remember it. She understands that sometimes he will forget things on purpose just so he can speak to her, ask her about her son, who is almost finished high school, and who lives with his father. She knows where everything is. "It's 2017," she says.

"I'm aware of the year."

"You can't say some things."

"You're my safe space," he says, feigning love.

She controls the information that filters to him. And through him. She tolerates his excesses. He considers her loyalty to him one of the more pleasant mysteries of the world, the sum of a series of actions he might never understand. She knows the man outside the office. A kind man. "You have to be careful," she says.

"Do you see who's in the White House? What the English have done to themselves?" He could go on. He'd felt it recently, he'd seen it: The assholes ruled the world. Everyone was shouting. There was a surplus of anger.

"We are neither American nor British," Vachon says. Her voice is soothing. She is speaking to a child.

"That's exactly what Canada is," Reed says.

"But we're in Quebec," she says. She looks at him with a mixture of disappointment and indifference.

"I want coffee," he says.

"And after that?"

"I may want another one."

He re-enters his office and takes a deep breath. He has spent much effort giving his office status. Making it feel larger than it is, creating within it something that will be remarked upon, a space that goes beyond feng shui to herald an understanding of the philosophy of power.

He hates the rug. It is a cheap carpet trying to be a shag carpet and it is sad and tired looking. The vibrant orange pattern has turned to rust. The shag carpet at home, that's a shag carpet, that carpet is the very definition of shag, rich and deep, a source of joy. Running your hands though that thick shag is to feel a kind of life force.

Vachon returns with his coffee and she places it on a granite coaster on his desk and she looks his way, knowing he will not thank her, knowing he is incapable of gratitude, knowing that he sees gratitude as weakness. As defeat. They make eye contact, and that is enough for her. It's a game to him.

He sits again and reaches for his coffee and takes a sip. He rereads the email and closes it and opens another one. He reads it and puts his coffee down and then he selects all the unread emails and deletes them and he feels giddy with the finality of what he's done.

He declares email bankruptcy once a day. He enjoys declaring it.

He enjoys making work for others.

Vachon returns and she places a folder on his desk. "What's this?" he asks, though he knows exactly what it is. It says so in large letters right on the folder.

"This is the new hire's report. You asked her to complete one, and now it's done and here it is."

"What else?"

"She'll be here in two minutes," Vachon says. "This one is a good hire." She smiles as she turns to leave, and Reed manages a quick smile as well, at least with his eyes.

Vachon exits, and Reed reaches for the report and wonders if he should put a coffee stain on it. Optics are everything. He angles his coffee mug and allows a small stream of his Javanese Arabica blend to drip over the edge. He prefers the old-school coffee. The good coffee, he calls it. These third wave fancy coffees his younger employees drink, with names that sound like computers with feelings, taste bitter and smell worse. Good coffee is good coffee. It doesn't need improvement. The desire to make things better, even things that are good enough, is evolution's revenge.

When the promise of better exists, what you have is never good enough. He thinks that's what marketing is. What it exploits.

He presses the coffee mug down on the coaster on his desk. And then he picks it up, opens the report to a random page, and puts the mug down on the matte paper. He twirls the mug in place and then lets it sit there, and he waits for the stain to spread, to show evidence of his own industry. The meaning of who he is and that he hired this woman, this girl, because she has good hair, but also because she was rude to him and spoke her mind, and he liked that.

Vachon is back at the door, and sometimes he feels like she never really leaves that place, and he says, "What?"

"Miss Lemay is here to see you," Vachon says and she leaves, and Lemay walks in.

"Nice tie," Lemay says, standing by his desk.

He touches his tie impulsively, not that he wants to, but he does, she's flattered him, because he's already off his game, but the tie *is* nice, his wife bought it for him in Paris, it's silk and heavy with material.

Lemay stands and waits for him to invite her to sit. She is not tall, but in her pumps she's at least six feet. Her hair is dark and shiny and full, shoulder-length. Her hair astounds him. "Sit," Reed commands, and she does. She sinks into a chair that renders its occupants much smaller than he, and there is a moment's surprise on her face and then she composes herself because she has understood her boss, his games. No doubt she's been warned about the pettiness that she will have to claw through in order to achieve anything. The HR person will have told her that her ambition would need to overcome many obstacles, without naming those obstacles.

Reed closes her report and tosses it her way. "Read it to me," he says.

Lemay studies his face and registers surprise. "Excuse me?"

"Just start."

She opens the report. "Did you like it?"

"That's a stupid question."

She frowns, registering multi-level regret.

Reed leans back in his chair. He does this slowly, extravagantly, and he puts his feet up on his desk. Lemay studies his shoes, and Reed notes this. "Check out the socks," he says, and pulls up a trouser leg.

Lemay takes a look and the reality of something hits her, of Reed perhaps, a newer more crucial realization of the kind of man he is and the kind of crap she's going to have to put up with before she can make a name for herself here. Her eyes belie the resolve she came in feeling.

"The socks are British, I think," he says, admiring them. "I love stripes. I like to study the patterns of the stripes. The interplay of colours. Socks are the new ties. They're so soft, it's like my feet are in a duvet. They make me so happy, I might never need therapy."

Lemay clears her throat and puts a strand of her hair behind her ear. She sighs and steels herself.

"Don't read it, just summarize it," Reed says.

Lemay looks at him. She closes the report and puts both hands on it, like she's covering it up.

Reed sniffs the air. "Is that deodorant or perfume? I can't tell."

"Sir?"

"Some scents are so ubiquitous now. Like citrus." She is flustered, and this disappoints him. He wants her to work out. He sees genuine potential in her. "Go on. Let's hear it."

She clears her throat and straightens her back. Her spine. "This company can be more profitable with a more data-driven revenue collection model," Lemay says slowly but confidently, trying to do her job, to impress a man studying the pattern on his socks. "Not just collecting data, because we do that, but collecting it in a way that we can learn from it. Building our own operating systems, instead of the off-the-shelf software we currently use, I believe we can increase efficiencies and margins while also collecting invaluable data about our current customers. This will give us intelligence. Plus, then we have a new product we can sell as well."

"Continue," Reed says. He picks up a pen and drums it up and down a leg.

Lemay looks at the pen and she cannot remember anything else in the world. On the pen is an illustration of Betty Boop diving into an inkwell. Lemay realizes something even more profound. Each thing Reed does teaches her something new. This is like a class. He is instructing her in something, but she doesn't know what it is.

He can tell everything she is thinking and wonders if she's wasting his time or if it's the other way around.

"I have also identified five data points we are not collecting but should be."

"Your report is boring," Reed says. "It's like you're trying to put me to sleep."

"Sir?" Lemay says.

"You need to do better."

"My report suggests we could cut fifteen percent of our operating costs within twelve months. Perhaps sooner."

"If you do it in six, you'll be a fucking hero."

"Sir, did you read this report?"

"You've been here a week, Lemay, please don't ask me questions."

"Did you?"

Reed sighs. "I know what's in it. I know the answers you want to provide here. I'm like Yoda. I know things just by squinting my eyes." And he squints his eyes to make his point, and he thinks Lemay is about to cry.

Instead, she sits up, her spine so straight it could cut bread. "This is about costs and efficiency. It is everything you asked of me. It's why you hired me. It is a blueprint for the future of this department and of this company."

He yawns. "You drink decaf, don't think I haven't noticed that," he says, and he points his finger at her, and she recoils, slightly, and he knows he has won. "Go. Leave your report, and go."

Lemay flips through the report, almost as if she's reminiscing about the writing of it, the week of labour it represents, the years of schooling that made it possible, and she stops at the page with the coffee stain. She looks at Reed, and he's staring into her with laser eyes now, and Lemay smiles, finally, again, like she understands, or wants to understand. The rules. This game. She stands and hands him her report.

"Don't fuck around," he says.

"No, sir."

"Work your ass off, even if it means you don't get any dates." Reed chuckles at how inappropriate this is and that he thought it at all.

"No social life, understood."

And then there is silence, and the meeting is over. Lemay doesn't know if it's gone well or not, but she hasn't been fired, and Reed is still staring at her with a violent intensity. "Do you have a budget?"

"It's on page twenty-one."

"Send me another report. No. A memo. Let's call it a memo. Bullet points. What you need. Promise it gets done in six months" —

Lemay tries hard not to beam.

— "and I'll get it approved."

Vachon appears at the door, and Reed nods. "Miss Lemay," Vachon says, and Lemay is startled to see Vachon there. Vachon extends a hand, not to offer it, but to lead Lemay out, and Lemay moves toward the door. Vachon shuts the door behind her, and Reed is alone, in control, amazed at what he can do and who he can do it to. He walks to his window and takes in the city, thousands of people doing thousands of things all for one common purpose. He could use some Japanese fried chicken. Karaage. He's going to get some for lunch today. It's his new thing, has been for months now, but he still feels the excitement of first love. He reaches for his coffee and grabs the mug and stares at the world, a content man. And he farts.

He doesn't work to win the affection of the people under him. He has friends. More importantly, he has a family. A group of people he loves without reservation, who love him and call him Bobby. It's not just enough, it's everything. His job, as he sees it, is to extract money from people. That's the system. His year-end bonus isn't a sign of affection, there are no morals attached to the winning of a larger bonus, there is only the math. He works here because of the money and because he's belligerent in the crafting of ways to elevate his employer's prosperity.

And now he has a meeting to lead.

Vachon had placed a copy of the agenda on his desk, and he studies it and then crumples it up and tosses it in the garbage. He steps out of his office. "I'm going," he tells Vachon, and she feigns interest, and he marches toward the meeting room and he reaches for the deer antler door handle and struggles with it because it was meant to be struggled with, and he enters the room and takes his seat at the head of the table. And then there's silence. "Where's Matita?" he asks, and on cue someone struggles with the door and finally it opens, and she is on the other side, apologetic without apologizing. She enters and takes a seat next to Reed. She is thin bordering on death. "Item one," she says.

"There are no items," Reed says. He pushes the agenda away and leans forward. "I'm going to say something simple. Numbers are facts, and the facts are results. Your work *lives* in the numbers. And the numbers need to be better. Because what you do isn't open to interpretation. It's not *art*. It's math. You stick a dollar sign in front of the math and you have *business*. In this department, you create numbers. This company creates opinions, but *you*, all of you, create numbers. You might make poor dietary choices, you might be going through a divorce, or your boyfriend left, or you like fucking barnyard animals, and that's your problem, what you do in your life is your problem, but in this office, your job is about numbers. That's why our jobs are so easy. Numbers don't change. They are permanent. They have never changed. The Hindus invented the zero, the Arabs did the rest, the Chinese created an abacus. The first writing was about accounts. We have numbers. Not excuses. Other departments make excuses. Other departments enjoy the opportunity to make excuses seem plausible. We work with numbers. And numbers are facts."

He pauses and thinks about standing. But he's not sure what that would prove. He wants to do something dramatic. He remembers once, when he was first promoted, at the first meeting he ran, in this room, how he brought everyone donuts, he had coffee brought in, he was pleasant. He wanted allies, and harmony, he may have even used that word, but within a few days he had learned the truth, learned that to run a department, an important department with the sole aim of enhancing cash flow, that nice wasn't going to do anything. That math was all the nice he needed. His boss, upstairs, the CFO, didn't care about the donuts, about the quality of the coffee, about employee satisfaction. He just wanted to see the numbers.

And now Reed is this. Feared. Low scores in every anonymous employee survey. The kind of man with a trail of unflattering nicknames whispered as he strutted past his amazingly productive employees. These people had made him. Enabled him. They received substantial bonuses every year.

His system works.

Reed stands. He reaches for the paper he's pushed away and he crumples it up and tosses it to the other side of the room. "Fuck this agenda," he says. "Respect the math. That's your only job!"

He heads for the door and he opens it without trouble and he doesn't bother to close it. He walks to his office. Vachon's eyes roll north; she knows better than to ask why he's back so soon. He closes the door to his office and returns to the window. He looks out at the city. He feels a tinge of remorse for the way he has to be, for what he must do to ensure things work. For the importance he must project. The authority he must feign. He studies his reflection in the window, a man who is king of his tiny realm, even if he is not, just a duke, really, if he's being honest. And he is. He's always honest with himself. It's why he's going to enjoy a Scotch when he gets home.

A scoutmaster. He's nothing more than that. Not royalty.

A scoutmaster thinking about Japanese fried chicken.

Chapter 2

Bobby pulls his Mercedes into the driveway. The car isn't flashy — it's a dull brown, and he bought it used, but he's kept it in good condition, and he's proud of the implications of owning an old Mercedes. Abbie, his son, says it makes him look old. But Abbie is only eighteen, and Bobby thinks most eighteen-year-olds don't know much and Abbie, perhaps, even less.

The driveway slopes down slightly at first, a car length, and then it drops off, a continental shelf, toward a subterranean garage. Bobby never parks in the garage. Neither does Mimi, his wife. The window on the garage door is darkened, painted over in black. With his interest in photography, Abbie has announced his intention of clearing the garage out of the boxes of old clothes and cleaning agents and never-used sports and exercise equipment, and turning it into a darkroom, though none of his photos has ever left the digital realm, and he doesn't know anything about the alchemy of transforming film. His intention, so far, is limited to the blackened window.

Bobby grabs his leather satchel and exits the car. He studies the house, notes the creeping clematis crowding out the buckeye shrub, the sad state of the geraniums in the flower bed between the driveway and the front walk, and tries to remember to tell Mimi about it. She cares about these things. Though, lately, she hasn't had time to pay much attention to anything. Including him.

The house is large, as all the houses on this street are, all the houses in this neighbourhood; there's money here, though not obscene money, just the kind of money that no one could honestly resent, admirable money, the end point of the middle-class dream, the wealth brought on by hard work, and not luck or inheritance. A neighbourhood of accomplishment rewarded, large split-level houses surrounded by lawns, and close enough to downtown to not feel overly suburban but suburban enough to not have good restaurants. It is at that point where Montreal stops feeling like Montreal, where finding a decent baguette becomes a chore, where the rhythm of the city gives way to something more somnambulant. More English than French.

Two storeys, with a den in the basement. Five bedrooms. Three baths. Red brickwork, a gabled roof. A stone walkway. A small front- and a generous backyard, large enough that Bobby and Mimi have thought about a pool, but that just means dealing with Abbie and Dee, their daughter, and their teenage friends and pool parties and the cleanup, and, no, both Bobby and Mimi shudder when they think of that. Of their backyard and what it might become and the reality of teenage girls in bikinis, though neither of them can picture Dee in a bikini, she's too self-conscious, even for a teenage girl, and they're worried about her. They're worried about Abbie, too, but for different reasons.

Bobby studies this lawn, the lawn that his wife used to care about before the business, before her success, before that success overtook everything. It is messy, but in the manner of something that was once well mannered and was then let go, like a Hollywood starlet two months after the realization that she's too old, but not yet ready to fight her destiny because she's afraid of needles. Mimi used to tend the lawn to ignore her business, to run away from her problems, to channel her grievances; Bobby always knew he was in trouble by how much work Mimi had put into the flower beds.

He wants to hire professionals to manage the aesthetics of the place, the topiary, but Mimi will only consent to the Sicilians coming by in their red pickup trucks to mow the lawn, and so the lawn is impeccable, front and back, while everything else goes to waste, distressed like once-fashionable jeans. Salvatore, the head gardener, implores Bobby, at every opportunity, to allow them to replace the flowers, to fix things, to touch them, but Bobby says "Mimi," and Salvatore knows what he means because he fears her, he has tasted her wrath and it's not something he wants to taste again.

Bobby puts the key in the door and opens it and places his satchel on a small bench by the closet. Mimi found the bench at a yard sale in the Laurentians and had it reupholstered by her guy, a Swiss retiree who lives on the first floor of a triplex next to the shuttered electronics store near the highway exit in Ville Saint-Pierre, and it looks simple but in a kind of majestic way, with purple velour cushions on top of chipped stained wood, cut solid and square. Bobby hates the thing; he does not share Mimi's taste in furniture, but this is her thing, everything is her thing, and he does not have the desire to invest the energy in replacing any of the furniture.

The house overflows with stuff; Mimi used to make ugly stuff her business. She tried the bricks-and-mortar route and for almost a decade, ever since the kids were off in school, she tried to make it work. She didn't listen to Bobby's criticisms of the strip mall she chose to house her business, its lack of traffic or of an anchor store, or even a good grocery store, or the fact that almost everyone shopping at the mall was old and already owned their own kitsch, a word Mimi always resented, because she wasn't selling kitsch, never was, she was selling collectibles and antiques and homeware, found objects that she knows others want, and then elevated that. She started in figurines and ended up in Danish teak, objects that were *objets*, she taught herself about furniture, she did the work, she went to the shows, she travelled, and she's moving that stuff now online. She's become an important seller of mid-century modern furniture, runs the kind of place that magazines and other websites describe with overused words like *hidden* and *gem* and *hidden gem*. But the store itself was a place to fill your middle-class house or student pad or bachelor apartment, and Bobby needed to support her, not criticize.

Especially not now. Not when all of Mimi's instincts have been proven correct. Not when her dismal retail space with its criminally low rent is only a front for a back warehouse staffed by immigrants shipping goods to people just like Mimi. Not when Mimi knows what her customers need, her tribal sense of taste. Mimi has taken something she knows nothing about — the internet — and used it to become a minor baroness, the kind always ignored on peerage lists but always there, in the corner, royal by association, or marriage, or by the happenstance of birth, or, today, fodder for low-level gossip and, perhaps, reality television.

She is becoming something else; her business has gone from curio to desirable, and Bobby's fear is what happens next. What if she becomes someone else as well? Because she lives her work. She *is* her work.

Her low overhead in a hard luck strip mall that smells vaguely mouldy and of cheap plastic and whatever powder or ointment the aged put on their skin has been a salvation to her, to her business, to a business that insists on lots of space and cheap labour and a lack of caring about certain things while obsessively caring about only one kind of thing. Once, Mimi didn't know anything about a spreadsheet or a computer or about selling anything to anyone that mattered.

He smells Mimi's cooking. She is home and cooking, and his first thought is: She's cheating on me. Then that thought is gone, and he realizes that why she is cooking matters less than the fact that she is, that the house smells of her brand of fusion cooking, "for our fusion family" she always says, a little west a little east, a little south a little north. She taught the children geography through spices and the panoply of noodles in the pantry: Abbie still thinks of noodles becoming spaghetti by way of Marco Polo. He knows that tomatoes and potatoes are native to South America. He knows the chicken is from Southeast Asia. He knows about the origins of pepper (India) and apples (Central Asia), that hamburgers are not German and neither are frankfurters. Mimi has taught Abbie that food is culture and that everything else, even language, is a construct of the marketplace.

Dee has always seemed embarrassed to know any of this. Or to resent that she does.

Bobby removes his shoes and heads to the bedroom to change out of his armour, to complete his transformation, to remove the antagonisms of the day and throw them in the laundry hamper.

"Do we have wine?" Mimi calls out. She wants wine; she wants to announce something, and she wants to have a drink announcing it. Abbie won't care, he's so into the opposite of what makes her happy, but Dee, she worries about Dee. She tries not to. She tries to remember what it was like to be a teenage girl, but the world is too different, her reality was too different. Dee lives in a world where girls start shaving their pubic hair the moment it sprouts. Mimi worries for her daughter more than she thought she ever would, about her daughter's difference, about Abbie's as well, about the perception of her family, the oddness of it, and it drives her to an unpleasant amount of distraction.

Abbie and Dee are both adopted. Mimi had never wanted children, and Bobby convinced her that adoption was a kind of compromise, a mid-point, and a way to perhaps help the world, to shelter some unwanted, unfortunate souls.

Abbie is from Ghana. Bobby and Mimi travelled to an orphanage in Accra, and Bobby became ill, and Mimi fell in love with Abbie immediately, and they named him Abena, which is West African in origin and also recalls Mimi's father's name, Akito, and once Abbie had been brought to Montreal, Mimi and Bobby knew they would need a girl to complete their family, and the paperwork was started, and two years later they found themselves in another orphanage, this one in a city outside of Mumbai, where they were presented a tiny girl, whom they named Devandhra, because they had seen the name in a local paper, and Mimi had noted how lovely it sounded. Bobby had become ill in India as well, an anecdote that felt safe, a family heirloom, until it wasn't, and everyone grew tired of its telling.

Bobby enters the kitchen dressed in jeans and a T-shirt, and he kisses his wife. She slaps his ass with a spatula. "Thank god that's silicon," he says, but Mimi is too busy sautéing noodles and onions. "We have wine," he says, and Mimi cracks an egg into the noodles and starts stirring vigorously. "What's the occasion?" Bobby asks finally, and Mimi puts up a finger, and he waits and has to remember to breathe because his wife seems excited about something, he can tell just by the sheer effort she is putting into folding the egg into the noodles.

"I have passed a milestone," Mimi says. She looks at him now, and she lets out a sexy growl.

"Are you calling a press conference?" Bobby reaches behind the counter and produces a bottle of white and places it in the fridge.

"Silly."

"It's that big?"

"It's this big," Mimi says, pointing to the food she's making.

"Can I retire?"

Mimi feels like breaking into song. She knows he's asking facetiously, but, yes, maybe he can start thinking about retirement. Bobby's worked long enough, and he hates his job, and what has the slog given him? Materially, it has worked for him, for the family; he has provided, or, as he puts it, he has done his duty. She would never tell him this, but he must know that one day her success will engender a discussion that will be as uncomfortable as it will be liberating. They will discuss finances and quality of life and happiness. Her happiness versus his. Their collective happiness. He will have to say out loud what they both know to be true, and how he handles this will delineate their future, will map out the survival of the family. But that's a big, big discussion, and she doesn't know if he is up to it. "You'll retire when you're old," she says.

Mimi attacks the noodles once more. She shakes the wok and grabs the handle and gives the food a professional-looking flip. Bobby retreats down the carpeted steps to the sunken living room and seats himself on the red couch, a sexy Italian sectional, and leans his head back. The day is still with him, he could use a drink, but Mimi wants to open some wine, and he can't mix Scotch with wine. He shuts his eyes and tries some of the hippy-dippy breathing exercises Dee always wants to share with him, *it's better than alcohol,* she says, always, and he never does them. Not because he doesn't think they'll work, but because the advice is coming from Dee, and she's too young to know that things can be better than alcohol. But he feels shame for always thinking this of her, for dismissing her ideas on the basis of her age. For thinking it, even. And he makes a point to show her he can do this. He can try. Being a father is about appearing to care even when you don't, he thinks, or is that love? He's not so sure. Perhaps it's both, or perhaps fatherhood is love and nothing more. But Dee is a sixteen-year-old girl, and her advice is substandard, that's the word he thinks of, and this makes him feel more shame. Even adults give substandard advice, and so Dee's age shouldn't mean anything to him; she's his daughter, and he loves her.

Mimi is humming now, loudly; she's in a tremendous mood. She plates the noodle dish and opens the fridge and takes out a stainless steel bowl of chicken breast marinating in spices and vinegar and she dumps the contents onto a cutting board and she chops the chicken up expertly. She cleans the wok in the sink and returns it to the burner and the water hisses in the heat and burns off. She watches the beads of water pool in the centre and vanish, magical mushrooms of smoke rising and disappearing faster and faster, and when all of the water is gone, she pours in some peanut oil and tosses in a handful of garlic and ginger and then the chicken and she's back at it with the spatula, stir-frying vigorously.

She can't wait. She can't wait to reveal what has happened to her family. She can't wait for the moment when Bobby realizes the pressure is no longer on him. This is her gift to him. Her announcement is not about her, it's about him. She thinks this and laughs.

Of course it's about her.

She plates the chicken. It is done. She opens the heating drawer at the base of the oven and in it goes. "I'm doing so fine," she sings to a tuneless nothing. This lack of talent, this negation of voice, was one of the things that endeared Bobby to her, an entertaining part of the genesis story that brought a man named Roberto to a woman named Manami, her awful voice attempting Helen Reddy's "I Am

Woman" in a karaoke bar in the basement of a shabby convention hall in Paris. They always possessed an unbeatable genesis story, a kind of topper in their early days of boasting and explaining themselves, their existence as a couple. The moment when love splashed over them and kept going until they happily drowned in it.

"Where are the kids?" she calls out, half out of exasperation. A part of her doesn't care because she knows they won't. Abbie has his own thing, and Dee is unimpressed by money in a way that her middle-class upbringing allows her to be.

Bobby tries to calculate the cost of one finger of Scotch in relation to the wine he will soon consume.

Mimi wonders whether or not she should add a vegetable. She worries her meal lacks balance. And Dee has been so awkward with meat lately.

Bobby is thinking a finger of Scotch won't craft collateral damage.

Mimi decides the broccoli is a good simple choice, and she opens the fridge and fishes it out of the crisper drawer.

Bobby makes a firm commitment to one finger of Scotch. He ends up with two fingers.

The front door opens and it's Dee. Both of her parents can tell this just by the heaviness of her step. Dee is small, petite even, but her step is that of some giant long-extinct thing. No one else in the family has locomotion so influenced by gravity. "Hi . . ." she calls out, but by the end of the syllable her voice is already trailing off, she's saying this out of habit, and not necessarily to initiate conversation.

Bobby comes into the front hall cradling his Scotch. "Hey, DeeDee," he says, but when he leans forward to offer a kiss, she's already past him and thumping her way up the stairs, toward her bedroom.

She runs into her room and closes the door and drops her bags and drops herself onto her bed. She buries her face in her pillows and she's thinking, thinking, she's been thinking this thing for weeks now, and she wants to continue thinking it because thinking means she doesn't have to do anything about what's being thought. She turns over and stares at the ceiling. She slides her phone out of her back pocket and checks her text messages and smiles and responds to a message and puts the phone down next to her. She picks it up and taps an app and then she turns on the stereo on her dresser and turns up the volume and she doesn't hear what's playing. She doesn't care. It's too loud to think. She likes that. She's been using words like *complicated* a lot recently; it's this word that's filling her head now, and she hates when things are complicated, she much prefers simplicity, she prefers just a voice and a guitar, or a piano, to a full band. She doesn't much like her mother's cooking, it's all too fussy and spicy and full of flavour for her, the opposite of simple. When her mother sticks to Japanese, it's simple. Her mother's miso soup is clean and simple. But she rarely cooks Japanese.

Dee's room is simple. Her walls have never been adorned with posters or pages cut out of magazines or printed off the web. She has a smart white vase, something her mother bought for her in New York, on her dresser; it holds a single flower. A carnation. A photo of her family on the dresser. The small desktop stereo. A hamper for her laundry. She doesn't even own many clothes. Never mind that she doesn't like most of the things people wear, she just doesn't like clothes. She doesn't see the big deal.

She reaches for her phone and turns off the stereo. She can hear her mother cooking, humming tunelessly, she definitely has something to say. Dee can tell. Why else would she even be home at this hour?

She gets up off her bed and walks over to her closet and takes off her shirt and stares at herself in the mirror. She removes her bra and takes in her top half, the unimpressiveness of it, and she hates that she does this to herself, the self-criticism, that she cares about so little, but she cares that her nipples are off-centre, that they curve up, that this bothers her, and it bothers her that it bothers her. It bothers her that she has never liked her breasts. That when they started growing in, she felt fear and disappointment but never . . . joy. And she also realizes she sees them differently now, as something sexualized, and that she is perhaps a bit too old to have never exposed them to anyone sexually, that they have never been held and kissed and licked, and this is really what bothers her most, that she wants to share them with someone and that she hates them at once. She stares at them and then covers them, slowly, and she hates that, too, and she sighs and thinks about laughing, but she's too sensitive for that, for finding anything here funny. She wishes she could laugh.

She stomps to her dresser and opens a drawer full of white T-shirts in various cuts and puts one on. She knows her father will fight with himself over whether or not to ask her to wear a bra, about the propriety of it. Abbie will tell her to put on a bra without looking, and her mother will tell her, once again, about the nice lady at the shop in the mall, an old lady with a way of making everyone feel at ease about buying lingerie, about how she can talk other old women through the pros and cons of lacey underthings, how she always brings up her native Belgium, and the depravations of the war, or how she used to dance, and before you know it, you've bought a bra you don't need, but chances are it's not white or cream or something boring. At least it's a sexy bra.

Downstairs, Bobby sits on the floor in the living room, on the lush orange shag, nursing the Scotch because he's not going to pour himself another one, he's happy with the fumes. With his free hand, he rubs the carpet, caressing it, drawing patterns, losing himself in its well-groomed depths. He leans back against the couch; he's never liked it but he also long ago stopped arguing with Mimi about what goes in the house. It is her house. Even though he's now home more than she is, this is her house, and it is full of her stuff. The house is an extension not of an aesthetic but of her business, and in that sense, it is an extension of who she is, and this is fine with Bobby. He has done his part. He had bought the house. He had helped when his help was most needed, and during this time the house became hers in the same way that he once considered the family his, though that is not something he would ever admit. Out loud.

He thinks about the email he didn't delete. The hieroglyphics of office talk. He takes a gentle sip of his Scotch.

> *From: Lamontagne*
> *Reed. Meeting re new hire big deal my office 9h15.*

He has replayed this over and over, and it makes him ill. Lamontagne never wants to see him because they have nothing to say to each other, nothing to share or plan or improve or negate. One man is superior to the other by way of responsibility, hierarchy, a paycheque. They may share similar goals, but the goals are understood. The contract Reed abides by ensures a lack of communication, a gulf, made more possible by his being on another floor, a lower floor, a physical nod to hierarchies and rules and customs.

big deal

What is this about, who is it about, and why is it a *big deal*? And what does it have to do with him?

His work is easy in the end, when it is deconstructed and laid out, like parts of heavy machinery, on a pristine floor. The demands made of him are simple, or he has always thought so, simple and transparent. The mystery of his work, of his company's work, lies not with him or even within him, and so this talk of a big deal, even some cryptic allusion to something larger than himself, is worrisome. It means an event meant to belittle, both him and his work, and an invitation to an understanding that is beyond him, that should be beyond him because it is beyond normal expectations. Bobby is not in line for anyone's job. He is where he is. He does what he does. He generates profit. The company thanks him with a comfortable chair. He loves that chair.

He downs the Scotch and crawls over to the bar cart and pours himself another. Two fingers. And he studies his drink, the amber of it, and he thinks of the meaning of that email and how much it has bothered him, only he's realizing this now, the implications implicit in it, and how he doesn't like it, the foreboding in those few words, and he is upset he didn't realize it before. He sips his drink. And the front door opens and it is Abbie. He stands to greet his son.

Abbie throws off his shoes and sees his father. "Hi, Dad," he says, and smiles and runs up the stairs to his room. "I'll be down in a sec," he shouts down.

"Abbie!" Mimi yells from the kitchen, but he's already gone, up to his room. "Get the kids, dinner's ready," she says.

I don't understand, he thinks. He doesn't understand much lately, the whirr of the world, both inside the office and out. He's been thinking about the velocity of things lately.

He puts his glass down on a teak side table and hikes up the stairs. He knocks on Dee's door and then he knocks on Abbie's. "Dinner," he says, and right now, for all that is around them, this might be a scene from a sitcom from the '50s. Except the world is in colour and no one is wearing a cardigan.

Dee opens her door. "I'll be down in a sec," she says and closes her door.

"Abbie," he says, this time with some authority. "Dee."

Dee exits her room and thumps down the stairs. Bobby can hear his son unpacking his backpack, clicking things, the sounds of a young man being industrious and forgetting the world around him. He hears Abbie turn on his computer. "We're eating, just so you know," he tells his son through the door. "And your mother has something important to announce."

Abbie opens the door. "I just have to upload some stuff. I'll be down. Start without me."

"Your mother has an announcement to make."

"What kind of announcement?"

"I don't know. But she's been cooking and singing. And she made me open a bottle of wine."

Abbie knows what she's about to announce. Or at least he thinks he does. He's the only one in the house she trusts with news of her business. And he doesn't really care about it. Nor does he feel bad for not caring. "Five minutes max," Abbie says, and he closes his door.

Bobby heads downstairs. In the kitchen, Mimi is taking plates out of the warming tray. "We're eating in the dining room," she says, and she winks and Bobby remembers his Scotch and retrieves it from the side table in the living room and gulps it back.

Dee is sitting at the dining room table, a large block of wood Mimi found online from a Quaker carpenter in the Townships; it sits under a modern light that is more sculpture than functional, a blown glass and faux crystal thing that looks like something one might find on the floor after a botched surgery and throws an orange hue on the room. Bobby has never liked eating in this room — the light makes the food look unappetizing, burnt even — but Mimi has set it up now, for her announcement, with silver trivets the shape of branches, linen napkins, the good silverware, smartly mismatched, scavenged from the street sales of Paris. "Well, well," Bobby says.

"Please get the wine glasses," Mimi orders, and Bobby opens a cubby in the wall to retrieve three wine glasses, and a goblet for Dee.

"That one always makes me feel so special," she says, and both parents smile at her sarcasm and everything it implies.

"Where's the boy?" Mimi asks.

"He said five minutes," Bobby reports.

Mimi sighs and brings out the last dish, the noodles, and places it on a trivet, one she'd found at an estate sale in Toronto, silver with tiny inlays of mirror and red stone. Faux-Moroccan, she called it. She sits. "It's always nice to eat in this room," she says. It's something she might say about any room in the house; she has styled it, every single bit of it, and she embraces her surroundings completely.

Bobby pours her some wine. He can feel the first stirrings of the Scotch, and he regards the wine with trepidation. He pours himself a small glass. Mimi is waiting for Abbie, and she is now thinking perhaps the news isn't that big. Maybe it's only big to her. Maybe her news is nothing like she imagines it to be, her perceptions clouded by the success she foresees, she knows, the success that laps at her shores like the waves on a beach. Like that resort in Costa Rica, where the sea was dish-soap warm and the kids were away at camp and she and Bobby drank cocktails with umbrellas and ate barely palatable food and danced under the moonlight, a couple auditioning for an ad for ED meds. That's what success looks like to her. Better yet, it tastes like a margarita on that beach, the one in Costa Rica, that's what it looks and smells and tastes like, and that image is fading, she's losing sight of that beach.

Abbie runs in, his gaze on his phone, and he sits and finishes typing something and then looks around at how elaborate the settings are, the three courses, the condiments arranged near his setting, the wine glass in front of him. He places the cellphone in his pocket. "Whoa," he says.

"It's Keanu," Dee says with sisterly disdain.

Abbie places his phone on the table. "So this is, what?"

Bobby looks at Mimi and urges her to get it over with.

"The food is going to get cold," she says.

And so they reach for the food and attack it in their own ways, personality by mastication, a biological unit sharing sustenance in an age of abundance. Abbie drowns his noodles and chicken in sriracha, his broccoli in soya sauce, and Mimi always resents the amount of flavour he feels he must add to her food, to any food, nothing is ever good enough for him, it shows a lack of respect, each squirt from a bottle a middle finger to her and her family and her ancestors, and just when she goes far enough, once she reaches a place where her son has violated her entire culture somehow, she dials it back and decides to merely see his behaviour as proof of a still-unsophisticated palate.

Bobby sees in Abbie's hot sauce habit a kind of unthinking. Both parents, then, think *something* of their son's activity, one they watch almost every day, and yet they have never shared their thoughts on the matter.

Dee picks at the noodles. She eats her broccoli. She doesn't enjoy the food. Not because it's fussy — it is — but because something tells her she shouldn't. Eating is complicated, too complicated; she hates what everything she ingests seems to do to her ass. That's the worry. She worries about her ass. About its size, more specifically. She worries about her ass more than she does her asymmetric nipples. She doesn't even like sitting down for extended periods of time. Her teachers call her fidgety. She bemoans her aversion to exercise. She wants to be healthy without having to work for it.

Bobby licks at his wine and then just decides to down the glass and pours himself another. "Take any of your pictures today?" he asks Abbie.

He always calls them "your pictures." Bobby doesn't see them any other way. They are not "photos" or part of a "project" or a hobby or "art" or even just "pictures," they are Abbie's "your pictures," a kind of code that Abbie understands and resents and tries to ignore.

Abbie has built a following on social media by posting photos of smokestacks and chimneys. Often accompanied by fruit. He places the fruit, oranges usually, at the base of the chimneys, and he shoots. The city is full of ancient industrial sites awaiting gentrification, in the midst of gentrification, of transformation. It is all he does.

"Down near the canal," Abbie says, and he reaches for the bowl of noodles again.

Bobby has nothing to add to this, he never does, he's just happy his family still eats together; he knows the dinner table is a sanctuary, and in too many families he knows that sanctuary has been violated, exploded, replaced by cellphones and TV and media and stuff. At the Reeds' family table, there is no stuff. Just family.

Mimi takes a sip of her wine and as she puts her glass down she brings it back up and takes a bigger sip. She puts her glass down. "I hired another employee and my site just cleared a million and a group of investors wrote me and are sniffing around and are asking if I'm open to investment." She returns to her food.

Bobby, Abbie, and Dee stop what they're doing and turn their heads her way. "Mom?" Dee says.

Mimi puts down her chopsticks and studies the faces of her family, and she chews the food in her mouth, she over-chews it, and now she wishes she hadn't taken such a dainty bite of chicken, the piece was small enough, but she had to bite it, that's what she was taught, and now she can't make it last long enough and as she thinks about it, the protein is absorbed by her body and her mouth is empty and feels desert-dry. "The business is doing very well," she says. And she manages a smile. She takes another sip of wine. "I received an email from this man representing a group of investors here in Montreal."

To Abbie, this might be the most interesting thing his mother has ever said to him.

"Angels," she says. "They're a group of angel investors."

"What does that mean?" Bobby asks.

"A choir of investors," Abbie says, impressed he remembers something from school.

"I had to look it up," Mimi says.

"What are they exploring?"

"Dad, don't be so dense," Abbie says. Mimi takes this as interest, and it makes her bolder.

"They noted my sales, overall, they found my site by accident, someone's girlfriend or something bought a lamp from me, then they studied my website, they've been visiting the site every day for over a month, and made some calls, so I don't know what that means and don't ask me how they know what I'm moving on my website and they said they were interested in pursuing discussions about the potential of my business. They invest in e-commerce mostly, which is what I do, I suppose."

"That's kind of awesome," Dee says, and Mimi now wonders if she is happier that her children are both showing interest.

"Thank you, Dee."

"What does that mean? They want to buy your business? What do they care about the potential of your business?" Bobby asks.

"Dad, you're not getting this at all," Abbie says, picking up the bottle of sriracha and pouring it over his noodles with monsoon-level intensity.

And Bobby probably doesn't. He has to admit this. It may be the Scotch mixing with the wine, but more likely it's that he doesn't know why anyone would want to invest in his wife's company. "How are you even on their radar?"

Mimi takes his hand, if only to feel him and not let her perpetual resentment take over; Bobby has never fully understood what she does, or even why she does it. His lack of interest in her business has seemed to her like some wall he's constructed, for reasons she doesn't understand. "Honey, people like them are successful because nothing is too small for them. They see things others don't. That's the game."

This is where Bobby dislikes talking work at home, least of all around the dinner table. He regrets encouraging Mimi to speak now. Not that he has ever been capable of silencing her about anything. It's why he loves her.

Bobby is unsure if this is a joke. If perhaps he should be concerned for his wife. It's not this easy to make money. It never has been. He knows Mimi has worked hard, but she's just selling . . . furniture. She used to sell awful porcelain figurines. Her storefront sells almost anything. It's like a garage sale in there. He hasn't visited her website in a long time.

Dee fidgets in her chair, picking at her noodles, worrying about her ass, about her breasts, about this girl in school. She's worried overall. She's not even sure if she's happy. "Mom, I'm so proud of you. Can I be excused?"

"You hardly ate."

"I ate all my vegetables."

"Dee has body issues," Abbie says, stuffing his mouth.

Dee punches her brother in the shoulder and wants to perhaps shed a tear or two, or a dozen; she'd really like to get to her room, or just check her phone — she needs to talk to someone who understands her.

Mimi nods, and Dee runs upstairs. Abbie shoves an enormity of food into his mouth and pours some wine and adds the wine in his mouth as well, and Bobby can hear the food and wine sloshing about inside and he squeezes Mimi's hand. "What does this all mean?" he asks, watching Abbie chew and chew and chew.

"I don't know."

"They have money?"

"They *are* money."

Bobby is trying to remember everything else she has said, everything else his wife blurted out in that second, the world that came out of her mouth, the meaning of all of it. And then he recalls the word *million*. "A million what?"

Abbie stops chewing. He thought he'd heard the same word. An impressive word in any context.

"A million dollars."

"A million dollars," Bobby says blankly.

"I hit a million dollars."

"In what?"

"Sales. I've moved a million dollars' worth of merchandise online. I sold my first million. I've sold a million dollars' worth of stuff."

"When?"

"Since I opened the website."

"You opened the site what?"

"Fifteen months ago."

"Fifteen months."

"That's amazing, Mom," Abbie says. He scoops some chicken and puts it on his plate and showers it with sriracha.

"And if I keep going like this, at this rate, I'll hit two million in less than four months. Five at most."

"Five." Bobby can't tell if he's stunned or if he's more, if somehow the world feels different to him, if Mimi is still Mimi. For reasons he understands and dislikes all at once, the sight of Abbie drowning everything in hot sauce is very comforting right now.

"That's what they noticed, I think," Mimi says.

"Who?"

"The investors. They noticed the growth curve. Somehow. The speed. One of them said, 'Ikea started as a mail order business and then went bricks and mortar and you're doing the opposite.'" She unclasps her hand from his and reaches for her wine and downs it and pours herself another glass. "He was talking about my business and Ikea at the same time. He was trying to flatter me, but still. Look, it might be nothing. I've never been approached by anyone like that before." She finishes her wine and stands. "I think I need to get to work," she says.

"Now?" Bobby sees her heading to the wastelands of the strip mall, to the weed-encrusted asphalt, that forlorn parking lot the wind always seems to howl across, even when it's not windy.

"Now," Mimi says, and she gets up and leaves the room and heads to the basement, to her office, and Bobby feels the first pangs of self-pity. Or stupidity. He can't tell which.

"That's big," Abbie says. He burps and takes his plate and walks off toward the kitchen. "That's really big," he says.

Bobby knows it's big. He understands the bigness in what Mimi has said. He sits alone at the table. He thinks about businesses he doesn't understand — like Ikea, or billion-dollar websites, or magic — about things that shouldn't work but do, about businesses that defy common sense and yet become bigger and bigger and more powerful, about people who invent things no one has heard of only to sell them to someone else no one has heard of for more money than is fathomable, about the notion of success and its fluidity, about the meaning of something that is in many ways without a standard definition, and he picks at his noodles. He wants to be the first at understanding something, just once, the person making the discovery — not the last man standing because no one has chosen him but because he has survived. Success equates understanding, it *is* understanding, it is about conquering your surroundings and bending them to your will, to you, that's what success is, that's what the definition should be: Success is not about winning, it never is or has been. Success is about not being lost.

He refills his wine glass.

The table is a mess. He sips his wine and takes it all in. His wife is downstairs at her desk, staring at numbers on a computer screen, or finalizing the purchase of a table from a lady in Manitoba, or negotiating the sale of something dusty and forgotten from a dusty and forgotten corner of Slovenia. She does that. She finds valuable things and then creates more value. He wonders if she meant a million gross or net. He doesn't know that he has seen any material proof of his wife's success. The family still runs on his money. He's sure of this. He's proud of this fact. That it's still his money that makes things hum here. That pays for the food they have eaten, the remnants of which he now has to clean up.

Chapter 3

Reed arrives at work earlier than usual. He parks in his regular spot and throws his keys to the attendant, Vince, who has three kids, lives on the North Shore, and owns an above-ground pool he installed four years ago. Reed knows this from the minor chit-chat that has been the extent of their socializing over the past decade. He also knows Vince likes his coffee black, but weak, that he has a soft spot for croissants, and that his mother makes a fine zeppola. Vince knows almost nothing about Reed. Except that his wife is Japanese.

He greets the security guard. He doesn't know this one, he's new, but thinks he's Haitian, given his accent, or the little he's heard of it, and if he never knows who this man is, it won't bother him because Reed feels sincerely that he knows too many people, that there are too many people to discuss things with, and he's not anti-social but he feels like he's hit a wall. He's reached that age where weekends are about sleep and long weekends are about more sleep, where rest becomes the central part of your culture, and where knowing too many people just gets in the way of that culture. Whenever Reed feels the need to remind himself of something important, he almost always thinks, I have an adult son.

Reed steps into the elevator and pushes the button that will take him up to his office. His transformation is almost complete. The elevator will take a little under a minute to lift him hundreds of feet in the air, its doors will open, and he will step into a different world.

The office is empty; it hums with the stuff inside the walls. He is the first one here, and this pleases him. He heads to the kitchen to search for cookies, and he finds many snacks but no cookies. Singh, probably, has filled the snack drawer with some odd collection of Indian snacks that look appetizing but also don't, the packaging feels polluted somehow, befouled, and there are two empty UPS boxes next to the coffee machine, and then Reed remembers last night, while brushing his teeth, while half listening to Mimi tell him about two new Sri Lankans she had just hired for her shipping department, how he had drifted off, and he wonders if this was fair of him or not, if he was being a bad husband or a good husband and just being a bit too male. And then Mimi had said something about UPS, something *against* UPS — who can be against UPS? — and he spit out his toothpaste and turned on the tap, more than he needed to, because he loves his wife, but her shipping problems are *her* shipping problems. She brings her work home, and he doesn't think it's right — she works from home too much — he thinks the house is sacred, the family is sacred, but her business is her life, an extension of who she is, and that is also why he doesn't listen, because he has an image of his wife, an indelible drawing, and he wants to retain that image, because it's real, it's her essence.

Reed walks quickly to his office and sits in his chair and waits for his bottom to sink into the leather. He powers up his computer. He checks his watch. He has an hour until his meeting with Lamontagne. He reads the email again and then waits for the night's email to populate his inbox, the spam from different countries, lately it's been Turkey and, he's just discovered, Moldova, and each time he sees them pour in, he wonders as to the success of these ridiculous-sounding missives, the idea that anyone would contact the wife of a dead "Nigerian prince" so she can move money to a stranger's bank account just to take it all back. Has anyone become rich off this? Are there subdivisions outside the cities of Nigeria housing spam millionaires?

Lamontagne's email remains inscrutable. Reed logs in to the company server and checks the daily account sheets. He yawns. He sees a file in his inbox and reaches for it. Vachon has delivered the minutes of yesterday's aborted meeting. It is three lines.

What does it mean that Mimi has already moved a million dollars' worth of product? Does he understand what this means to her? To them? Does her success, or whatever she's calling it now, mean anything to the family? Who runs the world now? The people who make things or the people who lend you the money to make those things? What happened to banks? Going to a bank for a loan was something you did, something you had to do. You went to the money. Does the money come to you now? Reed would like to know who rules the world so he knows what to run away from when things come crashing down.

Vachon walks into the office with his coffee. "You're early," she says. She doesn't like not knowing what he's doing. It's part of what makes her so good at what she does, and also what makes her annoying.

"I had to catch up on things."

"What things?" she asks, putting his coffee down.

"I have a meeting, apparently." Reed reaches for his coffee and takes a long gulp and then makes a face in a show to Vachon that he is drinking a subpar coffee.

"It doesn't sound like much."

"What do you know?"

"No more than you."

That is a lie. She knows far more than he does. He knows this, and he knows that she knows it. They both enjoy the dance, even while it exasperates them. "What do you know?" She also ignores his coffee problem.

"There's a new hire."

"I know."

"I heard something about new org charts."

Reed leans back in his chair. His heart is beating faster, and he doesn't know if it's the caffeine or this news. "New org charts?"

Vachon shrugs and puts the files on the desk in order. "I don't know anything else."

"What kind of new org charts?"

"I don't know. Stop asking so many questions." She wants to leave. He knows she knows something and that it is existential; she's uncomfortable.

"This affects me, doesn't it?" he asks, sipping his coffee, willing himself to like it. "Us." His voice is coated in empathy, like excess paint on glossy abstract art.

"I don't know. Please." Vachon has been promised something. At some point, possibly overnight, he feels her loyalty has wavered. She has improved her station in this company, and now she can't tell him what she knows. Her loyalty to him, and more importantly his loyalty to her, has not been worth anything. Their relationship is the barren wasteland of a never-ending Arctic.

Reed stares into her soul. She can't look at him, and she retreats until she is out the door. And now Reed can see the future, or some of it. A bit of it. He can see the part that doesn't include him. He is not going to last here. I'm being paranoid, he thinks, and a part of him would like to believe this, but his instincts tell him he's in trouble.

Not knowing the lay of the land is when the hunter becomes the hunted.

He looks at his watch and stands and sighs. He smooths his tie. He takes another sip of his coffee, and stares into the cup, at the brown liquid, looking for answers to a question he's never thought to ask, and he stares until he realizes he's never believed in any of this stuff. He's not superstitious. He puts the cup down and pumps his arms, as if he's about to kneel into the starting blocks before a hundred-metre race. Get a grip, he says to himself; he's nervous, and the idea that someone might meet him for the first time while he's in this state washes him in humility — he's wet with it, which is also how he feels in his armpits.

He walks out of his office. He walks toward the elevators. He reaches the elevator and pushes a button and waits. He wants to believe in something now. He wants to belong to this place. His blood is in this place. He has slogged through the mud for this place. The most vile kind of mud. The elevator doors open, and he steps inside.

Chapter 4

Mimi parks her car in the reserved spot by the entrance to the warehouse. She has to pay for the spot, something that bothers her because no one, except for her or her employees, would ever want to park here except if they were hiding, or needed a place to have sex, or sell drugs, or park a car for a reason other than parking a car. It's behind the mall, and that she has had to pay for it, that the landlords extract money from her, for real estate that is otherwise worthless to them, because they know it is worth something to her, galls her. Every morning.

Recently, she's tried to stop thinking about it because she has learned to stop worrying about the things she can't control. She has learned to prioritize and not internalize. She's a walking aphorism, and she laughs about that, among other things, because she knows that the line between business advice and life coaching is as fine as Dee's thin hair. Or finer. She has learned not to give in to the demand of worry. She has learned that her attention must be earned. She has learned what will make her happy. The answer is usually a mix of power, control, and wealth.

The mall's owners are Persian brothers who emigrated after the revolution, or, more accurately, because of it. And instead of a place like Los Angeles or Toronto, cities where they have family, they found a Montreal overrun by what they considered under-valued land. They found strip malls neglected after years of misuse, relics sitting atop good land, centrally located, and they wondered why anyone would ignore such assets. Because the land was the gold mine and the strip malls nothing more than commentaries on urban neglect. Mimi dislikes the brothers, not because they don't care, but because their neglect of this mall is so naked, and more than once Mimi has nicknamed the older brother — the brusque one, the one who talks money and says no at least ten times for every time he says yes —The Ayatollah, called him this to his face, usually after he has said no to something Mimi deems reasonable, and this is not something that has in any way endeared her to him or to the other, more polite, brother. Whom she calls The Butcher.

Most consider the brothers to be nice people. They are pillars in the local Persian community. They support after-school programs in underprivileged areas, some not so far from the mall. They donate time and money to local museums. Mimi knows they don't deserve their nicknames. Still, she hates them.

The mall has lost its anchors; there are no large grocery stores. The hardware store closed five years ago. The pharmacy expanded into the spot vacated by the hardware store, but that's at the other end of the mall, the fancier end, *fancier* being relative, far from the low-rent hodgepodge around Mimi's *boutique*. A large dollar store has moved in to the spot left barren by the grocery store and next to it, a kind of permanent flea market, something so tawdry that the locals would rather hop on a bus and head to the nearest

Walmart, that even the sellers who display their wares, who try to earn their living, would rather they do so someplace else, anywhere but here, in a flea market with lights so yellow they feel like projections of sickness. Jaundice. Beside the flea market, a coffee shop run by Bangladeshis who sell more samosas than coffee, which is just as well. And next to the coffee shop, Mimi's store, a failed attempt at harnessing her obsessions until the internet came along, and she figured the neglect she herself heaped upon her store, and the cheap rent, all of it, all this desolation, didn't matter anymore, because on the internet her store was as desirable as Louis Vuitton. Or she would make it so. She saw on the internet the permission to be passionate again, to find people like her, to sell anything she wanted, because now she could. The internet had destroyed the boundaries of geography.

Mimi enters the warehouse and manages to make it through to her small desk without attracting attention. She slips her purse under the desk and opens the door to her store and steps inside.

The windows are dirty, covered by the grit of an untended parking lot, but still unable to hide the grime inside. The threadbare red carpet, the shelves buckling under assorted housewares and lamps and clocks and wooden tchotchkes. The counter, once white, now a kind of rust-coloured slab, she doesn't remember what material it used to be. But what other store would sell coffee table books about contemporary German design, Dutch mid-century dining chairs, teak trivets, PVC lampshades in bright colours, designer umbrellas, French bras, antique brass nails, high-end Japanese blenders, pink juicers from Mexico, stainless steel tie racks, a collection of Civil War era adzes, and pornographic prints from Germany? That is the inventory just along one wall.

She checks her watch; Esme will be in soon, the only person Mimi knows who admits to being happy working the front of her store, though Mimi doesn't quite believe her, she can't because believing her means not knowing what she thinks she knows about the world. But Esme's been here for over a year now, which Mimi doesn't quite believe either; and not having to worry about this part of the business is a surprise party for the kind of people who like surprise parties, which Mimi is not, she hates those people, and always wonders what kind of infinite sadness they're hiding behind the open-mouthed smiles and forced laughter.

A back wall covered in area rugs. A floor starting to sag. Shelves bending gracefully under the weight of her mismatched inventory. She feels affection for the store, for the pretense of it. It is the reminder of her start, the alpha, a touchstone, and no matter what it is or might become, the love she feels for it is eternal.

And she steps back into the warehouse. Here is her empire then, the guts of it, the computer terminals and servers and printers. The stacks of shelving running the length of a long industrial netherworld, the product, the multicoloured hue of tasteful curation, the stuff people want. A small alcove used as a photo studio of sorts to shoot and post.

Activity,

She feels warm. She watches her staff, and she feels something beyond maternal. She doesn't know what it is, but she feels it. She feels something that works its way into and out of every part of her, a force, like water, and it makes her whole. Nothing else has made her feel this. She will never admit this to Bobby, to the kids, but they don't make her feel the way this warehouse makes her feel. Sometimes these thoughts make her think she's a bad person. It is a question she asks herself more than anything else. But then she plugs herself into the hum of this room, a room that is never devoid of industry, that is always responding to someone somewhere, and she gets that feeling again, she dives into that feeling and it surrounds her with life and she feels alive. More than alive. She feels immortal.

In this warehouse, she feels her place in the world.

The new employees are working the shelves, a newly arrived Sri Lankan couple, literate but with no language skills. None. Their English is like deciphering the dialogue in a badly dubbed movie; Mimi is always having to interpret what she hears from them, to imagine what they are saying, involving a lot of contextual analysis. They are married, the Sri Lankans, and from what she understood, Sampath worked as a chemist and Kalpani was a nurse and they left behind a large bit of land as their country was torn apart by war, and they wandered the world until they ended up here, shipping Mimi's stock to her growing army of customers. Just the fact she has to hire overqualified immigrants fills her with the kind of idiotic joy that led her to make a three-course meal for her family last night.

When does she normally cook?

"Hello, Sam," she calls out, and Sam waves and then his wife's head emerges from behind a stack. "Good morning, Pani."

Karim is at one of the computers, printing out packing slips, his feet hooked around the legs of his chair. Mimi has asked him more than once why he doesn't play basketball and he keeps telling her they didn't play it where he grew up in Algeria, but Mimi finds it odd when tall people such as Karim don't play the one sport that venerates height above all else. Karim, however, is too gentle to consider any sort of athletic endeavour. Mimi has often wondered about Karim, his sexuality, what a gay man must go through in a Muslim land, what a Muslim must go through in a post-9/11 world, what a tall gay man must go through anywhere, anytime, how all of these things converge on Karim with astonishing force, or it would be astonishing were he gay, but Mimi doesn't know that he is — he's married with a baby, though even with that you never know. And she knows that gay people can be just as athletic as anyone else. But Karim's long and slender frame forces her to reconsider her own notions, especially her preconceived ones.

Esme enters the warehouse and removes her jacket. She always dresses as if it's spring, no matter what the season, and the mother in Mimi worries about her, about her lack of regard for something as elemental as weather, about how this must point to some need for an internal reset. How it shows Esme is not comfortable with her life.

"The Ayatollah's in the store," Esme says.

"Why?" she asks, knowing Esme can't possibly know the answer to this question.

Mimi walks to the door, her radar askew. She opens it, and The Ayatollah is there, holding an umbrella, one of hers, a taupe-coloured Chanel. "Mrs. Reed," he says, dipping his head.

"Mr. Khalili."

He looks at the umbrella as if this will make his presence here comprehensible. But it doesn't. He sets it down and leans on the handle.

"Is there a problem?" Mimi asks.

The Ayatollah stumbles now, in his own way, because he's too self-assured to stumble, or stammer, outwardly, too much a believer in his own superiority, sharply dressed as always. "My wife needs an umbrella, it seems."

"And you would like to buy this one?"

And then it's as if he remembers he's holding what he needs and he places it back in a rack of mismatched designer umbrellas. "No, no, not this one." He composes himself and he is The Ayatollah again and he's smiling that smile that Mimi has always thought meant he would eat a child. His belly is proof that he has eaten many. "I don't know anything about these things. I don't know where one would go to purchase a real umbrella."

"You were just holding a real umbrella. A Chanel."

"Yes, maybe, but I can't buy her an umbrella here." He leans in now, as if to emphasize his point, to ensure Mimi is aware of where here is. To let her in on an elemental secret.

"That umbrella is as good as any you will find downtown."

"But I would have bought it here."

"And it's cheaper."

"That's because your overhead is so low." He says this as if this is her fault. It's an accusation more than a fact. Though it's also a fact.

"Then you should go downtown," Mimi says. Esme opens the door and walks in and sits on her chair behind the cash. "Or Westmount perhaps. Or Outremont."

"I am trying to avoid the trip," The Ayatollah says. Mimi realizes that his desire to purchase an umbrella for his wife is going to become her problem. "Traffic," he adds. "This city and its endless idiotic roadwork. One day a road is open, and overnight it is closed and torn up, and they force you on a detour that takes you through neighbourhoods you have never even imagined."

"I have a business to run," Mimi says, and Esme lets out a laugh and covers her mouth.

"Mrs. Reed," The Ayatollah says, hoping that she will do . . . what? What does he expect of her?

"Mr. Khalili."

Esme is ready to laugh again. She watches this as if watching theatre. Her hands look ready to come together in applause.

Mimi and The Ayatollah stare at each other, each one aware that the other will do nothing to resolve what seems to each of them to be trivial. The Ayatollah looks at the umbrella again. He picks it up. "As much as it may surprise you to hear from me, I'm not cheap." He says this while wearing a bespoke suit she is sure he had made in London.

Mimi defers to this admission, but only because she'd like him to leave.

"I'm full of surprises."

"I'm sure you are."

Esme makes the sound of someone who takes pleasure in everyone's pain but her own.

And then a long moment of silence. Of desperation and defiance. Of resolution.

"Where can I tell her I bought this?" he asks.

Mimi wants to smile, but she doesn't want to give him the satisfaction. Not reacting is going to make him angrier. His defeat will be all the more crushing. She's going to treat him as an equal. She will help him construct his fiction. He will need her, eventually, to keep the transaction hidden, its secrets locked in the dustballs that swirl at her feet right now. She looks at Esme. And Esme readies the bill.

Chapter 5

Lalonde will save him. This is what she does. She fixes things. She anticipates and acts and accomplishes, and she does all this with the graciousness of a lace curtain fluttering in a gentle breeze. She makes the world run. Lalonde will save Reed.

Because Reed needs a tissue. He cannot enter this meeting with a nose containing substances in need of ejection. Of all meetings, this one, especially, demands that he exhibit strength. Stature. Stamina. He needs a tissue.

Because of this building's construction.

Because of the modern building code. The hermetically sealed modern building. This one, like all modern buildings, holds back the natural world with a mandated hyper-efficiency, and this renders the inside sterile, a universe of industrially recycled air and half-truths. We live in an age where air is no longer good enough,

Reed thinks, has thought, has ruminated on long occasions sometimes over lunch, outside, as he looks at the building, as he studies his home away from home, and then sometimes upon entering the building, when he feels the change in the reality of the air for the first time that day, just as he changes his own reality and becomes someone else. The processed environment. He has thought about our age, the Processed Age, where we create new realities to replace the natural realities we have destroyed, first artificially, and then less artificially, and then we return things to their natural state, often with great fanfare. We congratulate ourselves for doing the right thing. For coming full circle. More often, he thinks, we congratulate ourselves for the journey taken and not the mistakes made.

But the air in this building is fake, engineered, processed. And because of this, Reed sometimes finds he needs a tissue. How often has Vachon entered his office as he's blowing his nose, as he's studying what this faux environment has produced inside of him?

He walks the corridor from elevator to office and opens the door, carefully, he opens it, and Lalonde is not at her desk. Nor does Reed see a box of tissue. He can't walk past here, he must announce himself, and then Lalonde must call Lamontagne, and then Lamontagne must allow Lalonde to invite Reed into his office, and then Reed can walk to Lamontagne's office. Hierarchy demands process. Protocol.

"Mr. Reed, how lovely," he hears, and he turns, and there is Lalonde, her smile, saintly is the only word to describe her countenance, there is no other, and Reed feels somehow relieved, because Lalonde is going to save him.

"Madame," he says, and he bows his head, that's what he always does, but now he bows it more graciously, with more obsequiousness, and Lalonde wonders what's coming, because she is hard to surprise. "Would you have a tissue handy?"

Lalonde takes her seat. "Normally, yes," she says, and she picks up her phone to dial Lamontagne.

"You don't have one?"

She dials one digit. Because Lamontagne is important, and important people have one-digit numbers on the internal system. "Mr. Reed is here," she says. "Very well." She puts down the phone and looks up at Reed and smiles again, the effortlessness of her grace is truly a wonder of the world. "You are good to go."

"Can you think of anyone? Who might have a tissue?" Reed wonders if Lalonde senses the desperation of his predicament. He's sure she can because she knows everything.

"Are you alright?" Lalonde asks with genuine concern, or what appears to be genuine concern, because everything Lalonde does seems genuine even when it's not.

"I need a tissue."

"I can find a box, I suppose."

"I don't want to walk into Mr. Lamontagne's office and have to ask for a tissue first thing."

"It's just that I've announced you."

"And I thank you for that."

"It's always a pleasure, Mr. Reed."

And Reed leaves the comfort of Lalonde, hesitantly, and he walks slowly toward Lamontagne's office, studying the path before him, scanning the area for boxes of tissue, worried, unsure of whether to tilt his head back, protecting himself from the inevitability of gravity. He hears Lalonde's voice again and he turns, and she is walking toward him, holding a tissue, her warm smile melting all the ice in the world, and Reed accepts it. "I found some in my purse," she says.

"Thank you," Reed says genuinely; he is not going to utter words with more sincerity today, he already knows that, and he brings the tissue to his nose, and he blows into it.

Lalonde holds out her hand. "I can take that," she says.

Reed looks at the tissue crumpled in his hand and feels naked. Ashamed. "It's alright."

"Mr. Reed, I'm a grandmother." Lalonde laughs and takes the tissue from him and turns, spins really, and returns to her desk.

Reed knocks on Lamontagne's door. Lalonde has already announced his coming, but the etiquette of arrival is a complicated one. "Come in, Reed," he hears, and he opens the door. Lamontagne is at his desk, looking smaller than a man of his station should. Lamontagne is tall and has a runner's physique, but his desk is comically large, the kind of desk that seems like it was brought to this city in another era, possibly aboard a steamship, and coupled with Lamontagne's fondness for low chairs, Lamontagne often looks lost, even smaller, in the process of being swallowed by a desk that has turned sentient. Sitting in a chair before Lamontagne's desk is a woman dressed entirely in black. Except for her shoes. They are leopard print. It is all he can see. The leopard. How she might run in them. But that is impossible, what with the heels. She stands and faces him.

Reed knows he should extend a hand, but Leopard Lady threatens him somehow: that a woman with loud shoes is sitting in his boss's office for a meeting that has been advertised as big news means that she's the big news and he is not.

"Andrea," she says, and she holds out her hand.

Reed takes it. He shakes her hand. She offers something firm and manly, Reed thinks, though he also thinks that's probably not the right way to describe it, he thinks her shake is firm and corporate and not limp, he thinks her dress fits her a bit too well, and he thinks, damn, she's in my head already and I'm a pig.

"This is Roberto Reed," Lamontagne says. "Reed, this is Andrea, um, Deewey . . ."

"I prefer Andrea," she says. "We're not a football team, right? Ideally, we should be a family."

"Danza . . ."

"It's pronounced Dan-ner," Andrea says. "But it's spelled D-A-N-K-I-E-W-I-C-Z," she tells Reed.

". . . kiewitch . . ."

"That's an odd way to spell something so simple sounding."

"Evolution," she says. "America."

"You're American." Reed feels more threatened.

"Doonkoo . . ."

"Mr. Lamontagne, it's alright," she tells him. "The family name thing is oddly sexist, don't you find?"

"I'll stick with Reed," Reed says. "It's what I'm called here."

Lamontagne looks up at them and he stands and suddenly he is the boss, he takes over the room, the bespoke tailoring of his navy blue suit announces itself as a command, as the centrepiece of all that's important, and he smiles. Everything about Lamontagne suggests grooming, and self-importance, and intelligence; his smile is confirmation of both his position and his humility. Her name has defeated him. He's letting his underlings know that he knows. "Sit, please."

Reed and Andrea sit. "Coffee?" Lamontagne asks.

Reed wants a coffee, he needs a coffee, but if Andrea isn't going to ask for one, neither is he. "I'm okay," he says. "Thanks."

"I'd love a coffee," she says.

Lamontagne picks up his phone. "Two coffees, my dear," He looks at Reed. "You're sure?" he asks, and Reed plays this decision over and can't figure out what will announce weakness more, so he goes with confidence and nods his head. "And perhaps some biscuits. Thank you." Lamontagne puts the phone down and sits in his ridiculously low chair and almost sinks below the horizon of his continent-sized desk. He stares at them, smiling some more. "Reed, um, Andrea . . ."

She beams. Lamontagne's face registers the shock of the newborn. "Look at you, you're already making changes around here!" He laughs.

Reed wishes he'd asked for a coffee. He knows indecision is weakness, but he's not feeling mentally strong.

"Reed, Andrea is from our Seattle office."

Reed looks at Andrea again, the leopard pumps, the plunging neckline, the feline neck, and he wonders if she always dresses this way or if this is Make-an-Impression Day. The door opens, and Lalonde enters carrying a silver tray with two coffees and two plates of biscuits, places the tray on Lamontagne's desk, serves Andrea and Lamontagne, places two plates of biscuits at either end, and leaves, all without a word. She knows it's Reed who refused the offer of coffee. And she knows he regrets it.

"Andrea has moved to Montreal."

Reed understands that not only will Andrea impact him somehow, in a way that he already resents, but also that he is being diminished right here. In real time.

"Andrea used to head up HR and operations in Seattle."

Reed doesn't care what she's done in her past life, not at this moment, though he also realizes he's going to have to study up on her, that he's going to have to search the crevasses of her past to pick at her today. That he has never heard her name in any corporate talk surprises him most of all.

"She's the one who tried to install Tapas Tuesdays," Lamontagne says, laughing, and now Andrea laughs with him, embarrassed, certainly, she brings her hand up to her face. Tapas Tuesdays were a poor attempt to suck up to HQ and to instill culture in an environment where culture isn't important, where only the work is important, the results, and what you do after work is your problem, and if you want to make friends, great, but we're not going to help you.

"We don't hold that against her," Lamontagne says. "So much so that she's been promoted to SVP, R&P, ENA."

Reed has worked hard to get to Vice President, Revenue & Procurement, Eastern North America, and now Andrea has leaped in from Seattle and they've given her an *S*. He looks at her and hopes he appears composed. "Congratulations," he says, as genuinely as he can muster.

"I'm looking forward to working with you," she says.

She knows everything about him. He knows this. He hates that he doesn't know who she is, that he has never even considered anyone from the Seattle office a threat, that he hadn't even thought of Seattle, ever, in any professional way.

Lamontagne clears his throat. "You'll be reporting to her from now on." Reed turns his attention to Lamontagne. His boss takes a sip from his coffee. "You sure you don't want a biscuit?" he asks.

Reeds shakes his head. He slumps. He doesn't care if they can see it. He doesn't slump enough to slouch, but he displaces less air in the office. He feels as if he's been shot, but only after a large goon with a silly accent has pulled out all his fingernails with rusty pliers. Andrea picks up her coffee and takes a giant gulp. "Listen, Roberto," she says.

"Reed," he says. He looks at her, at her lips quivering just above the lip of the coffee cup. He watches her take another gulp; she loves — and needs — her coffee, and she puts down the cup.

"I don't want you to look at me as your boss," she says.

Reed wants to throw the most unspeakable insult at her stupid red-lipsticked lips.

"Even though I am, now, officially."

And the insults grow more unspeakable.

"Tell me something," she says.

Reed sits up. He does this out of habit and a kind of respect, a grudging respect, for the system, for what has happened even, for how casual and carefree Lamontagne seems behind his desk. Reed admires Lamontagne's complete nonchalance. Admires the fact that he's just fucked up one of his soldiers and he doesn't care. "Sure."

"What do you hate?" Andrea narrows her eyes. She's serious now. And for the first time, Reed realizes she's much younger than he is.

"Where do you want to be in five years?" Reed replies.

"We just met," she says.

Lamontagne stifles a laugh.

"That's what I hate," Reed says. "That question."

"Where do you want to be in five years?"

"That one. It's pointless."

"It's a standard question."

Reed has never even thought about the question. He's never been asked it. He's asked it of his underlings many times. It comes straight out of the HR manual. He can only imagine how many times Leopard Lady has asked it. "If you ask it, you're inhuman. Because most people don't know. And if you answer it, you're lying. You're bullshitting."

"Of course you're bullshitting. It's a bullshit question." Andrea picks up her coffee again and cradles it in her hands.

"That's what I said."

"That's why it's important," she says.

Lamontagne bites into a crunchy biscuit. Crumbs scatter from his mouth.

Leopard Lady has zagged on Reed.

Reed wishes he were better at chess. Or at playing defence. He's been playing offence for so long he's forgotten how to get the puck out of his zone. "Where do you want to be in five years?" he says, trying to smile.

"We're not here for the conversation."

Reed feels the menace in her voice, even though he knows it isn't there. He wishes he had asked for a coffee so he had something to occupy his hands. Andrea puts down her coffee and takes a biscuit and dunks it in her coffee and puts the entire thing in her mouth. Slowly.

"Why do you want to hurt me?" Reed asks.

"I don't even know you," she replies, her mouth full.

"So why are you here?"

"A promotion."

"And a well-deserved one at that," Lamontagne says.

"Why are you really here?" Reed asks.

"Where do you want to be in five years?"

"Come on," Reed says, sighing.

"How about this," Andrea says. She sits up straighter. "*What* do you want to be in five years?"

"That's also a bullshit question." Reed is questioning his place in the universe, and so now, watching Lamontagne and Leopard Lady enjoy their coffee and biscuits, he's wondering what star went supernova to put him in this situation. Andrea Dankiewicz is payback for something he doesn't realize he's done. He followed the rules, and now this.

"I know," she says. "We both know it's a bullshit question."

"So why are you asking it?" Reed sits back. He glances at Lamontagne who has a look on his face like he's pleasuring himself underneath his desk. This conversation is turning him on. Andrea stares right through Reed's facade. She can see him naked. "You are operating at a level I should probably admire," he says.

"You should admire me," she says, the tiniest smile on her lips.

"You have to earn my admiration."

"The *S* in my title means you should admire me."

"I don't even have to respect you." Reed appreciates that she can play this game. He'll give her that. He's just never had to speak this way with a superior.

"You have to admire and respect me." She finishes the last of her coffee. Lamontagne bites into his crunchy biscuit again. He has sunk farther into his chair.

"You have to earn both."

"I'm going to call you Roberto," she announces.

"Me too," Lamontagne says, laughing. "Roberto! There, I said it." He delivers this statement with the look of a child who has discovered a magician's secret. Reed watches his boss, a man who has taught him that work is a blood sport, who has encouraged him in everything he's done, a man who collects medieval weaponry and keeps an autographed poster of Bruce Lee in the entrance way of his home, Reed watches as this man's belly shakes from a deep and satisfying laugh.

"What do you hate?" Andrea asks.

Reed sighs. "Nothing," he says. "Andrea."

Chapter 6

Dee dislikes school. Not because she's bad at the school part. Her grades are strong enough to keep her parents at bay — her mother calls them "acceptable" — and she excels in subjects she never thought she'd excel at, like math and science. She hates the rest of it. She hates walking the judgement of the corridors. She hates that the hallways on the third floor are called The Catwalk. She hates that she cares so much about things she knows she will not care about when she gets older. That she shouldn't care about now. Abbie's told her. He warned her that she would care about the wrong things, that high school is about caring about the opposite of what you're supposed to care about, and here she is caring about her body. She hates that she has become one of those girls whom parents are warned about. Obsessed with her body image. God, she hates her ass.

She hates school because she hates large crowds. She hates malls and shopping and going to concerts. She hates that people in school think she's odd because she hates shopping. And that the ones who admire her for this stance are people she doesn't like. She hates that she's popular with the wrong people.

She hates the *idea* of social pressure.

The school she goes to is a French high school, a polyvalente, because Dee wanted to get away from the kids she grew up with. None of them were going to French school, and so Dee's decision had been made. That part she doesn't regret. She doesn't regret the few friends she has. She doesn't regret that her school is farther away from her house than the English high school; she figures this gets her out of the neighbourhood. High school is what it is, a funhouse mirror of bad things. Maybe it's good that her school is farther away from home.

Her best friend is most likely the only girl in Montreal named after Coco Chanel. Coco's mother is from France and worked in fashion. The kids tease Coco Chanel about her name. Because of this, Dee calls her by her full name and never just "Coco."

Dee and Coco Chanel hang out in Dee's room often, and they speak about how much they hate school or about boys though Dee doesn't think about boys nearly as often as Coco Chanel does because that would be impossible to do. Coco Chanel tells Dee her ass is fine and Dee tells Coco Chanel she has such lovely skin and Coco Chanel tells Dee about the crazy-expensive cream her mother lets her use and that's why her skin glows, because of this stuff, she doesn't even know what's in it, but she's sure if she did she would have to stop using it because it's probably been tested on something cute like bunnies. But it's not Coco Chanel's skin that Dee thinks is beyond her reach. It's her ass. Coco Chanel's ass is everything Dee's is not.

A friend of theirs, a girl named Clémentine, who was born in Cameroon and plays piano and has impossibly long, graceful fingers, calls Coco Chanel "CC," and Dee disapproves of this with an intense irrationality. Dee knows it's stupid, she feels like she might smother Coco Chanel at times, smother her because she's so dear to her, because she feels so much *affection* for Coco Chanel, but then Dee recoils; she knows she's being creepy, and she doesn't want that. She can never lose Coco Chanel.

Coco Chanel's locker is across the hall, so when they speak to each other, they're speaking over the tidal sludge of students shuffling to their own lockers, or to their classes, or to lunch, or to the school yard, or just shuffling to get from nowhere to nowhere; it's what they do, nihilism is just a shuffle away in high school.

The locker next to Dee's belongs to Sam, an unfortunately tall boy, unfortunate because at this age some boys don't understand the mechanics of their changed bodies, the distance from brain to limb so far, the possibility of nervous digression that much more possible. And then to complete the picture, the wispy onset of moustache, the gangly limbs, and, to dress it, an endless collection of flannel shirts and T-shirts sporting obscure hip labels. The lack of any kind of tension between them means they can speak freely and openly; Sam can make Dee laugh, and Dee offers Sam advice about things she knows nothing about. Dee knows Sam is going to grow up and be very rich. He's smart, he doesn't care what anyone thinks of him, he can build complicated gadgets out of parts of things.

Dee's other neighbour is Val, a Vietnamese girl with an unfortunate lisp, long dark hair, the most expensive taste in clothes, and an overprotective mother. Her parents own two depanneurs, that gateway for so many immigrants, but Val has issues, she harbours some deep-seated anger; Dee can never tell if it's against her father or her mother or both, and Val channels her anger by hanging out with some questionable guys. At least, they are questionable to Dee. Coco Chanel thinks Val is the coolest girl in school, not just because of how she dresses, but because she doesn't seem to give a shit about anything and treats everyone with equal venom. Dee thinks Val is going to get hurt a lot more before she finds herself. Or figures out what makes her angry.

Val's petite ass also reminds Dee that she hates hers. Dee hates so many things, but when Val gets going and starts pouring out her venom because she knows Dee will listen, Dee is reminded that her hatred is shallow, less visceral; that it has less meaning, it doesn't block her from anything, it doesn't occupy space; that the hatred of her own ass is nothing compared to Val's issues, to the tar she wants to pour on the world just to see it burn.

But Dee hates that Val has such a nice ass.

Val says, "These assholes, they're all 'what do you know, you came off the boat,' and I don't even know what that means, you know? Like what boat, we flew to this stupid country." She slams her locker shut. She stares at Dee expecting a response.

Dee says, "They don't understand, maybe," and she says it with a weak understanding of what Val is talking about because she's thinking of how Val looks in her jeans. And then Dee says, "Where'd you get your jeans?"

After school, Dee and Coco Chanel head to the park near Dee's house. They will hang out on the sun-warmed bleachers by the basketball courts and watch the boys play. Sometimes girls play, but they all seem short and wide, and Coco Chanel makes fun of their girth without once thinking that Dee sees herself the same way, without knowing that Dee internalizes what Coco Chanel says about these girls because she doesn't know that Coco Chanel doesn't see her the same way, she never has. As far as Coco Chanel is concerned, Dee is close to perfect, only slightly heavy, but in a healthy way. She has never seen Dee any other way, and one day Dee will see that too.

She will see how not fat she is, how the standards she sets for herself are impossible, how Coco Chanel treats Dee as she would anyone else she thinks is close to perfect. That is, normally. But there is also the fact that not all of the girls playing basketball seem to be as hopeless as Coco Chanel makes them out to be. Dee thinks some of the basketball-playing girls show promise, though not on the basketball court.

Dee and Coco Chanel sit on the bleachers. "Look at those fine young men," Coco Chanel says. She points to the far side of the basketball court, to three teenage boys, Black, lithe, and fit, their skin glistening with exertion, glowing almost. "Look at the tall one," she whispers.

Dee looks at them; but more than that, she looks at Coco Chanel looking at them. She watches how mesmerized her friend is. How Coco Chanel is feeling something right now that Dee has never felt. Coco Chanel once accused Dee of being asexual, and Dee doubted that was even a thing and then she looked it up online and found that it was a condition, a movement, a new group of people who had just realized they were a group of people. She was not asexual. But she was not so into sex, or at least, into it at Coco Chanel's level, at the height of what Coco Chanel sees and feels. Dee has sexual feelings, but she's not sure she has them for other people. She'd like to be sure about this. She feels small beside Coco Chanel's constant craving.

Dee looks at the "fine young men" and, yes, she can see that the tallest one is unnaturally handsome and graceful and has the body of someone who could star in an ad for designer underwear. "I'm watching him," Dee sighs, for Coco Chanel's benefit, because she's not really watching him. The boys wear such baggy shorts, even their gym shorts are baggy, there's nothing to see. It's all torso and no ass.

Coco Chanel returns her gaze to the far side of the court. Dee hears her purr and she's certain Coco Chanel is going to do something that might embarrass both of them a bit later, or soon, she can't tell, but she also knows Coco Chanel is fearless.

A ball comes skidding toward the bleachers from the far end of the court. The three fine young men watch as it stops before Coco Chanel. She stands and reaches down to pick up the ball. She stares down the boys and juggles the ball in her hands. She starts to walk toward the far end of the court, slowly. Dee watches as Coco Chanel walks the ball toward her quarry. Her auburn hair glows in the sun. Her red top appears tighter now. The young men stand around, their hands on their hips, wondering what this white girl is going to do. Except the tall one. He knows. Dee can tell by the expression on his face that he knows already. He's studying Coco Chanel, and Dee knows that Coco Chanel has already registered this. Dee watches Coco Chanel's ass as it gains something, an extra wiggle, her long legs leading her forward, relentlessly, toward the boys. Coco Chanel knows what she wants. Dee can see it in her ass.

Chapter 7

Abbie exits the metro with his friend Saul Zederbaum. The Zederbaums and the Reeds have been neighbours for almost twenty years, since before Abbie and Saul were born. The Reeds bought their house after they married, and Eitan and Channa Zederbaum were the first to greet them, offering them a very dry apple tart, the first to invite the Reeds over for dinner, the first to befriend them in a neighbourhood that was surprisingly indifferent to newcomers, even though the neighbourhood itself was new. Channa became pregnant around the time Mimi had conceded to the idea of adoption, and she would discuss this with Channa, as sisters almost, and their bond deepened after Saul's birth and after Abbie had been brought home, and then deepened further when Channa admitted to Mimi that she could bear no more, that Saul's birth had damaged her insides, and that this caused tension with her husband, because one child was never enough, not in their community. And though Bobby and Mimi could never invite the Zederbaums over for a simple meal, they take them once a year, the week before the Zederbaums' anniversary, to a kosher steakhouse near by, an act the Zederbaums never forget, even though their acts of kindness, if kindnesses must be ranked by quantity, far outnumber those of the Reeds.

So Abbie and Saul have grown up together. And though they could not be more different — Saul has graduated from cégep and is planning for med school — their friendship is a diamond, shimmering, permanent. Which is why Saul is with Abbie. Exiting a metro station named after a notorious anti-Semite, a Catholic priest who urged Quebec's women to gift the nation with many children and nothing else and is now someone whose name blesses a major metro station in the middle of the metropolis.

Abbie gathers his bearings and then motions for Saul to follow. "Past the church and then past the market," he says. And so they walk. Past the church. Toward the market and the stalls hawking cheeses and Thai soups and saucissons secs and gladiolas and then beyond it.

Saul has helped Abbie before, but not here. Not in this part of town. A part of him knows he tags along just to see things he might not otherwise see. To experience a life that he can feel slipping away. The last vestiges of his youth.

Abbie walks with purpose down the street. His destination is near the end of the road, an abandoned industrial site on the verge of redevelopment, of newness. And of a certain obliteration. "Why the rush?" Saul asks, as a joke certainly, because Abbie has long complained about the speed with which Saul moves about the world, the constant sense that he knows where he is going and why.

"It's another ten minutes," Abbie replies, and he checks the map on his phone to confirm his lie and finds that his lie is not all that white.

They pass an old mattress factory that has been turned into a tasteful condo. They pass an old brewery that has been turned into a new brewery. They pass an old tool and dye factory that has become a failed attempt at a tasteful condo. They pass cafés. Many cafés. They pass an old city garage now occupied by the type of offices that look like they accept payment in alternative currencies. Joggers. Young people, not much older than Abbie and Saul, already comfortable in their jogging gear, in their yoga pants, in their adulthood. These people are on the other side of a wall that Saul wants to climb and Abbie doesn't even want to acknowledge.

"I've never asked why," Saul says.

Abbie isn't listening. He's checking his phone to see how his prior posts are doing, to see if he has reached new people. To feel the validation that comes from strangers. His work reaches out to the world, to something that is beyond himself and his understanding of it.

"What?" he says.

"This."

Saul speaks in a manner that makes you think you've missed half the conversation, and in this Abbie believes hide the makings of a true man of science. If that's indeed what Saul wants to become. Abbie does not know how this squares with Saul's religion, but Abbie will be the first to admit he knows little about Jews and religion and science and belief. He just knows Saul won't eat anything that isn't produced in his mother's kitchen for fear of contamination. Abbie thinks it ridiculous. But he also knows that his father stopped barbecuing pork years ago, out of respect. And he respects that too.

"What do you mean by this?"

"Why do you do this?" Saul gestures outward, to the world, to the end of the street. "I have my theories, but you never tell me why. I always ask, and you never answer."

"It's my thing. I don't know."

"You say that every time."

"Because I don't know."

"But you keep doing it. You shoot these things with the stupid fruit."

"I don't know."

"You are obsessed with dicks."

Abbie stops. He turns to face Saul. "I'm obsessed with . . . what?"

Saul smiles. "You've thought this through. You have a plan. Come on."

"What are you talking about?"

"Long things. With balls."

"Why does anyone do anything?" Abbie asks the question this way just to get Saul to shut up. Because there's no answer to what he's asked, and he knows Saul has to think about it. And because Saul does think. He's a serious person. He was born serious. Their childhood photos often depict a smiling, bubbly Abbie next to a Saul who seems to be contemplating the existence of everything around him. Abbie makes jokes. Saul tries to decipher them. Abbie is sarcastic. Saul seeks out the cause of that sarcasm. Abbie laughs. Saul wonders how one can justify laughter. And it is because of Saul's almost Spock-like demeanour that Abbie finds the source of his friendship. Saul is entertaining and steadfast and loyal. And in Abbie, Saul finds everything that he is not.

"Like, every time I ask why you keep kosher, you don't answer."

"That's a complicated question," Saul says.

"So there you go."

"But it's also not complicated."

They walk down the street until they arrive at their destination. The street here is a construction zone in the making. Fenced off sections of field, demolition, flyers for theme nights at local bars, for concerts, for tastings of a new batch of local cheese at the famous cheese shop in the market, restaurant openings. Sketchy jobs. Weeds. Pyramids of dirt covering concrete pilings long ago abandoned to the elements. If earthquakes are the intersection of geology and human history, this place, right here, is where archaeology and market forces mingle.

"They aren't dicks," Abbie says.

"Okay."

"Stop saying that."

"What am I saying?"

The thing rises beyond a larger, sturdier wooden fence upon which, affixed like a promise, is a rendering of an architecture that sells a better life, a rendering of a way of living that is beyond what you have imagined until now and quite possibly may not be able to imagine again. A kind of campus for singles and upwardly mobile types, with rooftop pools and landscaped gardens and a club, a nightclub as a part of the complex. A condo project as a promise of sexual gratification. You can point your camera at the rendering and download plans and a pitch that will make you feel sexier than you have ever felt.

"This is not right," Saul says, and Abbie rolls his eyes. He finds an opening in the fence and walks through. The smokestack rises toward the sky, alone, surrounded by a field of weeds and rubble. Beyond the field, the parkway and bike paths of the canal, and on the other side of the narrow water, more greenery and more condos.

"This is not right," Saul says again. Now he's shaking his head.

"Saul," Abbie says, not with reproach but with a tone that suggests his friend needs to lighten up and trust the world.

"Thematically."

Abbie takes his tripod out of his knapsack.

"I know you understand what I'm saying."

Abbie takes his lens case out of his knapsack.

"Your art is not here."

"What are you talking about, art?" Abbie asks. He stops removing things from his knapsack.

"Your photos, at least the ones you post, they are about one thing. Your theme is obvious, and the fun in what you do is to see how many ways you can explore that theme."

"Dicks."

"Okay, whatever you do, even if they're not dicks, and they are, but even if they're not, your photos are . . . consistent."

Abbie would like to take Saul's musings on his photos as a compliment. Saul *is* complimenting him. "You think more about what I'm doing than I do," he says, and hands Saul the tripod.

"You can't tell me you don't know what you're doing," Saul says. "Even if I believe that you have no idea, you can't lie like that. You have a plan, you just won't admit it."

Abbie removes two oranges from his knapsack. He hands them to Saul. "This is a perfect chimney," he says.

Saul doesn't try to hide his exasperation. "Look!"

Abbie looks. He's been here. He knows what he's doing.

"All of your photos, all of the chimneys, they are always surrounded by renovations. Or by new buildings. The smoke-stacks are survivors. You make consistent statements, if they aren't dicks, fine, they are statements, and then with the fruit thing, you make another statement. But it's always the same. You are making a narration about, what, the economy, hard work, I don't know, but it's a theme. Your photos share a common meaning."

"Saul, shut up," Abbie says.

"That's brilliant," Saul says.

"No, really. I've been here. I scout these things. When I take a photo, finally, it's because I've thought it through."

"But you just said you don't know what you're doing!"

"I just see the final photo. That's all. So, I know what I'm doing in that sense."

"See?" Saul points his finger in the air to make his point.

But Abbie does not see what his friend sees. "Saul . . ."

"You admit to thinking about it."

"For fuck's sake, Saul."

"Look!" Saul says.

"Look at what?"

Saul points to another rendering, this one a billboard angled toward the canal. "What don't you see in that drawing?"

Abbie studies it. He knows. There's no chimney. "So what?"

"Abbie!" Saul is despondent, for a reason Abbie doesn't understand. He'd suggest buying him a hot dog, but he doubts he could find a kosher deli in this neighbourhood.

"They will tear it down."

"I know."

"You are not in the preservation business. You document survival."

"I thought you said I was doing dicks." He's heard this before. Saul is not the first to point out the phallic nature of his project. His photos are online. Of course, he's heard it. A lot more than once.

Abbie takes the tripod from Saul and sets it up. "Saul, just relax. And go stand about ten feet away."

Saul sighs and does as he's told, shaking his head, battered by an uncaring and unthinking world. A godless world of gentiles. "Here?" he asks.

"I'm not doing themes," Abbie says. "Or art. I'm not an artist. I post photos online. That's not art."

"Maybe I don't know what art is, but what you're doing sounds like the definition of art. To me."

Abbie has never thought of art. Of what is art and what is . . . what's the opposite of art? What is a hobby? When does a hobby become art? Who decides what is and isn't art? How does something end up in a museum? Does an artist have to admit to art for what they do to be called art? When does an artist become an artist? Why did Van Gogh die poor? When did people consider what he did worthy of respect? Who decided it? Why do the rest of us listen to them? Where does art begin? Abbie doesn't know. He suspects no one really does. And he resents Saul for raising the idea of art.

Art sounds old-fashioned. He's taking photos and posting them online and building a following. He enjoys the likes and validation. He has no idea what comes next.

"They're going to tear this down," Saul says. As if he's lamenting this, the future of this smokestack-free land. The absence of the past.

"I know," Abbie says. The wind picks up, and the garbage flies around the field. A hundred yards away, joggers, families on bikes, urban joy on a pleasant day. "Hold the oranges."

A heavy-set man approaches. He wears a lime-green polo shirt and slim-fit jeans that are a bad decision if nothing else. His belly objects to them. He lights a cigarette. He is the face of the gentrification that will eventually surround them.

Abbie takes his camera out of his knapsack and screws it on to the tripod. His bag emits an odour of old fruit. "You shooting a campaign?" the man asks, taking a deep haul of his cigarette.

Abbie doesn't know how to respond to what sounds like a reasonable question. "Hi," he says.

"So this is what?" the man asks.

Abbie looks at the scene before them. "I like chimneys," he says, shrugging like an eighteen-year-old. "Smokestacks. Industrial stuff."

"Are you pro pollution?" the man asks. "Because that's ballsy."

"I don't like smoke," Abbie says, and the man takes a drag from his cigarette and tosses it to the ground.

"So you're what, an artist?" He exhales an industrial amount of smoke.

Abbie winces at this word. Saul smiles as broadly as he is capable of smiling, which isn't much. "It's more like a hobby, I guess."

The man steps on his cigarette butt. "Okay," he says, satisfied. He coughs a smoker's cough. "I look at that stupid thing all the time." He coughs again and clears his throat. "I walk the canal every day for exercise. I see you with the camera, and I think maybe you're with the developer. I'm thinking of investing in a condo here. I can't wait until they tear that thing down," he says, and he walks back out of the lot and toward the canal.

Abbie watches him waddle through the lot, picking his way above and over the junk and refuse. Where did he come from? "The oranges," he reminds Saul.

Saul does as he's told. He's done this before with various fruit. Saul needs Abbie, for this reason, for the lack of reason, and Abbie need Saul, to take him seriously, to measure himself against as they become adults, to retain a totem of his childhood close by. Theirs is the essence of friendship. "He called you an artist."

"He didn't call me an artist."

"Artists create art."

"Lower," Abbie instructs.

Saul lowers his hands. The oranges are the most colourful objects in this place. Abbie looks into the screen and adjusts his lens. He pulls the tripod back a little. "Just a little bit lower," he says.

Saul makes his own adjustment. "Okay?"

"The light is perfect."

"The shot's not perfect."

Abbie takes a shot. "I'm not going to tell you how to practise medicine, Dr. Zederbaum." Abbie takes another shot. "A little higher now."

Saul raises his hand. "I'm a long way from becoming a doctor," he says. Though he smiles at the thought.

Abbie refocuses the camera. He studies the sky. He takes in the surroundings. This is a rare chimney surrounded by nothing. There is nothing here to obstruct, to contrast to, to suggest what once was or what has become. This shot is pure smokestack. It is the purest shot he will ever take. This shot goes beyond smokestack nostalgia.

Purity. His friend utters inconvenient truths. Abbie has thought everything through, even though he won't admit it. Not even to himself.

He unscrews the camera from the tripod and lies down on the ground. "Saul, bring the oranges toward me," he instructs.

Saul walks toward Abbie. "Where?" he asks.

"Keep coming."

Saul takes another step forward.

"More."

Saul takes another step forward. And then, on Abbie's monitor, the perfect shot: the oranges take up the bottom of the frame, and the smokestack reaches toward the cloudless blue sky. Saul disappears, his hands barely noticeable in the frame. There are three objects in his photo. Three ideas. Everything he has been thinking. "Stay where you are," he says.

Purity.

Saul stops. He looks up at what he imagines his friend is seeing in his camera, and something registers for him. He smiles. Understanding overcomes him. He tries not to move; he's become an expert at holding his hands steady. Abbie takes a shot. And then another. And then he plays with the focus and takes another shot. And another. He's laughing now. The perfection of what is happening. He keeps the shutter down, and his camera whirs away, taking photos, an entire series of them, and then he notices a flock of birds in the sky, they fly into his frame, and he takes his finger off the shutter and tries to decide if the birds work or not, he can't tell, and Saul looks at the sky and sees the birds. "They don't work," he says.

Abbie takes a shot anyway. And then another. "We'll see," he says. He stands. He puts the camera around his neck. He dusts himself off. He follows the birds until they land at the far end of the field, amidst what has become a swamp. Saul places the oranges in Abbie's knapsack.

"I'm sorry," he says.

Abbie looks at his friend. This is what they have. These moments. "Fuck it," he says. He picks up the tripod and breaks it down and stuffs it in his knapsack. "Can I buy you a soft drink or something? A juice?"

Saul nods. He stares up at the smokestack and smiles again. "I don't know if it works," he says.

Abbie understands that his humourless friend is trying to tell a joke. That he knows this puts more of a smile on his face than is necessary. He puts his arm around Saul. He thinks about the photo he has taken, about how it will look, and he feels that he has achieved something.

Even if he knows this photo will be different from all the others he's taken, that some in the community that appreciate his photos and follow his posts online will object; they will repeat Saul's complaints, and they will say it with all the bitterness internet anonymity allows. He knows that. He looks back at the smoke-stack again. He welcomes their comments. Their investment in his hobby. In whatever he's doing.

Chapter 8

Mimi buys the largest roast chicken she can find at the small Lebanese meat counter at the far end of the strip mall. She adds a container of tabbouleh and an oversized flatbread. She's had no time to prepare anything lately; the mere act of cooking something, let alone something so elaborate, was the importance of her announcement the other night made clear. Bobby used to cook — it was a significant part of the second stage of their courtship — but he has long stopped practising the art, and asking him to look after dinner involves pizza more and more often. Not that a store-bought roast chicken is much different. Mimi simply prefers it to pizza.

Bobby is already home, sitting on the shag carpet in the living room, a tumbler of Scotch in hand. He rubs his free hand along the carpet, the feel of it hypnotizing him, freeing him from Leopard Lady, her clutches; he gets the sense he's fallen into a trap and

Leopard Lady has been brought in to devour him. He smells the food Mimi has brought home. But he doesn't feel like eating. Not when he feels like someone else's dinner.

"Honey," Mimi calls from the kitchen. She says this as she has since they fell in love, in a manner that announces their bond, the familiarity of a marriage sailing along on a glassy sea. She unpacks the food. She spoons the tabbouleh into a serving bowl. She places the flatbread in the oven to heat. She takes out a cutting board and plops the chicken on it and finds the kitchen shears and cuts up the chicken and plates it on a serving tray. "Are the kids home?" she says.

Bobby doesn't know. He hasn't checked. He hasn't changed out of his work clothes. He went straight for the Scotch, and he hasn't left the carpet. "I'll see," he says. He attempts to stand and he feels the creak in his knees and he finishes off his Scotch. He heads upstairs slowly. He knocks on Dee's door.

"Yes?"

"Your mother wants to know if you're home."

Dee says nothing because it's obvious she is. Bobby doesn't move, knowing she's in there, a part of him wanting her to stay in her room, behind the door, safe from Leopard Lady. "Dad?"

"Yes, you're home, I get it."

"Are you okay?"

Dee is sensitive. Bobby loves that about her. Her sensitivity drives him crazy, but it's also her most endearing quality. She swims through life with a deep sense of empathy. She cares about everyone. She feels injustice. "Yes, thanks for asking."

He still doesn't move away. He leans his head on her door. Not to listen in but to rest. He's tired. Bobby thinks about bed, about sleep. About being horizontal and the comfort of the mattress, of being enveloped by the duvet, of losing himself in repose. "Dinner's ready," he says.

He walks to Abbie's door and knocks on it. He hears voices inside. Saul opens the door. "Hello, Saul," Bobby says.

"Hi, Mr. Reed."

Bobby has long asked Saul to call him Bobby, and for whatever reason Saul has refused. "How are your parents?" he asks.

Saul shrugs, which means they are fine, why wouldn't they be?

"We're eating soon," Bobby announces.

Saul turns to Abbie, and Abbie nods. His face is buried in his keyboard. "Five minutes," he says.

"I think the chicken is halal," Bobby says.

"Thank you," Saul says. "But that's not kosher."

"I think it's a similar process." Bobby and Saul have danced this dance before.

"It's not."

"I mean, it hasn't been blessed by the right kind of person, or whatever one does with these things, I understand that."

"Thank you for the invitation."

"It's not just the chicken."

"It's not just the chicken," Saul says.

"I understand," Bobby says, in retreat. "I always do. Long ago, your mother explained in great detail why it was impossible for your family to eat at our house." The kinship Bobby has felt for Channa, odd perhaps, he'd always felt perhaps it was odd, that he didn't feel close to Eitan. Saul is their only child, a rarity among Orthodox Jews, Bobby and Mimi both understood that; and when Channa admitted her medical issues to them, one evening across the fence in the backyard, and Mimi had invited her over, and the three of them had sat in the basement and commiserated, Bobby had known to leave the two of them alone so that Channa could let her grief pour out, safely, to another woman, one who wouldn't judge, and one with no contact to the community.

"It's the way we are," Saul says, almost apologetically.

"We all have to believe in something," Bobby says, even though he doesn't believe it, and he turns and makes his way down the stairs. He enters the kitchen and kisses Mimi.

"Are the kids home?" she asks.

"Both of them. Abbie said five minutes."

"Abbie always says five minutes."

Mimi taps her husband's ass and then pushes him away and she opens the oven to check on the flatbread. It looks like it's about to burn. She reaches in to pull it out. Bobby watches her do this with the beginning of alarm. She grabs the flatbread by the tips of her nails and flips it out of the oven and onto the chicken. "There," she says, surprised by how well that turned out.

Bobby closes the stove and shuts it off. "I can't handle the heat," he says.

"Then get out of the kitchen," Mimi says, handing him the chicken and flatbread.

He places the chicken on the table. Mimi will have no announcements tonight. He's grateful for that. He wants to speak more of her impending riches, but he also doesn't want to talk to *her* about it, he doesn't want to discover that *he* is suddenly not the important person here, that his work is no longer necessary, that he is no longer necessary. No longer vital. He hates that he thinks this way. And that others may make these decisions for him. "Smells good," he says.

"Has it been five minutes?" she asks.

Saul descends the stairs, and Mimi looks at him and smiles, surprised and not surprised that he's been in her house this whole time. "Bye, Mrs. Reed," he says, and waves, and he's out the door.

Abbie walks into the kitchen and opens the fridge and buries his head in it, searching for his condiments. "We're out of sriracha?" he asks.

"I don't use it, how would I know?" Mimi replies.

"What are we eating?" Abbie asks.

"Chicken. Tabbouleh."

Bobby walks to the pantry and produces two unopened bottles of the hot sauce. He places one on the table by Abbie's placemat. "Where's your sister?" he asks.

"I'm not her keeper," Abbie says.

"Dee!" Mimi shouts.

Dee enters the kitchen. She punches Abbie on the shoulder. She kisses her mother. She smiles at her father. And then she rubs his back. And she takes her seat. Mimi puts the tabbouleh on the table, and Dee spoons a heaping mound on her plate. And then she is about to start eating, but she looks around and waits. She puts her fork down. She stares at her father, noting the worry lines that crease his face.

Bobby acknowledges Dee's concern. "I'm fine," he says.

"Who's not feeling well?" Mimi asks. Her great concern is that she lets her work take her away from her family, and lately she's felt that she's done exactly that. She hates that she finds any domestic concern a distraction from her work. She brings a jug of water to the table and takes her seat.

"Your husband," Dee says, and now that everyone's sitting, she digs into the tabbouleh.

"I'm fine," Bobby says again, this time in Mimi's direction. Abbie tears a piece off the bread and stabs a drumstick. Mimi serves Bobby and herself. The family eats. Bobby studies their eating, how unceremonious it is, how the joy of family eating is just about doing private things in a group setting — survival turned into community. Mimi pours water for everyone. Dee finishes her tabbouleh and reaches for more.

"Have some protein," Mimi tells her.

Dee shovels another mound of tabbouleh onto her plate.

"Did you take your pictures today?" Bobby says, and Abbie dies a little inside and adjusts his outlook; again, he's making constant adjustments, it's all he does.

"I took Saul down to the canal," Abbie says.

"The canal again?" Mimi asks.

"When's the last time you've been down by the canal?" Abbie says.

Mimi has to think. She doesn't remember ever really being there. She's been to the market many times, and she once went to a restaurant near the canal. She often shops the antique stores on Notre-Dame, but she realizes she doesn't even know what the canal looks like, she doesn't know if it's wide or what. "Never," she says.

"Many years ago, we biked along the canal," Bobby reminds her, but she can't remember biking with Bobby anywhere, let alone by the canal.

"I don't remember the last time I was on a bike that wasn't stationary," she says. She's a member of the health club at the strip mall, a dank basement of thuggish Russian immigrants developing their thuggish-looking biceps and too-old-to-be-there dyed-blondes all trying to get into the aerobics class led by the cute Haitian owner. Who used to dance ballet before he got tired of touring. Mimi can't recall the last time she stepped inside the gym. She works. She works and buys prepared meals for her family. And she doesn't feel guilt, because she doesn't believe in guilt.

"The canal has what I need right now," Abbie says.

"I don't even know what that means," Bobby says. He tears off some bread and shoves it in his mouth. He wonders how long his son is going to do this, take these photos, before he realizes he might need a job, or money, or a life.

"It's what I'm doing now."

"What are you doing now?"

"Here we go," Dee mutters.

"Dad," Abbie says. He doesn't want to have this conversation. Not now. Not when he needs to work. He's thought about what Saul said, and he understands that Saul is right but he's also wrong, *this is how art happens*, Abbie told him, and realizes he'd just referred to his work as art, in his room, to Saul, and Saul felt vindication. And Abbie feels his work is in a new place and means something more than he'd realized.

"I worry," Bobby says. "You were never a great student, but now you're not even in school."

"Dear . . ." Mimi says.

Dee wants to leave the table but knows she can't.

"It's okay if you don't get me," Abbie says, playing for peace; the women at the table notice this, but not Bobby, because Bobby is not reading his son right now, he's playing The Concerned Father, or perhaps The Angry Father, or perhaps he's The Distracted Father, which he knows is worse.

"I don't know what that means either," Bobby says. He feels about to blow, about to go off on something that is probably unfair, but his son is, what, not who he had expected he might be, not on the cusp of adulthood, and Bobby tries to channel this anger, the poison that he feels might be welling up inside him, this thing that he has felt for so long and now, for some reason, that now wants to explode out of him, and he works to contain it, to keep it inside, because it's not a real feeling, it cannot endure because it is so poisonous, and then he sees Leopard Lady, he sees her rise above them all, an ancient goddess of malevolence, or power abused, and he understands what he's doing, what's happening to him, and he tries to climb down. "DeeDee, you can go," he says because he knows she wants to leave, she's wanted to for a while; it feels like the kindest thing he can do for her.

"Thanks," she says, and she takes her empty plate and puts it in the dishwasher and runs up the stairs to her room so she can stand in front of the mirror and examine her body while she digests her dinner and texts Coco Chanel.

Abbie stabs at a thigh this time. Mimi watches her son with a maternal sense of wonder. She takes Bobby's hand to try to calm him, and this simple act does calm him. Bobby takes a gulp of water. Abbie douses his chicken in sriracha.

"Abbie posts all of his photos online," Mimi says.

Abbie looks at his mother. He does not know that she knows any of what he does.

"They're remarkable photos," she continues. "And he has many followers or fans or whatever they're called." Mimi has taken pride in Abbie's output. She feels there is honour in art, if that's what her son is doing, she's not sure, but creation is honourable and timeless, and if she thinks long enough about this, she realizes, this is how she sees her own work: Curation as creation. She is birthing something, by herself, it's all her. All of it. "I don't know what he's going to do with them, either," she says, "but he seems to be doing *something* with them, so let's see where it goes."

Bobby is angry with himself, he realizes. The digital age has rendered him mute and old and worthless. Not because he is against the computer but because he does not enjoy it. He feels his attention tugged too far, the elastic manner of his mind snapping. He does email. He looks over spreadsheets. Occasionally, he reads the news. But he prefers the newspaper. Though lately he finds he does not want to know. Anything. The world upsets him. He figures this is a sign of age. Or perhaps the world really is worse.

He is angry with himself because his work life is crumbling and his wife is on the cusp of a form of success he never quite grasped and his son lives a life he doesn't know about. How did this happen? He worries for Dee; she's the youngest, so his worry for her feels normal, he's merely worried about her teenageness, but suddenly he's worried about himself, about his contribution to this family, and the fact that his wife knows what their son is doing and he doesn't. Why *doesn't* he know? What's wrong with him that he doesn't know what Abbie does and that he doesn't care? Bobby had thought he was just minding his own business.

That he was being *polite*. A good father. "That's excellent, then," he manages.

"It's all there for everyone to see," Abbie says, something he's never said before because he's never thought of the accessibility of his work this way, but it's true. His work is public. The internet is a public place. All those people commenting on his work are strangers. *His mother has seen his work.*

"I don't even do Facebook," Bobby says, to justify something to himself, to his son, who he knows is disappointed, who has seen this exchange between his parents and has noted the imbalance in interest. Bobby can feel the world move through space. It might be time for another Scotch. "I have a LinkedIn account, I think."

"I just wonder where it's going," Mimi says, but she's saying this in the manner of a viewer, dispassionate, curious. She's not worried for her son. Not because of his photography. It's never occurred to her to worry. He's young. He's smart. He makes her laugh. He brings out a kind of maternal something inside of her that Dee has never managed. Mimi doesn't try to analyze. She worries about him on another level. She watches the news and realizes she has a Black son. A brown daughter. These are things she cannot imagine for the simplest of reasons.

"I do too," Abbie says. "But I think I might know. I got something today. Saul helped me. *Saul*." His cutlery filets his piece of chicken with a scalpel's precision. Abbie has never liked animal fat to enter his mouth. He thinks he gets this from his mother. He has grown up watching her eat, and she cuts her food with the delicacy of a surgeon.

Bobby shoves more bread into his mouth. He can hear Leopard Lady laugh at him. He can hear Mimi laugh at him. He can feel Abbie's ultimate indifference; he fears his ignorance will be taken as something worse than it really is. "I need a drink," he sighs. He stands and heads to the liquor cabinet. Mimi watches her husband walk away from the mess he's created. She blames herself; she's been far too consumed by her own work, by her own incipient success, to notice this. To notice that something is changing in her husband. That he is bearing some kind of weight at work, and that he's bringing it home. Or perhaps she hasn't missed anything. Perhaps he hasn't been like this. Perhaps he's simply had a bad day. She can't tell the difference. Because she hasn't been paying attention.

Chapter 9

Karim glows in the blue light of the computer monitors surrounding him, his face contorting in a mixture of pain and rage that is his version of normal, the way the world always finds him, because the world causes in him the makings of severe gastric distress. He is almost always clutching the right side of his stomach while making these faces. Mimi wants him to see a doctor. He says it's because he reads the online comments on his favourite Arabic-language websites. "The problem with crazy people is they are so entertaining," he winces.

Mimi drops her purse next to the chair and takes her seat. "Your face shows signs of great pain," she says.

Karim notes his boss and says the night was good to the company. "And our first order from Denmark," he says, pained. "For a chair made in Denmark. The world is crazy."

"What else?" Mimi asks.

"The spreadsheet is on your desk," Karim says. He works early; he has a baby at home and he can only sleep at work, he says. So he arrives early, sometimes in the middle of the night, and he sleeps on a carpet near his desk until the first shift shows up, usually Manuel and Sam, who almost always bring him a coffee from the Tim's that sits like an island oasis in the middle of the mall's nostalgically expansive parking lot.

Mimi scans the spreadsheet. She keeps selling the smaller stuff and not enough of the big stuff. She wants to move more furniture. She fears she has too much stock. She has elderly customers who still purchase the collectibles. The porcelain statuettes. She should stop selling those, she's selling ugly things to old people, basically, but they move, and she can buy them for cheap and sell them at a silly markup. When old folks discover the convenience of online shopping, they are like children in possession of their first credit card. But that chair. To someone in Denmark? That's what she wants. She wants to hear that because she wants to know she can pull this off. That chair was shipped to her six months ago. And she's about to ship it right back.

Her eyes fall to the bottom of the page. "Karim!" she calls. She calls with urgency, as if she's just seen something horrendous happen right in front of her, perhaps to one of her children. She almost trips over her purse as she runs toward him. Karim meets her between their desks — it's not a great distance, perhaps ten feet, but room enough for the filing cabinets that hold all of the records and proof of their fiscal existence (Karim has called it the most important place in the warehouse) — and she shoves the spreadsheet in his face and says, "Is this true?"

He smiles.

"And you just told me about the chair?"

"The chair was important." He smiles some more. She can see his teeth. And she wishes he'd do something about them; she pays him more than enough to see a dentist. Karim is too important to her to fall apart. She thinks she is about to be big enough to give her employees health insurance.

"Is this true?" she says again, and she looks at the number at the bottom of the page, the receipts from the previous twenty-four hours, and it is a number she has never seen before. She would hug him, but his modesty would never forgive such a thing, and he's too tall, so much taller than she is, she must think at least once a day, and she also knows that hugging him would really change the dynamics around here, she might lose some authority, these are immigrants here, all of them, even her, and you just don't hug, not when you're the boss. You show concern and compassion, empathy, even, but you don't hug. And then the practicalities of success rain down on her like hail. "Can we handle this today?"

"Sam is on it."

"Is everyone coming in?"

"Sam is on it."

"Do we need to hire again?"

"Sam is on it."

Sampath is never on anything that needs to be done unless Mimi drags him toward it. And so Mimi's skepticism is on high alert. "Sam's on it?"

"Yes."

She stares at Karim as best she can given the height difference. She is a bungalow to his skyscraper.

"I told him," he says.

"Sam."

"Sam is on it."

Mimi checks the number again. As if perhaps it might have changed back to something more reasonable. Less momentous. As if the number might not be a confirmation of what's been happening, of this business she has birthed, that it's not a number she has simply dreamed up. But it's real. It's right there. It is magical and inviting. She wants to dive into it and go for a swim.

"Where is Sam?" she asks.

Karim shrugs. He points toward the shelves. The product.

Mimi heads toward the shelves. Three rows of shelving, each fifty feet long, three high, right up to the ceiling. The shelves at the front of the warehouse house the small stuff, the knick-knacks, the original product, what got her going, the Hummels and figurines and cheap and general kitsch from Germany and Poland, always that part of Europe, always, the kind of decoration that looks benign and useless by day but grows menacing in shadows.

The middle of the warehouse is home to the larger stuff, and here Mimi started to get into furniture, six months in, once she had some cash flow, first via stools and then she happened upon a factory of inflatable beanbags and she took the stock and she turned it over and found more and she had stumbled upon a nostalgia for beanbag chairs without realizing it, then she started selling bar kits, and then bar chairs, and then coffee tables, she kept finding this old stuff that people wanted and she sold to them.

And then, a few months back, she sharpened her focus. She decided to sell what she loved. Or more of it. And so the back of the shelves house the expensive furniture, the collectible couches and divans and chaise longues, the designer chairs and footstools and the Dutch mid-century modern armoires and sectionals and stereo cabinets and wine cabinets and chairs and coffee tables and dining tables. The more she looked, the more she found. She would travel just to source a new set of abandoned furniture. She joined fan groups online, and she sold this stuff — to a lot of gay men, especially, why she couldn't tell, but it had to do with taste, surely, with an aesthetic sensibility that appreciated furniture that could be so simple and so pleasing to the eye all at once, a design sensibility with style and curves if needed. There seemed to be no rules to Dutch mid-century modern, but there were, she knew there were, they just weren't so strict, like, say, the Quakers.

Mimi finds Sam doing inventory in the third row. He's a short man with dark skin, the darkest Mimi has ever seen on a person; she's convinced he's darker than black, that in a certain light he appears blue, or almost purple, with wavy, unruly hair and the makings of a pot belly. He laughs at odd moments, like after someone asks if he might want a coffee or had he seen the hockey game the night before. Pani also works the shelves, supervising inventory and shipping anything that could be considered "small." Half the week their shifts don't match up. And when they don't, Sam is withdrawn, a lesser man. His jokes feel less sincere, and because of this, they make more sense.

Sam was a chemist before immigrating. Kalpani a nurse. She has tried to pass the nursing exam, but her poor French is a wall before her. She has failed twice. The government French classes are pointless. Mimi has found her a tutor, and after work three times a week, Kalpani visits the home of Madame Sala, who lives in a condo two blocks from the mall, and whose home smells of cardamom and lavender, and whose French is Parisian and perfect, and whom Mimi has ordered not to teach her charge too well, lest she pass the test too soon.

Sam's accent is so thick, Mimi has often imagined spreading it on a sandwich. Her multicultural menagerie is the result of using a job placement agency with a large immigrant clientele. The Ayatollah directed her to the agency, and as the business has grown, Mimi has come to rely on it more and more. Karim is the only one employed in anything resembling his field. The rest of them, all of them, probably, are working beneath their station. And Mimi understands if any of this funding comes through, she probably has ample business acumen around her without even realizing it.

"I have seen them," Sam says, as Mimi approaches him. "Oh boy." His belly heaves, and he breaks into his awkward laugh, nodding his head, as if to acknowledge something that can't be acknowledged.

"Are we okay?"

"Sure."

"Karim says you're okay."

"Karim is correct," Sam says. "We are okay."

"How are we okay?"

"Mrs. Reed, you worry so, so much."

Sam was a *chemist*. What does he know about inventory management? About shipping? She understands why Sam can't find a job as a chemist in this country, but she still sometimes asks herself if it has to do a little with him.

"I have made the calls. All hands on deck," Sam says, laughing half-heartedly. She thinks he's laughing about the image of the warehouse as a ship. She thinks. Humour is a bridge to someone else, a kind of empathy, laughing *with* someone, that takes empathy and a willingness to inhabit another's reality. Navigating the neural pathways that lead to laughter, through culture and language and understanding. Mimi is Japanese. She spent her adolescence in France. Her humour is everywhere and nowhere. Specific and not. She finds American sitcoms beyond her reach. Especially the ones today. They rely on *discomfort*, on someone else's pain. She was the only person she knew who didn't understand *Seinfeld*. Slapstick will make her laugh, but not cruelty. She doesn't understand the idea of finding humour in someone else's tragedy. Bobby had told her that; he'd said the essence of comedy is pain. This seems to be especially true in Japan, where the pop culture is about humiliation. And the Québécois, their humour is just too closed off and insular.

It assumes a greater familiarity than American humour assumes. Growing up in Paris, she took to the truly dumb French humour. The raunchy slapstick that was an ocean away from the chatty movies she watched with her parents. She appreciated the films of Tati. But the Québécois. Their version of dumb was just . . . dumber.

Perhaps she just doesn't have a sense of humour at all.

"What if today is as good as yesterday?" she asks.

Sam stops laughing. "That's a very good question." He starts nodding his head side to side, as if he's warming up for the uneven bars. "We are okay," he confirms.

"And the day after that?"

"Then we have to get help, maybe," he says.

He doesn't laugh. Mimi notes this. "Thank you," she says. "Tell me if you need anything." She turns and walks down the row again, eyeing her inventory, her business. Studying it. She closes her eyes and listens to the hum of the warehouse. It is her hum. The sound of the sum of her efforts. She hears Sam start to laugh again. She hears Manuel dancing; he doesn't walk, he dances. She can hear Karim printing something out. She closes her eyes and sees herself embrace the entire thing.

And then she hears more activity. The arrival of Ximena and Joy. These are all the hands on deck right now, this is the totality of what Sam believes is enough. Mimi does not think he can have the orders out of the warehouse within the next two days. She does not believe any of it can get done. She does not think Kalpani and Ximena can clear out the small orders and then assist the men with the larger items. They only have one lift. Does she need another one? Does she need more things or more people or both? She reaches her desk and sits down and wishes she still smoked. She wishes this often.

Esme enters the warehouse and hangs up her coat. She hides her lunch in the fridge next to the water cooler. Mimi waves Esme over. "If the store is dead, come back here and help out," she says.

"Like packing things?" Esme asks.

"We had our best day ever, and they might need some help back here."

"I wouldn't know what to do," Esme says, her body contorting into a concave shape, like a tall vase melting.

"You would help." Mimi smiles. "Spend an hour in front. If no one comes in, close up shop and come back here. Or I can handle it."

"Really?"

Mimi takes Esme's hand and gives it a squeeze. It's all she needs to do. Esme's body starts to take shape again, as if she's being inflated. Mimi wishes Esme would do something with her hair, anything, something more interesting than what she has now, which is nothing, a limp mass of shoulder-length blonde hair. Mimi nods and Esme regains her hand and walks to the store to open it. She stops at the door and turns to face her employer. "The Ayatollah was out front," she reports.

Mimi raises an eyebrow. "I'm surprised he's awake."

Esme doesn't understand why Mimi would say this; both brothers work out in the gym every morning, and Mimi knows it. "He wanted to thank you for the umbrella. He smiled even. His wife was pleased."

"She was pleased?" Mimi asks, suddenly defending women's honour the world over.

"His words," Esme says. "And then he made small talk. He suggested you sell art. He says you'd be good at it. Then he said you had good taste. Maybe he's on new meds."

Mimi has thought about selling art as well. It's been a recent low-level thought, a thought but not yet a thing, but that's not the direction her life seems to be heading in, not lately, and she might have taste but there's study involved in this, lots of it, or at least an eye for something, and she has no time to develop another eye. Eventually, she's reasoned, she will ditch the cheap stuff that launched the business and sell the expensive furniture and perhaps even more expensive furniture, not antiques, but collectibles and fetish stuff, the kind of furniture people travel to purchase, and then, perhaps, art, yes, and all online, in a kind of ethereal invisibility, the demon-haunted freedom of the modern age, all out of this drab and drafty warehouse. No one will suspect a thing. That's what she wants. She wants to surprise people.

"He's a fool," she says.

She smiles. Both Esme and Mimi know she's being dramatic. They both understand that Mimi will never say a nice word of either brother, that she is, quite probably, incapable of it. But only Esme understands that Mimi, despite everything she says, under her breath, behind their backs, to their faces, that she respects them. Grudgingly, but still. They have succeeded because of the bad decisions of others. They saw gold where someone saw garbage. And Mimi understands the similarity. The parallel trajectories. She is aware of it. She would just never admit any of this.

Chapter 10

Reed walks into the office. He stops at the front, before a long aisle that leads to his desk, and he takes in the faces. His employees start to seize up, every morning the same, like squid on a hot grill. Every morning he wishes he had a toothpick, to heighten the black-hatted-outlaw-moseying-into-town feeling he gets on his slow amble to his corner office. He had learned how to lead with fear from his first boss, Monsieur Clément, almost fifteen years ago, and he had learned it from his boss, the amazingly belligerent Catalan Señor Cabal, a tiny man who roared like a lion, who believed in the possibilities of fear, in its power, sent over by an expertly run Catalonian financial logistics company to purchase a poorly run local accounting firm because it saw a beachhead to a continent and was going to run roughshod over a surprisingly weak market-place and own it. Señor Cabal believed in blood and paying with it, that employees you abused and who still bled for you were worthy employees. Reed is the sum of this company's DNA, and his success is a perpetuation of the belief that fear trumps love, that blood must run, that an unsettled employee is a productive employee, that someone who is abused will in turn abuse the people whose money is needed to make the company grow.

Vachon greets him by his office, with his coffee, and she's squirming, too, which worries Reed, because Vachon is his rock, she's the source of his strength, the one who eliminates his own fears.

Why is Vachon crying?

"Why are you crying?" he asks.

She hands him his coffee and turns away. Reeds watches her as she waddles toward the kitchen, and he turns, and Leopard Lady is standing in his office, staring out the window. "You have quite the view," she says.

She turns to him and smiles. Her hair has changed, Reed notices. It's bouncier. Perhaps bigger, if that's possible. It's as if she stepped into a time machine and journeyed to the '70s just to visit the salon. She seems not just taller, but older. Not more mature, just older. He can't stand that she is in his office. Using up his space with her big hair. But he has to get used to her, he knows this, she is his reality now, the future of this place. Lamontagne has sicced her on him for whatever reason, and if Reed wants to prosper, he needs to do it alongside this person. This imported thing.

"You have a nice smile," he says. He thinks that's a good opening. He's already pleased with himself for having said it.

"I'm not your wife," Andrea says. Her smile is gone and she sits herself down, and he really thinks she's going to find a cigarette behind her ear or something and start smoking. Right here. In his office.

"I didn't mean it in a husbandly way." Reed wants to sit down, but it feels wrong. He wants to see if she's going to stand up again.

She must feel the imbalance as well. The cosmos isn't aligned while she's sitting. "You know what I mean."

"No. I don't. Are you trying to pick me up?"

Reed decides he's going to sit down. She was so polite in Lamontagne's office. "Excuse me?" he says, sitting in his chair. He notes the give, the physical reminder of his station. Of why he's worked so hard.

"Are you flirting with me?"

"I said you have a nice smile." He shrugs. He should have started this conversation with aggression. He understands this now. Reed takes a sip of his coffee. Then another one. He stares at her, trying to discern the mood in his office. She's shooting arrows with her eyes. "And, no, I am not," he says.

"So, you don't want to have sex with me?" Andrea smiles now, again, leaning back in a chair she knows is uncomfortable and why it is so, but she's here to win. She's not going to give Reed the pleasure of showing discomfort.

"Sometimes I say things out loud that I shouldn't," he says, mystified.

She stands and returns to the window. She stares outside, and Reed takes another sip of his coffee, and he watches her watch the world. "Then you think I'm fat."

"Now that would be inappropriate."

"You said I had a nice smile." She turns to face him.

"And you do."

"We work here, in the same office." She leaves his office and returns with an envelope.

"What the fuck is that?" he asks. He fully understands the finality of what is about to happen. He wants to loosen his tie.

She stares at him. She wants an answer from him, and he doesn't know the question. "I think you don't know how to speak to a woman," she says. Her hands are on her hips. Reed cradles his coffee, looking up at her, she is looming above him, even though they are separated by the country that is his desk.

"I think you're right," he sighs.

She puts the envelope on his desk and leans forward. "I feel sorry for your wife," she says. She steps back and sits down on the uncomfortable chair. She's surveying the carnage she has wrought, how Reed has sunk into his own chair, how it looks like it's going to swallow him up like a carnivorous plant.

And then she turns her attention to the envelope on his desk. "You have an entire floor of employees here who are terrified of you. Who would be so much more productive if they weren't working out of fear."

"What's inside the envelope exactly?" he says.

"Fear is not leadership. It never has been. Fear breeds all sorts of things, and none of them are nice."

He reaches over and pulls the envelope toward him. Slowly.

"We cannot be about fear any longer."

Reed opens the envelope and unfolds the letter. It is signed by HR. He doesn't read it. His company no longer values what he brings to it. Leopard Lady isn't just the messenger. She's his replacement. Queen of the new order.

"I've been here more than fifteen years," he says.

She softens slightly. She's completed the most difficult thing she will have to do today. She knows it's over. "We are giving you something, and now you have to do something with it."

He's never thought about this conversation. Never planned for it, never imagined he'd be told to leave, even though he has told people to leave himself, and people have left him, because they did not like what he offered, which he accepted. He always did. It was the price, the sacrifice everyone had to make, most of all him; no one ever acknowledged his sacrifice. He did not have the empathy to imagine himself on the receiving end of anything like this. "I'm useless to the rest of the world," he says.

"You don't believe that."

"I think you do."

"You think I do a lot of things," she says. "I'm sure I'd surprise you."

"You just did."

"We can offer counselling as well," she adds, which feels unnecessary, like garnish.

"I don't know where I want to be in five years," he says, almost smiling.

"Okay." She stands. She looks like she's ready for a drink. She checks her phone. "All that before 10 a.m.," she says.

Reed wants to laugh. He wants to build a bomb and launch it at someone too. Though he feels like he's done hurting people. And perhaps that's important. "Do I get a party?" he asks.

Andrea shakes her head. "The severance is extravagance enough."

He should read that part of the letter at least. He wonders if he has to call a lawyer or something. He reads the letter. He is to vacate his office by noon. He is going to be paid a lump sum and then his salary for another two years — they have lawyer-proofed this process and ensured minimal fuss. He's being bought out. Benefits for eighteen months. Technically, he's being restructured out. Lamontagne is quoted at length. He thanks him. Attributes a certain amount of the company's success to Reed's lengthy stewardship. History is being rewritten, starting with this letter.

Reed leans back, still studying the letter, and contemplating the idea of not working. Of telling Mimi the news. How does he tell her he was fired from his job? The company thanks him for his loyalty. He wants to say something about that word. He wants to discuss the finer aspects of irony. With Leopard Lady. But when he looks up from the letter, she's gone.

Chapter 11

Saul fishes around Abbie's backpack, searching for what he has dubbed the "right orange." There are only three oranges inside. "These oranges suck."

"They do not," Abbie says, willing to accept that Saul might care about these details more than he does. And wondering why that is. He looks up at today's chimney again, a graceful giant of a tree trunk, tapering to nothing as it reaches toward the sun, in the parking lot of an old flour mill now housing ad agencies and young people and sports cars and scooters and electronic bikes and motorcycles.

"You can't do these photos with banged up oranges," Saul says. "Your photos are about regeneration and dicks."

"I wish you'd stop saying that."

"We passed a depanneur, right?"

"You're not buying oranges at a dep."

"Don't deps sell oranges?" It's conceivable that Saul has never been inside of a regular depanneur, though Abbie doubts it.

Abbie would pack up right now, but that might upset Saul, and preserving the peace feels more important than the shot today, even though this smokestack is just short of glorious. Saul has put something inside of him, a search for meaning, almost, Abbie's not sure, and then the knowledge that his mother is watching, that she knows . . .

Saul's certainty is a totem, something to aspire to, perhaps. Though Abbie does not wish for Saul's life. Far from it. The pressure his friend must face, from his family, his community, is, to Abbie, unfathomable, the seafloor under an ocean on a distant planet.

"See if you can find the proper oranges then," he says. And Saul checks his pockets for change and heads to the parking lot exit, to the street, toward the magical depanneur that might sell beautiful oranges.

A group of people, men and women, leave one of the buildings to gather around an ashtray and smoke. They are all in their twenties and oddly glamorous, or the women at least appear this way to Abbie, women who know what is happening in the world, combing it for trends to package to everyone else and sell. One of them, tall and slender, Japanese, Abbie thinks, with long jet black hair, dressed in the loose-fitting grey of Japanese fashion, white Stan Smiths on her feet, and Abbie recoils from what he feels when he sees her, which is partly his mother, but also partly the thing he keeps inside him, that thing that says she is his type. He likes the look of fashionable Japanese women, he likes Japanese fashion, and the oddity of it, the awareness this brings out in him, has always brought out in him, melts him every time. It is the reason for something, he doesn't know what, but it explains something about him, explains why he prefers taking photos and assembling his community online rather than interacting with actual people. Except for Saul. Who feels safe.

He's heard men end up marrying their mothers. But his attraction to Japanese women, or even women who dress in Japanese fashion, was something he wasn't even aware was a thing, he had to look it up, he had to discover the look he found sexy was . . . *Japanese*. Every time his mother asks why he doesn't have a girlfriend, he wants to laugh and cry and jump up and down and fall onto the couch of a psychiatrist.

I'm turned on by my mom and I take pictures of dicks, he thinks, and his head falls between his overly hunched shoulders.

He holds no other affinity for Japanese culture. Not anime. Not Shogun movies or Godzilla or yakuza slashfests. No great love for the food or music. No desire to visit and get lost in the warm neon glow of Tokyo. There is simply this: an inconvenient attraction. And his work consuming him. His personal life is this. A Nikon DSLR. Some landmarks. A computer. Social media. A website.

Saul returns. With a paper bag. "Oranges," he says triumphantly.

Abbie can't tell if he's blushing. He feels like he is. But no one could tell anyhow.

"There was a fancy fruit stand next to the dep."

"How'd we miss that?" Abbie says.

"We weren't looking for it."

Abbie has his camera set up. He is aware that the group is watching him. And that some of them are walking toward him. He busies himself behind his camera. "Hold them up," he says, trying to concentrate on what he sees on the screen.

Saul does as he's told. "They are beautiful oranges," he says proudly.

"Take a step back."

Saul does this.

"Higher. Just a little." Abbie can feel the eyes of the group behind him. He stands and turns, expecting the tall Japanese girl to be hovering right there, but there is no one. The group have returned inside, their smoke break over. He has imagined more embarrassment. He sighs, relieved, and turns again to take a shot. He moves the tripod back a little now, struggling to find the angle. It's a tall chimney. He takes another shot.

"I go to school soon," Saul says, for no reason than to say it. Perhaps to believe this is happening to him, to make it real by saying it out loud. His parents are sending him to New York. He will live with family in Brooklyn. He is going away and will return, someday, a doctor. If he ever returns.

"I know."

"Who will hold your oranges?"

Abbie straightens up. He hadn't considered that. Does he have to construct a device of some sort to replace his friend? Is there anyone else he can ask? Impose upon? Does the question imply he is going to take these photos for the rest of his life? Is that his plan? "Maybe no one," he says.

"Maybe you'll change your focus," Saul says.

Abbie shrugs. Uncomfortable. Feeling like the punchline to a joke he doesn't understand.

"No more dicks?"

Abbie doesn't know. He feels shame. He feels the beginning of something else, the makings of a shift. For the first time in a long time, he wonders where all this is going. He feels the burden of something. A heaviness. Confusion, perhaps. He worries he can't do this by himself. "Stop calling them that," he says.

Chapter 12

Dee studies her turkey sandwich with apprehension and returns it to its plastic home. She's never hungry now, not because she doesn't like food, but because she doesn't trust it, and that can cause problems, if not health issues, though Dee likes to think they are more mental health issues, and the fact she knows this offers her great comfort because it means she doesn't have real issues, only imagined ones.

Clémentine opens her Tupperware and out wafts an exotic smell, topped with peanut, at least to Dee's nose. She peers into her friend's Tupperware to find an unappetizing stew. "I will eat your sandwich," Clémentine says, and she reaches for it with her lovely fingers.

"I don't care," Dee says, because she doesn't, and she hopes Clémentine doesn't think she's going to want the stew, whatever it is, because the look of it is turning her off.

Clémentine bites into the sandwich and closes her eyes. "I like this bread," she says. It's a simple whole wheat, store bought, but Clémentine is tired of baguettes, tired of the seriousness with which her mother treats all baked goods — her mother, who is on a first name basis with her boulanger and who, Clémentine has found after months and months of trial and error, would never buy a loaf of sliced bread. Ever. And that kind of bread is the sin that Clémentine most desires.

Dee watches Clémentine eat. She watches her friend inhale a simple sandwich. She watches her mouth chew the bread, the slight smile on her lips, and Dee notices how lovely Clémentine's skin is, how perfect. She notes how her chin just stops being cleft and how gracefully it slopes down toward her neck, like a child's slide at an amusement park.

Coco Chanel joins them, loudly, bumping into Dee, who is lost in the angles of Clémentine's neck. Coco Chanel reaches for the Tupperware of Cameroonian stew. "What is this?" she asks.

"Ndolé," Clementine says, as if this answers the question.

"That sounds like a sad instrument," Coco Chanel says.

"It has nuts and kale, I think, and chicken. And spices. My mother makes it once a week, and I bring it to school once a week, and you ask me what it is once a week."

"And I eat it once a week," Coco Chanel says. She takes a spoonful and squeals. "Dee, have you had some?"

Dee can't imagine eating anything, let alone something with the colour palette of this Cameroonian thing. "I'm not hungry."

"You're never hungry," Coco Chanel says. "My dear, honestly, if you keep this up . . ." she doesn't finish because she has said the same thing too often and she knows her friend is unhappy with herself, and she can't break through to her because Dee will only accept help when she's ready to accept it. That's the way things work. They have discussed this, and Coco Chanel has told Dee she is tired of the conversation and then initiates it again.

"Clémentine, you must ask your parents to invite me for dinner one day," Coco Chanel says.

"I have, CC," Clémentine says. "You always say no."

"You always invite me when I have something else planned," Coco Chanel protests, shoving another spoonful of the stew into her mouth.

"You always have something planned."

"That's true."

Dee needs to leave. She feels the urge to go outside. To be alone. To change her immediate scenery. She feels a kind of panic welling up inside. She stands and feels unbalanced.

"Where are you going?" Clémentine asks.

"I don't know," Dee says. She feels hot suddenly, or stifled, something. But she needs to get outside. She needs to breathe.

Val joins her friends and sits. Coco Chanel pushes the Tupperware toward her. "Try this," she says. Val studies the stew and produces a bánh mì out of a paper bag.

Dee backs off and heads for the exit, out of the cafeteria, down a flight of stairs, and then out into the schoolyard. She walks to the edge of the yard, and then she's on the street, walking toward a park, her regular refuge, a small green space accessed by a dirty alley between ancient apartment buildings, a park populated by mothers and their newborns, the entrance a parking lot of expensive-looking strollers, but it's where Dee goes, because she's invisible there, a young woman without a baby, a non-person.

She finds her tree, a half-dead maple doomed to permanent shade by the cliff of an apartment building that rises behind it. She checks for dog shit, and she sits and leans back on the desiccated trunk of the tree. Birds scatter and come to rest on a maple on the other side of the park. She's hungry, she knows she should eat, that turkey sandwich was fine, her father had made it with love, because he loves sandwiches, perhaps not as much as Japanese fried chicken, but he loves sandwiches and he will always put care into even the simplest assemblage of whatever he places between two slices of bread.

Not all of the kids in the park are accompanied by their mothers; some are accompanied by their nannies, and in this neighbourhood, the nannies are Filipina, all of them, and the two groups, the mothers and Filipina nannies, almost never mix, though the kids do, they play together, because kids will do that, they will play. The kids don't know the caste system of the park or of the mothers and the nannies, some of whom are probably mothers as well, but their children are thousands of miles away, surely, and Dee has often wondered what these women feel, to be relegated to nanny from mother, to be treated as help and not as some child's world. Dee sees this division every time she's at this park, and then she thinks of the Filipino kids in her school, because she knows there are Filipino kids — they once got chastised by the school's principal because they ate all their food with a spoon, that was what they were taught, but the principal went off on some amazingly insensitive diatribe about foreign eating habits and what these kids were doing to the other ones, meaning, really, the white ones, but once the story made it to the media the principal had backed off, she had to, because she looked like the embodiment of intolerance, even when she tried to explain she was doing this for the kids, she was saving them from a lifetime of hardship, as if eating rice with a spoon were like being afflicted with leprosy. And Dee wonders if the Filipino kids at school have mothers who work as nannies and if they do, are there jealousy issues, or is being a nanny just another job? Like being a teacher.

She studies the scene, the apartheid the mothers impose here, their separation from the nannies a wall built of race and class and status. Dee is drawn to one of the nannies, perhaps the youngest of the lot, and short, like Dee, but lithe, she probably shops petite, and her skin, it reminds Dee of Clémentine's skin, the smoothness of it, and the way this nanny's nose barely forms, her face is centred by the idea of a nose, like a doll's nose, and when she smiles, which she seems to do often, Dee feels something, somewhere, deep inside, and then, suddenly, the nannies are all naked, the park is full of naked Filipina nannies, and they are all ignoring Dee, and Dee studies them with an embarrassed attention, until she's not embarrassed anymore, and then the nannies are clothed again, and Dee realizes that the nannies have noticed her watching them.

Dee buries her head in her hands. Why is she thinking of everyone's skin so much? Why is she so obsessed with the size of her ass? Why are all her friends better looking than she? Why is she not eating? Why is she in this park, in the shadow of the wall of a giant apartment building, imagining naked nannies? Why is she here?

In the distance, she hears the peal of the school bell. Lunch is done. She has ten minutes to get to her locker, retrieve her books, and get to class. She leaves the park and runs toward her school.

At the street, she waits for the traffic to part, and then she finds herself too close to the traffic and she has to stumble backward and then she is on the sidewalk and she realizes she's been struck by a force, something out of the sky, or the universe, she is wrapped by a blanket that feels cosmic, more real than her own reality, a shock of stars and planets and suns and dark stuff, all the stuff, everything, she hits the ground with the realization that she is not the same anymore, at least she doesn't think she is, she doesn't feel the same because she's just been told how she is and what she is, her body has just told her, her mind has processed something that means her awareness is a new kind of awareness, she has looked into a mirror and can see for the first time. She is the same but different.

She is whole. She hits the ground, her ass hits the ground, and she sits there, staring at her school but not seeing it, the traffic unusually heavy, or perhaps she's never assimilated the traffic this way, as heavy, as unusual.

Something has just been confirmed. Or perhaps was always there, inside, simply waiting to be found. There was a before and an after, and she has just passed through that place. She was under water. And now she is breathing. She remembers to breathe.

She's just figured out who she is. Just like that. She's thought it but never voiced it. Never felt it. She's contemplated it. And now she's been shot with the knowledge of who she is. Of what she thinks. Of how she's wired. With self-realization. She drowns in the reality of who she is. Of what she is.

Oh my god, she thinks. She feels lighter and heavier all at once.

And then the world makes more sense and less sense. And she achieves clarity and fog. And she tastes joy, she tastes it, the flavour of it floods her, it is sweet and like love, and Dee doesn't know if now is a good time to cry or yell with the joy she tastes or what. The joy that is pure joy, meaning it contains fear and ache and pain and love and clarity.

What does one do at a moment like this? What are the rules for this kind of thing? Maybe there's a book. Or a website. There's a website for everything. There are too many websites for everything.

And then she wonders who she can tell. She wonders who she can tell first. Who she tells first is the important thing here. Does she tell anyone? Should she wait? Is she sure? Because she feels sure.

She's trying to think of all the things that make sense now — like why kissing boys has never been a big deal, and the talk of sex all around her, how could there not be talk of sex when your best friend is Coco Chanel, how none of it excited her because none of it spoke to her. And she's trying to take in this knowledge, she's breathing funny, she realizes that, and the sound of the traffic is all around her, and then the school bell goes off again, she's officially late, but how can she go to school now?

Nothing matters and everything matters all at once. She wants to make sure she can breathe, that she *is* breathing. She puts her hand to her chest and she feels her heart, she feels her beating heart, it feels like it's going to jump out of her chest and slap her across the face and tell her to smile some more.

And she smiles.

Dee knows who she is, and she doesn't know what to do about it. She doesn't know anything. She has entered a life for which she doesn't understand the rules. First things first, she thinks.

She stands up and dusts off her ass.

First things first.

Chapter 13

Abbie's bedroom is a true darkroom, absent of natural light, and in the sense that all of his work, all of his manipulations, his editing, the work that transforms a picture into a photograph, is done in this space, in this darkness. In his room.

The centre of the room is lit by three monitors, and by Abbie's laptop, which is either on his bed or on the floor by the bed. And his tablet, which is almost always on his bed. And his phone, which is always by his side. And because the room is screenlit, the light, when there is any, is blue, a cool light that renders the space otherworldly, like a cartoon villain's icy lair. Abbie refers to his room as a lair. He has since he was a child, in order to scare Dee so she would stay out. But his room is not evil. It houses magic.

Wires criss-cross the floor like the transit map of a city with antiquated but serviceable infrastructure.

Abbie performs many ablutions to each of his photos, and each of these requires study and contemplation and effort and vision. Saul may use words like *art*, but Abbie speaks of work, without purpose, which Saul says is another definition of art. A hobby that has evolved into the very definition of work — though uncompensated, unless Abbie counts the digital likes and hearts and thumbs-up as currency.

Following this form of currency, Abbie could consider himself wealthy. But he doesn't. Because his pockets remain lined with intentions, and intentions alone. Digital love never put food on anyone's table. What he is doing can't be seen as anything more than a step. Toward what he doesn't know. Every day he has asked himself when he would stop this, when he might return to school and study something that might lead to something tangible, acceptable. His father had used that word once, had said school was created to get you an acceptable job — he'd said this as a kind of validation for school and the system — and to allow you to live an acceptable life, the kind of thing that keeps us going, us meaning the world, and Abbie had managed not to laugh, or lash out, because what his father was saying was so obviously ridiculous. But then Abbie navigated the rocky field of his own self-doubt every day, the questioning of not just his work (and there was that word, always, looming, a vulture awaiting carrion), but also the path he seemed to be on, how alone he felt, how eternal being alone always felt.

Abbie's not scholarly, or social, despite almost always being the most pleasant person in the room. Saul is his only true friend, the only one whom Abbie feels comfortable enough confiding in, about anything, and there is something about Saul's combination of intense familiarity and absolute otherness that has allowed Abbie to see him as his confessor. And Abbie has found in Saul a level of friendship that he's not sure he's bothered to seek from anyone else. Abbie was a person of multiple acquaintances. And now he is also a person who decided not to attend college, to take photos of smokestacks in gentrifying corners of Montreal, and to post them online, for strangers around the world to see and, if they were so obliged, to approve of, with a tap. Or a stroke. Or a push.

Abbie is eighteen, and he doesn't know whether that means he can continue searching his heart for his place in the world or if he has to make decisions and sit down and get to work. His mother is a searcher and always has been; if she is here, in Montreal, it is because she found herself here and allowed herself, her life, to happen. His father is different, a man who imposed a way of life on himself and then convinced himself he was happy. Neither of his parents have anyone else to blame for their mistakes. And their search, their mistakes, their meeting, has resulted in this: Abbie, alone in his room, staring at a photo of a smokestack, wondering if the sky is not blue enough, if the contrast between the smoke-stack and the buildings surrounding it is not high enough, if the saturation of the orange tint from the sunshine is warm enough to express what Abbie wants to express here, the mix of decay and rebirth, the marriage of old and new, the permanence of loss. Society's failure of remembrance. The meaning of progress. And its inevitability.

The phone buzzes, and it's a text from Saul. He wants to know if Abbie wants to come over and watch TV. Saul knows Abbie doesn't watch TV, but this, too, is part of the friendship: Saul will keep asking, and Abbie will come up with another dumb excuse, and perhaps one day, when the cosmos is aligned in a particular way, Abbie will say yes, in the manner that perhaps one day Saul will prove to Abbie that God exists, or that Abbie will be able to convince Saul to eat bacon.

I'm this close to solving the Palestinian issue, Abbie texts, and Saul returns this with a *LOL*. Abbie checks his email. Half the new messages are spam. Another three are notifications from social networks he has long abandoned but never deleted. There is one from a stranger. He opens it.

Dear Abbie Reed,

My name is Etienne de Bosch. I write to you from the Galerie de la Man, a contemporary art gallery in Mile-Ex. Some months ago, a colleague brought your work to my attention and I must now admit to being an admirer, and I wonder if you already enjoy representation at the gallery level. My research indicates that you do not, but my research was cursory: i.e., I googled you. The Galerie de la Man has long championed young artists of all expressive fields and mediums; this is, indeed, our specialty, using our extensive PR network to create the proper buzz and to launch careers. While I do not know what your plans are for your photographs, or if you are indeed serious about them, I do know there is a quality to your work that demands attention. In any case, if you are amenable to it, let's talk. Please call to arrange a meeting. I promise to keep it casual.

Sincerely,
Etienne de Bosch

Abbie puts the phone down. And then he leans back until he falls to the carpet. He picks up his phone and reads the email again. He doesn't know if he is breathing, the physics of life are suddenly unknown to him, or more mysterious than they were a moment ago. Before the email from Etienne de Bosch.

And then he closes his eyes and conjures pictures in his mind of things he never thought he had the right to imagine. Of being invited to a party he didn't even know existed. Of success, even though he is uncertain what that means. Of being adored in person. Of people throwing themselves at him because his work moves them to do so. Of what it means to do what he does and realizing he has to figure this out for himself. Of entering someplace, a room, where everyone is clothed but him. Of becoming a photographer without knowing the first thing about photography; he is self-taught, after all, and hasn't much been interested in the history of his hobby. Just chimneys.

He laughs. He laughs because he has been made insecure so quickly, by an email, nothing more. He needs to speak to Saul.

There is a knock on the door. He hadn't realized anyone else was home. And suddenly he feels shame, or foolishness, at least, for imagining these things, for letting himself get carried away by a simple message written by a stranger, by feeling the exhilaration of possibility, by feelings of insecurity brought on by exhilaration. "What?" he calls.

"Let me in." It's Dee. Abbie looks at the time. Either school's let out early, or Dee's in trouble. Or getting herself into it.

"Okay," he says.

Dee throws open the door, steps into the room, slams the door shut, and throws herself on the floor in front of her brother. She stares deep into her brother's eyes, a beatific smile on her face. Abbie thinks she kind of looks like the Mona Lisa, and he suddenly realizes that his look might be mirroring hers.

"I'll go first," he says.

"No, no, no, please, no," Dee says, grabbing Abbie's hand, bringing it to her face, and he feels how soft her cheeks are, and then he looks into her eyes, closer, and realizes it's possible his sister has been crying, that it's not softness he's feeling but moistness.

"What happened at school?" he asks.

"Abbie, please!"

"But why are you home?"

"Please, don't ruin this moment!"

She lies next to him. They stare at the ceiling together, both with tremendous news, neither knowing what the other knows, or how big their news is, or how their lives are about to change. Dee takes some deep breaths.

"A gallery contacted me," Abbie says, unable to wait any longer. He had to tell someone, and Dee seemed like the right person. Her news can't be bigger than that, right? He can't imagine the news she could have that might be more important than what he's just said.

"Abbie!" Dee sits up and punches her brother on the shoulder. He rubs it and sits up and sees that Dee is welling up, again, she might be crying already, and he leans back against his bed.

"Sorry," he says. "What's your news?"

"I don't know that I can tell you now."

"Dee, I'm sorry, it's just a big deal, it just happened, out of the blue, and I haven't told anyone yet, I was about to go tell Saul. I'm happy you're here. I'm happy I told you first."

Dee's face is buried in her hands, and Abbie starts to realize that perhaps his sister has something big to announce. Her body language is wrong. She's misshapen, almost a question mark, and she's shaking — it's subtle, but she's shaking, he can see it — and his alarm rises another notch. "What is it?" he asks.

She's crying now. Sobbing. Tears stream through her fingers and drip onto the carpet. But she may also be laughing. Abbie can't tell.

"Dee?"

She reaches out to him. He takes her hands, and she rubs her wet face on her shoulders. She's smiling. "I'm so scared."

"Are you okay?"

"I just know I can trust you."

"Did you do something?"

And now she laughs. She laughs and sniffles, and Abbie stands up to find some tissue. He searches the darkness of his room and finds a box on the floor on the other side of his bed and brings the entire box back to his sister. She grabs a handful of tissue and wipes her face. She blows her nose. She crumples it all up and tosses the wad in the direction of her brother's trash can. The tissues fall to the floor, halfway to nowhere. She takes a deep breath. "You can't tell Mom and Dad."

"What happened?"

"Nothing happened, you can't tell Mom or Dad."

"I can't tell Mom or Dad, okay."

"I can't believe I'm about to tell you this."

"Stop with the dramatics."

"But this is dramatic. This is the definition of dramatic."

Abbie struggles to imagine what his sister is about to tell him. In a second he pictures all the possibilities, all of the life-changing things that a girl her age might possibly be able to say, and none of them seems important to him. At least not as important as his news. "So?"

Dee stops breathing. Abbie watches as her face changes colour. As life is sucked out of her. As her eyes start to bulge. As her body tenses up, screaming for air, begging for Dee to breathe out again. Waiting to exhale. "I'm queer," she says in a breathless whisper, before exhaling again.

Abbie still thinks his news is bigger. "Okay," he says.

Dee waits for whatever she thinks Abbie is going to say now but soon realizes he's not going to say anything else. Has she done this wrong? Should she have used a more formal word? She doesn't feel like crying anymore. But she wants to feel the moment, and Abbie has somehow diminished its gravity. "That's it?"

"Okay," he repeats, shrugging this time. He reaches out to her and offers a hug, but even that feels insincere to her. "You're a lesbian. That's great. Now you know who you are. I'm happy for you."

"You don't think that's a big deal?"

"It's only a big deal if you want it to be a big deal."

"I think it's a big deal."

"Then it's a big deal."

"Wait. I think it's a very big deal."

"Then it's a very big deal."

Dee stands. "You're not being supportive." She wanted something so much more. This is the most important thing that has ever happened to her, and it doesn't appear that her brother thinks so. "Like, not at all," she says. She might start crying again.

Abbie sighs. He's probably underplaying this, he realizes that, but he also genuinely doesn't believe this is a major thing. It is for Dee, yes, but the sooner you understand and acknowledge your sexuality the better, and from that standpoint, it's only a big deal in the sense that his sister is bound to be happier because of her realization. And if she's at the age where she can make these realizations, then surely she is far more mature than most people her age. As long as she doesn't find herself attracted to Japanese women. He thinks this and doesn't know if it's funny. "Dee, I'm happy for you. That's one. Two: I've got your back. Always. You know that. Three: Yes, this is important to you, and I'm sorry I'm not making a bigger deal out of it. Four: Not everyone in the world is cool about these things, and I'm sure you know that. But I've got your back, I told you. Five: I don't know what five is." He thinks. He knows he had five points to make. "Five: I love you." He says this knowing she won't remember the last time he told her this. He's not sure himself.

"Thank you," she says. "And you suck."

Abbie takes her hand and squeezes. He knows he can't tell her more about the gallery now. About the email. Because that will make it seem like he's trivializing her discovery. But the thing is, he's just discovered something about himself too. And not even Saul, for his own reasons, will truly understand that Abbie has recognized he's an artist. What he's doing is not a hobby. It's a thing. A stranger has validated him with a cryptic email. Saul would laugh. He has definition. It's a way of seeing the world and interpreting it and fashioning something that he hopes the world will see and understand and appreciate. He hugs his sister. She hugs him and buries her face in his chest and starts to cry again.

"I think I'm scared," she says.

He hugs her harder. He squeezes her. He wills his love into his sister because he's scared too. Not for her. She'll be fine. He knows it. He's just not so sure about himself. He kisses her on the head. She squeezes him until he feels her life force. Until he understands that his sister feels like a new thing, and that one road mastered means a new and different road ahead.

Chapter 14

As her children are at home lost in waves of self-discovery, and as her husband gathers his things to clear out an office that is no longer his, Mimi opens the door and enters the warehouse and takes in the smell. She's always done this, and there is a smell, but it's nothing in particular, it's a ghost smell that hints at dust and dirt and cleaned furniture, there are chemicals in the air, and then if someone has microwaved their something, there is that, and with the makeup of her staff, some of that food is smelly, some of that smell sticks to things, and she has often wondered about setting a policy, broadly, because she doesn't want to single out anyone by their ethnicity, but also because of this there is no food policy. She walks toward her desk and watches Karim rise from his desk and walk toward her with purpose. He hands her a spreadsheet, showing the previous day's orders. Mimi's eyebrows arch up, as if pulled by string, and she looks at Karim, and he nods. "I must speak with you," he says.

He turns and heads for his desk, and Mimi follows. She waves to Sam and Manuel, then to Ximena, then to Joy and then she is at Karim's desk. Karim sits and then stands and clears his throat. He is visibly nervous. "We had another spectacular day," she says. He is sure to speak to this, about his need for support, an assistant, something they have discussed would happen eventually, and Mimi is thinking this eventuality is about to be addressed.

"We did."

"You should hire an assistant. I'm giving you permission."

"I can't." Karim slouches. When he does, and he does so when he's about to speak an uncomfortable truth, his shoulders droop and his neck bends forward, and to Mimi's eyes, at least, he looks ridiculous, like a sculpture hacked out by a hack artist. "I can't." He sighs.

If he's about to quit, or if he's about to negotiate a raise, Mimi has to do some math, right now, and she's prepared to do so, because she can't lose Karim. "You can't what?"

"I need this work, I love this work," he says. He's rubbing his hands, creating friction out of tension, out of whatever it is inside of him right now.

"Karim."

"My wife is pregnant again." He pauses. Mimi knows this, of course, and watching him is to watch an actor try to collect his thoughts, to recall lines he has rehearsed but has forgotten before a full house. On opening night.

"Karim."

"I'm overwhelmed."

"We can hire someone today." Mimi has, in fact, visualized this conversation, she has prepared for it, she read about it in a book, about preparing for the inevitable conversations by having them, with yourself, imagining what the other person is thinking, empathizing without forgetting your own needs, and so she's had this conversation with herself, but she can't make it work if Karim is going to play dead.

"I want to stay. But sometimes I think it would be better if I didn't have a job that I care about this much."

"Right now. We can hire someone. Now. Do you know anyone?"

"I don't know what to do."

"You need a drink." Karim looks at her and sees the smile on her face. She knows he doesn't drink. "Or at least some mint tea."

He stares at the ground. Thinking. He watches Mimi's smile grow and then retreat as she begins to doubt the outcome of her joke. "I should drink something," he says, the idea of a smile forming on his lips.

"You will have a department eventually," she says. "You need help, I know. You run this place." She wants to be human, even humane, but never overly friendly. She doesn't know if she's succeeded. Of all the business books she's read, all the books on leadership, the ones written by men are all either irrelevant or don't speak to her, and the books written by women assume too much, like money, or status, or almost always imply young children and nannies, and she never finishes them. She doesn't have the attention span or the patience for platitudes and aphorisms. "Are we okay?" she asks, hopeful, because she wants Karim to regain his senses, and then she wants to study the spreadsheets, analyze the orders, have a real conversation with Karim about the numbers, as opposed to this conversation. Are all young fathers like this? she wonders. "Because I don't like that this is the first idea you get whenever you feel pressure."

"I have no pressure at home," he says.

"Don't quit on me, Karim."

He stares at her, and she just wants to sit and get on with things because they are now in that place where productivity goes to die. This is when she starts to feel the insecurity of her station.

"We also need to hire in the warehouse," he says, finally. "Perhaps more than one." Mimi tries not to show her relief. "We also have to consider, at some point, a real human resources person. We are growing. Something happened the last few weeks. Everything is up."

"Do you need a raise?" She asks because she'd rather offer it than lose him. She knows he will not ask, not until it's too late, not until he's gone to a place that offers no respite from his doubts.

Karim doesn't answer. Because he can't. He has been brought up to earn what he's given, not to ask, but to receive.

"I'm offering that as well."

"Thank you."

"Ten percent," Mimi says, doing math, quick math, where she knows she's getting the numbers wrong; she needs paper at least, but she's spending money because she's making money, she understands that part of the equation. "And get yourself an assistant. And see about the floor. And I'll consider a human resources person. I'll run some numbers tonight."

Mimi nods, and Karim nods, and she walks to her desk and takes a deep breath and sits. She studies the spreadsheet and realizes, quickly, that her company is on the cusp of something much larger than an investment from strangers, much larger than anything she has ever imagined she could achieve. The sales are independent of online advertising; they are coming from everywhere, literally. She sees an order from Morocco and one from Brazil, and she sees herself atop the world, sitting peacefully, the picture of serenity, her world growing bigger and bigger, like a flower properly watered, and she's doing the watering.

She has managed this with no marketing or PR. No media outreach. With a website that Abbie has told her does not work well. And yet people are finding her. Consumers. Important people are finding her and telling their friends. She has purchased ads on Facebook and that's it. On Google when she remembers. She doesn't have time to plan this. Anything. She barely has time to eat.

She logs in to her email and within an hour has approved orders for merchandise from three new suppliers, has cruised her preferred auction site and purchased three mid-century modern sofas, has approved the purchase of art nouveau lamps from a collector in Kentucky, has made plans to visit a design convention in Toronto and speak at a marketing conference in Boston. She checks on the store, and Esme says a Hasidic man came and bought all the crystal wine goblets, every single one, and now they have no more lead-free crystal wine goblets. Mimi asks Esme whether she would like to become Karim's assistant, and Esme says no, with a look bordering on disgust, and Mimi thinks at least she asked; she thinks Esme is too smart to stay in the store, but with Esme at the store Mimi doesn't have to worry about it. Then she authorizes Karim to create a kind of boardroom somewhere. She needs a place to meet, not just with her own employees but with the investors, should they ever come, because if their interest is real, they will visit, to study the warehouse and crunch their own numbers while in the place, because she has seen how math can be contextual, how a number gains meaning when the thing it represents is in front of you, when it loses its *abstractness* and becomes real, becomes a tangible thing with obvious meaning.

She wants to call a meeting and tell her entire staff, all of them, that she appreciates their work. She wants to tell them she loves them, even though that's probably not true and would break her rules of leadership. But she wants to because that's what she feels right now, a kind of love, of this place, of her business, of the life she has created here, not just for her, but for all of them, of what an idea can construct, the power of it, how she has created another family here, literally out of nothing. She tells Karim to call a meeting. She just wants to talk to everyone. She knows they're working hard. She tells Karim that with his raise perhaps he should have a new title. She asks him to think about what that title should be. She wants to celebrate but not look too eager doing it. She wants her staff to see this growth as natural, a progression. And to expect more of it. She needs to tell her staff this.

She texts Bobby to ask him to pick up dinner. She waits for a reply, which he always does, he always texts something almost cute, he'll write *okey-dokey* and not *okay*, or he'll write *if you so command* and never *yes*, or he'll write something simple like *I love you* when she asks him to pick up milk. He makes *I love you* into a non sequitur, and she loves him for that, but today he doesn't respond, she tries calling, and he doesn't pick up — the phone never connects — and she resigns herself to thinking about dinner, to the planning of sustenance for her family, and she feels exhausted suddenly, it tsunamis over her, and then she prepares for her staff meeting because it's a thing and it's happening, and she makes a note in her phone to pick up dinner and then she decides she will leave early, she will address the staff and then leave, she will fulfill her business needs and her family's needs. Tiger Boss. Tiger Wife. Tiger Mom.

The employees assemble by the front wall. She stands on a stepladder. She tells her employees about her appreciation of their efforts, their work, how well the company is doing, how their effort translates directly to the happiness of strangers around the world, and how that happiness results in even more business, more work, more money, because you can sell the best thing ever invented but if you don't deliver it properly, no one will ever buy it again. And as she tells them this, she sees before her an ocean of blankness, a world of it, these are not people who are accustomed to telling others what they think, certainly not their superiors, and aside from some head-nodding from Sam, head-nodding in that subcontinental way that makes it seem like he's agreeing with you and ignoring you all at the same time, there are no reactions, none, except when Mimi tells everyone about Karim and his promotion, that he will be hiring an assistant, that he will also be hiring a new hand, at least one, for the floor, and that she will be looking at the shipping department as well, something that just occurred to her, because if she sees a bottleneck coming, it's in shipping, and so she announces it, and then she says as the company grows she will look into a benefits package and insurance and more, and that gets a reaction as well, and then she asks anyone if there are any questions, and Manuel congratulates Karim, and there is a murmur of congratulations from the group, and then Sam says the same thing, and there is another murmur. Karim beams, literally, he is like a flashlight; either he has whitened his teeth recently or they have grown in size or both, but there is light emanating from his mouth.

And then the meeting is done. If no one has anything to say, she has nothing to add. Mimi waits for Karim as he accepts handshakes from his colleagues, and then he turns to her and his smile disappears. "I'm very happy," he says, deadpan.

"I'm going to leave early today."

Concern lines Karim's forehead suddenly.

"Everything's fine," Mimi says. "I'm just going home. To take care of dinner. It's my turn." It's not, but she would never admit that. It's Bobby's turn, but Bobby's not answering his phone or even acknowledging her, and a mother is a mother, budding empire or not.

Karim's forehead loses the topography, and he thanks his boss once again, and here Mimi is again tempted to hug him but instead she says, "You deserve it." She picks up her purse and says, "Start the hiring process."

"It's started," Karim replies, heading for his desk, Mimi close behind.

"There should be new stock tomorrow, we'll need the photographer."

He sits at his desk. "I booked her last night."

She rests her fingers lightly on his shoulder, barely touching him, her mouth scrunched up as if she's sucked a lemon. How does one show affection properly in this environment, with a man this large, across a cultural chasm? "Thank you," she says, and taps him on the shoulder once more.

And she heads up front, to check in with Esme, who did not attend the meeting because she refused to close the store, *Because that's bad business*, that's what she had said, she was telling Mimi what was good and bad business, and Mimi did not argue because she was addressing the warehouse, and Esme seems to have no desire to leave her stool behind the cash, where she reads photocopied zines put out by her friends and plays games on her phone.

Mimi opens the door and peaks in. "I'm leaving," she tells Esme.

"The Ayatollah was here again."

"And did he purchase anything?"

"He looked at some ashtrays."

"He doesn't smoke."

"And then The Butcher showed up, and they spoke, whispered to each other, and then they left."

"I'm leaving."

"You told me."

Mimi closes the door and walks the warehouse to the exit. She takes a last look at the cavernous room, at her *thing*, at what she's created, at the reality of commerce, and she leaves. She walks to the car. She pushes the button on her key chain that unlocks her car door.

Mimi throws her purse onto the passenger seat. She turns the ignition, and the car idles. Her car sits there as she decides where to go, what to feed her family, what direction to launch her vehicle, and considers the ramifications of the dinner itself. She is tired by the domestic side of things. By the abundance of choices she has to make everywhere. All the time.

She decides on the traiteur a few blocks away, ready-to-eat dinners prepared by a chef, a charming Frenchman who once owned one of the most well-reviewed restaurants in town, a place that seemed like it would transcend trendiness because the food was so good, but he closed the place down, surprising everyone, tired of the hassle and low margins, the increasing number of no-shows, the paperwork required for everything, the bureaucracy of begging for this and that, the simpletons from the city who revelled in making difficult things more difficult, the taxes, the fees, the feeling he had that disaster loomed every day, a shadow he couldn't outrun, all of this Mimi read in a tell-all kind of interview he granted upon opening his ready-to-eat counter, in this neighbourhood of all places, away from his regular clientele, which was mostly franco, mostly gay — he had been on the doorstep of the Village — to start fresh, because by moving to NDG, to an unfashionable street, between a fruit store and a pizza joint, he was going to live and die by his food and his service. He had wanted to enjoy cooking again. And for Mimi, and many like her, especially the harried working mothers, the matrons of the west end, this man had been like a gift. Plus, he was cute and spoke with the kind of Maurice Chevalier accent that makes anglo women weak, and though Mimi had lived in France — she considered herself more franco than anglo, really, but not in Quebec's unique demographic sense — she, too, found his accent more than charming. This was a man who could make her dream, a little, not quite fantasize, but then again, fantasy was a function of desire and need.

Mimi parks in front of the traiteur, the rush hasn't started yet, and she walks in and studies the day's offering on the blackboard. She's thinking perhaps a lasagna, it's so good here, and so large, and it's fancied up with mushrooms and even truffles on occasion, and then a beet salad, with some garlic bread; she has it all planned out, it's happening, she can time this so that dinner will be on the table before seven, but as she studies the blackboard she sees everything is changed, the menu is different, the food has become some French-Korean mélange, and everything in glass behind the counter is, what is some of this stuff, she can't even tell. "What happened?" she asks the girl behind the counter, who must be new here; Mimi's never seen her.

And the girl is confused by the question. "To me?" she asks. She looks at her hands for some reason, Mimi notes this, she studies her hands with definite guilt, and Mimi thinks for a moment this girl behind the counter, who is tall and plain with straight and thin blonde hair, her face studded with freckles, has just had sex with someone she's not supposed to have sex with.

"To the menu," Mimi clarifies, with alarm, though she's trying to hide this. But she's alarmed. She can feel it. The hair on the back of her neck is pulling at her skin.

"Jean-Marc changed it up," the girl notes, not very helpfully. "He felt like a change. He said he needed inspiration again."

"Where is Jean-Marc?" Mimi asks, before she knows why she's asking, before she realizes she's lodging a complaint, if that's what she's doing.

The girl's face gets longer now, perhaps confused, again; this girl lives in a world where confusion is never far away. "Jean-Marc?"

"Is he here?" Mimi can feel the girl's eyes on her forehead. She must look frightening.

"He's in the back," the girl says, pointing toward the kitchen with the élan of someone who has failed their audition to model sports cars.

"If it's not too much trouble, I'd like to speak with Jean-Marc," Mimi says. "He knows me."

"You want to speak to Jean-Marc?"

This girl might start crying. Mimi takes a slight breath and tries to centre herself. It's going to be okay, she thinks, because this is not a big deal; and she looks at the girl and tries to affect sympathy. "It's okay. I just need to ask him if he can do something special for me."

The girl has either been told to avoid this very situation, or hasn't been told it could happen, but either way she doesn't seem sure of what to do. She backs away from the counter, slowly, and turns and enters the kitchen. Mimi is alone in the store. The morning's bread is by the side wall. Three empty tables line the space by the window. The blackboard lines another wall. It isn't even a blackboard, just a wall done in blackboard paint, but the result is effective. Muffins and cupcakes line the countertop. Behind the counter, a small fridge with exotic juices and eaux petillantes from around the world. But it's what's on the blackboard that is upsetting Mimi. Gochujang-spiced coq au vin. Cold noodles with duck confit. Kimchi-infused minestrone. A Korean pissaladière. Heat-and-serve bulgogi beef on buttered noodles. Kimchi mashed potatoes. Scallion pancakes. Surely those can't travel well. Spring rolls. Shrimp-stuffed tofu balls. Fried rice. Korean sausage salad. Chili potato soup. It goes on and on.

Jean-Marc enters the store from the kitchen, sees Mimi, and breaks into a gallant smile. He looks like he's about to sing the climactic song from an overly long musical. "Madame Reed!" he exclaims in a show of genuine happiness.

Mimi leans over the counter, and the two exchange a two-cheek kiss. "Bonjour, Jean-Marc."

"Madame Reed, is everything okay?"

Mimi leans in as if about to share an important secret. She feels childish about what she's going to ask already. She's a professional woman, and Jean-Marc is a professional as well, both are successful, though he may not know about her success, she doesn't brag. Both have France in their blood. "Where is your lasagna?" Mimi says meekly.

Jean-Marc breaks into laughter. Mimi doesn't understand the humour in what she's asked. The girl enters the store from the kitchen, and seeing Jean-Marc laugh she loses her worry and seems to grow taller still.

"What's so funny?" Mimi asks.

Jean-Marc stops laughing, or attempts to, and seeing the concern on Mimi's face, tries a bit harder to regain his composure. "Oh, Madame Reed."

Mimi has nothing to say. She's asked a question. Then she says, "And the salads. Your beet salad!"

Jean-Marc shrugs. "I'm trying something new," he says. "I thought, I'm tired of cassoulet; this week, let's do something different. I've been eating so much Korean food. I love it very much. And we finally have good Korean in this city. Not far from here, even. So I thought, why not, I will mix it up. I will cook what I love. I've been experimenting with a kind of what I call 'cuisine de bistrot coréenne.' And this week, voilà, let's see what happens." He smiles the smile of a man who would never doubt the righteousness of what he believes.

"But you can't just lose everything from your menu," Mimi says.

"Madame Reed," Jean-Marc says. His tone is conciliatory, approaching seductive. "I can do whatever I want here. That's why I opened this place. For the freedom. The liberty."

"But you have to transition to this. You can't just say 'no more beet' salad one day."

"Madame Reed."

"I came for the lasagna." She says this with a tone that evinces panic, and Jean-Marc hears it.

"I may have one in the freezer in the back."

"And what about the salad?"

"Try the new salads."

"But I want the beet salad."

"So far I have not found a satisfactory way to combine Korean spicing and beets."

"But —"

"I have some green beans, mixed with Korean spices, almond slivers, and garlic."

"That won't go with the lasagna." He is suffering a delusion, she thinks. He should not be making Korean anything.

"No, you're right." He turns to the girl and asks her to get a family-sized lasagna out of the freezer. "Just make a salad."

"The point was to not make anything."

"I understand."

"You should put the freezer out here and stuff it with frozen food. Like lasagna. Your lasagna is wonderful."

"I want to. I thought about it when we were opening."

"But you didn't."

"Aesthetically, I don't see how it will work. Freezers are so ugly. I didn't have the heart to ruin this room with an ugly appliance. Unless I can purchase a beautiful freezer."

Mimi thinks she knows where to find one. A distributor out of Italy. Turin, if she remembers correctly. Because Italians *would* make beautiful commercial freezers. And because of all the people who might walk into this store, she would be the only person who might know this. "I'll give you a number."

"A number for what?"

"A distributor I know who carries beautiful freezers."

Jean-Marc raises an eyebrow. "Such a thing exists?"

"I think so. Italian."

Jean-Marc considers this for the amount of time it might take him to mentally undress a new customer. "I can make you a salad. Fresh. But I don't have beets."

This is an entente, Mimi thinks. This is how wars are averted, labour disputes solved, marriages saved. "I will have the number for you by the time the salad is ready," she says.

Jean-Marc reaches out across the counter, takes her hand, and kisses it. "This is a lovely exchange, Madame Reed," he says. He smiles and looks at her with love, or more to the point, with *I want to love you.* His look is the prelude to seduction. To undressing.

The girl returns with a lasagna. "I am going to make Madame a salad," Jean-Marc informs her, with a misplaced dignity. And he returns to the kitchen, and the girl looks at Mimi and her confusion is back, Mimi can see that, and Mimi blushes, or at least she thinks she does, because Jean-Marc is all sex, she feels like perhaps they've just had a kind of sex.

Mimi has long thought cassoulet is one of the more overrated items in the French culinary arsenal. She agrees with him there. Fuck cassoulet, she thinks. And then she retrieves her phone from her purse to hunt down the name and number of the man in Turin who will ensure there will be lasagna no matter what delusion Jean-Marc is suffering.

Chapter 15

Bobby hears Mimi enter the house, where she'll find him in the living room on the shag carpet, nursing a Scotch. Bobby shoots back his drink and pours himself another. "Hi," he says, trying to work up the courage to face the scenario in which he admits to his wife that he has just been escorted out of his office, that he no longer has a job, and that he heard some of his charges cheer as he was leaving. They *cheered.*

"Home early?" Mimi says as she rushes to the kitchen with Jean-Marc's lasagna and salad. She turns the oven on because this lasagna takes forever to cook, and then she enters the living room and sits on the corner divan.

"I'm home early," Bobby says, with an audible slur, the first sign of his inebriation, though he is still thinking clearly enough to wonder if he should stop and maybe just take a shower. "So are you."

"I just needed to get out," Mimi says, feeling the buttery soft leather of the divan, an angular but elegant modern teak from Germany with smoke-coloured cushions and a red throw over the back. She thinks about how little she paid for it and how much she could get for it now, triple the price maybe, and she slots that away, a debate she needs to have with herself between love and need.

Bobby can't tell her. He's going to take a shower. He might have another glass first, but he can't tell his wife, not yet, and not necessarily because she will care — she's a realist, and she knows that nothing is forever; she said so on their wedding night, something she's told him she regretted saying — but because he must first decide how he feels about his new status, how he will confront this change, how he will admit this to himself, how Leopard Lady came to his office and fired him and how he didn't see her coming because he was too comfortable, he forgot the first rule of the job, about always being alert to opportunity, yes, but also to danger, a basic SWOT analysis, it was what made him a success and now he is out of work and he needs to re-evaluate his thinking, confront the fact that he doesn't know who he is anymore. Maybe he never did. Maybe he's being dramatic.

Maybe he should be relieved. He's thought this as well. Relieved of not having to play that game. Become that person. His employees cheered for a reason. They had every right to. That realization hadn't stung as much as he thought it might. He is amazed how quickly the job is falling off him, like water.

He needs a shower.

Mimi can tell he's holding back, something is bothering her husband, because she knows him too well; but she also knows well enough to let him announce what he needs to announce on his own terms. She has never pushed Bobby to do anything, ever, she believes this, even though Bobby might object if she said it out loud. "I'm going to put the lasagna in the oven, and then I'm going to take a shower."

"We're having lasagna for dinner?" This is what comes out of Bobby's mouth, but what he's thinking is he should take a shower with his wife. He hasn't touched her wet skin in a long time, they've both been so self-absorbed, and a shower with Mimi might be the tonic he needs. Or craves.

"The kids are home," Mimi says, as if she knows his thoughts.

"No, they're not."

"Listen." Mimi puts a finger to her lips, and, yes, Bobby hears something, movement, almost like mice, but then it's steps, and that can either be Abbie or Dee, but it's a step, and then there's another one.

"I hadn't heard them."

"You came home, sat on the floor, and opened a bottle of Scotch."

"I opened the bottle before I sat on the floor. And I got myself a glass." He drains the glass and sighs. He leans his head back on the couch and closes his eyes. He contemplates his worth as a man.

Mimi stands and walks to the kitchen. Bobby listens to Mimi take something out of a paper bag, meaning she went to that French chef's place she keeps talking about, and then he hears her open the oven and slide something in, and then she's in the hallway. "I'm going to take a shower now," she says.

"I'm going to have another drink and then I'm going to take a shower too."

Mimi smiles and heads up the stairs. She thinks it would be nice if her husband joined her in the shower, but she doesn't say anything. She's not worried about the kids, but she will not push Bobby. She pushed when they were younger, when both of them pushed because both of them were hungry, both of them wanted pushing, because both of them were in the mood for push and pull and poke and tickle.

If her husband wants her, he will follow.

But he doesn't.

He wants Mimi, he's never stopped wanting her, but his want has had to share space with other things, its importance has dropped on his list of priorities. He doesn't know when this happened, but it did, he feels less of a man for even acknowledging it, and even though his desire for his wife hasn't died, he feels as if a part of him has, that part that put her first, that part of him that could taste her and smell her and imagine her fingers running up his legs, her nails digging into him, that part of him is buried by layers of bad decisions, by complacency, by his own sense of not being the person he once was — a feeling that has endured far longer than he realizes — no longer being the person who met a strangely erotic Japanese girl in Paris while at a conference, the confident man who pursued her, even though her father was his host, a potential client, no longer being the man mesmerized by the beauty of her and then dazzled by her intelligence, by a woman who could debate him about anything in two languages and more if he knew more languages, by the skill with which she could make a martini without breaking eye contact. He pours himself another drink, he shoots it back, and he wills himself to get up so he can join his wife, so he can touch his wife, and then he hears Dee's laughter — he thinks it's laughter — and he decides no, because he still feels funny around the kids, despite their age, perhaps more so because they would know, as they surely must, no one believes they are the result of an immaculate conception, even though he and Mimi adopted their children, so that technically, no, there is no physical proof to anyone else that they have ever enjoyed each other, but then he thinks that at least when Mimi's done with her shower he's going to watch her dry off, and then he's going to get in the shower himself and sober up. And with that decision made, he pours himself another drink.

Mimi leaves a trail of clothes as she makes her way to the bathroom. If there's a room Mimi and Bobby have splurged on in their home it is here, the ensuite bathroom; Mimi sacrificed a walk-in closet for the expansion, but she wanted it, the heated floors, the dual sinks, the luminotherapy shower, the bath with the spa jets and headrests, the ceramic tile from Spain. There had been talk of using up a part of the bedroom as well, for an exercise bike, but then Bobby talked her out of that, he called exercise bikes the graveyards of good intentions, and Mimi respected the idea of what he'd said, if not the idea itself, and so they had saved a few thousand dollars.

Mimi shuts the overhead lights and turns on the luminotherapy unit. The room is bathed in a warm orange glow. Then she turns on the water and she steps in and she bathes in light, she looks like a tourist attraction, and she lets the light and the warm water work its way into her body, inside her thoughts, until her warehouse and the tension — she's willing to admit she feels tension — wash away and she becomes what she is, a woman, naked, alone, letting herself melt into an element. The lights change to red, and the mist in the room takes on the look of that lighting that exists in all horror movies just before the bloodshed, but here there is no blood being shed, not that anyone can tell, just relaxation. The validation of ambition.

And then, despite the luxury of her surroundings, perhaps because she can feel every drop of water hit her body, or can feel the rays of light infiltrating her pores, she thinks about work, about hiring new people, about a new system to handle orders, about some software Karim's told her about to help with the logistics of what they do, about an old-school furniture restorer way out in the East End, past the stadium, that apparently is a magician and can make a piece of shit shine like gold. She's thinking these things, and she opens her eyes and turns off the shower.

"Towel yourself off very slowly," she hears from the mist, Bobby's voice, and for a moment she is brought out of herself, out of her work.

"You had an invitation, mister," she says.

"Very slowly."

She steps out of the shower. Bobby flicks the switch and he sees her, and she sees him. He adjusts the settings for the floor — he's always liked the floor warmer than Mimi. He takes off his shirt. Bobby would like nothing better to push his wife back in the shower. Take her with him.

Mimi towels off. She doesn't listen to Bobby. He had his chance, and he decided he'd like another drink. Her mind is at work again. "Dinner should be ready in an hour. I'll be downstairs working."

Bobby admits he saw this coming. Mimi's work is everything now. He had the luxury of leaving his work at the office; Mimi has no such luxury. "All work and no play."

"I know, I know, I'm terrible." Mimi balances herself on one foot while she towels a leg.

Bobby looks away. He loves that his wife can still make him dizzy. The sight of her. Right here. Or maybe it's the booze, he thinks.

She walks toward him. He takes her in his arms and rubs his hands slowly down her back. She kisses him, and he feels himself grow moist from her shower-warmed body, and then she's off him. She reaches for her robe and wraps herself in it. He's disappointed, but, again, he's thinking the kids are home, a few feet away, separated by tile and gyprock and plumbing and wiring. And then he's thinking about his job. Or the job he once had. And Mimi leaves the bathroom and starts picking her clothes off the floor, and Bobby watches her do that, wonders how he is going to tell his lovely, hard-working wife that he is unemployed and perhaps even unemployable, that everything he has worked for has been destroyed by a woman with a fondness for leopard print pumps.

Mimi drops her robe and wiggles into her underwear. She searches for a bra in her drawer of an Italian commode-style low-slung chest supporting a space-age mirror held together with brass fixtures that she found at a garage sale while in Philadelphia for an antique show.

Bobby realizes his wife and he are the same, that their connection is through their work and no longer through the kids or through each other. Mimi searches another drawer for her sweatshirt, the simple white sweatshirt she is sure to stain during dinner. Her clothes bear the scars of years of sloppy eating. Of Bobby's entertainment.

Mimi watches Bobby watching her. "Take your shower," she instructs, with the hint of a smile, with sympathy perhaps, but then she's out of the room, and Bobby stumbles out of his pants and underwear. He enters the shower and sets the water high. He's never touched the luminotherapy buttons. He's not even sure what they do.

Chapter 16

And so the family gathers for dinner. Mimi pulls the lasagna out of the oven. Dee places the bowl of salad in the middle of the table. Abbie distributes cutlery. Bobby, his hair still wet, sets a jug of water next to a carton of orange juice. Mimi places the tray of lasagna on a trivet and slices into the pasta and cheese.

Abbie reaches for the salad. "Just wait," Bobby says. "Wait for your mother."

The son sits back. He tries to imagine Etienne de Bosch, what she looks like, she sounds sophisticated and artsy and everything he would imagine a gallery owner to be if he ever imagined gallery owners. And he tries to imagine the gallery, but he can't, he can't even picture Mile-Ex, which is supposed to be cooler than Mile End, which isn't cool anymore, just gentrified and at the beginning of ossification, like so much of that part of the city.

Dee pours herself a glass of water. Juice has too much sugar. She's read there's more sugar in juice than in soda, which she won't drink, either, just water, never bottled, that's marketing, water shouldn't be more expensive than stuff that uses water as just one of its ingredients. Dee is not going to tell anyone at this table what she's told Abbie. Telling him was a door to legitimacy, to making it real, but she can't tell her parents, not while eating lasagna, which doesn't seem like the kind of food a family should be enjoying when one of the kids tells her parents she's just discovered she's gay.

Abbie looks at his sister. He knows she's not going to announce anything here, they've talked that part through, he respects his sister enough not to push her, but a large part of him wishes she would, right here and now, if only to see the reaction of his parents, but also to then talk about the gallery, to change the subject and save his sister and promote his own story at the same time, to be able to look at his father and say something snarky without sounding snarky, to share someone else's belief in his work, but that won't happen, not now, and he doesn't want to announce anything until he's spoken to Etienne de Bosch, who grows more fanciful in his imagination every time he thinks the name.

"How was everyone's day?" Bobby asks. Dee lets out a snort. Bobby knows that means something, but his heart is not into probing, not now, not when he has a secret, not when the husband and father sitting down with his family is a different man than the one who sat down with them yesterday. This is dinnertime. With the family.

"I'm hiring," Mimi says. She has distributed lasagna to everyone. She produces a bowl of freshly grated parmesan and a smaller one of chili oil. "That was my day."

She looks toward Abbie, and he can't tell if this is because she wants him to ask for a job or if she wants him to go next. He helps himself to salad. He doesn't feel the need to speak. He wants to have the gallery's interest in his back pocket. He looks into his mother's eyes. "That's great, Mom," he says. "Is this because of those investors?"

"This has nothing to do with them. That hasn't happened yet, and it might never happen."

"You're like Joe Businesswoman," Dee says.

Yes, Mimi thinks. That's exactly what she is. She's going to be successful. She's going to march over the world a conqueror. She's going to show her family, the ones still alive, but especially her father's side, who never approved of Bobby, who never approved of her marrying this Mexican-Scottish Montrealer, whom an uncle called "a mongrel." That side of the family, scattered across three continents, is going to hear of her, each one in their local paper, and Mimi realizes suddenly she has a plan, a poor reason to succeed, but a goal, she wants to get her story out, she wants to achieve the kind of success that will make her an interesting story in media around the world, or at least on three continents, because she wants her family to read her story without knowing it was there, she wants them to absorb her story, and she wants them to choke on it, a little, not much, but enough to scare them. She needs a marketing person maybe.

"Mom?"

That's Dee's voice. Mimi shakes off her reverie. "Yes, sorry?"

"What's the chef's name?"

"What chef?"

"The guy who made this."

"He's French from France," Bobby says, as if to help, but it's all he can say, he needs to show he's a part of this conversation without appearing a part of it.

"Jean-Marc?"

"That's it," Bobby says flatly, smiling in the most sincere manner he can manage.

Abbie can tell something is off with his father. He's not all there. His tone is distant. He can't imagine what it could be. He's never known his father to have a problem that he brought to the table. He can't imagine how much his father has hidden from him, because he's sure he has, and he respects him for that, he has always listened even if he hasn't supported, but he has never discussed his problems at this table. As far as Abbie can tell.

"Jean-Marc has changed his menu completely, everything's Korean all of a sudden! I had to beg him for a lasagna," Mimi says.

"Korean's so hot right now," Dee says. She knows this because she read it online. And because Coco Chanel keeps talking about a Korean barbecue not far from her house. With a cute waiter.

And they eat silently. Each in their bubble. Each with their thoughts and concerns and dreams and dilemmas. Each a chrysalis waiting to break free.

Bobby needs another drink or he needs to go to bed. He needs to speak to his wife, but maybe he can wait for the morning. Or maybe not. Because he can tell her tonight and sleep in tomorrow. The idea of it, of sleeping in, feels like something earned, a step toward recovery, or, perhaps, the beginning of a descent. Then he realizes tomorrow is Saturday. And then he's back to Leopard Lady and the calculation and of course she did the deed at the end of the week. He chews his lasagna like a cow chewing its cud.

Abbie needs to get in touch with Etienne de Bosch. And he will right after dinner. Etienne de Bosch is now giant, an amazon, in red heels, buried in scarves. But he's going to have another piece of lasagna first. He cuts himself a piece and douses it in chili oil.

Dee needs to speak to Coco Chanel. Urgently. She needs to tell her. She needs to unload on her friend because she knows her friend will hug her and support her and say the right thing because Coco Chanel always says the right thing.

Mimi needs to calm down. Mimi needs to listen to what her family is saying. She's not even sure if they are saying anything. Mimi is thinking about hiring people and about the size of her warehouse and about the angel investors and about her own small-scale plan for global domination, and she is thinking about how surprising that faction of her family that would be surprised by her success already tastes like the most delicious thing she has ever put in her mouth.

Chapter 17

Dee walks to the park and sits on the bleachers waiting for Coco Chanel. She is going to tell Coco Chanel and then she's going to wait for her friend to tell the world because, as much as Dee loves Coco Chanel, the girl cannot keep a secret, it is not in her DNA to hold things in, which is why she loves her and why she's so exasperating and why Dee feels this is the easiest way to get this over with, because she has to. Coco Chanel is the last door Dee needs to open and walk through.

On the other hand, her parents are a wall. She doesn't know how she's going to tell them. They already don't know so much about her, about her obsessions, about things she thinks and doesn't think and wants and doesn't want. She is still their little girl and sometimes her father, especially, will say as much, he will use the words *little girl*, she hears it when he calls her DeeDee, and a part of her is comforted by this sentiment, but more and more she needs to stop hearing it. They need to see her for what she is. She just doesn't know how to tell them properly.

Dee feels a tap on the shoulder. It's Coco Chanel. She's wearing a white linen blouse that is transparent enough to show off her lacy cream-coloured bra. She's wearing a denim skirt that stops at the knees. And flip-flops. To show off her toes. She is very proud of her feet. Coco Chanel is always dressed a few weeks too early in terms of weather — the sun is setting, and the night's chill is a real thing, it's still only May — but she has never let weather dictate her wardrobe.

Coco Chanel greets Dee with a two-cheek kiss. She smells good, Dee thinks, and then she stops thinking it because she needs to not think of Coco Chanel in that way. "Are you okay?" Coco Chanel asks.

"Thanks for asking."

"Your text was frantic."

"No, it wasn't."

"All caps and like a million exclamation marks."

Dee takes a deep breath. She's just going to tell her because that's the only reason she's told her friend to meet her at the park. Coco Chanel is already looking toward the basketball courts, and the boys are returning her gaze; Dee understands there is a time limit at work here.

"I figured something out," she says.

"Okay," Coco Chanel says, staring at the boys.

"I need you to look at me."

Coco Chanel turns her head slowly toward her friend. "Are you okay?"

"I'm fine." Dee hesitates. She hesitates because her hand is on the doorknob and she doesn't know what lies in wait on the other side.

"So?"

Dee takes a deep breath. Because now it is out in the world. "I'm queer."

Coco Chanel puts her hand to her mouth. Almost as if to stifle a laugh. Dee has no idea what this reaction means. And then Coco Chanel starts laughing. She *was* trying to stifle laughter, and she has failed and is now laughing. Dee doesn't know whether to feel humiliated or insulted or worse. Had she imagined Coco Chanel's reaction, laughter would not have been in the top five. Or even ten.

Coco Chanel hugs Dee and squeezes, and Dee feels the energy that her friend is transferring to her, it's like sunshine, and Coco Chanel shakes with laughter, and then Dee is laughing as well, but only because her friend is laughing so hard.

"Why are you laughing?"

Coco Chanel releases Dee. She has laughed herself to tears. She wipes her eyes. "I knew it!" she says, a huge smile on her face. "I knew it, I knew it, I knew it!" She hugs Dee again, and again Dee feels warmth though now it's tinged with something else. Shame perhaps.

"What do you mean you knew it?"

"I suspected it," Coco Chanel Chanel says. "Not just me."

"Who else?"

"Clémentine. Val. Even Sam."

"You mean you've all been talking about this? Like, is Dee a dyke? This is what you guys talk about?"

"Not all the time." Coco Chanel takes a hold of Dee's arms and stares straight into her eyes. "Look, we figured it out. I figured it out. We haven't been talking about you all the time, don't worry. But when it comes up, it comes up. We knew." She hugs her friend again. "I'm just happy for you." Dee does not return her friend's hug.

"What do you mean 'when it comes up'?"

Coco Chanel releases her. "Dee!" she says, annoyed.

"When would it come up?"

"Dee, please."

"Like you're in science class and then you guys start talking about whether or not I like girls?"

"Only Val is in my science class."

Dee wants to not care. She wants to be flattered. She's new to this, to being the subject of gossip. She's never thought she's done enough with her life to provide fodder for any kind of gossip, but this is juicy, the frantic whispering surrounding her sexuality. She wants to blush. She feels like she should. She also realizes she might not care too much. She's more comfortable with this than she understands.

"We didn't know how to bring it up. Okay, I didn't know. I wanted to. I wanted to ask." Coco Chanel is staring deeply into Dee's eyes, trying to convey empathy and support and love. "But how do you ask your best friend 'Are you a lesbian?' You know?"

"At this point, it's more theoretical," Dee sighs.

Coco Chanel breaks into a raucous kind of laughter, as if she's just heard the world's most fantastic joke, and she bends over and clutches her knees. Dee watches her shaking back, her back really is perfect, her spine is like a thin rope on a floor made of marble. Dee turns her head to watch the boys.

Coco Chanel sits up and hugs her friend again. "We're going to find you a girlfriend, girlfriend!" she says, almost like she's on the sidelines cheering, waving pompoms.

Dee wants to laugh at this thought. Because she's pretty sure Coco Chanel can find her the right girl.

"You're free," Coco Chanel says, with a hint of admiration.

"I haven't told my parents."

"You must tell your parents." Coco Chanel grabs Dee's arms once again. "You must."

"I will. It's still new. I just figured this out."

"When?"

"I was across the street from school."

"Today?!" Coco Chanel screams again. She stands up. "You figured this out today?"

"I left the cafeteria at lunch."

"You figured it out during lunchtime? Today?"

"I was coming back to school. I went to the park and I heard the bell and I was coming back to school and then bang, like someone punched me. I almost walked into traffic!"

"And you didn't tell me?"

"I was late for class!"

"And after? You had all afternoon."

"Where? Right in the hallway?"

Coco Chanel thinks about this. "But after school then."

"I came home early." Dee can't help but smell whatever perfume it is that Coco Chanel is wearing right now, and she's pretty sure she doesn't like it. "You were with that guy."

"So?"

"You were flirting with him."

"So? You're more important."

"I didn't want to interrupt."

"Dee!"

Coco Chanel is going to make a very difficult mother, Dee thinks. Her kids will not be able to hide anything from her.

"I'm telling you now."

"You must tell your parents."

"I told my brother."

"And?"

"I have a cool brother."

"You do. I love his photos. All that sex."

Dee can't help but think what she looks like next to her friend. She looks butch next to Coco Chanel's casual elegance, her effortless sexiness. Dee wants to be sexy. She wants to be confident, and through that confidence she wants to be sexy. She needs new clothes. "I need new clothes," she says.

Coco Chanel smiles as if told she has won a vacation to Bali. "Yes!"

Dee smiles too. She reaches over and hugs her friend. "I'm kind of happy," she says, an admission she has not made to herself yet. But it's true. She's going to tell her parents. It doesn't matter when. Until she has a girlfriend, perhaps it doesn't matter. She needs to let her new self sink in. She needs to slow this down. But she has clarity. And she has happiness. A kind of happiness. And lightness. She feels lighter. She releases Coco Chanel, and they smile at each other. And then the sound of a bouncing basketball is too much, and Coco Chanel looks in its direction, and it's as if she's already travelled far away, to another world. Dee would like to do that. She would like to hunt the way Coco Chanel hunts. She wants to be a hunter. She wants to start hunting. She wants to be hunted. Dee wants. She realizes now she has been drowning in confusion for so long. And now she wants to drown in something much simpler. She wants to drown in desire. She wants to want.

Chapter 18

Bobby throws off his clothes, slinks into bed, reaches for the remote, and turns on the TV. He flips through the sports channels and turns off the TV. He buries himself under the pillows and imagines himself walking downstairs, calmly, to fix himself a cup of tea, sitting on the old couch within sight of Mimi's computer, and telling her, in an even voice, about his new status as an unemployed man.

Or he can press the pillows down on his face until he has trouble breathing.

He tosses the pillows. He sits up. He pushes the blankets away and sets his feet on the floor and sits up. He buries his face in his hands. Why is this so hard? He didn't quit, he was fired, for reasons he doesn't even need to understand because he has imagined a plot encompassing offices on either side of the ocean, a plot so complicated and base and naked it has its own soundtrack. Those stories, of men who, once fired, continue to get dressed every morning and leave the house and then spend their days in coffee shops, are starting to make sense to him. Because he can see himself doing exactly that. He can imagine himself living a lie. It would not be so different from the lies he constructed at work. From the self he had built up. Only to see an interloper from Seattle knock it all down.

He stands. He's kept his secret long enough: he's going to tell Mimi. He should have told her immediately, or at dinner, but he didn't, and now he will. He is the not the kind to hide secrets. Not of this magnitude. Mimi once told him she would know if he'd ever cheated on her and he would never have to tell her, though she'd prefer if he did: She knows he can't keep a secret. She knows him too well. She knows him better than he knows himself. It's a cliché, but it's true. And he realizes that though she has no idea what he was like at the office, she could never have imagined the transformation in him. He was unrecognizable. Jekyll *and* Hyde.

He pulls his pants back on, grabs a T-shirt from the dresser, and opens the bedroom door and takes a deep breath and heads to the kitchen to brew a cup of tea. Or two cups of tea. She might like that. They have some genmaicha in the cupboard. He'd like that too. Something gentle. Thoughtful. The right kind of tea makes Mimi close her eyes and think of something far away, a long time ago. Her parents, perhaps. Tea is her soul food.

Bobby fills the kettle and searches the cupboards for the Japanese teacups. He finds them, and then he finds the genmaicha and tea gloves and fills each glove with the right amount of tea and places them in the cups. Mimi turned him on to tea; it was her first act of assimilation, a step toward their union, the first sign he had that he was being drawn into her essence. She had invited him to her apartment, and she had made him tea, and they talked through the night, and in the morning he said he would make her eggs if she had any and she said she had some sausage in the freezer and that was the beginning and the end of their courtship; they would not be married for another year, but after that night they both knew their marriage lay before them, it was just a matter of when.

The kettle starts whistling, and Bobby pours the water into the cups and waits for the tea to steep. He knows Mimi doesn't mind loose tea at the bottom of her cup, but this is cleaner, she's at her computer, working, perhaps she'd like a biscuit. He searches the pantry for tea biscuits and finds a box. An old box. He makes a note that they need tea biscuits. He might go shopping tomorrow. Maybe he'll make tomorrow's dinner. Maybe he'll do actual housework, and maybe he'll take his mind off the work thing. He's still getting paid. He's going to get paid for a long time. He hasn't yet appreciated the enormity of his severance. He'd never have approved something so generous. Was their extravagance saying something about him or about them? He isn't sure. But that severance buys him time. Which, he realizes, is what it is meant to do. Time and trouble.

He removes the gloves from the cups and places them in the sink. He steadies himself and heads for the basement. At the base of the stairs, he watches Mimi as she stares into her screen. She has a hand calculator by the keyboard. Her fingers caress the tiny buttons on the calculator as she reads charts off the screen. In her yoga pants and baggy sweatshirt, she could be a college student.

He places one of the cups on her desk and walks to the old couch, a couch from before Mimi's business — the basement is a graveyard of unwanted, discarded stuff — and sits. He sips his tea and watches her, and for the longest time she doesn't acknowledge him at all, she continues reading whatever it is that's on the screen, and then she reaches for her tea and brings it to her mouth and she inhales and closes her eyes and takes a sip. "Thank you," she says.

"I have something to tell you," he says.

"I know."

"I was going to tell you before my shower, and then after it, and then at dinner, and then I didn't."

Mimi stops looking at the screen and looks at him. "What is it?" she asks, gently.

"It's hard for me to say."

Mimi says nothing. Bobby knows she's not going to force anything out of him. That's not her style. She doesn't force anything with words. Just by her presence. He knows that if he says nothing and retreats, she will return to her work and not even think about his reticence.

And he thinks, just do it. He's going to push this out with the help of a slogan. It's on the poster on the wood-panelled wall opposite him. From when the basement was more the kids' rumpus room. From when Abbie was mildly athletic. The poster is white. The slogan is in the colours of a rainbow. *Just do it.*

"I lost my job." He exhales. That's done, he thinks.

"You were fired?" Mimi asks. Now she displays some concern. She puts her tea down and gives her husband all her attention. Bobby can feel her eyes on him.

"Yes. This morning. I was fired."

"Why?'

"I don't know. And I've thought about it and I don't care. I was fired and that's that."

"You had no warning?"

"Maybe I did, and I didn't notice it." He hadn't thought that yet, and now he's going to need to rewind every single meeting, every single comment, every email from the last few months to see if he had been too arrogant, or comfortable, to have seen it coming. If he was too lost inside his armour. It is possible he had received a warning and deleted it during his daily email bankruptcy. "I don't know. They brought in a new person. A woman from Seattle. Transferred from the Seattle office. I met her yesterday, and today she fired me."

"She's your replacement?"

"I guess."

"So." Mimi leans back in her chair. She picks up her cup and takes another sip of her tea.

Bobby blows on his tea and takes a sip. "I don't know what to do."

"I envy you," she says to his surprise. "Treat it like a vacation."

Bobby would like to do that. He would like to not feel his entire being has been attacked, that he has been cut down like a tree, an old tree covered in rot. "The severance is very generous. Insanely generous."

Mimi smiles. He doesn't know why she's smiling. "We'll be fine." And now Mimi stands and walks to her husband. She kneels on the carpet in front of him and puts her hands on his legs. She runs her hands up and down his thighs. Squeezing his knees. She doesn't want to show it, but she might be happy. She can demonstrate her worth now without stepping on toes. Without upsetting her husband. "We'll be more than fine. And so will you."

Bobby sighs. "I don't know."

"You'll be fine."

"I feel cut off at the knees."

Mimi stops touching his knees.

"I feel like I didn't realize how much I'd internalized my job until they told me I didn't have it any longer."

Mimi kisses his knee.

"Some of my employees clapped as I left. I could hear them. Clapping. The door closed behind me, and there was applause."

"Dear . . ."

Bobby leans back and closes his eyes. He feels no better for having told Mimi the truth. If anything, he feels worse. He feels worse right now than the moment he read the letter in front of Leopard Lady.

"You will be fine, dear. Honestly. If you feel this way, it's good. It's good that you're no longer there."

"They led me out like a criminal."

"What about all your things?"

"They're going to box up my things and send them to me. They took my phone, honey. I mean, I've had that phone number forever, and they took my phone." That, more than anything, had upset him most. They had started to peel away at his identity when they kept his phone. He feels silly for feeling that way. For feeling it now.

"I tried calling you about dinner."

"There you go. See? I don't have a cellphone."

"You'll get one." Mimi stands. "A new number. A fresh start."

"I'll never remember a new number now."

"You can sleep in," she says. She leans over and kisses his forehead.

Bobby sighs, deeper. He feels lost, again, still, permanently. He sips the tea.

"And then we can talk. When you're ready."

"About what?"

"About what you want to do." He's not ready. She can see that. This just happened. She may have to wait a long time. "Maybe you work with me. Us."

He's never been to the warehouse. She has told him about it, but he has never been beyond the door behind Esme's perch. His curiosity was never profound enough, and he wonders if that makes him a bad husband.

Mimi sees an opportunity where Bobby sees nothing. Mimi's business is a success, people want to invest in it, and she knows she's not just understaffed but perhaps wrongly staffed, and she sees another opportunity here.

Bobby's real fear is that Mimi is just as awful at work as he was. He was a monster. His employees had applauded his departure for a reason. He had been taught to be a monster, and he was, he was an awful human every day in that office, and he was rewarded for it until it was not the way to do business any longer. Then, he was worse than a monster; he was a dinosaur.

He sees his own pity.

"Call your friends. Go out. Recharge." Mimi marches on. She's going to be optimistic. She's going to lead Bobby out of this, even as he sinks deeper into a funk most foul. He's going to let her burn her energy on him, and then at some point he's going to realize he's being selfish and he will change. And then. Only then. It's all mapped out. They are playing their roles. Their married roles.

"My friends," he says.

"Go. Get drunk. Do they do that anymore?"

"My friends," he says, again. Which ones? Where? Where would they go? When's the last time they went out for drinks with them? Would they go to a bar? Where did middle-aged men go for beers these days? What does an unemployed man do for fun? What is he like? Who is that man?

Bobby watches Mimi's mouth curl into a smile. Does she recognize me still? he thinks. He feels incomplete, smaller. The incredible shrinking man.

Mimi returns to her computer. She sits, her face awash in the blue glow of her screen. Bobby sips his tea and watches Mimi study whatever it is she's studying. He watches his wife work.

Chapter 19

Abbie looks toward the sun, and sighs the sigh of the lost, and wonders where the gallery is. He's not familiar with this part of the city, he's never considered it before because he's never had reason to, and now he's navigating a neighbourhood that doesn't even seem like a neighbourhood, more like an assemblage of forgotten things, a row of houses here, an empty lot there, an industrial building, a warehouse, a construction site and then, suddenly, a piece of *architecture*, a photo from a magazine with a heavy cover and matte paper, and then back to a nondescript duplex, a lot overgrown with weeds, an abandoned building awaiting its fate, and then, suddenly, an obviously trendy restaurant, a café, a salon that advertises beard trims and waxing, and then a return to nothing.

Abbie is in possession of the address, it's in his phone, except he can't find it. He took the metro to Park Ex, and then he was lost, reliant on a map on his phone, now losing battery life, and he's forgotten his charger, so unlike him, a sign of nerves, of the understanding of the possibilities that await. What he realizes is the map has not taken the obvious shortcuts around here, through the weed-strewn empty lots, the parking lots, the dead-end streets. And so his path isn't efficient, and as he follows the prescribed route, the route he is beholden to take because the phone in his hand tells him so, because it is his master, he feels lost, not temporarily displaced, especially here, and doubts set in, because they must.

And then his phone tells him that he has arrived at his destination. He stands before an ugly two-storey building that looks like a botched layer cake baked by an apprentice, with cream-coloured brick. The garage door is the only indication that perhaps there is something to this place, something different, as it takes up most of the street-facing wall and surely the first floor is not entirely made for cars. A small sign — in exceedingly small lettering, low-contrast white on a cream background — announces the gallery. The door is by the side. Abbie takes a deep breath.

He enters a space of oppressive whiteness. The floor, the rugs, the furniture, the walls. The ceiling. The stairs that lead to a second floor. The curtains blocking off the garage door windows. The garage door itself, which opens, rolls up to open the gallery to the world as needed. Abbie closes the door behind him. "I'll be right down," he hears, and he imagines Etienne, glamorous, descending the stairs, and he wonders why he hasn't googled her, why nothing he would normally do has been done, why he's behaving like a child, and, he thinks, perhaps it's because he is one.

A door on the back wall opens, and a person struts toward Abbie. He can't tell if this person is Etienne, he can't tell if this person is a he or a she, he can't read a thing about this person. This person is short. And roundish. On the round side. Almost like a punching bag. Dressed in a loose-fitting black . . . something. Abbie thinks it's a frock. With loose-fitting black pants that flare out to impossible dimensions; one could hide a good-sized dog inside these pants. This person is wearing white Keds sneakers. And this person's neck is surrounded by a multitude of scarves in a multitude of colours and a multitude of materials — Abbie had imagined scarves at least. This person's hair is short, jet black but speckled with grey. This person's face is expansive — the nose takes up a large area of the face, and the eyes are large as well, large and grey. The nose overtakes the small mouth in a cartoonish manner. "You must be Abbie," this person says.

The voice is raspy but gives no hint to its gender. Abbie had been sure Etienne was a woman. He extends his hand. This person's hand is soft. This person has amazingly large hands.

"I'm Etienne," this person says. "Welcome to the gallery."

Etienne leads Abbie to a white couch in the middle of the room. Etienne sits on a white chair facing the couch. "Can I get you something to drink? Coffee? Water? We might have some juices."

"Thank you, I'm fine," Abbie says. He's looking for a hint. He should have googled Etienne. He's full of regret, and he should be full of wonder.

"Did you find us okay?" Etienne asks. "It's tricky around here, what with all the cul-de-sacs and empty lots."

Abbie waves his phone and then puts it down on the small white side table next to the couch. Abbie decides Etienne is a woman. He's just going to go with this hunch. She must be, he thinks.

"Of course," Etienne says, adjusting the scarves around her neck. "No one's lost anymore." She laughs, sarcastically.

Abbie doesn't know what to do with his hands. He rests them on his legs and then he clasps them together and then he puts them on this side and then he crosses his arms.

"I'm glad you could come on such short notice."

"I couldn't ignore your email," Abbie says, as honest as he can be. There's no use in trying to be someone else here, he thinks.

Etienne is far more sophisticated than he is, than he'll ever be. Last night, thinking about Dee, about the courage it took her to admit what she did, Abbie had decided to act his age. He had decided to greet this meeting, this situation, with the awe it deserved. If that meant he was going to look like an eager puppy lapping at Etienne's feet, so be it.

"Yes, there's a good story here," Etienne says, sitting forward now. "We have a new board member. She recently moved to Montreal. A very dynamic young woman. She says to me, 'Look at these,' and she shows me your website. Well, I saw what she saw right away." Etienne slaps Abbie's leg and starts to howl. Her laughter is canine. "I saw your vision of the city, the juxtaposition of old and new, the symbolism, the phallocentric ideology of gentrification, of industry, of change. So I thought, let's see what we have here."

Abbie sits stunned.

"I'm sure people think you're just shooting cocks and make it all seem so obvious."

Abbie remains stunned.

"I'm guessing you don't print these out," Etienne continues. She clears her throat the way, well, the way a man might, or a heavy smoker, which Abbie realizes perhaps she is. He is just now smelling her smoky funk, noting the contrast of it to the white tranquility of the space. "That's my guess, but I could be wrong."

"You're not wrong," Abbie says meekly.

"Okay. No problem. A lot of the art is in the printing."

"I have never considered myself an artist."

"Of course not." Etienne stands and waddles over to a desk and opens a drawer and takes out a tin of mints. She pops two in her mouth and returns to her chair and sits. "We should sit outside, in the sun, and talk about what we see in you."

"What do you see in me?"

"We hardly know you!" Etienne says and barks some more, until the barks become wheezes and then she is silent. "Do you want to learn?"

"Learn what?"

"To be a photographer."

Abbie sits up. "Yes."

"You have to learn about what you can do," Etienne says. "You must learn about the possibilities of your craft. You must find your own limits and then your own needs and then your own vision. How to mould a photo into an actual thing, into a work of art."

"I work with the photos quite a bit." Abbie may have said that defensively. He's not sure. He wants to remain humble. But he does know *some* things. At least on the computer.

"Yes, of course you do." Etienne puts her hand on Abbie's leg again. "Don't get me wrong." Etienne smiles, and Abbie returns the smile. He doesn't know what they're smiling about. He looks at the hand resting on his leg. He registers something, he knows he's doing it, trying to be himself and trying not to be. "Let me end your confusion," Etienne says, "because I know you're wondering: I'm a man."

"I knew that," Abbie stammers.

"I have to clear that up for some people. And I don't mind."

"I didn't —"

"I was born female."

Abbie hadn't considered that.

"But I never felt like a woman. If you understand."

"I wasn't even" —

"I was born in Germany. I have lived in New York. And Brazil. But now I live here, I'm Québécois."

— "thinking about" —

"I can change nationalities, change who I am. I am a modern. Global."

— "that, honestly" —

"I just thought I'd get that out of the way. Because I can make it difficult. I get that. And because we're going to be friends."

— "it never even" —

"Just so you know who you are dealing with. So there are no secrets between us."

Abbie stops trying to speak. Etienne stands up. He gestures for Abbie to do the same, and Abbie does and follows Etienne toward the door on the back wall. They enter a small unlit room, and then Etienne opens another door and they are in a lovingly manicured backyard. Multicoloured deck chairs are scattered around a small fountain. The lawn is surrounded by rose bushes. Beyond the roses, a large brick building rises up, casting shade over half the yard. "Have a seat," Etienne says.

He sits on a deck chair next to a small table upon which sit two packs of Marlboro Golds and an ashtray overflowing with stubbed-out cigarettes and ashes. Abbie sits and watches as Etienne lights a cigarette. He offers Abbie one, and Abbie refuses; he's never smoked and he's old enough to know he shouldn't start.

Etienne lights up. His lighter is in the shape of bloated Vegas Elvis. "I don't mean to scare you," he says.

"About what?"

"I don't mean to scare you about art. Using big words. Concepts. I don't mean to imply you're not a photographer either. Or that you don't put any effort into your creations. It's quite obvious that you do."

"Thank you." If nothing else comes out of this meeting, the fact that someone like Etienne can acknowledge his work will be enough for Abbie.

"I speak four languages and I just talk very fast and sometimes that freaks people out."

"I'm freaked out enough as it is," Abbie says, easing into reality.

Etienne explodes with laughter. A cloud of smoke exits his mouth and he hunches over, coughing. He gathers his breath. He takes another haul of his cigarette and then he places it on the ashtray. "This gallery doesn't specialize in people like you. Or I should say it hasn't in the past. We show new artists, but they're already developed. We're their big break. It's a different kind of thing, the promotion of new art. It's even a different kind of grant, when we apply for grants, which we do, like all galleries. But now we are thinking we should start introducing raw artists to the world. Go beyond what we're known for. Extend. Surprise. Our artist bios tend to emphasize schooling and training. But with you, it's next level. It shows a way forward. All this social media. It's a shift. Like a new school. Our thinking is that we should start this change with you."

Abbie thinks about things he never thought he had a right to think about. He starts to think about a career. About what that means. About being an adult.

Etienne coughs and continues to cough for half a minute and the cough transforms itself into barking. "Yes," he says, surrounded by a cloud of smoke. He reaches for the cigarette, it's only half done, takes one last puff, and then stubs it out and turns to Abbie. "I want you to meet with a photographer," he says with a serious tone, a tone Abbie has yet to hear. "He is a bit of a legend. He's fully digital, and yet he produces these prints . . ." Etienne's voice trails off, as he imagines the prints. And he stays there, in this reverie, until he is out of it, and he lights another cigarette. "Your work reminds me of his. He will help you. Teach you some basic things. About printing. And then if you want to know more, that's up to you. He's very difficult. I'm warning you now. Nothing will be forced. Everything is free will. Freedom. Your freedom is the most important thing. Without freedom, art is nothing. Without freedom, you become a commercial photographer. There's nothing wrong with that, but it's not art. That's a different story. Art and commerce. I bore myself just thinking about it. But you, here, you need to learn how to create prints of these works of yours."

Abbie has always envisaged his photos on a large scale. He has imagined his photos, immense and overpowering, hung on a white wall. He has imagined them looming over anyone and everyone who might look at them, but mostly looming over him, the photos dwarfing him in the way he often feels dwarfed by the smokestacks themselves. He wants his fruit to overwhelm, to heighten their colours to the point of garishness, he wants even the fruit to make the viewer seem small, he has imagined all of this and more, and now he is sitting with a person who is going to unlock this vision, this desire he is only now realizing is a strong force within him, a fire almost, and he wonders if this is what art feels like. If creating art is like controlling fire.

And he thinks about emerging. He feels that when he leaves this place, whether it's in a minute or an hour or a day, he will have become something else, he will emerge from this place as another person.

"We have an opening in our schedule," Etienne says. "The fall. I was working on a show, and then the artist's mother died in a car accident, terrible tragedy. I'm not sure she should have been driving to be honest, but the artist has taken it very hard, they must have been close; anyhow, all this to say we have this opening, and your name came up and here we are."

"This fall?"

"November. Here, that's practically winter. Early November. It's a good time if you think about it. People are thinking about Christmas. Even collectors have to buy presents."

Etienne is talking about people buying my photographs, Abbie thinks. He grips his chair like someone realizing for the first time how rickety a roller coaster can be.

"But look, we're getting ahead of ourselves." Etienne barks, stubbing out his half-smoked cigarette. "November is very soon, I know. Normally, a show takes at least a year to put together. At least! But we're stuck, and you're here." He stands now. "Come inside. Let's see if we can hook you up with the photographer. He's tricky. But he enjoys teaching. I don't know why. But you — we need to get to work. We have arrangements to make." Etienne waddles for the door. "We have to sell you," he says over his shoulder. "At least you have this social media thing happening, right?" He turns to face Abbie. "People still care about social media, don't they?"

"I guess." Abbie smiles until his face hurts. He smiles as wide as he's ever smiled. He feels his face split in two and a new face crawl out. The end of the beginning. Or the beginning of the end. He can't tell. He feels a before and an after. He can't feel his feet hit the ground as he follows Etienne inside. "Some people care. At least, that's what they tell me."

Book Two

Want

They always say time changes things,
but you actually have to change them yourself.

— ANDY WARHOL

Chapter 20

Bobby has found the vacuum cleaner. He's found the cleaning closet, something he knew existed but couldn't ever imagine, like Shangri-La, or the smell of a porn set. Inside the closet, not just a vacuum cleaner, but assorted environmentally sound liquids, rags, cleansing pads, dusters, mops. The accoutrements of civility.

The regular housecleaner, Martha, almost a member of the family, *almost*, someone who had entered their house three times a week for the last decade and washed and scrubbed and dusted and made their home look clean and proper, had to return to Jamaica for a family emergency. It sounded bad, something about her brother, and Bobby had told her to take the time she needed, they would survive without her, and he thought he could do the cleaning, the family could do it, he'd said, but he'd really meant him, he would do the cleaning, it would be cathartic, and he told Martha not to worry.

I can do this, he thinks, and he finds an outlet and plugs in the vacuum and searches for the button that will turn it on and he presses a button and turns a knob, but this vacuum cleaner is *designed*, it's German, he thinks, and it's so well-designed he can't figure out how to turn it on. He finds a switch on the bottom of the handle, where his hand would be were he already vacuuming, and he flicks it, and the machine comes to life. It's an amazingly silent vacuum, he never thought a vacuum could be so quiet, and he wonders if it works at all, and he starts vacuuming, slowly, and it seems to be — it's not that the carpet in the hallway is soiled, but the carpet where the vacuum has been seems cleaner, it seems transformed, the after is better than the before — and so he continues; it's him and the vacuum. This isn't so bad, Bobby thinks. I can do the whole house quickly; what does Martha do all day? And then the hallway is done, and Bobby feels a satisfaction he has not felt since Lamontagne told him his work had earned the division an unforeseen profit and that he was in line for a bonus that would make his knees weak. And he takes the vacuum to the living room and the shag carpet.

Martha had warned him about the shag. There's a setting on the vacuum for deep carpets, the pictogram shows a shag rug, and he finds it and turns a knob so that it is pointing to the right pictogram and away he goes, he's cleaning the shag. The sun pours into the living room, illuminating the rug, and Bobby can see bits of dirt in it, it's shag and it *captures* things, things *live* inside its shaggy depths, and now he can see the vacuum's accomplishments, its effectiveness. He'd like to retract whatever dismissive thing he'd said about the vacuum cleaner every time Mimi had lauded its virtues because this thing sucks dirt like a tornado sucks trailer parks. And it does so with love: this vacuum cleaner tugs at the shag but then releases each strand tenderly; it's as if this cold appliance *cares* for the shag.

Bobby zooms through the house, riding the vacuum cleaner to a finish line of unexpected pride. The joy of tasting a new pleasure. He returns the vacuum to its magical closet home, and he takes a long look at the duster and he grabs it and he starts dusting the house, the shelves, the tops of doors, behind books and statues and Hummels, the tops of cabinets, the dark recesses of the entertainment unit in the bedroom. He cleans the toilets. He's seen it done before, on television, and he feels a previously unimagined kind of paternalism in cleaning the receptacles for his family's various wastes. He scrubs the sinks. He dons an apron and readies himself to tackle the kitchen floor. He gets on his knees and becomes intimate with the tiles of the kitchen floor.

Abbie comes home. "Dad?" he asks.

Bobby stands. He bounds up. His apron is festooned with butterflies and both know it is ridiculous looking, even when not worn by a human, let alone a man who hasn't shaved recently. "Hi," he says, not embarrassed exactly. "Martha had to return to Jamaica. Something about her brother."

"He's having surgery," Abbie says. "His stomach exploded or something."

"I'm always the last to know."

"And you decided to clean?"

"Someone has to."

"Okay." Abbie gives him the most skeptical look he can muster, which doesn't take effort because he has never seen his father clean — this is a man who can barely load the dishwasher. He sees what unemployment is doing to his father, the changes that accrete, the transformation that becomes suddenly apparent, like continental drift on a time-lapse camera spanning millennia, and he backs away, and he runs up the stairs and heads to his bedroom. And once Bobby hears the door close behind his son, he gets back on his knees and prepares to once again pray to the Platonic ideal of a spotless kitchen floor.

He refills the bucket with water and cleaner that is environmentally sound and biodegradable because the family held a meeting once, and Dee made a presentation about the environment and the chemicals in standard household cleaners and ended her speech with "we can afford it" — meaning the family could afford to be green, which Bobby thought ironic, and that led to a broader discussion about class and "the right thing" and intent and virtue and whether or not only the upper middle class could afford to care about a healthy planet and if that was the case, wasn't it a strange kind of hypocrisy, after all, if you could afford to be green that meant you could afford all the things that made the world less green — and blue — and Dee had run from the room because she wasn't making a class statement, she just wanted to do the right thing, she was the young one, she was the one who was going to pay for it, and she'd said this with Abbie in the room, as if their difference in age had become a chasm, and Abbie had joked about feeling old, which is when she started screaming, and the next day Bobby and Mimi drove around the city — an irony they also recognized — and found the products Dee had suggested, and the ones they hadn't found, they bought online and had shipped, which Bobby also noted, but they'd used the products since that time and had never once complained about it, and the environmentally friendly products had not made their house notably cleaner nor had they made it notably less clean, but there was a consciousness at stake as well, and that part of the equation was priceless, and then there was Dee, and that part was even more priceless.

It had been a week now, and Bobby was discovering some truths about himself, the mythology that he had built up around him like the walls to a fortress. He had been liberated in so many ways, but it had not felt like liberation. Mimi kept telling him he was free, but he felt, perhaps, like an Iraqi after hearing George Bush peddle freedom from far away. Technically, he was free. In reality, he was prisoner to his own expectations. His own disappointment.

He finishes with the floor and he crawls out of the kitchen and lies on the hallway carpet and he thinks he should finally tell his friends, someone, just call someone up and tell them. He sees in this moment the value of social media, of what his family had told him so many times, that social media was more than people complaining about breakfast and screaming at one another, though there was that as well. Without the internet, Mimi didn't have a business, and Abbie didn't have an outlet for whatever it was that Abbie did, and Dee would probably spend more time watching TV, or trying drugs, or chasing after the wrong type of boys. Bobby's friends have told him to get on Facebook at least, and he has resisted, and now that resistance is a point of pride, and they chastise him for it. He saw his old circle of friends grow closer, he saw that he was slowly excluded from things, not because they didn't want to see him, but because it was easier not to. Bobby had reached an age where he hardly even picked up the phone, and now he didn't have a cellphone; he'd made no effort to purchase a new one.

He heaves himself up and walks to the phone and he tries to remember Jonathan's phone number, because Jonathan is his oldest friend, and the fact he can't remember the number says more about himself than anything else. He puts the phone down and thinks. He's had trouble remembering phone numbers since they went from seven digits to ten, even though the area code is easy to remember, that's not something one has to memorize, but the three extra digits short-circuited something. He wonders why this isn't a bigger deal to people, this ten number thing.

Jonathan and Bobby have known each other since high school. He is Bobby's most enduring link to his youth, a miracle, he thinks. Perhaps Jonathan had once thought that as well. Jonathan lives not far from Bobby, not far from their old high school; they had lived just two blocks from each other growing up, and Bobby never forgets to remind his friend that he'd introduced Jonathan to his wife, that he'd introduced them because he'd slept with her first, and when that hadn't worked, because there was nothing to work, Jonathan had asked about her, and Bobby called her up — her name was (and still is) Gail — and told her about Jonathan. She knew who he was, and then it was up to the two of them, and a decade later they were married. Now they have a son in university, in the States, and another son just entering the architecture school at McGill. They own a condo in Florida. And a cottage up north. Jonathan owns his own company. Gail teaches history at a private school.

Bobby finds them both boring in their success. But Jonathan remains that link to his past, and he feels closest to him, even now. He doubts that Jonathan sees Bobby in the same way, because no one sees Bobby in that way.

Bobby finds his phone book, a jumbled up mess of pages and scribbles he's kept on his bedside table since he's had a bedside table. He sits on the bed and finds his friend's work number. He picks up the phone and pushes the number in, and Jonathan's secretary answers and patches the call through.

"Hey, hey!" Jonathan says, because he always greets Bobby that way and has for more than twenty years.

"We haven't seen each other in a while."

"That's not my fault."

"I didn't say it was."

"I should put the phone down now, call the newspaper, and tell them to write a story about the fact you picked up a phone."

"Ha ha."

"Are you okay?"

"Of course I am."

"Then what the fuck?"

"What does that mean?"

"Did someone die?"

"No one died." Bobby doesn't know why he's called. He's not going to recount the story of his life over the phone. He's not entirely sure that's why he picked up the phone. "Wanna go for a drink?"

"How's Mimi?" Jonathan asks.

He's trying to be civil, Bobby thinks, and he probably should be as well, be civil, not shoot straight for the back and forth of old men. "Mimi is great. Her business is going very well. I don't see her much it feels like. And Gail?"

"She wants to stop teaching. She's not even fifty, and she wants to retire."

"She said she wants to retire?"

"Not in those words, exactly. But what else is it?"

"You can change jobs without it being a retirement," Bobby says, with some force. "It's called a life shift or something. When you want change." He thinks that he will get a new phone tomorrow. Something about Jonathan has made him realize something about himself. He's just not sure what it is.

"Sure, let's get a drink."

"I can understand the urge to move in a new direction." He worries he may sound too sincere.

"I'm not criticizing her," Jonathan says.

"I mean, good for her."

"Where do you want to go?"

"I don't know. Where do people go for drinks?"

"There's this place I go with the boys. Not far."

"What boys?"

"My boys."

"You go out with your kids?"

"Why wouldn't I go out with my boys?"

Bobby has no answer for this. How could he? What kind of father is surprised that another father likes to go out for drinks with his grown children? "I just remember the boys as kids," Bobby says, sliding across the crease for the save.

"And your kids?"

"What about them?"

"What are they up to? Abbie must be heading off to college, no?"

"Abbie is not sure what he wants to do," Bobby says slowly, trying to make Abbie not sound like a dropout.

"I hear that," Jonathan says. "I travelled, remember? If he's unsure, he shouldn't do it. School without direction is a waste of money."

Jonathan had gone to Mexico and then found a job on a cruise ship, travelled to Europe, spent some time in Sicily, picked up enough Italian to make himself popular in the right cafés, and then stuck out his thumb and discovered himself. That's what he always said, he'd discovered himself. And that discovery led to business school and then a job and then his own company. Jonathan had always taken risks. He'd navigated change with an ease that Bobby had always envied. What if Abbie is doing that now, taking risks, discovering himself, only he's doing it through a camera? What if Abbie is happy? Why can't Bobby bring himself to understand his son?

"Friday?" Bobby asks.

"Saturday's better."

"I can do that."

"Good then."

There is silence between them, as sure a sign the conversation is over as any.

"Everything's okay?" Jonathan asks.

"Stop fucking asking that."

Bobby hangs up and lies on the bed. I am lost, he thinks. He's willing to admit this. Not to anyone else. He's not sure he has anyone to admit this to. Who could listen to this message? Who is there to burden with this information? He misses his parents. For the first time, he feels like an orphan, a child alone in the world, adrift. He misses his parents. He misses his mother's cooking. The smell of the house. The intent nature of his father's listening. The concentration. No one listened as deeply as his father had.

Chapter 21

The sun finally hits summertime strength. Dee has just felt it and she wiggles out of her shorts, takes off her top, and Val whistles. Dee slaps her, but inside she's beaming, she's never been out in a bikini before, and she feels comfortable in her skin. She's convinced this helped her during her exams even, and now school's out, and her mother wants her to work for her, she promises to pay her properly, and Dee's going to do it. She's a girl in a bikini and she's going to have money in her pocket and the summer's ahead of her.

"Girl," Val says, admiring her friend's sparkling silver swimsuit.

"Shut up."

"That's the bikini."

"I don't look fat?"

"Shut up."

Dee opens her eyes. The sun burns through them, and she sits up to rummage through her bag for her sunglasses. She puts them on and lies back again. "Not even my ass?" she says. Always her ass.

Val lies next to Dee. The sun beats down on them with purpose. There is nothing more magical than a Canadian sun, than the Canadian summer overall, the miraculousness of this kind of heat after so much cold. Dee knows her father always says that Canada isn't underpopulated, that it's a miracle that anyone lives here at all. "Where's Coco Chanel?" Dee asks, because she wants Coco Chanel to see her in the bikini, and she wants Coco Chanel to comment on it, because this bikini is critic-proof, it is the best thing she's ever bought.

"She said she was going to get some wine, as usual," Val says.

Coco Chanel is not yet at the point where the drinking has gotten her into trouble, but Dee isn't sure she would let her friend get to that point either. Coco Chanel can walk into any depanneur and buy a bottle of cheap white, because in Montreal that has always been possible for certain girls in certain deps. Coco Chanel knows the ones that are sympathetic to her or, even better, indifferent; that's what she thrives on, the indifference of those around her, because indifference is what permits her to act the adult.

Val opens a paper bag and pulls out a round doughy thing, about the size of a golf ball, and passes it to Dee. "What are these?" Dee asks.

Val shrugs. "I think the guy said gluten balls, but that sounds dumb."

Dee takes the paper bag. "It says they're vegan."

"So, vegan gluten balls?"

"Is gluten vegan?"

Val reaches for her phone. "I'm going to look that up."

"No, seriously."

"I'm looking it up."

"Like gluten-free vegan balls maybe makes sense."

"Gluten is vegan." Val shows Dee her phone.

Dee bites into the ball, a combination of an egg-free dough and sugar. Lots of sugar. And perhaps vanilla. "It kind of sucks," she announces.

Val takes one from the bag and sniffs it. She puts it down.

"It sucks a lot," Dee says.

"That bikini."

Dee loves that Val seems mesmerized by her bikini. She doesn't know if she is turning her friend on, but the way Val studies her is kind of world-changing. "Shut up."

"That's going to get you a girlfriend."

Dee hadn't thought of it in that way and is annoyed that sex remains theoretical.

"Coco Chanel is trying to set you up."

"Shut up!"

"And Clémentine too. She said she knows girls."

"She knows girls what?"

"Like you don't try and set up people."

"I'm not listening."

"Just because Coco Chanel is trying to find a girl for you."

"It's out of her comfort zone."

"I don't think anything is out of her comfort zone."

Dee turns over to sun her back. She adjusts the bottom of her bikini for maximum sun. She had a sexual dream involving Coco Chanel, and she remains deeply ashamed of this. She's sure if she were to tell Coco Chanel her friend would love this news, would be flattered by it even, but the dream felt wrong, as if Dee were breaking rules, and in her confusion, she had avoided Coco Chanel for two days because she couldn't look at her properly, not without remorse, without the knowledge that she had imagined something that lay beyond the invisible line she shouldn't cross.

Coco Chanel arrives wearing a top as transparent as cheese cloth and a red check kaffiyeh around her neck and down her front to cover her breasts. Not always successfully. The kaffiyeh is not a political statement, though in this neighbourhood it is, and Coco Chanel knows it. Since the late spring, she has paired it with this shirt, and when she wears the shirt, she doesn't wear a bra. The shirt makes that obvious. But the kaffiyeh's positioning is also strategic. She whistles.

"Thanks," Dee says, proud of herself. Of the chutzpah she's showing now, slowly, the comfort in herself that is the result of her epiphany.

"You're going to get a girl with that."

Val snorts.

"You think?" Dee asks, playing coy. Because she would like that. She fears her only future sexual activity will be online, watching others. She knows enough, and she's old enough, to understand the difference between online and real life. Sometimes she feels like she's failing at real life.

Coco Chanel pours wine into one of her cups. She downs the contents of the cup in one gulp and pours herself another. "I think you're hot," she says.

Val snorts again. And rolls her eyes so hard she sees the inside of her head.

"No, really. You are. Look at you. And that ass. I know you don't like it, but get over yourself."

"I don't know what girls like," Dee says, admitting something that has been bothering her. She can't tell, from what she's seen, from the queer porn sites she's visited; she's not ready to interact with anyone, not yet, she's not ready to chat with others, to click on the links Coco Chanel keeps sending her, the links Val keeps sending her; even Clémentine has been sending her links. All of her friends are visiting lesbian chat rooms and websites and message boards and, yes, looking at porn, so much porn, but not the lesbian porn for guys, not "girl on girl." But Dee wouldn't know. She can guess the content of each site — Coco Chanel sends her links with a synopsis of what she's seen — by the URL, but she can't bring herself to click one because she can't bring herself to admit that her straight friends are helping her explore her own sexuality. Each email with another link makes her feel passive, hopeless. A loser.

"Beth is a dyke," Coco Chanel says before taking another swig of wine.

"Shut up," Dee says.

Beth is a neighbour. She lives near the end of Dee's street and goes to the English high school. Dee has known her since they were kids. Beth has strange parents, the subjects of rumours and gossip. Innuendo. They are both professors, Dee thinks.

"I found out," Coco Chanel says proudly. "My neighbour goes to her school. She knows her. She told me about Beth."

"No really, shut up."

Beth is tall and blonde and athletic. She was one of the first girls in the neighbourhood to play hockey, to play with the boys. She plays basketball and volleyball. She is smart. The girl other parents might hold up as an example if perhaps her own parents weren't such outcasts.

"She's been out for a year," Coco Chanel says.

Dee is annoyed by the homework her friend is doing on her behalf. As if the endless text messages and emails weren't bad enough, as if Coco Chanel's obsession since the moment Dee told her didn't bother her enough. "Maybe it's obvious. All those sports."

"Just stop."

"I don't want to believe the stereotype," Coco Chanel says, "but she's an athletic girl. She's good at all those sports. My friend told me she's like a hero in the school because her teams do so well. So at least no one's picking on her."

Dee does not have it in her to change the subject. She would listen and even be interested in this news were it delivered by anyone else. But who else would tell her? Who else would know? Who else would consider this news worth telling her, in this manner, not as some rumour but as good news? "Just stop," Dee says again. And she opens her eyes and sneaks a peak at Coco Chanel and she sees her pour herself yet more wine, and their eyes meet, and Coco Chanel smiles at her friend and Dee returns the smile because they both know what's going on and because Dee knows that Coco Chanel is telling her this news about her neighbour, is doing this work on her behalf, because she is her friend, her best friend, and that's what best friends do. Dee understands this, and she slides her hand across the blanket and she finds Coco Chanel's free hand, the one not holding the plastic wine glass, and she gives it a loving squeeze. And then she slaps it. As Coco Chanel brings her cup up to her lips.

Chapter 22

Bobby has been to the new butcher, the one that lists the names and locations of each of the producers from which it procures its ethically sound animal products. He's making meat loaf, and he takes the making of it seriously. He had elevated the idea of meat loaf long before the idea of comfort food had been pushed as an antidote to fussiness. He dons his apron. He piles the ground chuck, veal, and pork in a large stainless steel bowl, adds spices, cracks two eggs into the pile of meat, and covers it all with panko. He folds everything together, gently; he learned long ago not to overhandle the meat in meat loaf — or meatballs — and he pours barbecue sauce in and folds the mixture some more. He tips it all onto a baking sheet lined with foil. He pats the meat into a loaf. He also learned long ago to not stuff the meat into a loaf pan, and if anyone mentions the quality of his meat loaf, this is what he tells them, this trick is all you need to produce a superior meat loaf.

Bobby brushes more of the barbecue sauce over the loaf, and finally he pours some honey that's been spiked with ground chiles over the mass. He places the baking sheet into the hot oven and sets the timer. He cleans his hands. He cuts some organic carrots he picked up at the small market next to the butcher. He melts butter in a cast iron pan and adds olive oil, some apple cider vinegar, and a sprig of thyme. When the butter bubbles, he places the carrots in the pan and gives it a shake. He checks on the rice in the pot on the stove. He sits at the kitchen table and takes a sip of his Scotch.

His life had become domestic surprisingly seamlessly and quickly. He'd thought about taking up jogging. He'd always complained he didn't have time to exercise, and now he had nothing but time; he understands he never had the desire, that exercise was an activity that felt distant. He wasn't sure that exercise was worth it. What did good health get you? An extra year? Two? Did it even guarantee that? Did exercise equal time or did it simply grant purchase into conversations about being in shape? Because in the end, the only people who really listened were the other people exercising, a society of the fit, exercise being a lifestyle, under a larger umbrella of wellness, what a word, *wellness*, with its implication that everyone who doesn't subscribe to it is a fan of *un*wellness.

He was going to jog. It was just a matter of buying the right gear. Which he would do. That would be his errand tomorrow. He'd go to a running boutique and he'd purchase his uniform and he'd become one of them, he'd look the part, and perhaps in that pursuit he would gain entry into a world he didn't want to enter.

He stands and checks on the rice again and turns the burner off and starts stirring the carrots. He shakes the pan. He turns the exhaust above the stove to medium, and the steam from the carrots runs toward the fan, to its efficient disposal.

He pours himself another Scotch. He hears the door open and then the short steps running up the stairs and he knows it's Dee.

"Dinner in half an hour!" he yells. He's not sure if Abbie is in the house at all. Lately, every meeting with his son has elicited a kind of surprise, and Abbie has noted it and seems to enjoy the awkward serendipity of their encounters. Both kids have been supportive of his new life. They did not care about the firing, not because they didn't understand it but because he's their father, employed or not. That helped him, more than he realized, when first confronted with their indifference to the news.

Mimi has texted her expected time of arrival. This is how they speak now. Bobby's new phone doesn't do much, and he doesn't want it to, he doesn't want to become one of those people sitting by themselves, removed from the world, hunched over their phone. But Mimi texts more than ever. He has watched Mimi become consumed by her business, and each level of consumption is another wall constructed between them, another barrier to their communication. He has suggested date nights, and Mimi says yes and then forgets the suggestion, that it was ever mentioned, because she no longer listens, her world is lived in her head when she is not in the only world that matters to her.

Dee runs into the kitchen and gives her father a kiss. He reaches for her, but the Scotch has slowed him, and he misses, and Dee opens the pantry and stands staring at the delights within. "We're eating soon, DeeDee," Bobby says.

"Twenty minutes?"

Bobby reaches for his phone. "Sure," he says.

"Do we have any fruit bars or something?"

Bobby doesn't think they do, but he doesn't know, either, and this bothers him. Fruit bars are the kind of thing Mimi might buy if she were thinking of her family's needs. But Bobby wouldn't, he would never buy fruit bars, because he's not sure they are a real food, he didn't grow up with something called "fruit bars," and so when he goes shopping, which he does regularly now, they do not exist, not in the realm of the things he thinks he can buy when he steps into a grocery store. He thinks he lacks empathy. Perhaps he needs to ask everyone what they need and then go shopping. Perhaps he needs to go shopping somewhere beyond the local grocery store. "Is your brother home?"

"So is that a no on the fruit bars?"

"I didn't even know you liked fruit bars." He is sure he can buy them in bulk. He makes a note to head to Costco.

Dee turns to face her father. "I love fruit bars."

"I didn't know."

"You should."

"I do now."

"So do we have any?"

Bobby shrugs. He's not sure what a fruit bar looks like. He can't picture the packaging. Is a fruit bar the kind of thing that would even occupy the pantry? Is she looking in the right place?

"I can hold out."

"Is your brother home?"

"I don't know," Dee says, because she doesn't, because like her father, and like her mother probably, she never knows if her brother is home because his door is always closed. She backs her way out of the kitchen, keeping eye contact with her father, for no reason; she can't fathom why she thinks she needs to maintain eye contact with him, perhaps because she thinks it's polite, but really she just wants to get back in her room and continue finding different ways to explore her new self that involve actually meeting other new selves and not girls online who may or may not be girls. And she also wants to figure out if she should tell her parents about her new self, because meat loaf seems like the ironic meal, to her, at which to do so, and maybe she's backing out of the kitchen because this is the last time she'll be in the kitchen with her father while he believes his daughter to be heterosexual. And she finds this so silly she turns and runs up the stairs to her room and dives into her bed so her father doesn't hear her muffled laughter.

Mimi sends Bobby another text to say she's coming home. Early. She uses many exclamation marks, which is not something she normally does, and so Bobby thinks either she's had a great day or she's cheating on him. And he's certain she's not cheating, mostly because she doesn't have the time. He's never thought of this before, of her wandering away, but he's amazed by where his mind goes while he's dusting the shelves, or cooking dinner, or grocery shopping. He might be squeezing a pear to check for ripeness, but he's thinking, Is she cheating? Or agonizing over granola. Or canned soup. Why are there so many brands, and why is she cheating on me?

He checks the timer. He texts Abbie and Dee that dinner will be ready in ten minutes and he'd appreciate help. Dee is in the kitchen before he can register he's asked for anything, and she sets the table.

She thinks a rote task, a routine, right now, is a good nerve calmer, something to keep her mind from collapsing under the enormity of what she's going to share with her parents. Abbie texts that he's not home but is on his way and should be there in fifteen minutes.

Dee is in a T-shirt and her bikini bottom; it's become her uniform. Bobby is amazed that he's old enough to have a daughter who dresses like this, that he is the father of a young woman in a bikini. "Do you ever take that off?" he says pointing to her bottom and immediately he understands what he's asked. Dee looks at her bikini bottom and starts to laugh, and Bobby laughs as well, the words that come out of a parent's mouth change meaning as their children grow older, and at a certain point almost everything sounds inappropriate.

"You know what I mean." He slaps her on the shoulder lightly, more like brushes her shoulder with his hand, but he feels he shouldn't even do that, not when his teenage daughter is wearing half a bikini and a T-shirt.

"It's summer."

"I'm sure you won't be wearing it when you go work for your mother."

"It'll be under my pants," she says, smiling coyly, playing the daughter; she misses *play*. This is what the house lacks. A sense of fun. She's long complained about this. About this lack. About what they don't share.

The front door opens, and father and daughter lean back to see who it is. "It's me," Mimi says, picturing her husband in the kitchen, leaning backward, trying to see the front door, which you can't do from the kitchen, not from the stove, and not from the table, she knows because she's done it, too, and can't see anything. From the pantry, maybe.

She speed walks into the kitchen and kisses her husband and takes a good look at Dee's bikini bottom. "Does that ever come off?" she asks, but she's out the kitchen before she can hear Dee and Bobby laugh. "I'm going to change, and then I'll be right down," she calls, running up the stairs, always busy, always in a rush, because that is her life now; she has schedules, she has an agenda.

Bobby reaches under the counter and opens a cupboard door and pulls out a serving dish and spoons the carrots onto the dish. "Put the rice in a bowl," he tells Dee, and she does as she's told; she dances around her father and reaches up to get a bowl from the shelf next to the window that looks out to the backyard. She can see the Zederbaums on their deck, discussing something, they're always so serious, the parents, not Saul, Saul is cool, for a Zederbaum. Mr. Zederbaum is stroking his beard while he listens to his wife tell him whatever it is she's telling him; Dee can't imagine what Mrs. Zederbaum has to go through to kiss her husband, what with that beard.

Abbie enters the house. He peeks into the kitchen, weighed down by two backpacks, and waves. Dee sticks out her tongue at him. "Dinner's on," Bobby says.

Abbie runs up the stairs, three at a time, full of the day, of the photographs he shot along the viaduc, where the hounds of gentrification have yet to be unleashed and where, to his surprise, rise dozens of smokestacks in various states of disrepair, surrounded by nothing more than misery and the history of a city's obvious decline. He also spent time with Jacques; he's truly become his mentor, who is showing him how to process film properly but also, more importantly, how to properly print digital images, how to work the files and prepare them for giant prints. Etienne has agreed to subsidize the cost of the printing for a greater commission on the eventual sales of Abbie's work, and Abbie doesn't care, because this gallery owner is talking about the sale of his work as if it is a certainty.

Abbie drops his backpacks. Jacques has loaded him up with books, told him to buy the books he doesn't already own, told his liege to study the history of photography, of all photography, including industrial photography, has explained to Abbie that what he's attempting to capture is a take on something as old as the craft itself, that he is positioning himself in a long line of great photographers, and that to know what he's doing he should know who has done it before him. Jacques's studio is not far from the gallery. A new coffee shop has opened recently between the studio and the gallery, in the lobby of a building that houses tech start-ups.

Etienne de Bosch thinks Jacques can get Abbie ready in four months, which he knows sounds silly; there's not time for the proper promotion, but he feels Abbie's story is marketing in and of itself, and with his online presence, and the few outlets that have started to reference his work in the book report style of unpaid interns writing stories, he sees the splash Abbie can make.

The timer chimes, and Bobby opens the oven and sticks a knife into the meat loaf. It gives the right amount of friction and comes out shiny with fat, and the juices from the wound run clear. He pulls on the oven mitts and takes the baking sheet out of the oven and places it on the trivet Mimi had picked up at a ceramics store in Maine. "Dinner!" Bobby yells, once again amazed by his own domesticity, by how quickly he has become this, whatever he is, a man collecting a salary while making meat loaf for his family. More than once, he's thought, They disliked me so much they're paying me not to work.

Dee finishes her task and sits in her chair and waits. She takes a look around the room to remember the details she sees, the steam rising off the rice, the pile of bright blue napkins next to the faded blue of the bowl. Her father places the carrots next to the napkins. Dee watches him slice the meat loaf and plate the slices on a silver serving tray. "So fancy," she says, but her father isn't listening to her, he assumes she's talking to someone else, about something else, not about how he's plating his humble meat loaf on something Mimi might use for hors d'oeuvres if company were coming, if indeed they invited people to their house anymore.

Abbie enters the kitchen and heads to the fridge and takes a bottle of sriracha out and places it in front of his seat and sits. Dee puts her hand up, and Abbie high fives her, something they've been doing lately, neither knows why.

Bobby places the tray on the table, next to the carrots. "Honey!" he yells, and he sits. He takes in the sight of his children, they are adults now: Dee is a woman, she can't stop revelling in it, and all the time he's heard of girls blossoming he now understands the word, the sentiment, and how sexist it is, because boys don't blossom into men, they become men, it's far more direct, but women are flowers, and sometimes flowers don't quite make it, and men will always speak of women with a poetry that says more about what men want and less about the women themselves. I'm a feminist, Bobby thinks. "Where's your mother?" he asks.

And on cue, Mimi enters the kitchen and takes her seat. "Meat loaf?" she asks, with neither disappointment nor anticipation, just a settling of facts, more for herself than for anyone else. She serves the table. Bobby watches as she does this, a bit insulted by her gesture; he made this meal, after all, why is she serving it? And as he thinks this, he realizes the lunacy of it, the silliness of what his mind is producing, and he pours himself a glass of water and drinks it down.

Mimi serves everyone: one slice of meat loaf, a few carrots, some rice. Abbie reaches for the sriracha and squeezes it out over the meat loaf. "You haven't even tried it yet," Bobby says, insulted, he feels an insult in every gesture, every act of normalcy, this is his family, this is how they are, why is he taking everything personally?

"I had a very interesting conversation today," Mimi says. No one says anything, and Mimi continues. "I met with one of the potential investors. He told me what I lacked. Very matter of fact. That's how he put it: What I lacked. What the company will need to succeed. How I'm understaffed. Not by one or two people but by at least ten, he figures, and then he told me he could see more, maybe twenty people. The systems I don't have. The things I'm not doing that I need to be doing." Mimi watches as Bobby digs into his meat loaf. He's looking at his wife, but she can tell he's enjoying his meat loaf, *his meat loaf*, she thinks it might be his favourite thing in the world though he'd never admit it.

"This man told me what I need to do to get his group's money. Because I'm not there yet. He told me that straight out. I'm not there, and so no one is investing in my business. And then he told me what would happen if his group agreed to back me eventually. He closed the door but he left it open, in other words. He told me about the steps, the work, how quickly things might change. He told me I needed a team just on the website, and he listed these jobs I didn't even know existed."

Dee can hear her mother talk, but in her head she is rehearsing her speech, her grand entrance. This is where the future starts, she thinks, this is where I can start to live openly as I am, because once I tell my parents, my new life can really begin, I can embrace myself, I can be who I am, I can do the things I want to do. Dee plays with her food, but she can't eat, not as she prepares for her announcement, as she leads up to the moment, she can't eat any of it, because she can't have anything else inside of her, there's already so much.

"And he presented a sample timetable, what would be expected of me and my current employees, and he said I should perform a very rational assessment of their capabilities, because if I continue to grow and follow his advice and make the changes he is asking me to make, and if his group backs me, my employees are going to start working for a very different company, they'd better be ready for changes, and he hinted that he didn't think they were ready."

Abbie can hear his mother talk, but in his head he's replaying what Jacques had said about Abbie's place in the history of photography. Abbie devoured a catalogue from an exhibit in Toronto about the history of Canadian industrial photography. For the first time, he saw himself in a continuum of work, an aesthetic, he'd started to see the flaws in almost all of his photographs, some of which could be fixed digitally, but some of which meant he'd have to reshoot chimneys he'd thought he'd shot perfectly. He used to succumb to the illusion of perfection. Jacques speaks of this illusion as if it's a real place, where lesser talents lose themselves, The Room of the Illusion of Perfection, because there is no such thing as perfection, he said, there is only the moment and what you bring to it, but it can never be perfect because if it were you would never take another photograph again. Jacques told Abbie he had to visit Boston eventually and see a collection of industrial photography at Harvard, even though there was a website about it, he had to see the photographs in person, experience them.

"He's telling me about PR and marketing and the team I would need for this, and he was very serious; he said I was going to be the face of the company, the brand, and then he told me if we did things properly, either we'd get sold to someone big, like Amazon, or we'd become big by ourselves."

Bobby is thinking of the word *househusband*. He's stuck on this. He's about to go out for drinks with an old friend, and he's going to call himself a househusband.

Dee doesn't think her mother is going to stop talking. Her mother's mouth has not stopped moving. Like Dee, Mimi hasn't touched her food. Dee is sure her mother is talking about her business, but surely that's not as important as what Dee has to say, to announce, she has to say something about who she is, after all, *she's* important, isn't she?

"And I don't think I have the room for all of this, for what he's suggesting, so I'm thinking I have to convince the bakery next door to close, or I move, but I don't think I'm going to find another place as cheap and convenient, it's not just convenient for me but for everyone who works there. And speaking of work, Dee, I can't wait for you to start next week."

Abbie reaches for another slice of meat loaf and squeezes sriracha on top.

Bobby thinks the carrots could have used more honey. He's worried that no one is complimenting him on the meal, and he notes, finally, that neither Dee nor Mimi has touched their food. Abbie will eat anything. He needs someone to say something about the food.

"I'm just so energized, that's all I can say, even though there's a lot of work ahead, more than I thought, maybe . . . ."

Mimi sighs, and Dee sees an opening but then she notes her mother's mouth, it's going to open again, and perhaps *her* opening is closing, this might be her only chance. "Mom and Dad, I'm a lesbian," she says, and she says this so quickly, it sounds like one word, what she's really said is *momandadimalesbian*.

And then there is a moment of silence.

Abbie puts his fork down and stifles a laugh, he's been waiting for this, but he didn't quite think it would happen this way. Over meat loaf.

Bobby stops thinking about himself and stares at his daughter. He pictures her as a baby, he can see her swaddled in the orphanage, her head a ball of thick hair. In rapid succession, he revisits the milestones of her life, or at least the ones he remembers, a home movie about Dee, right up to this point, right up to moments ago when he asked her about her bikini. That exchange is already a memory. He's reminiscing about something that just happened. Her declaration has made him instantly nostalgic. And he wonders if this is what will make her happy. He wonders how long she's known. He has so many questions for his daughter. He feels neither relief nor shame or whatever a parent might feel when his child announces they are gay. He wants to reach out and hug her.

"No, you're not," Mimi says. She digs into her food, finally.

Dee is silent. She is stunned. She looks to her father, but he's looking at his wife. Dee searches. For meaning. She feels something. Lost. Her mother has denied her existence.

Abbie is surprised himself. By how quickly his mother has dismissed what must have taken a lot of courage on Dee's part. By the fact she said it. He'd thought their mother would be the supportive one. He reaches under the table and takes Dee's hand. His thumb caresses her wrist.

She squeezes back. Hard. She squeezes his hand so she doesn't feel alone.

"Excellent meat loaf, dear," Mimi says.

Chapter 23

Mimi watches her daughter rush off, on the verge of tears, and doesn't understand why Dee is so upset. She hears her husband say, "Oh, honey." She faces down the blank look of disapproval from her son.

What has she said that was so awful?

This lack of understanding can't possibly be her fault, she knows this. "I have to work," she says, excusing herself, taking her plate, and making her way down the stairs, to her office, where she has to do some serious math, more math than perhaps she should be allowed to do unsupervised, she thinks, and she thinks this funny. I'm going to use that at some point, she thinks, to disarm the investors when they return, if they return, and she wiggles the mouse and her computer springs to life, the screen's blue glow like the submarine light of an underwater adventure.

She brings herself to a spreadsheet that the investor emailed her like he promised he would, a spreadsheet with dollars and costs and projections and possibility. The numbers are people, her employees, now and in the future, and the correlation between the right numbers and increased dollars. There is a column for her expenses, and the column assumes travel, it assumes that Mimi is away from Montreal almost half the year. The costs assume networks, keeping spotters on retainer, a system that manages not only the products she has already identified and ordered but also the products she doesn't even know about, products that she assumes are available but only in theory, products that are the epitome of potential; *Success is being right about the potential of things most of the time*, the investor had said.

The numbers are, in the end, people. To be responsible for so many, to be the builder of something upon which all these people will depend, to support their families, to be the thing that makes their lives happen, the pivot around which they will rotate. The sun. She is going to be their sun.

And then she's in Paris, and watching Bobby from across the room, or not Bobby but Roberto Reed, what an exotic name, she remembers seeing him as he made his way across a line of executives, shaking their hands, bowing to the Japanese men, his hands pressed together in front of his chest for the Indians, this was a man who'd been briefed and done his homework, a handsome young executive thrust into a crowd of middle-aged suits, sent to Paris for business, to meet these self-important men in the world's most self-important city, at least it was then. She was a translator; she could speak Japanese and French and English, and her Spanish was workable. And her father ran the show. She was translating and assisting him, and then Roberto saw her staring at him and she didn't look away, she continued staring at him, and so later, when he made his way to her, because every time he'd looked her way, she'd been staring at him, she was the one who'd spoken first, she remembers it clearly, his smile when she'd said, "Yes, I was looking at you," the slight blush she saw come over him, and that had been the start, and for four days she was his guide, and four days later, she saw him leave his hotel room, she'd been in his bed at the hotel, and they said goodbye but really meant au revoir.

She shakes her head. These thoughts come so easily. She remembers her father once telling her how his work taught him humility and his family made him feel important. She remembers the scene, she remembers her father's smell, the mix of tobacco and the woodsy cologne he had custom made at a parfumier in the Marais and the detergent on his shirts. She understood that he wasn't teaching her a lesson, that he was probably speaking to himself, trying to convince himself of something, trying to make sense of finding himself in Paris after a life spent in Osaka, and then suddenly Paris, embracing that city, creating a family, learning a new language, succeeding professionally, and still not finding happiness. Mimi knows her father was never happy. Not depressed, not how it's understood today, but just incapable of feeling good about his station.

She misses her family, she realizes. And she is making the mistakes her father told her he'd always regretted. She is making those mistakes here and at home. Mimi had worked so hard to not become her mother that she'd become her father instead.

Mimi stares at the numbers in front of her. The numbers are all potential. The future. Rules. Not just her rules but the rules of doing business. Of success. The discipline that money demands. Because money only wants more money. That is an equation she is starting to understand.

She was told she could play with the numbers, to see other potentials, other realities, other ways of seeing the future, he had said she should *crystal ball it*. He had said *Imagine your own success and then double it.* He had said *Don't worry about making mistakes, worry about not making them.* She scoffed. But whatever she thinks of him, however she imagines him living his life, however shallow she finds him, she cannot deny the reality that he is wealthy, that his success was built by the likes of her, by identifying businesses and ideas that were leaving money on the table because the table cost too much money in the first place. Whatever she feels about all of this, she can't help but feel flattered. And important.

What would her father say now? At this moment. Were he here, peering over her shoulder, at the math up on the screen of his little girl's computer?

Chapter 24

Abbie has never seen his sister like this. Not since they were young, at least. When he was too young to be conscious of her own youth, of being heartless without realizing it even while taking pride in making his sister cry. She's not crying now, but she is hurt, he can tell, hurt enough that she won't speak to him for fear of appearing the baby, again.

He texted her last night, after dinner, after she'd run from the kitchen, and he'd realized that their mother hadn't even realized what she'd said, the power of her words, because she'd been talking about her thing, and she wasn't listening to anyone else. He'd been doing the same thing, he'd been lost in his own world, in the history of the shuttered image, in technique, he'd been imagining the giant printers Jacques had shown him, the print he'd created as a test, seeing his work so large, two feet by two feet, and the potential of that image, of what he'd done, the art of it. He hadn't been listening to his mother, not really, and one day perhaps Dee will admit she chose the wrong moment to announce what she'd announced, but he couldn't blame her, he can't imagine a convenient time for something like that.

Everything is different.

Etienne de Bosch has convinced him that how he sees the world is valid and can change the way others see the world around them. Jacques is giving him tools, ones that allow him to see what might be or what is hidden in front of him. But his sister is showing him something else. She is showing him what it means to be alive. He needs to tell her. He wants to be her support. He needs to do more than send text messages. He hates that he didn't run into her room last night. Or that she didn't run into his.

He meets Etienne at a beer garden not far from the gallery. More a parking lot than a beer garden, with picnic tables and Christmas lights strung up, which must make the place look much nicer at night, more like a beer garden, but during the day, it's nothing, there isn't even any music, just lots of plaid and facial hair and tattoos and ripped leggings. Etienne sees his charge and raises his stein. Abbie walks toward him, notes the bright colours his patron is sporting today, tries to count the silk scarves around his neck and stops at six. The sunshine adds a burnished gold to the parking lot. To the weeds surrounding it, and the red brick industrial buildings that surround the weeds.

"It's like East Berlin after the wall," Etienne laughs.

Abbie might understand the reference had he paid more attention in school.

Etienne raises his hand and gets the attention of a server. Abbie thinks she must surely be a lesbian; she wears the close-cropped hair and white T-shirt of that kind of lesbian who takes their cues from James Dean. She probably listens to rockabilly, not pop, but then he's thinking, again, of Dee, and he doesn't know if what he's just thought of the server is offensive or not, he thinks about his sister, about her type, and he blushes, more out of shame than anything else. He feels overly protective of Dee right now because their mother has reacted to her declaration in a manner that makes no sense. "My friend will have a lager," Etienne says.

The waitress looks at Abbie, she's figuring out if she should card me, he thinks, he knows that look, and there are parts of town where he's still carded, though it's rare, it's one of those things that make Montreal so great, how sin is never judged, and the waitress says, "You're good?" and Etienne studies his stein and nods, and at that moment Abbie realizes she might be part Japanese, and a part of him runs away screaming, and the waitress saunters away toward the bar. She walks as if she has the biggest dick in the world between her legs.

"At night this place is hipster central," Etienne says.

Abbie doesn't know how one would find this place. He doesn't yet know the rules of discovery, of what one has to do to gain membership to the knowledge that exposes places like this to the wider world.

Etienne takes a chug of beer and slams the stein on the rickety picnic table. "October."

Abbie sits up. "What?"

"October. Your show is going to be in October. The third week. The vernissage is going to be on the Thursday. Your show will run three weeks. The board is on board." He smiles and holds it long enough that Abbie does the same. "We want to sell this properly, in terms of marketing. It's last minute, so the art press is going to be difficult, especially in Toronto; they're so organized. They respect their deadlines. But we need to make noise in some markets. New York. Get some galleries interested in you. But mostly local. Build up your name and profile. We want to make as much noise as we can in the small amount of time we have. Baby steps and then not-so-baby steps."

The waitress returns with Abbie's beer. He reaches for it and takes a sip. Avoiding eye contact with her. And then he takes a bigger sip. "You mean my work's going to sell?"

"Of course it is," Etienne says, laughing. "Why would we invest this effort in you if we didn't think your work would sell?"

Abbie wants to shrug; these are not questions he's even considered, he hasn't thought about business, he's only ever vaguely thought about perhaps selling his work, becoming something he's not, validated, seeing his photos vault from hobby to work, to object, to art.

"We are doing this because we think your work is wonderful," Etienne says. "And we think there is a market for it. And a future. We may see your future more clearly than you do."

Abbie takes a substantial gulp of his beer. The stein is massive, he knows he's going to be drunk at the end of it, and now he just needs to figure out how quickly he wants to get there. "I didn't see a future. I thought of it as a hobby."

Etienne laughs again. "When you delay your morning constitutional it ends up smelling really bad."

The thought of Etienne de Bosch on the can. Abbie has no idea what he means.

"Art!" Etienne says, loud enough that the few people at the other tables turn to look at him. "Your hobby, the thing you do, that's art. Don't you realize that?"

Abbie has had a difficult time with the definition of *art*. Shouldn't someone know that the thing they're doing is art while they're doing it? "I don't know."

"That's the point. Art is figuring out life." Etienne puts his beer down and places a hand on Abbie's shoulder. "No one knows what they're doing. That's the secret. We pay artists to figure things out for us. If you seem like you're doing a good job at it, people pay you. They pay therapists. They pay writers to write these stupid how-to books. We pay to learn."

"What do we learn?"

"What everything means. All this." Etienne orders another beer. It's possible he's drunk. "You are going to be a star," he says quietly. "If you need to learn something, learn that."

The waitress walks by, and Etienne de Bosch reaches for her and grabs her wrist.

"Do you have food?" he asks.

She looks at his hand on her arm. Abbie watches as her other hand forms a fist. Slowly. She's going to punch him. She's going to remember all the slights, all the times some man did something to her, made a comment, and she's going to take it out on him. Abbie stands up and pries Etienne's hand loose, and once she is free of him, she takes a step back. "We have tacos," she says, rubbing her wrist.

"Why must it always be tacos?" Etienne asks.

"I'm sorry," Abbie says, and with his apology she stops rubbing her wrist. She is only part-Japanese and she's heavy, and he can't think this way. He's hungry and he's not hungry.

"We also have a charcuterie plate."

"That sounds lovely," Etienne says. His words run together, not quite slurred, but with the sincere tone that precedes obvious inebriation. "What's on it? Ham? Some dry sausage? Some pickles?"

"Cornichons."

"And a smear of mustard?"

"It has two kinds of mustard. And housemade mayonnaise. And two kinds of ham. Some sausage, yes. Lardons. Some salami. Or salumi. I'm not sure."

Etienne starts to laugh. "Tremendous!"

Abbie watches the waitress rubs her wrist again; he can tell she won't forget Etienne's transgression. But he wants to finish his beer and get to the gallery. He's here because Etienne wanted to introduce him to some board members. "We'll have that," Abbie says.

She calms, again, visibly, and looks at Abbie and manages a smile. She stops rubbing her wrist. "He's here all the time," she says.

"I can hear you."

"He didn't mean to grab you like that," Abbie says.

"He knows what's on the menu."

"He's hungry."

"He's even had the charcuterie plate before."

"I'm right here. I can hear both of you," Etienne says.

"Why does he have to ask what's on the menu?"

"He's hungry. I'm apologizing for him."

Etienne stands up and opens his arms. "Come here, darling," he says.

The waitress stands her ground.

"Come on," he says, waving her into his open arms. "Darling, we can't be enemies."

"Why would you ask what's on the menu?"

"I was being optimistic. Utopian!"

"You treat me like a piece of meat."

"We're all meat, dear."

And despite her fist, despite the menace that seems to hide right under the pompadour, she hugs him, and Etienne de Bosch sneaks a peek at Abbie, his eyes sparkling with the triumph of a lion tamer who has just finished another successful show, and he says, "You know I love charcuterie," and then she slaps him on the ass, at which point Abbie realizes he's snuck into a movie theatre without knowing what was playing, that Etienne de Bosch is always in charge, and Abbie's put his own life in this flamboyant man's large hands, this man who's not afraid of anyone, because this is a man that was born female and he doesn't care what you think.

The waitress saunters away. Abbie cradles his stein, contemplating Etienne, contemplating the idea of him. "You know her," he says.

Etienne lights a cigarette. "I only love this place because I can drink and smoke at the same time."

Abbie knows how he appears, and around Etienne, especially, perhaps even for the first time, he feels *suburban*. He can't think of something worse, sitting here, surrounded by this attitude, by this aura, drinking beer, awaiting a charcuterie plate delivered by a tough lesbian, who is not his sister, his little sister, wearing her bikini and hanging out in the park with her friends, shunned by their mother, crying by herself in her room. Abbie can't get over his shame. His sense of not doing his job. His sense of being a bad sibling. A bad big brother.

The waitress returns with the charcuterie plate and a beer. "Anything else?" she asks in a tough, unaffected way.

Etienne explodes with laughter. "Go away!" he screams, and her frown becomes a smile, she winks at Abbie, and she ambles away. "Her name is Randi, and the answer is yes."

Abbie is unsure what the question was, and he doesn't bother with it, he doesn't need the feeling of exposure, of being outside of his comfortable box, of a publicly screened ignorance. Randi needed to look him over before deciding whether to card him or not, even though she wasn't much older than he, but she still gave him that look, and rather than confirm his innocence of the world, he ignores Etienne's cryptic message and eyes the charcuterie plate.

"Don't touch the salumi," Etienne says, slapping his hand away, laughing again, surely the beer is working its way into his brain with increasing effect.

Abbie knows he should eat. He eyes the remaining beer in his stein with a weary self-awareness. He reaches for something that doesn't look like salumi, which he's guessing is a kind of salami and he knows what salami should look like. He grabs a tiny pickle.

Etienne's puffy hand becomes a front loader. Abbie watches him shovel food into his mouth, he watches him eat his food, masticating, because Etienne doesn't close his mouth when he eats, and Abbie's hunger vanishes, just like that, he can see the puff of smoke that was once his hunger, emanating now from Etienne's neglected cigarette, perched on the edge of the table.

And then Etienne stops eating. "Listen," he says.

Abbie listens. There is music. It's German. It's vaguely familiar.

"Do you know the song 'Danke Schoen'?"

Abbie knows where he's heard it. "The one from *Ferris Bueller*?"

"What's *Ferris Bueller*?"

"It's a movie my father made me watch."

"It's a German movie?"

"What? No. The character Ferris Bueller sings 'Danke Schoen' during a parade."

Etienne hits a wall in his cultural understanding. "He's German?"

"He's American. It's set in Chicago."

"Ah, Chicago is a very German city." Etienne finds the nub of his cigarette at the edge of the table and takes a long, deep drag. "How old is your father?"

"He's in his forties."

"Was this a big movie?"

"*Ferris Bueller*?"

"That's the name of the movie?"

"*Ferris Bueller's Day Off*." Abbie remembers very few things from the movie. He remembers the parade and the song. He remembers the sports car crashing into a ravine behind a luxurious house in the suburbs. He remembers a character wearing a Detroit Red Wings jersey. In Chicago. He remembers that the actress who played Ferris Bueller's girlfriend was impossibly good-looking.

"I grew up watching French movies. I would watch them with my maman."

"My mother grew up in France."

Etienne raises his eyebrows. "She's French?"

"She's Japanese."

"From France?"

"Yes."

"Your mother's from France?"

"Paris."

"Your mother's from Paris?"

"She wasn't born in France. She grew up there. My parents met there."

"Your father met your mother in Paris?" Etienne doesn't know Abbie's genesis story. "So your father's Black?"

"My father is Mexican Scottish."

Etienne stops everything for a second. Abbie has never seen him this quiet. "Your father is what?"

"I'm adopted."

"Of course you are."

"So is my sister."

"Of course."

"What does that mean?"

"Nothing, nothing, okay, so your mother is Japanese and your father is Mexican and you are what then?"

"I'm an artist," Abbie says.

And then there is a pause. A conversation that has run its course. Like a river dissolving into the sand.

"Let's go," Etienne says. "Let's meet the board before they all leave." He takes the stein and brings it to his lips and tilts his head back and the beer disappears. "Drink up," he instructs.

Abbie tries to down his beer in a gulp, but he is incapable, it takes a few gulps, but he finishes it, and he feels the circular logic of the drink affect his footing, and as the closing notes of "Danke Schoen" fade out, Abbie smiles at the thought of his day so far, about the idea of what's to come, about the idea of what he's become, because there's always that. He's an artist now.

And drunk. Most definitely.

Etienne grabs some ham off the tray and smears it with the Dijon. He raises his arm to get Randi's attention and air-squiggles, and she nods, and Abbie wonders if he should eat but there's nothing on the tray that appeals to him; he knows Etienne has touched all of it at least once, and the meat is starting to sweat in the sun.

Etienne checks his phone. "I don't think anyone will be at the gallery," he says.

"So why bother?"

"Because someone might be."

Randi returns with the bill. Etienne pulls out a credit card from his pocket, and Randi inserts it into the credit card reader, pushes some buttons, and returns it. The modern paperless transaction. "I need the bill," Etienne says.

"So take it," Randi says.

"You rip it out."

"Don't start again."

"My fingers are so greasy."

"You just handed me your credit card, you pushed all these buttons."

"My fingers . . ."

She takes the machine from him and tears out the receipt.

"Place it in my pocket."

"Fuck off."

Etienne grabs the receipt from Randi with mock humiliation. "You never put your hands in my pocket."

"I mean it, Etienne."

"I used to be a woman. I know what you like."

Randi leans over, they exchange a two-cheek kiss, and she lurches away.

Etienne begins to walk toward the gallery, and Abbie stands and takes a breath before he runs to catch up. They walk side by side, silently, toward the gallery, a block away. Etienne takes them through a parking lot and then over a weed-strewn lot and then the gallery appears, like an apparition, the entire block feels like a mirage of culture surrounded by decay.

At the foot of the walkway to the gallery, Etienne stops and grabs Abbie's arm and turns toward his charge. "We have four board members plus myself. The newest member, she's the one who found you. You shouldn't be nervous. It sounds very fancy calling them board members, but that just means they are volunteers with connections or energy or good ideas. This isn't like a board for a bank."

Abbie hadn't thought of it as a board for a bank. He wasn't sure what a board did.

"They are all very passionate people."

"Great."

"They approve the budget. There were a few who weren't for this. For you. A part of it was politics. The new kid found you and pushed it, and I allied myself with her because she has good taste and she's energetic. But she's American. I think a few board members resent her. She's young and American and pretty and smart."

"I don't care about the politics."

"I'm only telling you this because there will be some board members who might not be . . . warm."

"I'm going to be nice to everyone."

"Well, of course you are." Etienne stares into Abbie's eyes now, deeply.

He resumes his march toward the door, and Abbie follows. They enter the gallery and find silence. Emptiness. "Hello?" Etienne de Bosch calls out.

"Upstairs," a voice calls, a female voice, Abbie can't tell if it's an American voice or not, but it's not a voice he's heard here before.

Etienne and Abbie climb the stairs. "I have a present," Etienne sings, and then they are at the top of the stairs and there is only one person in the room. She stands and Etienne walks toward her and gives her a two-cheek kiss. Abbie stays at the top of the stairs, waiting to be introduced, afraid suddenly, for no reason that he understands, but he's nervous, because he suspects this is the woman who found him online, who followed him from afar — from America! — and who is responsible for everything that has happened to him. The woman is dressed entirely in black, almost. On her feet, she wears shockingly high heels, her shoes patterned in leopard print. Abbie notes the skirt especially, the impossible tightness of it, and her glasses, he notes those as well, and the combination of the two does something to him deep in his belly, something he feels could become inconvenient.

Etienne reaches for Abbie, and when he doesn't find him he turns around. "Come here," he says, and Abbie walks toward them, toward the two most important people in his professional life; he's thinking about his professional life, and he doesn't know who he is anymore. "Abbie Reed, I'd like you to meet Andrea Dankiewicz."

Andrea extends her hand, and Abbie offers his and they shake. "I've long admired your work," she says.

"Thanks for everything."

"I'm happy and relieved, frankly, that Etienne has managed to make this happen."

Etienne gestures toward the white leather couch under the glazed windows, and they make their way toward it. "I could use a drink," he says, and Abbie sees these words as the first lonely snowflakes that herald a blizzard.

"There's vodka in the freezer," Andrea offers, and she marches toward the stairs. "Does that work?" she says, turning around and waiting for confirmation. As she turns, her skirt does something dramatic, or perhaps it doesn't, but Abbie sees it in slow motion, and he works to remove the thoughts cascading inside because he needs to not even think about anything other than his gratitude, to these people, to her, to whatever persistence she applied to create his future, to whatever fate brought her here from wherever she's from.

"There's wine too," Etienne de Bosch replies. "But vodka always works. That's its genius."

Chapter 25

The oversized parking lot surrounded by oversized buildings housing oversized versions of all sorts of stores. Hardware. Cheap men's suits. Lingerie. Sportswear. Office supplies. Wine. Womenswear. Menswear. Shoes. More shoes. And then, at the end, the discount warehouse, where people come and go, like spawning salmon, in both directions.

Bobby finds parking behind the store — no one ever wants to park behind — and he grabs an oversized shopping cart and he shows his membership card — an affectation this store has never lost — and then he's inside, the chaos of it, and he realizes perhaps he should have made a list because, outside of toilet paper and Dee's fruit bars, he can't think of anything they need, even though he had decided to make this trip because of a perceived need.

This place is designed in such a way as to disorient. The lighting. The electronics right up front. The chaos at every cash. The crowds.

Across the aisle from the electronic section, giant jars of all sorts of nuts. What psychological insight would put nuts and cellphones next to each other?

Bobby considers leaving. Can he make it through and just buy toilet paper and Dee's fruit bars and nothing else? Would he break the system by not buying something he doesn't need?

Just looking at the nuts and the candy and the snack bars, he begins to feel fat. He finds fruit bars immediately, next to granola bars, and he considers the box of fruit bars before him; he doesn't even know if this is Dee's preferred brand, or if Dee would even consider eating something bought here and not at the health food store, and then he sees the box as a commitment and he's not so sure he's willing to make it.

He turns the cart around and heads for the toilet paper. He has no qualms about committing to toilet paper. He passes socks and jeans and T-shirts, and then haphazardly designed cookbooks and more electronics, and storage containers and bins, and then he is upon the toilet paper, and he throws a giant package of it in his cart, he's sure they will not need more toilet paper for months, at least, and then he reads the packaging again, this is the brand they usually buy, not too soft — the girls don't like it too soft for some reason — but not too hard, either, three-ply. He can't imagine having to work in a company where toilet paper is a division, and teams of people have to sit and think about the mechanics of toilet paper each and every day. About the physics of defecation and particulates.

He wheels the cart past the toothpaste and the teeth whiteners, and there is a mirror conveniently placed there for customers to examine their teeth, their lack of white teeth; *Why aren't your teeth this white?* that mirror asks, and it asks it of everyone who dares look at themselves in it, and Bobby does, and he smiles and examines his teeth and wonders if they could be whiter. He thinks perhaps they could be. But who would he impress with whiter teeth?

He puts the smallest box of tooth-whitening toothpaste in the cart.

And a giant bag of pretzels.

A lovely older woman hands him a little cup of linguine carbonara and he tries some. He thanks the woman, and she says "It's twenty percent off today," and he considers this, and he takes a package. Then he takes another.

A giant brick of cheddar cheese.

A six pack of sriracha.

He returns to the fruit bars and reads the ingredients on different boxes of fruit bars, and then he spots a box with the word *organic* in giant letters, and he reads the fine print on the box and learns that proceeds from the profits are sent to Indigenous communities in South America, and he thinks he can sell that to Dee, and so he places the organic fruit bars in his cart.

A giant tub of peanut butter.

A pack of boxer shorts. He finds lately that he is in the process of transitioning to boxers from briefs.

He walks up to a short brown man handing out small cups of nacho chips and salsa, and accepts a cup, and then he walks to the fruit and vegetable section and places bananas, oranges, and apples in his cart.

He stands in front of a freezer overflowing with frozen pizza. We never eat frozen pizza, he thinks, there is a fine pizza place in the neighbourhood. They kind of like that pizza. He opens the freezer door, and then he hesitates and closes it. He's proud of his self-control. And then he looks inside his cart.

"Tell me about it," he hears, and he turns and sees a woman with her own overflowing cart.

He smiles. "I don't know how it happens."

"It happens every time."

"They're geniuses."

"The pizza in the freezer behind us is better."

Bobby turns and stares into the freezer, and from here it's hard to tell if that pizza is any better; in the end this is a frozen pizza in a box, after all, and he turns to ask the woman something else, but she is gone, she has continued her shopping, and then Bobby starts to seek her out, for whatever reason, without moving, he takes a good look at everyone in this aisle, and then he realizes she is truly gone, and that he is cold, and he starts to move, and he thinks, I am this, and he does not know what *this* is, but he is a man, shopping in a giant store, in a land of more giant stores, far from home, in the middle of the day.

His wife is busy building a lucrative business. His son is doing what he does. His daughter is a lesbian.

And he is this.

He looks again inside his cart, at everything inside of it, everything he has placed in this cart, of his own free will. And he wheels his cart to the freezer behind him, and he opens it, and he spots a box of four-cheese pizza, it's actually four boxes held together with tape, and he takes the box, and he throws it atop everything else already inside the cart.

Chapter 26

Dee knows this neighbourhood. She knows the people inside the split-levels and bungalows and colonials. She's walked the streets aimlessly, that's how she usually experiences it, and she's been doing so since she was first allowed out of the house on her own. She'd tell her mother she was going to the park, and then she would be beyond the park, walking, saying hi to everyone she met, because she felt safe, because this was her neighbourhood.

She knows that lately more Russians have moved here, Russian Jews mostly, and that's why there's a Russian bakery around the corner now, next to where the McDonald's used to be, the rare McDonald's that's closed, the one that became a community centre, a meeting place for the tall Black boys who live behind the centre, farther away from Dee's neighbourhood, the same fine young men whom Coco Chanel finds so delicious.

The Russians play loud music and go to synagogue every Saturday though not to the same synagogue as the Zederbaums because the Russians aren't *that* religious. The Zederbaums' synagogue is not far from the strip mall that houses her mother's store, but far enough away that the walk to it in the deepest winter must feel like an especially solemn pilgrimage.

At the far end of the neighbourhood, behind a row of houses that are owned almost exclusively by Italians, homes with stone lions guarding expertly manicured lawns and rose bushes, are the train tracks, which is why the Italians own those homes, because the backyards are triple the size of the other yards in the neighbourhood, backing as they do onto the tracks. And in the fertile soil of those yards, the Italians plant row upon row of tomatoes and zucchini and other vegetables, and every autumn the smell of tomato sauce wraps the neighbourhood in its sweet red blanket, and the empty boxes that once housed mason jars litter the front lawns on recycling day. And the kids from those houses don't hang out in Dee's park, they hang out in a little park by the tracks just next to the underpass and the fumes of the cars of thousands of commuters, and over time Dee has learned not to visit that park, because if you weren't from that street you weren't always welcome, though Dee had never tested this out, she'd just been warned, by other kids in the neighbourhood, by her brother, even by the Black kids who play basketball in her park, who'd said her park was the cool park, that small park was a literal dead end, and you had to be Italian if you wanted to even breathe in its foul air.

Dee has walked the streets of the neighbourhood enough to know these things, to know which houses hand out the best candy on Halloween, which ones house the loudest and crudest boys, and which ones don't.

She knows the house where Beth lives, and she realizes now she is going to walk by it.

She cannot forgive her mother.

Her mother's indifferent denial of what she'd said, how no one had come to her defence, not even Abbie, all he did was hold her hand, but no one was listening, no one, and she knows she shouldn't have blurted it out like she had, that had been a fuck up, she repeated that over and over to herself in her room, and then when she called Coco Chanel, it was all she could say, "I fucked up," because she certainly had: she'd fucked up a *moment*; she'd fucked up.

Clémentine had told her there was help. People could help her with these issues, trained people, but Dee had dismissed help, she wasn't going to ask a stranger how she was supposed to tell her parents this, plus she was sure, she was *confident*. She was just going to say it, at the first opportunity, and she had, and her mother had dismissed it, her mother's mouth had continued to move, to talk about whatever it was she'd been talking about, and her mother dismissed her and her entire sense of self. She'd said, "No, you're not."

Coco Chanel and Dee had debated whether that had been three words or four.

In her room later, lying on her bed, hugging her pillow, she'd laughed because she felt like a kid in a sitcom, the kind of sitcom that ends in group hugs, because she'd done all the things that teenage girls in those shows do: cried on the floor, kicked a threadbare stuffed animal, stared at herself in the mirror, hugged the pillow, texted her friend, put on her headphones and blasted some music, cried herself to sleep. She'd cried so much.

And neither Abbie nor her father or her mother had come to see her. And she'd never felt more alone in her own house.

Her phone vibrates. Val has texted her. *I'm worried about you, ma chère*, she says, and Dee feels the warmth that is friendship; her friends have been supportive and displayed concern as she navigates this thing; they are there, all of them, but no one outside the circle knows because some secrets are not gossip, some secrets stay secrets, they are too important to be shared with illicit whispers. Even though all of them are trying to find her a girlfriend.

Dee replies with a heart emoji, and then she looks up from her phone to get her bearings, and she is in front of Beth's house, Beth the volleyball-basketball-hockey-playing star, the high school athlete, the only other teenage lesbian Dee is aware of in the neighbourhood, though there must be some at her high school, she'd be shocked if there weren't, even in her grade, how does she not know any, how do her friends not know any, and why did her mother dismiss her so quickly last night, did she even hear what she had said, is it possible her mother had not heard her?

Would she really dismiss me if she didn't hear what I'd said?

No, you're not implies she'd heard, that she was responding to what Dee'd said, to exactly what she'd said.

Her phone vibrates again. Val has replied to her heart with a heart of her own. Dee replies with two hearts. Val replies with three. Dee replies with four. Val replies with a stop sign. Dee replies with five hearts. Val is freer than Coco Chanel, more willing to appear uncool.

I'm having a party, she writes.

Six hearts.

Not a huge party. My parents are going to New York for the weekend.

Seven hearts.

Saturday night.

Dee replies with eight hearts.

My brother said he'd dj.

Dee replies with a thumbs-up.

Okay?

Dee replies with two thumbs-ups.

She puts her phone away.

Dee makes a loop, she feels like she's patrolling the neighbourhood, but no one's out today, there's no activity, which she feels is kind of typical — she understands that where she lives is not exciting, that's been obvious to her for years now, but she is at the age where the paucity of any sort of activity is grating, where she is starting the countdown to exit, to a place where walking around the neighbourhood in circles is not an option because there's so much more to do, because there are destinations.

Her phone rings, and it's Coco Chanel. "Why are you calling?" Dee asks, because Coco Chanel never calls, she does everything via text or social media. Dee remembers when Coco Chanel made fun of Sam once because his phone wouldn't stop ringing, implying that using a phone as an actual phone was something only losers did.

"Hello to you," Coco Chanel says.

"Are you okay?" Dee asks, because an emergency is the only reason she can imagine her friend would deign to use the phone.

"That's why I'm calling."

"What's wrong?"

"No, I'm checking up on you."

"I'm fine."

"What are you doing?"

"I'm on a walk."

Coco Chanel doesn't say anything. Walking can mean a number of things. "Is everything okay? You can tell me."

"I'm fine." Dee switches ears. She continues walking, listening to her friend breathing, to her concern, even in the silence. Especially in her silence. "I'm still pissed off."

"You haven't spoken to her?"

"She's working all the time. She's so busy, it's like impossible. And I'm going to go work for her in a few days, and I'm still so pissed at her."

"You have to speak to her."

"When she's working she doesn't listen, like she's in another world." Dee can hear her own breathing, though the phone, and she stops walking and sits on the curb and wraps her free arm around her legs and curls herself into a ball. "I'm going to talk to her. I have to. I just don't know when."

"Don't worry about when, just do it."

"I just want her attention."

"Have you spoken to your father?"

"No."

"What's wrong with you?"

"I haven't spoken to anyone." Dee knows that's not entirely correct. "Just you guys."

Another long pause. The silence is a hug. "I'll call you later," Coco Chanel says. "Let's do something tonight."

"I'd like that," Dee says, thinking she might cry.

"Come over."

"Okay."

Dee hangs up her phone. She stands and looks at the sun until her eyes burn, and she starts walking again, the endlessness of it a salve to the numb feeling inside of her. She walks past Beth's house again. It is the same as hers, the same general construction, and she can imagine Beth inside, in her room, probably a room similar to her own, lying on the floor, dreaming of things, of nothing, of everything, trying to make sense of her life, though she probably has a shelf full of trophies and ribbons and workout equipment and the things that make her happy.

She walks past the house and decides to head home, to bury herself in her pillow and cry some more, maybe, or listen to music, or get naked and look at herself in the mirror. Or cry. She looks into her phone and for a fleeting moment she thinks about throwing it away, just heaving it into someone's yard, but she'll never do that, she'll never cut herself off from the world, from her world. Who would do such a thing?

And then she hears her name. She turns around, and it's Beth. She's jogging toward Dee. She's wearing loose basketball shorts and a white polo shirt two-sizes too large and flip-flops. She's so tall, so sculpted, so agile. Even at this pace Dee can tell Beth is all tense muscle. Beth is so comfortable in her body that her jog is full of grace, Dee can see that, and then, for the first time, she imagines her naked, she imagines what Beth must *feel* like, and she is shocked by the sensation this creates inside. Beth approaches her, looming larger and larger, more and more real. More and more possible. Dee is sure she's blushing.

She wonders what would happen if she just kissed Beth right here, just to try it. Is that even done?

Beth is close enough now that Dee can smell her, she's pretty sure she smells her, her sweet musk.

"So, is it true?" Beth asks.

Dee stares into her eyes. They are a deep blue, the colour of the water at the bottom of a lake. Beth's face is covered in freckles, and Dee imagines drawing connect-the-dots on her face, but with mascara, or lipstick, or soft ice cream. Beth wears her freckles like Cinderella wore her glass slipper. Dee doesn't say anything. Everything Beth needs to know is right there, in the way Dee looks at her.

Chapter 27

The door opens and it's Dee. Bobby tries to make eye contact with his daughter, and their eyes meet, but just as quickly Dee is up the stairs and into her room. He hears her door slam, and he wonders if he should speak to her, he knows he should, but first he has to speak to his wife because Mimi is oblivious to what she's done, to the severity of it, she may well be oblivious to what Dee said, and that might be worse, he doesn't know, how can he? Where in the parents' manual is this situation?

He downs his Scotch and soda and continues unpacking and shelving and trying to figure out where to put things. Scotch and soda is his new drink, the addition of soda has made it a cocktail, has been the respite from doing nothing, which is what Mimi has mandated he do until he feels he's over being fired, doing nothing is her remedy, but Martha's gone, so his job is to keep house, and that means he's discovered he likes Scotch *and* soda in the afternoon.

The phone rings, and he puts down the six-pack of sriracha and follows the ring until he finds a wireless handset on the dining room table. "Hello?" he says. He returns to his tumbler and walks it over to the bar.

"Hey, hey!" says a voice, full of genuine enthusiasm.

"Dude."

"We're having a reunion," Jonathan says.

"What does that mean?" Bobby asks. He finds his Scotch and fills half the tumbler with it. Then he re-enters the kitchen and heads for the fridge.

"That means I told a few guys what we were up to, and they want in."

"What are we up to?" Bobby reaches into the freezer for ice cubes.

"We're going out."

"Right."

"You haven't been out in a while."

"True." He opens the fridge and takes out a bottle of soda.

"Old times."

"We're old, Jonathan."

"That's why it's called 'old times.'"

"And you're calling to tell me, what?" Bobby mixes his drink with his finger and sits on the kitchen table.

"That our evening has expanded."

"How?"

"It's become more than two old friends . . ."

Bobby takes a deep sip of his drink. "Like who?"

"You name 'em."

"Jeffrey?"

"Yup."

"Stu?"

"Yup. You're good at this."

"Phil."

"Phil's in town this weekend, that's how this all got going."

"Barry."

"Yes."

"Drew."

"Drew lives in Vancouver."

"I know that."

"Drew is not in town this weekend."

"Sid."

"Sid lives in Toronto."

"So does Phil."

"Sid is not in town this weekend."

"Weng."

"I haven't heard from Weng in ages."

"Me neither."

"I hear he's in Boston," Jonathan says.

Bobby finishes his drink. He feels it now, and he worries about how being drunk, even slightly, may impact his dinner decisions.

"Anyone else?"

"Not so far."

"Lou."

"I don't know anyone named Lou."

"Neither do I."

"How are things?"

"I'm still trying to figure out what to do with my life, thanks for asking."

"Aren't we all?"

"Except I *need* to figure something out." Jonathan doesn't respond to this. Bobby knows his friend can't relate to his situation. Jonathan's had whatever crisis he's going to have. He had it long ago. He's successful. He coaches kids hockey. He works out. He has more cars than he needs. "I have to go."

"See you in a few days."

Bobby sets the phone down and takes in the mess he's made. He wonders if he's going to make another drink, or if he's going to go and lie on the shag rug and sink into it and never get up. He wonders if he should go talk to his daughter. He wonders if his son is home. He wonders if he should order Chinese for dinner. He wonders if he really wants to see his old friends, if he's in a good place to talk about the past, to bathe in the nostalgia the evening promises. A simple night out for drinks has turned into a reunion. He doesn't feel like he's putting his best face forward, not now. He's become a househusband. How is he going to spin that?

And how did this become a reunion? He's seen Jonathan. He's maintained a friendship with him. Through Jonathan he's kept up with Jeffrey and Stu and Barry. But the rest are tangential; he's not sure he was close to them in high school. They were Jonathan's friends. They were Bobby's acquaintances. Bobby has never been good about making friends and then maintaining friendships. He considers the energy needed to keep up with people he's never liked to be a kind of inefficiency, a cosmic joke, the result of the fear everyone has of dying alone.

Bobby grew up with an inability to make small talk. He saw that as a quality. And it has led him here and made him what he's become, who he is, a husband and father, anti-social, with perhaps one close friend in the world, a friendship he doesn't actively maintain, he can't be bothered, but now that he's home, he wonders, he thinks about Zederbaum, about how close he is to Eitan Zederbaum, a thought that surprises him because Zederbaum's otherness is there, always, laid out before them like the distinct form of his shadow.

He is drunk. And he has to get dinner. But more than that, he has to speak to his wife. He has to fix things. He wants to hug Dee, and he's not sure why he doesn't. He wants to assert his sympathy, but not in a way that undermines Mimi, and that's why he wants to speak to Mimi first. He is home all the time and he feels not in control of it.

He decides to take a shower. Because after that, he's going to drink a coffee and then maybe drive to get food and he's thinking he's even going to stop in at Mimi's store and try to talk to her there; it's possible she's not as busy at work as she is at home, isn't it? He wants to see what she's building, he's curious, he would never admit it to her, but he wants to see what her empire looks like. He wants to better understand his wife, he wants to understand her ambition because it's new, it's something that is flowing out of her, it's like someone put a Mentos into her Coke and that's Mimi, she's overflowing with ambition.

Bobby climbs the stairs. He walks the hall, past the family photos, the chronological neatness of his family assembled over the years by Mimi, the order, the simple frames, sometimes it's as if she were chronicling the partners of some blue-chip law firm, the photos go back in time to Bobby and Mimi's own parents and their children, and it is here where Mimi's family history feels more exotic and cosmopolitan. And yet it is Bobby's blood that has travelled farther, that has mixed more, intermingling both Old and New Worlds, a family with a Mexican spiced haggis in its lore, the jokes about what cumin does to the pale Scottish tongue, and then the inevitable comparisons of Scotch to tequila.

At the entrance to his bedroom, he stops and holds his breath. He listens for signs of something from Dee's room, of anything, of a reminder that she is alive and well, and he hears nothing, and he worries and enters his bedroom, sad, because his daughter is in pain, because he doesn't know what to do about it, because he loves his wife, because now it is Abbie he doesn't need to worry about; he's without a job, his daughter is in a deep and perilous pain, his wife is oblivious to the world outside of her work, and his son appears content with his lot, though Bobby would give anything to understand what that lot was.

Bobby walks to the washroom and strips down. He stares at his naked body in the mirror, notices a few more soft spots around his waist, thinks about jogging, again, he knows he's at that age where letting go means he'll never be healthy again, there is history in his family, heart troubles and tumours and all sorts of ailments that don't cut lives short, just create misery, and much of it.

There was a gym in his building downtown. His company paid for a membership, it was part of the benefits package, and he joined every year and never once set foot inside.

The closest gym that Bobby knows of is the dingy basement gym in the strip mall where Mimi works; he's sure there are closer gyms, though, and he can only imagine the clientele, and then he realizes he is going to let his body go to pot because he's a snob, one who would rather grow fat than sweat next to strangers, because he's like that, anti-social, he'd rather spend the money on his own equipment, and build a room at home, and hire a personal trainer to set up a regimen, than go to the local gym because gyms are intimate places and Bobby has trouble with intimacy.

He turns on the shower.

In the shower he lets the water work its wonders on him, he loses himself in the steam, and then he's hit, again, with full force, by the song he always sings to himself. He never admits this to anyone, it's his guilty pleasure, the shower concert, he's never even told his wife because he's sure the song is lost on Mimi, but he takes the shower head and launches into "Heat of the Moment," lip-syncing all of it, and as sincerely as he can.

In his head, his singing becomes more and more extravagant. He imagines he's on stage, and there are lights dancing about him, and the crowd roars and their lit lighters sprinkle the arena like fireflies in the backyard.

Bobby doesn't remember when this started. When he took his love of hot showers and turned it into an over-the-top performance of a commercialized prog rock supergroup from the '80s. He even mimes the synth solo — *a synth solo!* — and this is the thing he holds most private, of all the things, it is this. He has never considered sharing, he hadn't even considered it when he first met Mimi or more specifically when they'd become intimate enough that they were taking showers together, although they did that quite often, that was her thing, taking showers and baths and spending long afternoons wet together, and he hadn't told her then, he hadn't broken into song, and definitely not this song, this awful, acrid song, and that made it all the more special to him.

He sings this song with a sincerity that brings him to laughter, and that sincerity is the reason a movie might play it ironically, because it is so sincere, so awfully and painfully sincere. A soundtrack with "Heat of the Moment" is telling its audience something.

This time, he knows at least Dee is home, and so he sings the song in his head. And at song's end, he reaches for the shampoo. And that signals the beginning of the end of the shower.

He dances under the shower head for a final flourish and turns off the water. Bobby reaches for his towel, his towel is always blue, and he wipes his head and then wraps the towel around his waist. He steps out of the shower and considers shaving and decides he's not going to do it, why shave when he has no one to impress? He's been shaving diligently since he lost his job, he can't just give up on his routines because that would be giving up on life, but shaving, he's going to try a beard maybe, at least until Mimi demands he shave, and then he thinks he's not going to shave as a test. As a test to see if Mimi really is paying attention to him, to anyone, if she even enters this house anymore, especially when she's in it.

He hears a door open, somewhere in the hallway, and that means it's either Abbie, which is doubtful, or Dee, and he races out of the washroom and through his bedroom and into the hallway, wearing nothing but the wet blue towel around his waist, and there's Dee, wearing her uniform, a T-shirt and her bikini bottom. "Hi," he says.

"Hi," she replies. She can't look at him, he can see that, and he takes a step toward her.

"Dee, I just want you to know," he says, and then he stops because he's never had to rehearse this. To prepare for a moment like this.

She wants to look in his direction, he can tell, but she won't, or can't, or will never again, and Bobby takes a deep breath.

"I love you, DeeDee," he says.

She looks like she's about to drown in something he can't imagine. And he knows he should say something more, but he doesn't know what that something is supposed to be. He feels guilt about it, deep guilt, and at this moment he's never seen his baby girl look so alone. "I just thought you should know that. If you needed a reminder."

"Thanks," she says, the tears welling up.

He takes a step toward her and reaches out, and then she is in his arms and he is squeezing her, he is trying to consume her with his love for her, with his strength, he wants to tell her everything that needs to be said with the force of his hug. And instead of breaking down, Dee squeezes back, she hugs her father as solidly as he hugs her, and this sight, a man in a bath towel and his daughter in a T-shirt and bikini in a firm embrace is what confronts Abbie as he races up the stairs.

"Group hug?" he asks, and Dee chuckles suddenly, and this causes her to blow snot onto her father's bare chest. Bobby steps back.

"That's gross," he says to Dee's laughter.

Abbie makes a face and escapes to his room.

"I just showered," Bobby says, and then he hugs his daughter closer, until she understands what he's doing and now she pushes him away and steps back.

"Dad," she cries, wiping her tears. And she feels her hair and her suspicions are confirmed by the mucous on her fingers and she says "Dad!" this time like Bobby's baby girl, and now it is her father's turn to laugh.

Dee retreats from her father and walks to the washroom and closes the door, but not before she looks behind her and offers a look of gratitude and love. Bobby accepts her gift, because that's what his daughter is, that's what his children are, gifts, and the gifts they bring him are eternal, and he decides he's going to get dressed and then he's going to get Chinese for dinner so he can fulfill his duty and once again feed his gifts.

Back in his room, Bobby steps into the jeans he left on the floor. He picks up his shirt and sniffs it and decides he can confront the world with it and he pulls it over his head. He searches the dresser for his wallet and keys. He exits the bedroom. "I'm going out to get dinner," he announces, and he rumbles down the stairs and out of the house and into the car.

In less than ten minutes he is at the bar of the Chinese restaurant, a neighbourhood restaurant in the truest sense, never reviewed by anything other than neighbourhood papers and those odd vanity publications that appear and disappear like weeds in springtime, never a bad review, always a shout out to the owner, written up as a dear friend, always, but this place, Mr. Woo's — that's what everyone calls it, even though, officially, it's called Chez M. Woo: Mets Cantonais et Vietnamien — the local, where your grandmother is going to ask to be taken at least once a year because she "misses the egg rolls," packed on Christmas and Friday nights, but really a delivery and take-out place, and also a taste of home; so many who have moved away, and know better, who have eaten at much better Chinese places, at places that are not just better but more authentic, even more authentically Chinese Canadian, they will return, they will make the pilgrimage to Mr. Woo's to taste their childhood once again, to taste the nostalgia of the won ton soup and the General Tao chicken and the barbecue ribs and the glorious fried rice, because it is glorious, and every kid who grew up in this neighbourhood first realized the glory of that rice late at night, probably stoned, when the munchies were at fever levels, and the rice, especially the special with shrimp and chicken and barbecue pork, that is a drug in and of itself, it adds to your buzz and then you are buzzed again.

He takes a seat at the bar and delivers his order, and Mr. Woo himself pours him a Tsingtao. "Bobby, looking good," he says, as friendly as it is possible to be without smiling. Mr. Woo never smiles. He also greets all the regulars the same way. Everybody looked good to Mr. Woo.

"I've felt better," Bobby says, taking a sip of his beer.

"You look good; how you feel doesn't matter." Mr. Woo takes Bobby's order into the kitchen.

Bobby is the only person in the restaurant, aside from the waiter, a new one, a tall, lanky Chinese boy, probably a student, all young waiters must be students, and, at the cash, Mrs. Woo, who is looking much older than her husband, her back the shape of ancient mountains weathered by the elements.

Bobby takes a long chug of his beer. Something about drinking in Mr. Woo's makes him feel invincible, or at least young, which might be the same thing. His phone buzzes, and it's a text from Mimi. She's working late and won't be home for dinner. She had a late lunch at Jean-Marc's.

There's that name again. Mimi loves Jean-Marc's. Bobby downs his beer, he finishes it, and the young waiter sees this and speed walks to the bar. "Would you like another?" he asks.

Bobby nods, and the waiter fishes a bottle from the fridge behind the bar.

He stares at his phone. He brings the bottle to his lips and takes a long pull. Mimi is swimming away from the family, toward a horizon, while the water rises around her and her family, but so slowly . . . So stunningly slow is her swim that no one sees it, and everyone sees it, because with water you can always sense the slow rise, the coming of disaster, and that's what Bobby feels, disaster, he feels Mimi swimming and he feels like he's sinking and this is happening all at once.

Is she seeing Jean-Marc? He's dismissed the thought every time because he sees what Mimi is doing, how immersed she is in her work, in building what she's building, in the creation of a new kind of commerce. And Bobby wonders if his wife is seeing Jean-Marc on the side, in her spare time, which he knows does not exist. The mere suspicion feels wrong to him, but also symbolic, this is where we are, he thinks, in a space of unreasonable suspicion, of visions, of loss.

How does he recover from imaging his wife with another man? Is it fair to impose your fears, your suspicions, your neuroses on the person you love the most when you know it's all untrue? Because despite the ubiquity of the question, Bobby knows his wife is too honourable to lie. She has faults, they are all living under the cloud of her faults, but she is not a liar.

He reaches for his beer and takes another pull. Mr. Woo enters the room from the kitchen. "Another five minutes, Bobby," he says. He places a bowl of fried won tons on the bar, and another bowl of plum sauce.

Bobby takes a won ton. "Thanks," he says. He dips it in the brown-orange of the plum sauce and swirls it around. He brings it to his mouth. He sighs and then he bites into it.

Chapter 28

Mimi stares at flowcharts and bank balances as the day turns to evening, and as the shifts turnover and the Hispanic workers start — and she has wondered why her entire night shift is from different parts of Mexico and Central America — Karim walks to her space and makes his presence known. "I'm leaving," he announces.

"Good night," Mimi says, not looking away from the digitized spreadsheets in front of her.

Karim does not move. "I mean I'm *leaving*."

"I heard you," Mimi says, trying to understand the numbers, trying to finesse something out of them, making sense of what the investors are telling her, and the state of her own finances.

"I mean I'm not returning." Karim steps back. With finality. "Ever."

Mimi turns to face him. She tried to keep him before, and she succeeded, but not this time. His hands are balled into fists. The veins pop out of his arms. His resolution appears firm. She needs Karim, but no one is irreplaceable, she knows this. He is more replaceable than everyone back in the stacks. If they walk out, she won't ship. If Karim walks out, as he is threatening to now, she won't ship for a few hours. Maybe a day.

Karim looks at the floor. He won't be able to do this if he looks at her. "It's not good for my family," he says. He puts his arms behind his back and starts to move his right foot in circles. "For my wife. My children."

Mimi stands. She's not going to fight him. She will replace him with someone with the right kind of training and experience. Someone who can run this place without her supervision.

"I can have all the assistants you give me, but it won't be enough. My life demands something else."

Mimi has come to see Karim as a symbol of a simpler time, when she almost called the company Mimi's Hummel Hutch. He'd even registered the domain, and they were going to be downmarket forever. It wasn't her. A few collectors' conventions, and she'd decided to start devoting time to her other interest, to furniture, because the Hummel crowd was strange and old and sad and smelled funny and she could never see herself too comfortable surrounded by these people day after day, to make a living off them, to go through the act of caring about her customers. She wanted to love her work.

"Okay," she says. He looks at her, his boss, his ex-boss, and she can tell he's hurt she isn't putting up a fight. "You wanted to leave before. You stayed," she says, "because you wanted to. That's why I talked you into staying. That's *how* I talked you in to staying."

The tall Algerian shrinks before her. He deflates. "Miss Reed."

"But this time you want to leave. I can tell."

"I have to leave."

"Because you want to."

"Because I have to."

No one has to do anything, Mimi thinks. Her father had once told her this, explaining the difference between duty and choice, on the moment we choose and how we arrive at that moment, on our duty to others and family, and how duty sometimes trumps choice, how freedom is absolute but also finite. *No one has to do anything*, he had said. *But we always do something.* That was the second part of it. The second part negated the first part. While also affirming the first part. She's still not sure she understands what he meant. "I'll miss you," she says.

"Thank you."

She reaches to hug him, their size difference doesn't matter now, she's sorry to see him go, and as she sinks into the hollow of his chest — because he's hugging her, too, and hard — and sinks farther, she realizes she's not upset, or not as upset as she thought she'd be at this moment, because she saw this coming, and she wonders if perhaps she hasn't lost something inside of her, some feeling, empathy. Where is my empathy? she thinks. She releases him and looks up and smiles.

"Thank you," he says. He takes a step back and goes to turn. "Thank you for trusting me."

"Come back next week. We'll have all the paperwork done." She is unrecognizable now. To herself. Professional. Without emotion.

"I've completed the paperwork." He pauses. "I wasn't raised to quit anything."

"No one is," she replies. She waves him off. She's more upset by the hassle of replacing him. As if she doesn't have enough to do. To learn. She has to think about money. She has to borrow. She has to dip into her savings. She has to ask Bobby about their finances, to be reassured. She has to think about her inventory, about travel, about meeting people in different cities. She needs to hire some young genius just to handle her website and make it go so she never has to think about it again. She keeps hearing about taking her business to the "next level." She looks up and she wonders how far up the next level is. How high is too high? Karim walks off. Perhaps he had expected a going-away party, she thinks. Perhaps he had expected an announcement. But do you throw a party for someone who quits? He had called himself a quitter.

She wants a cigarette. She wants one with great intensity. She hasn't felt this twinge, not like this, since long before she'd even quit smoking. She stands and wonders where she can get just one, just now, and she opens the door to the store and then she's out of the store and in the parking lot and she sees two figures huddled near one of the entrances at the far end of the mall, and she walks toward the two figures, and there is smoke, she'll just bum one and regret it later, smoking is all about regret, after all, and as she walks closer to the two figures she sees that it is the Khalili brothers. The Ayatollah is smoking, and The Butcher is just standing with his brother. He notices her first, her approach, and she sees him say something to his brother and then they wait for her, for the oddness of the moment to come to fruition.

"Miss Reed," The Butcher says, and he bends at the waist in greeting.

"I didn't realize you smoked," she says to The Ayatollah.

"And you are here why?" The Butcher asks, because he knows she doesn't smoke.

"I don't smoke either," she says, trying not to seem too pathetic, her eyes still on The Ayatollah.

"I'm just here for the fumes," The Butcher says.

The Ayatollah knows why she is here and reaches into his pants and pulls out a gold cigarette case and he holds it open for her. She reaches in and takes a cigarette and puts it in her mouth and then she leans forward so The Ayatollah can light it, all the movements and gestures remembered, muscle memory, universal, across time and space. "Thank you," she says, and she takes her first haul, and the smoke sears her lungs and she closes her eyes and remembers the joy of guilt-free smoking, remembers the rush of the first pull of smoke, the slight dislocation, the fuzziness that envelopes the brain and then rushes out with the smoke as one exhales.

She opens her eyes. "I haven't done that in a long time."

"You should not have done it, then," The Butcher says.

"But then, sometimes, the business makes you do it," The Ayatollah says. "I have witnessed your stress."

"Karim just quit."

"He was the bookkeeper?" The Butcher says.

"If only that." She thinks about everything he did. He ran the place. She must ask him to return if only to train his replacement.

"You need someone, then?" The Butcher asks.

"Yes."

"You have someone in mind?"

The Ayatollah takes a last haul of his cigarette and stumps it out in the ashtray. "Do you?" he asks his brother.

Mimi takes another drag on her cigarette, a deep drag that allows her to forget and also to remember, and again, she thinks of her home, of the odour that trailed behind her father wherever he went, the smell of the bars that clung to a person like a tattoo, the pervasive smell of tobacco that takes her back to a certain time in Paris.

"I might, yes," The Butcher says.

Mimi has her eyes closed. She hasn't enjoyed anything as much as she's enjoying this cigarette in a very long time. She feels on the verge of a dangerous mistake.

"Miss Reed?" The Butcher says, bringing her out of her joy.

"Yes, sorry, I'm just enjoying this thing a bit too much I think."

"I can send someone tomorrow. Day after at the least."

"Who is this person?"

"A friend. She lost her job just recently. The company moved to Alabama or someplace. She's very good. Manager. Bookkeeper."

The Ayatollah takes out his cigarette case again. He lights another smoke. "This stress, Miss Reed."

Mimi smokes her cigarette down to the filter and throws it in the ashtray. The Ayatollah holds out his case, and she hesitates and then takes another and leans in for the light. "It's good stress," she says, blowing smoke away from the brothers.

"There is no good stress," The Butcher says.

"I need more space," she says.

"In the back?"

"I'm growing. I need more space."

"This is possible," The Ayatollah says. He eyes his brother with something approaching a smile.

"You are growing," The Butcher says.

"I am."

"Why do you insist on the store?"

"I don't insist on it. I just like it."

"It's nostalgia," The Ayatollah says.

He might be right, she thinks. But she resents that he's the one saying it.

"We can do something with the store, perhaps, and then, maybe, find you more room in the back."

"I don't need much."

"For now," The Butcher says.

For now, she thinks. Because he can see the future, just like the investors can see the future, just like Karim could see the future in his own way. She takes another drag off her cigarette. It fills her with something — with emptiness, if that's possible — the smoke slowly clearing out the jumble inside her head.

Chapter 29

They stare into each other's eyes. They sit at opposite ends of Dee's bed. Staring. Each exploring the other's soul with nothing but her eyes, their collective longing streaming from their eyes, everything they have ever wanted and every desire and every longing they have ever felt is belied by their eyes.

The room smells. Of nerves, perhaps, of some kind of energy, of youth, of the joy a sailor feels when spotting land after seasons spent at sea. The room swims in this aroma, this thing being secreted by two girls, by two girls who have arrived in this room, in this very situation, from two different paths, two paths that were consigned to permanent divergence until they weren't.

Dee and Beth stare into each other's eyes and imagine different things, different futures; they are both thinking of tomorrow and the day after that, but only one of them has to convince herself that *love* is too strong a word for what she's feeling. She's feeling relief, surely, this is confirmation for her, this moment, confirmation that she is not wrong, that her feelings, that her head is telling the truth, she is what she says she is. What she has always imagined herself her to be. Even when she couldn't possibly know. She hasn't changed. Only her self-awareness has.

"Have you?" Beth asks. Because she has. Dee knows about the divide on this question. About the imbalance.

This question is where the reality of Dee's self meets the reality of her actions. Even if she doesn't yet know if anything is going to happen. If she will touch Beth. Because she wants to.

"How long?" Beth asks. She has some calculations to make. She knows Dee's age, she knows because they have known each other for so long, because they were born just months apart, because she lives down the street. Just because.

"A few weeks ago," Dee says. "Before exams. I think it was May? On lunch break."

Beth lets out a giggle and brings a hand up to cover her mouth. It's a mannerism Dee has seen in her mother, and she's always considered it Japanese, but here is Beth, a tall Jewish girl, a jock, blonde with freckles, and those freckles are everywhere on her, at least the parts of her that Dee has seen.

"I just knew."

Beth leans backward and one of her hands almost slides off the bed and she catches herself and catches Dee's affectionate gaze and she looks down at the bed, or at her feet on the bed. "I'm a bit of a klutz."

"Right," Dee says. As if the sports star could be clumsy. "Hockey. Volleyball. What else? Basketball. Tennis?"

"I gave up on tennis."

"Klutz."

Dee would like to conduct this conversation naked, if possible, and she starts to realize she may not be able to do so here. In her house. She's never as much as kissed another person in her parents' house. She wouldn't know how to address the potential for disaster, how to enjoy a kiss while listening for footsteps.

"I don't like being the centre of attention," Beth says. And with that she reaches out for Dee and holds her hand and tries to remember everything that has happened in her life up to this moment because she knows it is a dividing line, this is her before and after, an actual one, where she *becomes*. This is the moment she will tell others about, this is her first time, even if she has had other first times, it's not as if she hasn't fooled around with boys, but, unlike her friends she has never fucked a boy, this is the first time for her, the first time that matters, that means more than just two strangers exchanging fluids, even if they don't kiss right now, even if she doesn't think this is the right moment, because she's nervous, she's in her house and it doesn't feel safe, she's in her mother's house, and her mother has denied her only daughter her own sexuality, her own expression of self, she does not feel a part of this family right now, she feels a part of Beth, and the heat from Beth's touch, she can feel it now, the heat that emanates from her hand, from the point of contact, she wants to jump out of her skin. But, more importantly, she wants to jump Beth.

Dee leans forward and Beth leans toward Dee and their mouths meet and at that moment Dee forgets everything that needs to be remembered, or that she had tried to remember just a moment ago. Beth's hands move under her shirt, and Dee feels a kind of release, a mixture of joy and pain and relief and the world grows sweet, she smells something sweet in the air, even though she can taste Beth and Beth tastes like . . . raisins, and a little bit like sweat, she licks Beth's neck and Beth tastes like sweat, but at that moment Dee hears music. Her room is filled with music, it's an odd kind of music to choose for a soundtrack to something so important and then she realizes the music is coming from Abbie's room, he's playing his music at crazy levels, probably because he thinks he's alone, and now Dee is thinking of Abbie just as Beth's hand is about to start an exploration that Dee wants so much, and they're kissing, but there's Abbie's music, he's been listening to very dark Norwegian metal or something, she forgets what he calls it, he says he doesn't like it but that it gets him pumped and he likes the idea of these Norwegians growling at their devil, and now Dee realizes she's thinking about her brother and Norwegians and she pulls away from Beth, and a string of spittle forms a momentary bridge between their mouths and Beth says, "What's wrong?"

"My brother's home," Dee says, and she's trying to remember to breathe because so much is going on and she wants everything that is happening to continue but she also feels like her brain is going to explode.

"Does he ever come in your room?"

Dee takes a deep breath. She's going to start gasping for air soon, like now, like soon. "No," she says.

Beth kisses Dee once more. "No problems," she says.

Dee would like to believe her. And she wants the moment to be perfect, though she doesn't know what perfect means, she's worried she might be overthinking things, but then she hears another deep-throated howl from her brother's room and she jumps off the bed and starts pacing. "This isn't going to work," she says.

"It's okay," Beth says, and even though they're the same age, she sounds years older.

"Fucking shit this isn't going to work, and I want it to so much."

"It's okay."

"It is *not* okay." Dee feels like she might melt down, everything inside of her is a jumble of needs.

Beth stands up and gets in Dee's way to stop her from pacing. She hugs Dee, and Dee stops what she's thinking, again, and she lets Beth hug her, she accepts the hug and she sinks into her, she closes her eyes and sinks into Beth, she breathes her in, her scent, she wants to melt inside of her, she can't believe how strong her feelings are, her confusion hovers over her, it surrounds her, and she just hopes she doesn't do anything awkward.

"Meet me later," Beth says.

"Where?"

"Text me after dinner."

"I can't even think about food."

"I have a practice tomorrow morning, so I can't stay out late."

Dee feels like Beth is already her girlfriend. She doesn't know how Beth feels, and she's too afraid to ask. All they've done is kissed. Did they even do that? Was that really a kiss? Beth might see Dee as a toy for all she knows. "Okay."

"Okay?"

Dee sighs. She's sure she's going to mess this up, she's going to say something that is going to remind Beth what kind of girl she's dealing with. "When did you know?" she asks.

"Last year."

"But did you know for sure?"

"I kissed a girl." She pulls away and she smiles. "And I liked it."

And then the two of them are laughing and swinging each other around and singing a song about girls kissing girls, a song that might be an anthem if it hadn't stirred up the hormones of frat boys everywhere. And above them both, over the sounds of their laughter, are the grunts and bombast of Abbie's Norwegian death metal, except he's listening to it ironically, and next door, his sister and her girlfriend are singing their song in the sincerest manner possible.

They twirl each other around until they are dizzy, dizzy with so many things, and Dee falls to her bed and Beth stumbles into Dee's dresser, and she picks up Dee's bikini top, the one Dee never wears, and she holds it for a while and Dee stops laughing and says, "Stop it," because she's embarrassed, for no reason, but she is, she feels like her brain isn't working properly now, that Beth is doing things to her she has no right to do, making her feel things so new she can't tell if she's confused or not, she's confused about being confused.

"Show me something," Beth says.

Dee has to ponder the meaning of this request. She notices the silence. Either Abbie has left suddenly or he's grown tired of the music, which is what tends to happen. She hears the front door open. "Crap," she says.

"Guys?" It's her father. He's home. He said he was getting Chinese. And he's done it.

"Wait here," she tells Beth. Dee opens her door and walks to the top of the stairs. "Hi, Dad," she calls.

"Is Abbie home?"

"I think so."

"I got Chinese."

"I have a friend over."

Her father does not respond to this. She can hear him in the kitchen opening containers, the rustle of a paper bag, the fetching of plates and cutlery. Dee retreats to her room. "Wanna eat over?" she asks.

Beth shrugs. "I have practice."

"Were you going to eat?"

"A protein bar. Maybe."

Dee shrugs. "It's up to you." She walks toward Beth and kisses her. She smiles and looks at the floor. "Whatever you want," she says.

Dee hears Abbie open his door and then he is at the entrance to her room. Dee and Beth look at him as if they've been caught, their secret revealed, though both are thinking how stupid that sounds. "Hey, Beth," Abbie says.

"Hey, Abbie."

"I heard Dad," Abbie says.

"He brought home Chinese," Dee says.

"You staying for dinner?" he asks Beth, smiling, but coyly, both the girls see that, they see he knows something, except Dee hasn't told Beth that Abbie knows, and Dee can see that her potential girlfriend is mortified. Abbie is the big kid on their street. Him and Saul. "You should," he says.

"She has practice," Dee says in an attempt to save Beth.

Abbie shrugs and descends the stairs, and Dee turns to Beth. "Say hi to my dad, at least?"

"I'll say hi."

Dee takes a deep breath: she feels nervous; she feels as if a light is shining on her. Dee is starting to feel that Beth is like a hop through the sprinkler on a warm and muggy day.

They walk downstairs and enter the kitchen. Abbie is already scooping fried rice onto his plate. Bobby sees Beth enter. "Well, hi there," he says. He stands and gives Beth a hug and a two-cheek kiss. "It's been a while."

"It has," Beth says, in that awkward way teenagers sometimes talk to adults when their elders act too familiar.

"I hear great things about you," Bobby says, at which Abbie stifles a laugh.

"She can't stay," Dee says.

It strikes Bobby that she's answered a question he hadn't yet thought to ask. "Oh?"

"She has practice."

"Oh," Bobby says, now understanding both the question and the answer. "Right. Of course. Well, that's too bad."

"Thanks for the invite," Beth says.

"Are you still a defenceman — woman? Defencewoman? What's the right word?"

"I have volleyball . . ." Beth says.

"Oh, sure, I'm just wondering."

"I play outside hitter."

"I used to play defence."

Abbie rolls his eyes. He's heard about his father's exploits, the self-aggrandizement, the memories lapsing into a kind of aggressive nostalgia.

"I have to go."

"She has to go," Dee says.

"Defenceman in hockey, though," Beth says.

"I suppose they'll get around to changing that someday," Bobby says thoughtfully. He bites into a giant piece of General Tao chicken.

"I don't mind," Beth says.

"No, but they'll change it. Because someone will mind." Bobby reaches for his beer. He's opened a beer. And he's opened one for Abbie as well.

Abbie's curiosity snuffs out his hunger. This upsets him. He's heard about Beth, but he doesn't know if it's a rumour, the kind of thing that grows on the streets out of jealousy. Beth is a success. She wins things. The community papers write about her. Of course a certain kind of person would start rumours about her. He's never given much thought to her regardless — he's not a sports guy — and what she is or isn't is none of his business. But he hasn't seen Beth in a long time, and his sister has announced her orientation, and now here Beth is, in his house. In his sister's room. Abbie would like to know if he should treat her as a friend or as his sister's girlfriend, both of which require indifference but different forms of it.

Beth waves goodbye. "Give my best to your parents," Bobby says.

Beth nods, and Dee steers her toward the front door. "Have a great practice," she says.

"Meet me by the tracks," Beth says.

"Where?"

"The little park."

"Where the assholes hang out?"

"They're cool, don't worry." Beth looks past Dee, then kisses her on the mouth and runs out the door. Dee watches Beth run. She watches the power in Beth's strides. The way her hair waves behind her like a flag. She watches Beth run away. The way she can feel the muscles tense on the backside of her ass, even though she has not felt Beth's ass, and she'd like to.

Dee closes the front door and returns to the kitchen. "I'm hungry," she says, sitting down.

And then they eat, three-quarters of the family. Abbie kicks Dee under the table, and she catches him raising his eyebrows. She smiles but looks away, toward her plate, at the multicoloured offerings of Mr. Woo and his kitchen staff.

"Beth is so tall," Bobby says, making conversation.

"She is tall," Dee says, with a mouth full of chicken.

Abbie stifles a laugh.

"Sports does that," Bobby says. "You grow up active, you get bigger. Exercise triggers these genes that would otherwise stay asleep."

"That's Dr. Reed to you," Abbie says.

Dee would like time to rush toward her meeting with Beth. She would like to will that time into being. Why does time move slowest when you want it to move fastest? When you are most aware of how slow it can be?

"We haven't seen Beth around here in a while," Bobby says.

Dee pours herself a glass of water. "I just ran into her on the street."

"Just like that?" Abbie asks, probing.

Dee kicks her brother under the table. "We like literally bumped into each other."

This causes a high-pitched guffaw from Abbie.

"She seems to be doing well," Bobby says.

The sounds of chewing, of cutlery. Dee takes another bite of her chicken and decides she needs to retreat to her room. She needs to speak to Coco Chanel. She needs to tell her about the day. This urge, to talk, becomes enormous, a welling inside of her, and suddenly Dee realizes that if she doesn't speak to Coco Chanel right now, she might throw up.

She puts her rice back in the container. She pushes her chicken back into the container. Mr. Woo always won points for using the old-fashioned paper containers with the thin tin handles. It was kitsch without intent. Nostalgia as the product of stubbornness.

"I'm done," Dee says, standing.

"You hardly ate," Bobby protests.

"I ate."

"Hardly."

"I did, honest, thanks for dinner."

"You're going to be hungry in a few hours," Abbie says, making a joke that Dee decides to acknowledge with a face.

"So are you," she says, and she leaves the kitchen and runs up the stairs and stops in the bathroom to pee, and while she's peeing she's thinking of Beth, and then she's thinking about how she's going to tell Coco Chanel, she thinks of the time Coco Chanel called her to tell her she had lost her virginity, that she'd slept with the cute blonde guy with the neat locker, like she'd said she would, only it had taken a bit longer than she'd thought it would because he was a virgin as well, and he wasn't sure he wanted to lose it with her, which Dee found funny and Coco Chanel found insulting.

Dee wipes and flushes and washes her hands and towels off and runs to her room. She closes the door behind her and grabs her phone and jumps onto her bed. She dials Coco Chanel's number and she waits for her to pick up, to answer, to pick up and then be ready to listen to Dee because Dee is going to tell her things she hasn't even thought of yet.

"Why are you calling?" Coco Chanel says.

"You won't believe it," Dee says.

"Are you okay?"

"Of course I'm okay. Or maybe. I'm fine, but maybe I'm not okay."

"You met someone."

"It's that obvious?"

"Oh my god." Coco Chanel says this in English. For emphasis.

Dee starts to giggle.

"Beth?"

Dee starts to laugh. She's nodding her head.

"You fucked Beth?"

Dee stops laughing. "I didn't fuck her."

"So you what?"

"I don't know. I was walking by her house."

"Like right after I called you?"

Dee has to think back to her life before Beth ran up to her. Did that life happen that recently? "Right after."

"Fuck off."

"I hung up, and there she was, running up to me."

"Oh my god."

Dee starts giggling again. "And then we talked and she came over and we stared into each other's eyes and then we kissed and then I realized Abbie was home and then my dad came home and then she had to go to volleyball practice, or maybe it was basketball, I don't remember, it was practice, something-ball, and now I'm just waiting for her practice to be over because we're going to meet at the park by the tracks." Dee remembers to breathe. "I can't wait." And then she remembers they'd made plans. "So maybe I can't come over."

"Dee," Coco Chanel says. Dee can sense the happiness in her friend's voice. "I just hope she's not a slut or something."

"I can't believe you'd say that."

"Because you never know."

"We stared into each other's eyes. We sat on my bed and just stared at each other."

"That sounds romantic." Dee can't tell whether Coco Chanel is being sarcastic or not.

"No really."

"Be careful."

"We kissed."

Coco Chanel is silent to this news.

"We kissed, and then again. Even at the door. We checked that no one was watching, and she kissed me. She. Kissed. Me."

Dee waits for Coco Chanel to say something. Her friend remains silent.

"Okay, I know, it's just once, it's just an afternoon, but I felt something with her, just staring at her, it was like we were getting to know each other all over again, getting to know each other in this new way."

"Be careful."

"Why would you say that?"

The friends say bye, and Dee hangs up the phone. She lies in her bed and buries her face in her pillow. She wonders if she's in love. There's a thought: What if she loves Beth? And is it possible to fall in love with someone so quickly, to fall so hard for someone you already know, and then just like that, you are in love, that person becomes another person, that person goes from being just someone else, scenery, to something much more important, to the thing you want more than any other thing, the object of a desire so deep you had yet to visit that place?

Is Dee in love? Or is she coming out, again, but on some deeper level, in a deeper more important place . . . was kissing Beth like walking through a gate, like leaving her home? Was kissing Beth like growing up? Or is Dee simply a horny teenager?

There's a knock on her door. She sits up. "What?" she asks.

"It's me." It's her brother.

"Okay."

Abbie opens the door and walks in. He stands in the middle of her room and takes it in. He hasn't been inside Dee's world in a long while. "So, Beth . . ."

"What about her?"

Abbie runs a hand through his hair. He's nervous, and Dee appreciates that. "Are you guys . . . ?"

"What?"

"Are you guys a thing?"

Dee can't stop smiling. She's just realized that. "I don't know."

"But maybe?"

"It just started."

"Like how recently just started?"

"Today."

Abbie sits on the floor. "Do you mind?"

"Don't be stupid."

"So you're, like, feeling all crazy because it's so new."

"I think that's how I feel."

"Like your insides are doing flips."

"Yes."

"Okay," he says, reassessing what he came into Dee's room to say. He can't tell his sister he's an expert; he's never been in love. And he doesn't care that he hasn't.

"Is that a problem?" Dee asks.

"I was going to have this talk about the difference between love and lust and play big brother about it, but you're not even there yet, and I'm not really an expert."

"I'm feeling both."

"Both what?"

"Love and lust." Dee listens to herself use the L-word and it doesn't register how simply it passed through her lips.

"Have you talked to Mom?"

And now Dee slouches. She lies down on the bed. She hugs her pillow.

"You should," Abbie says. "I don't know what she meant by what she said. Any more than you do. I don't even know if Dad heard it. I haven't talked to him about it either. Have you?'

"I think he tried to."

"You can't keep all this inside."

"I have my friends," she says, looking at her brother. "And you."

"We haven't really talked about it."

"I know you don't judge me."

"Dee."

He gets up and walks out and shuts the door behind him. Dee hugs the pillow again. She squeezes the pillow. And then she checks the time. She wills time to go faster, for her life to go faster, so she can get where she needs to go, which is nowhere special, just a park, where an old friend will be waiting for her, and where she will be introduced to the rest of her life.

Dee texts Clémentine. She texts Val. Both reply with variations on *I know, Coco Chanel told us, when are we getting together to* talk *about this?* She stares at herself in the mirror. She texts Coco Chanel. She gets dressed. She has to. She doesn't want to dress up, but she has to wear something more than a bikini bottom and a T-shirt. So she puts on a pair of jeans. And then she stares at herself in the mirror again, she turns around and looks at her ass, and suddenly her ass isn't important anymore, or not as important, and she realizes it hasn't been as important since school ended, since the spring started feeling like summer, since she made her silver bikini bottom a part of her uniform; something has changed, and it's not her ass, which is the same as it ever was, but something changed inside her, how she sees the world, how she sees the things she thought were important. When did this happen? Is the bikini that powerful?

She slides her feet into her pink canvas espadrilles. She brushes her hair. She takes off the espadrilles and searches for her flip-flops. She finds them on the far side of her room, near the window. She slips her feet into them. She checks the time. It's close enough. She'll walk slowly. If that's possible.

She opens her door. Her father is in the hallway. "Hi there," he says.

"I'm going out."

"Are you hungry? You didn't eat much."

"I'm fine."

"Where are you going?"

Her father never asks this. Why is he asking now? she thinks. What is he trying to get out of me? She shrugs. "I'm going to hang out with Beth," she says.

"It was nice to see her again."

She waits. Just long enough to make it not seem like she's blowing him off, which she is, and which she knows he knows she wants to do and is in the process of doing. "Okay, then."

"Don't be too late."

She finds her keys and then starts her walk to the park. Her slow, deliberate walk toward what feels like destiny. Past the houses she has walked past so often, split-levels and manicured lawns, past Beth's house, where she slows her walk still more, and then onward toward the park.

And then she's there; she always forgets how close it is. Psychologically, it's far. In her mind, the park and the tracks are the edge of the world and so best avoided. But it is only two blocks away, and one of the blocks is especially short, a city planner's mistake.

The park is full of strangers hanging out. She searches for Beth, and, not finding her, she stands at the park's edge, almost on the street, waiting. She tries to ignore the park and the people in it but without seeming like she's doing it. She stares into her phone, pretending to text. She clicks through some apps she hasn't touched in ages and wonders why she still has them. She checks her text messages and finds nothing, and then realizes Beth doesn't have her number, has no way of getting in touch. She sits on the curb and goes through her social media, learning things she doesn't need to learn, watching videos of others passing the time, using social media for the exact thing it is often criticized for, for ignoring the world, for ignoring the pageant around her, the kids who live by the tracks, threatening but not really, no one has bothered her, not yet at least.

"Hey," she hears, and she looks down the street and sees Beth approaching, her hair still wet from her post-practice shower.

"Hey," she says, relieved. But how relieved should she appear? How happy? How overjoyed? If anything, she's happier to see Beth than she thought she'd be.

She stands, and Beth leans over and kisses her. Dee is surprised by how public Beth is with this, they're just a few feet away from her house, but Beth doesn't care.

"Take that shit somewhere else," a voice calls out, and Beth searches the voice out, and gives it the finger, she gives the entire park the finger. Someone starts clapping. And Beth gives that sound the finger too.

"Come with me," she says, and she takes Dee by the hand and leads her to a break in the fence by the train tracks. She walks through the hole, and Dee follows her because it's all she can imagine doing, and then they are on the tracks. Beth leads Dee to a boulder between two sets of tracks and sits down on the side away from the park. In front of them, the darkness of nothing.

"What's on the other side?" Dee asks.

"It's a seniors' home, I think," Beth says.

Beth smells like Abbie's soap, which Dee has just figured out. They use the same brand, and this is going to be a problem. And she doesn't smell like shampoo. Her wet hair sits limp on her head and down to her shoulders. Why wouldn't she smell like shampoo?

Beth leans in and kisses Dee and grabs her by the shoulders. Dee melts into Beth. Is this where it happens? she wonders. Is this the place? Should I try and remember everything? Am I thinking too much? Her soap really does smell like Abbie's. She smells like my fucking brother, oh fuck.

She pulls away. She looks into Beth's blue eyes and understands the meaning of love. I don't want to overthink things. I don't want to overthink things. "What soap do you use?" she asks, and she cringes while asking.

"What?"

"I just know that smell, what is it?"

"Dove?"

"You use Dove?"

"Is it okay? Do I smell okay?"

Dee kisses her. The first time she's initiated a kiss. "It's fine."

"I can change it for you," Beth says, and this to Dee is akin to a declaration of intent. Of permanence.

"My brother uses it."

"Oh god," Beth says, and starts to laugh. "I'll totally change it."

"Because it's kind of freaking me out."

"I'll totally change it."

"And you didn't shampoo, so I just smell the soap."

"I don't shampoo," Beth says.

"That's impossible," Dee says.

"I did research! Shampoo is addictive. Like a drug for your hair. But if you don't use it, you go all natural again. You just have to take care of it. I use baking soda and some apple cider vinegar. And it's fine. Did my hair look shitty this morning?"

The way it was waving in the wind behind her, Beth's hair looked like she'd just come off the set of a shampoo commercial.

"I was shampooing all the time. I was killing my hair. And it's bad for the planet. It's dirty. Now I'm trying to figure out what soap to use. Maybe this helps."

Dee is listening to someone speak a foreign tongue.

"The first year sucks. Your hair even smells. I got away with it. I take like two or three showers a day. I'm the cleanest thing in the world." Beth leans toward Dee. "So, let's stop talking about my hair."

"I want this," Dee says, shocked by her own admission. Shocked that she's said such a sexual thing out loud.

"Even though I don't use shampoo?" Beth says opening her mouth. Her hand is already underneath Dee's T-shirt. She shifts her weight toward Dee, and Dee takes it. Inside, she feels the world's beginning. She feels a birth. A cataclysm. She leans backward. The ground shakes. It might be a train approaching. By the time Beth is on top of Dee, she is oblivious to the train, or to the gravel beneath her, or to the world.

Chapter 30

Abbie lives far removed from the Montreal of celebrity chefs, music scenes, and circus schools. He feels that distance every time he walks the final blocks to the gallery. The metro stop, one neighbourhood to the north, is a huddling of masses, a United Nations of ethnicities and colours and aromas and clothes. He wonders what would have happened had his family decided to live any place else, in any other part of town. What would he have become? Who would he be? The small choices that his parents had made, that their parents had made, that his birth parents had made, the unimportant moments that created the time and place for him, especially, as an adoptee, from an orphanage in Ghana and now this, an artist-in-the-making walking to a gallery that will exhibit his work and announce a new presence to the world. Or at least that part of the world that cares about such things.

He lives far from the Montreal people imagine when they hear the word *Montreal.*

Abbie lives far from the places that serve artisanal poutine, or craft beer, or roast duck in cans, though all those things are getting closer and closer, and will arrive, finally, in his neighbourhood when the rest of the city has moved on to other things. He lives far from the places people recommend tourists go to if they want to discover the "real" city. He lives far from a genuinely decent cup of coffee. Though he imagines good coffee will be the first sign that the neighbourhood is catching on to things.

His Montreal feels more anonymous, blank. He could look back now at the moment he took his first photo of a smokestack as his own way of reclaiming something he never had a right to claim. A past. He was telling a story about the city, sure, but perhaps himself as well. As someone without a known past. Without a connection to his biological history. And then, when he decided to place the fruit in the foreground of each photo, he was making another comment, reclaiming the memory of that which he'd never had, of the happy destruction he was starting to see, in the name of a progress that was lauded without inspection. Cheered because progress had to be cheered. And then, when he decided to document more and more smokestacks and chimneys, surely a sign of the city's economic recovery, but to do it publicly, and then to become a thing, an internet thing, and now to translate that thingness into somethingness, by documenting the unthinking, uncritical rush to modernity, that word again, *progress*, the equation of *new* with *modern*, when both require thought and backstories and more, he truly hadn't thought of making a commentary on masculinity. Not at first. He hadn't seen it. He's amazed at his blindness now, at the willfulness of his tunnel vision. The irony in his photos mirrored by the irony of his ascension to the position of artist. He understands the mechanics of what is happening to him now, he understands the arc of what Andrea and then Etienne de Bosch had seen, he understands that all art is supported by something approaching irony, or luck, by the same flimsy architecture that has been the subject of his photos. His art is art about art.

Abbie walks into a dep and buys a samosa. "Three for two dollars," the lanky man behind the cash says, trying to upsell. But Abbie isn't hungry, just snacky, and he kindly refuses the suggestion and walks out biting into the greasy, doughy dumpling.

He walks by a mosque that more than once had been accused of being a den of terrorists. He walks by a donut shop, the most Canadian thing in the world planting its flag among the immigrants, a conduit for assimilation. He walks by a souvlaki joint and then a Turkish sweets shop. And then he walks the underpass that would take him to the hodgepodge that is the gallery's neighbourhood, the unplanned streets, the abandoned lots, the dainty duplexes with yards still tended by Italian grandmothers shaped like tortellini. And always, the cool café, the restaurant that looks like a barn in the middle of farmland, the forlorn boutique selling impossibly white, ethically sourced shirts from Denmark.

Abbie opens the door to the gallery. "We're up here," he hears Etienne say, and he climbs the stairs, rubbing the samosa grease on his jeans. At the top of the stairs, he finds Etienne with Andrea, sitting huddled together on the floor, a bottle of white wine between them.

"Come here," Etienne says. "Would you like a drink?"

Abbie never knows what to expect when he walks into the gallery. He's here because Jacques is going to bring the first two photos that they have printed, and they are going to discuss framing options. Etienne wants to see the photos in the context of the gallery space. He suspects the photos have been printed too small, even though Jacques has followed his instructions, above what

Abbie's told him, because Jacques was told not to listen to Abbie, only to humour him, something he told Abbie in a moment of weakness, when he thought that perhaps some of Abbie's ideas weren't bad at all, and he was the artist, but he was not the boss, that was Etienne de Bosch.

Etienne pours Abbie a glass of wine. He lets out one of his high-pitched giggles, the kind that leads many to suspect he's drunk.

"A dealer from Toronto likes your work," Andrea says. "He said he liked it conceptually. He's in town and wants to meet you."

"And here I am," Abbie says. "I'm not going anywhere."

Etienne's phone pings, and he looks at the screen. "Jacques is on his way," he announces.

"I want to make sure the photos are right," Etienne says.

Abbie wonders why they wouldn't be right.

"They will be right," Andrea says. "But we want to ensure they are perfect. We haven't seen them printed yet."

"Jacques says they're not ready," Etienne says.

Abbie feels the way he felt when he realized he'd killed his pet turtle. He was fourteen, he'd never hurt anything, and he killed the turtle, his pet, his first one, José, because he'd taken it out of its tank and then forgotten about it, and then he stepped on it, and the sickening sound of the crack of its shell, and the feeling that travelled his body when he'd stepped on it, he'd never forgotten that feeling, it still made him ill. "What does he mean?" Abbie asks.

"That's what we're going to see," Etienne says.

"I hardly know Jacques, but I know he exaggerates everything," Andrea says.

"He's been known for drama," Etienne agrees.

Abbie does not recognize the Jacques they are talking about. "I saw the first two prints, and they're awesome," he says. "We worked hard on them. We fucked around with that first print for the past week. We tried it without hands even. We took Saul's hands out of it once and then I decided you have to see the hands holding the oranges, you have to see that artifice, the making of it, that completes the image, the story, it complements the narrative we see in the image. We talked about all of that."

"He's talking about the printing. Let's see," Etienne says.

Abbie finds a chair and sits on it. He has decided he'll drink the wine.

"Don't worry," Etienne says. "I shouldn't have said anything. Perhaps I should have just been disappointed in the print and sprung it on you. Surprise! Like those disgusting jumping spiders."

"You saw the prints?" Andrea asks.

Abbie nods. His knees feel weak.

"And you were happy with them?"

"I thought I was." Abbie sighs because now he doesn't know what to think.

"Jacques is the most dramatic man in the world," Etienne says with a flourish. "I'm going to get more wine." He runs down the stairs to hunt down another bottle.

Abbie has seen a room of his photos, all printed to his satisfaction, all rendered to the specifications, all perfect, he thought they had all been perfect, Jacques said they were as good as they were going to get, he had said something like, *nothing is perfect* and *Abbie knows the art comes from what we're willing to accept*, and he'd said Abbie's level of acceptance was high, he'd been impressed, he'd told Etienne, and Etienne had relayed this to Abbie, because Jacques was too old and too set in his ways to offer a compliment, but Jacques had let Etienne know that Abbie had it, he had the eye, he'd taken the lessons of the darkroom and absorbed them and quickly — he was an artist. And now something is wrong.

Abbie knows Andrea can see his confusion. It's on his face, in his posture, the way his fingers are not quite curled up into a fist, but close, how he taps his toes without hitting the floor. He can see everything and nothing right now. He sips his wine. And then he finishes the glass.

"We don't even know what Jacques texted," she says. "For all we know, Etienne's the one being dramatic."

Abbie hasn't considered this. Though there are only so many ways to parse *they're not ready*.

"When I first started following your work, I had no idea we'd end up like this," Andrea says. "I was still living in Seattle. I knew I was going to move here — it didn't happen suddenly — but I had no idea I'd take part in this. Or that I'd luck into someone like Etienne. I met him at a vernissage, and everyone was drinking afterward. I didn't know anyone. I hadn't started work yet. I'd just bought a condo. I was getting used to all the French everywhere. I hadn't started my French classes yet. And we were talking, and he called me the next day and he told me there was an opening on the board." Andrea sitting on the floor is a position that mesmerizes Abbie for what he knows are the wrong reasons. But as far as he can tell, Andrea is not Japanese, she does not possess the tiniest percentage of any kind of Asian blood, not in the slightest, and this reassures him. I'm normal, he thinks. A bit triumphantly. And then he realizes that Andrea's still speaking.

". . . I was surprised by how serious it was. I was surprised this place even had a board. But Etienne runs the gallery as a non-profit. He needs a board."

Andrea leans back on her elbows and stretches out her legs. "I think they resented me. Maybe they still do." She pauses and looks toward the blank wall. "I was new in town, and Etienne just nominates me for the board. It's his gallery, he gets what he wants. And I admit, I can see how that would be off-putting. I've been getting that a lot. The 'You Americans' thing. I get that. But anyway, then I saw that your work was going to interesting places, and your follower count was getting way up there, and then I realized, oh, Abbie Reed lives in Montreal!"

Abbie wonders if Andrea has a plan. If she has planned any of this out. He wonders this because he suspects she doesn't and that makes him feel better about himself. He also thinks she dresses really well.

"When I moved here, it felt like the most adult thing that had ever happened to me," she says. "I'm in my mid-thirties and I'm starting to feel like an adult. And then when Etienne asked me to be on the board that sealed it. How much more adult can you get than that?"

Abbie doesn't know. He's eighteen. He's lucky to live in a place where he can drink legally at his age.

A door opens downstairs. They listen as footsteps approach the stairs and then climb them. Abbie looks toward the staircase, and Jacques emerges, holding an oversized leather carrying case. Abbie's photos are inside, no doubt, and Abbie doesn't know whether he should stand or not.

"Bonjour, Andrea," Jacques says, carefully placing the case against a wall.

Jacques looks like he's just woken up, again, this is his look, and it's possible that he always feels like he's just woken up. "Abbie," he says, acknowledging his charge. "The photos are fucking amazing."

Abbie wants to smile, but he knows they work, he's seen the prints, and he doesn't want to acknowledge anything else. "Why does Etienne think they're not ready?"

"Why does Etienne think the world is flat?" Jacques asks.

"Jacques, Etienne says you texted him," Andrea says.

"I text him all the time."

"And you just texted him now?"

"I texted to say I was coming over. I didn't say anything about not being ready."

"Etienne said . . ." Abbie's facade is going to crack, if only because he never learned about crisis management or people like Etienne in school.

"Etienne can suck my dick," Jacques says. "Where is he?"

Abbie has never asked about Etienne's history with Jacques. That Jacques is important to this gallery, and to Etienne, is as obvious as the colour of the sky.

"He went downstairs. I think he's out back having a smoke," Andrea says, standing up.

Jacques storms down the stairs. They hear the back door slam open and then shut.

"Do they hate each other or love each other?" Abbie asks.

"They don't love each other."

"Then what is it?"

"It's a long story, and I don't know the whole thing but it involves a woman, I know that much, and it may involve Jacques's ex-wife."

"But Etienne . . ."

"He's been a man for a long time."

"Etienne?"

"He used to be married."

Abbie thinks this through. Not the marriage part.

"I'm starting to feel nervous." He says this out loud before he realizes he's doing it.

"I want to open this." Andrea's fingers inch toward the Velcro straps that guard the contents, Abbie's work, his future, a strap as guardian. As resistance. She takes one end of the strap in her hand but retreats. "Etienne would kill me."

Abbie can hear the muffled yells from the backyard. The shouts of two men.

"What's going on out there?" Abbie asks.

Andrea walks to the back window and looks out. "There's a lot of gesticulating."

Abbie joins Andrea by the window and watches. Etienne looks like he has the makings of a smile on his face. It's Jacques who's angry, or at least appears to be. "Jacques keeps calling Etienne a liar," he translates.

"About what?" Andrea asks.

Abbie strains to listen, but the window serves as a surprisingly effective noise barrier. "I don't know."

Etienne is laughing. He's hunched over laughing. His face is somewhere between pink and red. Jacques pulls out a pack of cigarettes and takes a seat on a lounge chair. He lights a cigarette. He stares off in the opposite direction of Etienne's laughter.

They watch. They watch Etienne turn redder from laughter, from an inability to breathe. He is coughing now, and still laughing, the aftershocks of whatever has set him off. He puts a hand in the fountain and dampens his face. He places his hand on Jacques's shoulder, and Jacques ignores him, continuing to stare off, toward a place in the distance that can contain his anger.

"I don't get those two," Andrea sighs.

"I just wish they'd get up here so we can take out the photos," Abbie says.

"Oh, fuck them already, let's do it," she says, and she makes her way to the case and undoes the Velcro straps and then the case is open. "Ready?" she asks. Abbie can hardly breathe. She closes her eyes. "You take them out," she says.

Abbie gulps some air. He walks over to the case and opens it wider and pulls out a photo. Jacques has brought the large ones, four feet by four feet, and Abbie places it gently on the floor. He stares at it. "So that's that," he says.

Andrea grabs him from behind. "Holy shit," she says.

"What does that mean?"

"That means holy shit."

Abbie loosens up. "Is that good?"

Andrea squats in front of the photograph. She studies it. "I've seen this one before," she says. "On my phone."

"Probably," Abbie says.

"It's just so large right here. It's hard to believe."

Abbie reaches into the case and pulls out the second photograph. It is one of the tall ones, mirroring the dimensions of a smokestack, with less of the surrounding buildings. He places it on the floor next to the larger one. In both, the oranges in the foreground, the joke, the statement, whatever one will call it; Etienne has taken to calling them "the balls" because he would, and because that is what they are, in the end — they are balls. Abbie and Jacques have printed a dozen four-by-four squares, another dozen tall photographs ranging in height from eighteen inches to four feet, a series of six two-by-two-foot squares, and another series of almost postcard-sized miniatures, to be mounted individually and framed, but almost like a collage, on the far wall of the gallery, an end point to the exhibition. If Etienne thinks there is a problem with these two, the others will have to be reworked and reprinted.

"There is no problem," Andrea says. "That's obvious."

Abbie searches the case for more photographs, but there are none. He wants to see his work on a wall. He wants the show to be mounted now. He wants the instant gratification of social media. He feels he's waited for a long time, for too long, he doesn't know what it is to wait for anything any longer, he can't imagine being a photographer in the days of film, when you had to labour just to see the result of a simple click.

Abbie doesn't know what to think. He feels like he's not in this room. He feels detached from this room, from himself, from the world. He's afraid if he closes his eyes he may wind up in another dimension and suddenly learn that everything in his life until now has been an illusion. His work feels, suddenly, like a distant thing.

"Remind me again how many pieces are in this show?" Andrea asks.

Abbie does the math. Does he count the small ones? "Thirty," he says. "And then a series of small prints. So, forty. About. I think."

"Right. We want to fill the room. Both floors. Comfortable but not crowded. These things need space," Andrea says. Abbie is realizing the level of her involvement in this. Andrea's efforts go beyond following Abbie's work from Seattle on her phone. Or showing his work to Etienne. She's more than a champion.

Abbie can hear Etienne's laughter, the wheezing, the gasping for breath. "Etienne hasn't seen these," he says.

Andrea grabs the wine off the floor and takes a healthy pull, draining the bottle.

Abbie reaches down and picks up the tall print and walks toward a wall. He holds it up.

"Steel," Andrea says.

"We have access to some distressed steel," Etienne says from behind them. Andrea turns to face him. Etienne puts a fresh bottle of wine on the floor and kneels before the photograph on the ground. He reaches for the bottle and takes a swig. "I think simple steel will work nicely. On the large ones. The vertical ones will get wood. Almost salvaged wood. Jacques says he can source that. The small squares should get black. But chipped. We have to chip them, make them look old. For the smaller ones, I'm tempted to go to Ikea."

"Where's Jacques?" Andrea asks.

Etienne waves the question away. He's still red from laughter. He stands and walks toward Abbie. "Are your arms getting tired?" he asks.

Abbie says nothing. He has never seen Etienne this serious. "What wasn't ready?" he asks, meekly.

"You won't believe," Etienne says. "He's a genius. But he's an idiot. He works hard, but he's the laziest man I know." Etienne clears his throat. He turns to Abbie. "Seriously, put that down before your arms cramp."

Abbie carefully sets the photo on the floor. Etienne takes another swig of the wine. "Jacques meant *he* wasn't ready."

"I don't know what that means," Andrea says. She stands and crosses her arms. Abbie can sense the shift in the temperature of the room.

"When he said they weren't ready, he meant *he* wasn't ready, that he was worried about rushing things, he didn't think he could do it, he said he needed a vacation — this is when I laughed, because his life is an endless vacation. But he says he needs one and he needs one now, *this instant*; he even said this, he said *this instant* or *immediately* or something ridiculous like that, before the show, *despite* the show, and because of this he's worried he's not going to have all the printing done for the show, there's too much work. He went on and on, and it was like watching one of those very talky movies from the '60s, you know, very nouvelle vague. I was thinking he was complaining about his life, because he's so busy, and no one pays him enough, and then he got so angry that I kept laughing, he left, and I could hardly breathe."

Abbie is going to slide the photos back in the case, and he's going to go to Jacques's studio. They don't have much left to do. They've done most of the work. At least he thinks they have. Abbie wonders why Jacques is nervous about finishing the job, or if it's just historical, or psychological, this complaining, something more about his relationship to Etienne and not about the work itself. Jacques is distant but surprisingly caring. His lessons in photography, in technique, have been intimate. He's not afraid to touch Abbie when they are working with the chemicals to process the smaller photos, which have been transferred from digital to film and are being developed. Or to lead his hand on the oversized touchpad. He holds his hand as they take the stylus together and trace contours of the photo on the screen in order to increase the contrast of a line, or to remove noise from the sky or to brighten a certain feature. Everything Abbie knows about photography he knows because of Jacques. Everything about being a photographer. Jacques pours everything he knows into his student. And he knows Abbie will soon leave him, crawl toward the ocean, and swim away. "Now, let's see the work," Etienne says.

Abbie steps away. He can't watch. He feels judged more intensely than ever. He feels Etienne's gaze all over him. He feels it inside. Andrea walks over to stand next to him. Etienne makes humming noises while eyeing the photo up and down, his head moving around the image like a cat following a laser beam. "Can you see it with the frames?" he asks. He turns to face Abbie, and his smile is generous. And loving. "Can you see it? These beautiful photos? Filling this gallery? This magnificent fucking art?"

Chapter 31

They drop out of the social engagement, one by one, lined up before the inevitable, like penguins waiting to dive into an unforgiving sea. Jeffrey had texted this morning. His youngest was sick. Bobby had been the first of the friends with children, and so the first to drop out of a social life.

Stu called. He had to fly to Miami at the last minute, on business, and he used the phrase *rain check*. Bobby and Stu had, perhaps, been closest in high school. They lived next to each other, and each knew the others' basements intimately. Stu bought his parents' house when they downsized and moved to a condo; he slept in the room he had been conceived in, and when he'd agreed to this, when his wife had talked him into buying the house, it felt as if Bobby and Stu had divorced in some way, because Bobby could not fathom what it would take to do what Stu had done, even if the house had undergone a drastic renovation.

Barry called Jonathan. They were having people over, and Barry had forgotten, and it hadn't occurred to him to check with his wife. This was wife number two and very different from wife number one, but there was a reason she was different, and Jonathan had warned Barry to watch himself, if he didn't want to once again be on the other, financially undesirable, end of a lengthy and unpleasant divorce.

Phil's father was in hospital with a possible pneumonia, and it didn't look good. He had emailed Jonathan, had contemplated the end of life and the idea of infinity, was thinking about god and an expanding universe. He hadn't spoken to his father in many years, after he had taken over the family business and changed the overall direction of the building supplies manufacturer and moved it to Toronto. But possible death was just that, and the man was Phil's father, and Phil wanted to ensure the will would not be a permanent reminder of their estrangement, and Phil knew his sister would be planning to lay it on now, she would attack their father's impending death with transparent sympathy. It had been a long email.

Bobby hadn't seen Mimi in three days. It felt longer. He sensed her crawling into bed at night, but he had not spoken to her. He remembered that she may have kissed him, it's possible he'd imagined it, perhaps last night, perhaps the night before. She had spooned with him, as well, after crawling into bed; she had pulled herself close to him and draped her leg across his, and had pushed herself into him, she had held him tight, but he doesn't know if this is something remembered or something imagined.

He's pretty sure he'd been sort of drunk every night before bed. He does know that she is up before him every morning. He can smell the lingering scent of her morning routine in the washroom, her towel damp, her toothbrush wet. Every morning her coffee mug is in the sink, half a pot of coffee still in the coffeemaker, the machine on; he appreciates the fresh coffee.

Mimi and Bobby have never been the kind to email each other, to call, to text, unless it's Mimi telling Bobby she's going to be late, which she does now every evening. He wonders if he feels her absence more because he's not doing anything, because his mind is free of the politics and realities of work, because he does not work. Because he's unemployed.

And Bobby keeps thinking of that stupid French chef whom he has never met but who seems to be feeding Mimi night after night, who seems to have become his wife's personal chef, and he pictures a dashing man with a well-groomed salt-and-pepper beard, his flowing hair hidden beneath a lampoonish toque.

Bobby is sure Jean-Marc looks nothing like this.

But Mimi sees him more often, the French chef, she sees him at least twice a day, when she might not see Bobby for days on end, despite the possible middle of the night spooning. This is a man who feeds his wife, and Bobby can't help but wonder what other hungers this man is feeding.

He knows, but he also doesn't know. He dislikes himself for thinking these things and he resents the reasons he thinks them.

Bobby estimates Mimi is working eighteen-hour days. Including weekends. He thinks she's working weekends. Because he doesn't know when the weekend starts now. The calendar is hazy, he recognizes the construct of the calendar, how it is geared around work, around the routine of labour and not around anything else; it is not a construct of the dreamer or the philosopher.

Time does not seem to exist for Mimi.

Time is all Bobby has. He owns time more than it owns him. He still hasn't learned to enjoy this, to appreciate the lack of time for the luxury it is, because luxury is the ability to not care about things like time, to enjoy the quiet that timelessness brings. What is more luxurious than quiet?

Bobby has spent afternoons on the shag carpet listening to the silence of his home and he knows he should enjoy those moments, he should appreciate the luxury of nothingness, but he can't, he's come to realize that maybe he'd like to continue terrorizing people in an office because he was always so good at that, he was good at being someone he was not, because it delivered results, and it continued to get him results until it no longer did. He misses the joy of eliciting fear. He misses the armour of the modern business suit.

He has thought about the shag. He has ruminated on it while lying on it.

He goes shopping once a day. Even if he doesn't need to. The pantry is overflowing with food. There are bowls of fruit in the kitchen and the living room. He has added a bowl of fruit to Dee's bedroom and another one to Mimi's worktable in the basement. And the fridge is crammed by the will of his dilemma. By overabundance.

Bobby finds the bar. It used to be something else, and he can't remember what it was, but he's been in the space, he's eaten something in this space before it became a bar. It's a pub now, with pub food, so he could still eat if he were hungry but he's not, he's been eating leftovers, heating up mysterious items from the freezer, trying to feed his kids because his wife is never home. Though they are hardly home either. Mostly it's just him.

Bobby walks in and seeks out Jonathan. His friend isn't here yet. He finds a table and sits. A girl in a tartan skirt comes over; the place is an Irish bar and the obviousness of this is only apparent to him now. He orders a Guinness and waits. This is a very anglo crowd, an anglo bar in an anglo part of town. The amazing thing about this city is this very same bar, with the exact same decor, could exist in another part of the city, farther east, farther north from here, anywhere but west, perhaps, and the crowd would be either mixed or completely French, and everything else would be the same — the tartan skirts, the mix of Irish music and pop metal from the '90s, the menu, the knick-knacks decorating the walls, the sports on the TVs. That is the parallel nature of language in the city, everything the same but different, but never different but the same.

And then a familiar face is before him. It's Singh. From the office. It takes Bobby a moment to realize this, to locate Singh in a different environment. "Well, well," Singh says, extending his hand.

Bobby takes his hand and they shake. "Singh," he says, flustered.

Singh has the kind of awkward smile on his face that one gets after having discovered their mother's sex toys. "Call me Vijay."

The waitress returns with Bobby's Guinness. "Here you go," she says.

"Amelia, let's have some whiskey, please. Shots," Vijay orders.

"Singh, it's okay," Bobby says. "Vijay."

"It's on me." Vijay looks toward Amelia and makes a gesture that Bobby can't read. Amelia heads to the bar to retrieve their shots.

"Call me Bobby."

"Come on, I'm the one still employed!" Vijay bursts into laughter, though Bobby sees it more as a joyful snickering, or at least something Vijay has kept inside for a long time.

"You are indeed. How's the office?"

Vijay stops laughing abruptly. "Do you really want to know?" he asks.

"That's a good question," Bobby says.

"Because if you really want to know, the office is wonderful. Things are more relaxed. Andrea has everyone very calm. She's very calming. She leads in a calm manner. She's like one of those smelly candles, you know? We're more productive."

"That's what she was brought in to do."

"And there's more laughter. Our meetings work. People feel friendlier."

"Is Vachon still there? Um, Isabelle?"

Bobby takes another sip of his Guinness. And before he knows it, half the pint is gone. He wonders where Jonathan might be.

Amelia returns with their shots. "Thanks," Vijay says. He picks up his shot glass and holds it out. Bobby picks up his, and they clink their glasses. "Drink up," Vijay says, and he tilts his head back, and the whiskey vanishes into his mouth.

Bobby does the same, all the while thinking perhaps Vijay has had the drink doctored somehow, that maybe he's going to find himself in an alley being raped by a dog while guys watch and exchange money.

"Let get some more," Vijay says.

"Are you here with someone?" Bobby asks.

"This is my brother's bar," Vijay says. "I manage it when he needs a day off. It keeps me out of trouble." And then the laugh returns, except this time Bobby hears a cackle more than a snicker. He hears the beginning of evil. "Isabelle works with Andrea now."

This guts Bobby. It means, what, that she had never loved him? Had he loved her? Is love the right word? Loyalty? Was he not loyal to her? He was always loyal to Vachon. She was his foundation. She was his. He thinks this and sees the folly in it. But that's what she was. She was his. Just as much as he was hers. Upon his dismissal, Vachon had been the only one to show any kind of emotion; when she had told him she would miss him, she had sounded genuine, and genuinely hurt. And now she was working with the woman responsible for his dismissal.

Vijay gestures to Amelia for two more shots. "Are you alone?"

It takes Bobby a second to realize he's being asked this question. "No," he says. "I'm meeting a friend."

"Great," Vijay says. "That's what this place is for: Meeting friends, having fun. Staying out of trouble. And getting into it!"

Amelia returns with two shots and collects the empty glasses.

Vijay holds up his shot glass. "To you," he says. "To whatever it is you did in that office, and to all the people you did it to." He downs his shot and slams the glass on the table.

Bobby wonders if he should drink his shot. Because he was a terrible person. Why wouldn't Vijay want to poison him? He had employed a management style that had long passed its best before date. He knew it, but it worked for him. He takes a sip of his beer instead. It feels safer now, but it's beer and beer is always safer. Bobby glances over at the entrance, hoping to see Jonathan. Praying to see his friend. I was like the office Trump before Trump became Trump, he thinks. He hopes his face does not betray this realization.

"Like that time you spiked the coffee with soya sauce. That was you, right? I just stopped drinking the coffee. Every morning, I bought from the coffee shop in the lobby. I became friends with the owner. Toast and coffee, every morning. And then I met his daughter. She would help out because he's getting old, and he doesn't trust his other waitress, so his daughter started working there to run the place. And now I'm seeing her! She's my girlfriend. For the last six months. He hates that she's seeing me. I mean, I'm not even white. He says to me, 'at least you don't wear that turban,' and so that makes me okay."

Bobby glances toward the front door again. Jonathan enters. Bobby feels safe.

"So all this to say, that stupid coffee trick of yours led directly to my meeting this awesome girl."

Vijay holds out his hand. He wants to shake Bobby's hand. Bobby looks at Vijay's outstretched hand and realizes what's just happened. The shots had been in celebration. He downs his whiskey, puts the shot glass down, and takes Vijay's hand. "I'm very happy for you," he says.

"That coffee trick was some fucked up evil," Vijay says. As if Bobby doesn't know this. "But silver linings, right? Cause and effect."

Jonathan reaches the table, and Bobby stands and the friends hug. "Jonathan, this is Vijay Singh. I used to work with him."

"Your brother owns this place," Jonathan says.

"That's right," Vijay says. He stands, and they shake hands. "Amelia! More shots!"

Jonathan and Bobby exchange glances. And smiles. "It's great to see you," Jonathan says.

"Hey, guys, whatever you need, just ask, okay?" Vijay says, and he collects the empty shot glasses and walks toward the bar.

Jonathan takes the seat vacated by Vijay. He stares at his friend. "How many shots?" he asks.

Bobby isn't sure. "Two?" he asks. He brings his beer to his lips. "I'm pretty sure we only had two."

Amelia returns with ten shots. Jonathan orders a Guinness as well. "Wow," he says. He takes a shot glass and holds it up. "Feels like high school."

When they were young, Jonathan and Bobby were the first ones to start drinking. To get together and drink for the enjoyment of it. Not with the idea of getting drunk but getting drunk as the side effect of drinking. Jonathan learned to make cocktails using a book he found in his father's library. His parents left him alone on weekends when they went to their country house up north. Especially during the winter, Jonathan hated skiing because his parents loved it so much. He'd seen his bar mitzvah as a way to get out from under the tyranny of the ski hill, and it had been; his parents had to respect his opinion on the matter, on any matter, after a two-year build-up of "becoming a man."

"Feels like high school," Bobby says.

They down their shots and reach for their beers at the same time. "Did you drive?" Jonathan asks.

"I walked."

"That's a walk."

"It's nice out."

"I took a cab. Just in case. And now look."

Bobby takes another pull of his beer. Alcohol wasn't important to him growing up, and he still doesn't know that it is, even though he drinks quite a bit, enough that he's aware of his consumption, of the amount, and each trip to the liquor commission sees larger and larger bills, and he's aware of that as well. So he's started just ordering what he needs from the liquor commission online. He's thankful they have a points program.

"Tell me . . ." Bobby says.

"What do you need to know?"

This is how they have always started conversations. Bobby asking for information. Jonathan asking what kind of information needs to be proffered. Time doesn't stand still, but men do.

"Which one of them was bullshitting?"

Jonathan takes a sip of his beer. "None of them," he says. "They were all within the realm of the possible. The only one, maybe, is Phil, but he also was the one who wanted to come out the most."

"Fuck them all."

"Phil was really pissed about not coming."

"He doesn't even like his father."

"Pneumonia. He's in the hospital. He could die. That's a lifetime of guilt."

"Guilt is overrated."

"Okay. Regret."

"Regret is not overrated."

Bobby orders another beer.

The two friends pick up another shot each. "Shit," Jonathan says.

They lean their heads back and down their shots. Bobby finishes his beer. Jonathan takes a long pull of his. Bobby can picture Jonathan chugging bottles at the golf course behind his house. They had found a spot in a valley bisected by a stream that separated the third and fourth holes. The valley hid them from the clubhouse and from everything and everyone else. They could build fires down there, by the stream, and they did, and they drank and got stoned and brought their boom boxes, and someone would always bring a guitar, and they would sing and laugh. They would bring girls and walk off with them into the thicket of trees surrounding the stream as it left the golf course.

It's a public golf course, and now the city is threatening to sell the land to developers, and Jonathan is one of those leading the fight to preserve the green space, out of nostalgia, sure, but also because he knows the developer and hates him.

"What's going on with Valley Meadows?" Bobby asks.

Jonathan's older brother and his friends had introduced the valley to Jonathan and his friends. His older brother's friends were more bohemian, freer, more prone to screw up in school for more idealistic reasons, and most of Jonathan's older brother's friends, and his brother as well, ended up in creative careers. One was even a legitimate actor, had moved to LA, and achieved a kind of success acting in infomercials. Jonathan's friends — Bobby's circle — had been more conservative, not politically, but in taking risks, in their desire to question authority for reasons other than making trouble.

"We're going to win," Jonathan says. "I'm not sure the neighbourhood can support the kind of development these assholes are trying to peddle. Now they're talking about keeping half the golf course, so a nine-hole public course and a smaller development. They're so desperate they're even talking about affordable housing.

Except it's at the end of the city, so anyone who lives there is going to need a car."

Amelia returns with Bobby's beer. Jonathan asks for another. Bobby reaches for his and takes a long drink. "Have you been reading about it?" Jonathan asks.

"I don't read the paper. I don't watch the news. I don't even turn on my computer. I don't know anything anymore. I vacuum. I think about what to make for dinner. I fold things. I shop. I think about our shag rug. It's amazing how many things need folding. Clothes, okay. But then towels. And linens. And tablecloths. Everything has to be folded and then put in its place.

Jonathan finishes his Guinness. "Dude."

"I know."

Jonathan leans forward. "Do you want me to ask around?"

"For what?"

"For you. For work. Do you want me to ask around?"

"I don't need to work," Bobby says.

"You want to fold?"

"I want to take this time to figure out what I want."

"Work with Mimi."

"Not a chance."

"Why not?"

This is the question Bobby asks himself more and more. The frequency of it, the conversation he has with himself, has become a cacophony. "We can't put our eggs in one basket."

"Right now, you don't have a basket, and she does."

"I got a great severance." He can't tell if he sounds defensive.

Amelia returns with Jonathan's beer.

Jonathan and Bobby do another shot. Bobby reaches for his beer. He can remember Jonathan calling him when his company became what he'd wanted it to become. Jonathan was squealing, he promised anyone who would listen that he was going to start to collect cars. He'd bought his parents' country house, tore it down, and brought in an architect who taught at Yale to design a new home. Bobby admires his friend's success, and he has to admit he admires his wealth more, but most of all he admires his calm. Success has given him serenity. Peace. Jonathan exudes peace. When he sweats, patchouli must pour out of him.

"I have a year," Bobby says. "At least."

"I bought stuff from Mimi once," Jonathan says.

Bobby feels a kind of defeat hearing this. Vachon works for Leopard Lady. And Jonathan purchases furniture from Mimi.

"I redid my den up north. Everything is from her site. Except the carpet and the wall unit."

Bobby feels unsupportive. Maybe he's jealous. He suspects something base in his reaction to what Jonathan is saying. It might be that he's afraid of what Mimi's success might mean to him. To them. To their marriage.

"A couch. A lounge chair. A great teak coffee table. A side table. A lamp. A clock. Maybe the bar set."

"Some investors approached her," Bobby says, because Jonathan might find this interesting, and because it's something to say, to show, if only to himself, that he knows, that he is involved in his wife's work, somehow, while spending his days prone on a shag carpet.

"I can see it working," Jonathan says. "She's hitting a sweet spot. It's well-curated stuff. I use words like *curate*. She has a good eye. I would invest in her company. If asked." He takes a swig of his beer. "Sometimes I wish I still smoked," he says.

"I never see her anymore. I don't even know what she's doing these days. I don't remember the last time I talked to her." Though he does. More specifically, he remembers the last time he should have spoken to his wife and didn't, the last time the family was together, sharing a meal, being a family.

"She's going to need you," Jonathan says. "You're a numbers guy."

"I *was* a numbers guy."

Amelia checks in. "Okay?"

"I like this," Bobby tells her. "This treatment." She smiles, not quite warmly, and she tilts her head.

"Another beer?" she asks.

Jonathan studies his beer. Bobby knows he needs another one. "Two more," he says. Amelia leaves. The friends lift another shot.

"I'm happy I took a cab," Jonathan says. He downs his shot. Bobby follows suit.

Bobby can remember waking in Jonathan's basement, or Barry's, or Stu's, and wondering what had happened. In trying to connect the forgotten moments, the friends built their mythology, adding layers of half-truths and half-measures, constructing a narrative that loomed larger and larger in their collective memory, becoming glue. Mortar. He reaches for his beer. He finishes it and stares into the empty glass, and he can smell the funk of waking up on the golf course, in the valley, of getting his bearings, of hearing birdsong, recoiling from the sunlight, and then the smell, of grass and the underbrush and sex and dirt, the memory of that smell envelops him now, the freedom of it, the realization that nothing bad could happen and never would.

"Find out the name," Jonathan says.

"Of what?"

"Of this group. Of these people investing in Mimi's company."

"You're serious." Bobby feels a strange sense of helplessness, speaking to a friend, an old friend, who has succeeded where he has failed, that's how he feels, as if he has failed; he's keenly aware of the feeling now, and he knows Jonathan is angling for information, for an investment opportunity, because he can think of these things, he can imagine depositing his money with other people, in other people's lives, to make more money, that's how the world works, and Jonathan has figured that out. And Bobby thought he had. Getting fired, the circumstances around his firing, how he hadn't fought it because of the generosity of it, he'd been fired and taken care of all at once, was the changing of an order he hadn't known existed. He'd represented something when it worked, and he'd represented the same thing when it had stopped working, and so he was kindly asked to leave.

"It's a small world," Jonathan says. "And Montreal's an island. I don't know everything that's going on here. I'm not hot shit like that. I'm not connected. But maybe a little. I'm lukewarm shit."

Amelia returns with the beers.

Bobby feels the room spin for a moment. If he closes his eyes right now, he's going to start floating through space. He attacks his beer and then half of it is gone. "I'm not working with Mimi," he says. He laughs at the idea, and Jonathan starts laughing with him. And then he's laughing because his friend is laughing. Because they have not done this in so long. Because it feels good, like the late nights in the valley. Before they started drinking wine.

"Remember that night . . ." Jonathan says before he is lost in the laughter, before the memory of anything is lost in the joy of the present.

Bobby feels the mingling inside of him, the happiness and the confusion. He is confused. He might be lost. He hopes it's temporary. He stands up. "I have to piss," he says, still laughing, his stomach starting to ache. His eyes filled with tears.

He walks to the washroom, squeezing his way past clusters of the semi-drunk, no one is quite fully gone yet, at least not those in his way. He passes the bar, and Vijay is there, at the cash, and he waves, and his ex-colleague waves back. "How's it going?" he asks, without expecting an answer, because no one ever does.

Bobby enters the bathroom and stumbles toward a urinal. He begins to pee and reads an ad placed at eye-level for a car. He's peeing, and there is an ad for a car, a Ford Focus, and he's sure this is not an ad that will ever work, but what does he know? Ads don't work on him, and he doubts they ever have.

He shakes and zips up and washes his hands and makes his way back to the table. At the bar, Singh hands him two shots. "We still have," he says.

"Come on," Singh pleads.

Bobby takes them and makes his way toward Jonathan. "Surprise," he says.

"This evening is going to take a turn," Jonathan says.

The friends down their shots and reach for their beers. The noise in the bar rises, somehow, and Bobby wonders if this is because he's more sensitive to it, because he's crossed another threshold in his drunkenness, or perhaps the bar did just get noisier, perhaps the music was turned up and so the voices had to rise with it.

And then Phil walks in. He heads straight to the table, a planet-sized smile on his face. Bobby notices right away that Phil has shaved his head, that bald Phil is now Phil who might be bald but you'd never know because he's shaved his head. Bobby stands and the two friends hug. Phil plants a kiss on Bobby's cheek, and Bobby strokes Phil's smooth pate. Phil turns to Jonathan, and they hug in turn, Jonathan also rubbing Phil's head and laughing. "What the fuck?" he asks.

"There's only so much you can do in a hospital," Phil says. He looks around for a chair. Amelia walks by, and Bobby grabs her and she looks at his hand on her wrist and he lets go. "Sorry," he yells. "Do you have another chair for my friend?"

Amelia almost laughs and continues her way toward the bar and she is engulfed by everyone and disappears. Phil walks into the crowd in the opposite direction, toward the entrance, and he exits the bar and returns moments later with a patio chair. He sits down. And he reaches for his friends, an arm on each. "Guys!" he says.

"Dude!" Jonathan yells.

"Shots," Bobby says. He pushes his last one to his friend.

"What about you?"

"Don't worry," Bobby says, and he reaches for Jonathan's last shot and drinks it down.

Amelia returns, and Phil orders a vodka tonic.

"Still with the vodka tonic," Bobby says. Phil is the most concerned with calories. He was concerned with calories long before anyone knew to be concerned with them. He jogs. He works out not to build muscle mass but to keep his shape. He's long boasted his physique means he can buy clothes wherever he wants and never needs to try anything on. He's a medium.

"Nothing has changed," Phil says.

"Except the hair," Jonathan says.

"It was pre-emptive."

"It looks good."

"It was done as a survival mechanism."

"I would fuck you."

"I know."

Bobby finishes his beer, which he's certain just arrived. His friends are already reverting to type. Two old friends talking is two old friends with a past but living in the present. Three old friends is like a time machine.

"How's your dad?" Bobby asks.

Amelia returns with Phil's vodka tonic. Bobby looks at his beer and thinks about the rest of the evening and what having another beer might mean, if it might mean anything at all, and then he orders another one. Jonathan demurs.

"It's not pneumonia. It's nothing. It's a very bad cold. He might have an infection. But it's not life-threatening. And then when that became clear, I left. Because come on."

Phil takes his vodka tonic and opens his mouth and it is gone. "Whoa, horsey," Jonathan says.

"I'm very tense," Phil says.

"I'd massage you, but I'm holding a beer," Jonathan says.

"You would love to massage me," Phil says. He puts his hand on Bobby's shoulder. "So? You lost your job?"

Bobby still meets people who ask him this, and so he still has to relive this news, his occupation now feels like living a reality he didn't choose and telling people how it came to be. "I lost my job weeks ago," he says. "A few months." He feels more drunk. "Things change. Everything goes well until it doesn't."

"So now what?"

"I have a great severance package. I'm still getting paid. I'm going to take my sweet time to think about next steps."

"I can ask around."

"Everyone says that."

"Just let me know."

"All you successful people." Bobby holds this thought to gauge Phil's reaction. The moment feels serious because people generally stop trusting their instincts when around the less fortunate. Bobby breaks into a smile, and so does Phil, and Bobby slaps his friend on the back.

"I'm serious," Phil says.

"Me too," Bobby says, laughing.

Amelia returns with their drinks. And three more shots. "I think these are the last ones," she says.

"I'm okay with that," Bobby says.

She leaves. Phil watches her walk into the crowd. "She has a nice ass," he says.

Bobby hadn't noticed. He hadn't once noticed his waitress's appearance, and now he is far too drunk to notice salient features. To notice differences. Things that might please him.

"How's Toronto?" he asks.

"Big and out of control," Phil says. "Like it's becoming more Toronto and less Toronto at the same time."

They were of that age where they could vaguely remember when Montreal was the bigger city, when it aspired to rule the country, before its aspirations shrunk, and it aspired to a kind of regionalism that was probably more suited to its station. It never bothered Bobby, the way it bothered many in the city, especially the anglos who stayed, but Bobby and his friends grew up understanding that power fluctuates, that nothing is eternal, that Montreal was a diminished place, and though they may never articulate it, they knew, it was something every Montrealer knew, it was bred deep into the collective DNA of the city and could be seen in the reflexive defence of the city's merits, and the way in which some people still put down other cities as unlivable, or worse. "I haven't been in ages," Bobby says.

"It's a construction zone," Jonathan says.

"I probably need a vacation," Bobby says. He's thinking out loud, but he hasn't been away in a year; the family rented a house near Cancun over Christmas, and it feels like a long time ago. Another life. The possibility of such a trip now is unimaginable. "I'm also hungry." He's sure this place has fries, at least. Something.

"We should go for a poutine," Phil says.

"You're just homesick."

"Yes, that's why we should go for a poutine. And a steamie. Oh god, I'm hungry."

"Next you're going want to pick up bagels."

"I already did that. First thing."

"Smoked meat."

"Yesterday."

"So, poutine."

"Holy trinity."

"A souvlaki."

"I hadn't thought of that."

"I was thinking we should go to the golf course," Jonathan announces with a smile.

Bobby is against this idea. Against the nostalgia-soaked potential of it. But he's not going to play curmudgeon. And he is coming around to the idea of a poutine. He hasn't had one in months.

"We can pick up poutine on the way," Phil says.

"We don't have a car," Bobby says.

"That's a good point," Jonathan says.

"I have a car. I've only had two drinks, so we're good to go," Phil says.

Bobby stands. He wants to pay. He hasn't been out like this in so long that he wants to pay for the privilege of it. For the joy it will give him. He reaches for his wallet. "Let me settle up," he says.

Jonathan grabs his arm. "Not a chance," he says.

"Let me, come on." Bobby feels the world make a revolution around the sun. He sits down. "I want to pay."

"Not a chance," Jonathan says. He stares Bobby down, and once he's sure his friend won't get up again, he reaches for his wallet and makes for the bar.

"I don't like why he's doing that," Bobby says.

"I would do the same thing," Phil says. He finishes his vodka.

Bobby is not a charity. He is unemployed, but he lives in a split-level house with a large yard and two cars in the driveway and two kids and a wife with her own business. He is wealthy enough to buy things and forget about them. Expensive things lie forgotten in his house. He can afford to pay for drinks for friends. He was expecting to pay. His friends are both successful men. And he was, too, until he wasn't. That's what he keeps returning to, the past tense of his success, of how he felt before and after his termination. His friends wouldn't let him pay for anything if he begged. They would never have let him pay. He would have done the same thing. He knows it. And that bothers him too.

Jonathan returns and joins the laughter. "At least I'm sober," Phil says. "Actually, that sucks."

They stumble out of the bar and onto the sidewalk. There is a poutine place down the block and they all know this and so they walk in its direction. "I had a great poutine in New York," Jonathan says. "I was so surprised to see it, I ordered, and it was fucking good."

"I don't like how it's become Canadian," Bobby says. "Like, it's not Canadian food, it's Québécois food."

"My friend was in Thailand, and there was poutine on the menu," Jonathan says. "I mean, if you're in Thailand, why would you eat poutine?"

"Would you order a pizza?" Bobby asks.

"No. I would eat Thai food in Thailand."

"In Thailand, Thai food is just called food," Bobby says.

Jonathan stops walking and hunches over in full laughter. Phil pulls a pack of cigarettes out of his pocket and lights one. He offers his pack to Bobby.

"I thought you quit," Bobby says.

"When in Rome," Phil replies.

How drunk am I? Bobby wonders. He takes a cigarette.

Jonathan is having trouble breathing.

"It wasn't that funny," Bobby says. Jonathan leans back against a tree. He holds his stomach as the laughter pours out of him. "In China, Chinese food is just called food," he says.

Jonathan's laughter reaches another level.

"I'm hungry," Bobby says.

He and Phil walk toward the poutine place. They can see it now, a dull and dirty sign in front of a small corner counter restaurant. Late night burgers and dogs. And poutine.

He turns to check on Jonathan. His laughter has died down to aftershocks. It's about composure now, or at least the attempt at it, regaining a semblance of comfort. After the laughter has become distress.

Bobby stands beside Phil, taking deep drags off his cigarette. He hasn't smoked in years, both officially and unofficially, and each time he inhales he tastes joy and regret in equal measure. He knows he will have another one before the night is out.

Jonathan reaches them. "You don't smoke," he tells Bobby.

"No, I don't."

Phil walks ahead, almost speed walking to his date with poutine. "It's not like they don't have this where he lives," Jonathan says.

"They have everything where he lives."

"Except good bagels."

Bobby and Jonathan enter the restaurant. Bobby recoils from the harsh overhead lights, and then the smell, of fried foods, he thinks he can see little balls of grease floating in the air, the smell is around him, and he feels like a planet, and the grease is the dark matter of space, the essence of everything.

Phil turns around. "I've ordered," he says.

Bobby feels poor again. Or malnourished somehow. Which is ridiculous given where he is.

Jonathan finds a table. The place is empty save for the sad-looking teen behind the counter. Until another man shows up next to him, an older man, burly, possibly Lebanese. Bobby joins Jonathan. "Slide over," he says, and Jonathan slides down the cracked faux-leather banquette, the upholstery a bright unnatural orange, probably chosen decades ago, it looks like it might have felt optimistic in the '60s, a kind of Howard Johnson level of optimism, but now it looks and feels like failure, or loss, or both. Neglect means both.

Phil brings a large paper bag. "We have two poutines, three steamies, and three Cokes. To Valley Meadows."

He turns and leaves. "I wanted to eat here," Jonathan says, fading.

"This was your idea," Bobby reminds him.

They slide out of the booth and head outside. "This smell is killing me," Phil says.

"The food will do the same," Jonathan says, sober, as if his laughing fit squeezed the drunk out of him.

"My car's just up the street," Phil says, walking ahead.

Bobby and Jonathan follow, stumbling their way toward a date with their youth. Bobby pokes Jonathan in the ribs, and giggles, and Jonathan pokes back, and then he's running toward Phil. "Can I have my hot dog?" he asks. "Please?"

Phil is taking his keys out of his pocket. "We're eating at the golf course," he says, with as much authority as he can muster, so that it comes out as a symbol of insincerity, and Jonathan starts laughing again.

Bobby has heard the paternal tone in Phil's voice, though he's not sure if the tone just means Phil is sober and trying to maintain control. "Don't puke in the car, it's a rental," he says.

"Well, just for that," Jonathan says, opening the passenger door.

Bobby opens the door to the back seat and slides in. He leans over until he's resting his head on the seat. He hears the engine turn over, and he feels the car drive away. And then his eyes are closed and all he can smell is the food in the bag, which is now a bag of gold.

And then he is being poked. It's Phil. "Wake up," he says, his mouth full of poutine.

Bobby opens his eyes slowly, unsure of his bearings. He sits up. He sees Jonathan by some trees, throwing up, violently puking up whatever he's just eaten. And then the smell of the poutine and the steamies hits him, and Bobby remembers. His eyes focus, and he sees they are just outside the golf course. Jonathan is puking by the train tracks, the same tracks that eventually run by Bobby's neighbourhood. The place is familiar but it's not. Because things change. "Where are we?" he asks.

"They put a gate up," Phil says. He offers Bobby a steamie, and Bobby takes it. He opens the car door and steps out.

"When did they put a gate up?"

Jonathan walks back to the car, wiping his mouth. "I need a Coke," he says.

Bobby bites into his hot dog. He studies the gate, the oddness of it, and he tries to understand why he feels offended by its presence. Because it offends him. This is a public golf course. It still is. He walks toward the gate and touches it. He peers through the bars; the parking lot is the same, as is the clubhouse. The gates seem to be protecting the shabbiness of the place, as if holding back some developer who wants to tear it all down and take it private.

"The gate is stupid," Jonathan says. Barely.

Bobby peers down the gate and notices that it stops. The gate is for show. The golf course hasn't changed. It's only developed a sense of pretension. "We can get in," he says.

"Guys, I have interests here," Jonathan says.

Phil exists the car holding a large Styrofoam container of poutine. "What do you see?" he asks.

Bobby points to the gap where the fence stops, behind a thicket of trees. He then looks in the other direction. The fence stops at the train tracks. This is neither a gate nor a fence. It's an intention.

Phil follows Bobby's lead and walks toward the gap. "Should we eat here or in the valley?" he asks.

"I'm not eating shit." Jonathan is leaning on the car, a can of Coke in his hand, close to catatonic.

"Remember when you could puke and then act like nothing happened?" Phil asks.

"Remember when you had hair?" Jonathan says.

"Ha ha," Phil says, turning to face the fence again.

"No, really. Guys. There's security."

"We can walk around either way," Bobby says. "Train tracks or go through the trees."

"The train tracks. Of course."

"I thought the same thing."

"I was getting ready to hop the fence."

"No, you weren't."

"I was mentally preparing myself to get ready to hop the fence."

Jonathan starts to throw up again.

"Not on the car!" Phil yells.

"The train tracks are easier," Bobby says. Meaning they are going in and are eating the rest of their food on the golf course.

Bobby and Phil walk toward the tracks. The hum of the night, of distant electrical lines, of backyard lights and garden parties and the gentle throb of traffic from the highway beyond the golf course and the train yard. The scrunch of dried and dying leaves underfoot. And then of gravel. Jonathan catches up to them. "I don't know if this is a good idea anymore," he says. Silently, the three friends make their way through undergrowth and then onto the tracks and double back, and they are on the other side of the fence, of the gate, in the golf course. "I don't remember if I locked the car," Phil says. He stops and Bobby and Jonathan stop and wait as Phil wrestles with the importance of locking the car.

"It's a rental," Bobby says.

And then they are bathed in lights. In flashlights. And they stare into them and are blinded. "Eh, les boys," they hear. A deep Québécois-accented voice. And the voice's author steps out of the flashlight beam. It's a cop. Not security. A cop. With a hand on his gun. Bobby begins to laugh. And then Phil joins him. "Poutine?" he says, offering some of his. Jonathan hunches over and throws up again.

Chapter 32

The cellphone vibrates. And then Mimi's cellphone becomes what one hears when one is lying in a rustic cabana on a beach, the kind of beach where the waiters don't wear shoes and the drinks come with tiny umbrellas. It is not a ring tone designed to wake one up in the middle of the night. But Mimi has just surrendered herself to sleep; her eyelids still flutter with consciousness, and so she hears her phone go off, and she curses, and then she reaches for it, and she pushes the appropriate button, and she brings the phone to her ear. "Yes?" she says, unsure.

"Honey?" It's Bobby. Why would he call now?

Mimi looks over at his spot in the bed and it's empty and she realizes she has climbed into bed and fallen asleep without knowing whether or not her husband was there. "Bobby?"

"It's a long story, but I need you to come to the police station and sign me out."

She sits up. She rubs the sleep she has yet to feel out of her eyes. "Bobby?" she asks.

"It's the one up near the mall."

"Why are you in jail?"

"Technically, it's not a jail."

Mimi looks at the clock on her bedside table. She's been in bed for maybe ten minutes. "You want me to do what?"

"I need you to sign me out of the police station."

"Why are they holding you at the police station?"

"That's the long story part."

"What did you do?"

"Nothing. I went out for drinks with Jonathan and Phil."

"Doesn't Phil live in Toronto?"

"Right now, he's standing next to me."

She tells him she'll be there. She hangs up and puts down the phone, and then she lays her head back down on her pillow and when she feels the sleep come, as fast as a train in a movie about a runaway train, she opens her eyes, widely, and she sits up. She gets out of bed and finds something acceptable to wear, and she gathers her purse and fishes out her car keys. There's a donut shop on the way; maybe she'll get a coffee. She wonders if she'll need money for bail. But she can't think. She disengages the home alarm and opens the front door. She tries to open the door to the car, but she can't. Until she realizes she's trying to open the door to the wrong car. She gets in her car and she pulls out of the driveway and she drives to the donut shop. She orders a coffee. The fact that she can do this without exiting her car is normally something that still amazes her, more than, say, Wi-Fi on an airplane, but she's too tired, too confused to be amazed, too worried. She's worried about what's happened; she can't imagine the chain of events that might lead Bobby to incarceration. She can't make sense of it because what she's doing seems so nonsensical. What could three grown men do to get themselves arrested in the middle of the night?

The police station is within a municipal complex that houses a suburban town hall and a library, surrounded by landscaped parkland and parking lots, further surrounded still by new family homes, and then mid-rise condos, all nondescript, all employing the bare minimum of any aesthetic standard. Across the street, a once giant mall, now truncated by an old folks' home on one side, or an assisted living centre, she's not sure what they call it. The entire complex has long bothered her, the affront of an unsuccessful attempt that led to settling for mindless mediocrity — unlike her mall, where no attempt had ever been made and so it came by its ugliness with more sincerity.

She parks the car and takes a sip of her coffee and then another. She leans back in her car seat, the coffee cup hovering just below her mouth. She breathes in the fumes. She wonders whether it's rude to take coffee into a police station because she does not know the rules of bailing out your husband in the middle of the night. She decides to take her coffee with her.

She enters the station. She's never been inside a police station before. She realizes this as she enters. She's never had to, for any reason, and the first thing she notices is this station, with her husband inside somewhere, looks nothing like the stations she's seen on television. The lights cast a dull yellow glow over cinder-block walls painted off-white. The reception area is painted black. Who paints reception areas black? The pallor of the place is that of a crypt, an old one, under an ancient city, the collected celebration of the dead. How welcoming! She walks to the front desk and rings the bell. Because there is no one to receive her at this reception.

She rings the bell again. Along a wall at the end of the front desk are two wooden chairs. She sits in one. She waits. She sips her coffee. Without the coffee this might be unbearable. In the light, the coffee looks like it's been blessed by pee. She resists the urge to check her email. She hears footsteps and she stands. "Hello?" she says into the void of service before her.

"Coming," she hears. A burly voice. French. And then the voice appears. He is a heavy-set man, with a thick moustache, eyes set deep within the fat of his cheeks. The buttons on his light blue uniform strain against the reality of his girth. Surprisingly gentle eyes. An artist's eyes, she thinks. There is sensitivity in them. "Oui, madame," he says, smiling.

"My husband is here," Mimi says in French.

"And who is your husband?"

"Roberto Reed," she says. "Bobby."

The cop stops smiling. "Yes, he's here."

"I'm here to get him."

The cop looks surprised, and she can't tell why, but she registers his look, it's right there. As if he were expecting Bobby in lock-up for a while longer. "And the other two?"

"I'm just here for my husband."

The cop motions for her to have a seat, and she does as she's told. He disappears down a corridor and Mimi is left again with nothing but her coffee. She takes another sip, a longer one, and then another one. She thinks she's awake now.

She watches the second hand race across the face of the institutional clock on the wall behind the front desk. She sells a similar clock. They look nice in certain kitchens.

She hears footsteps again, and she stands. Bobby walks into view, followed by the burly cop. He sees his wife and smiles and rushes to Mimi, and she reaches with one arm, the other one protects her coffee because right now that's more important, and her husband hugs her, tightly, and she tries to hug back, but she's watching her coffee. "I'm sorry," he whispers.

He releases her, and she looks into his eyes. He's still drunk, she can smell it, and she thinks he's smoked a cigarette as well, but he looks fine. He looks like he might while splayed out on the shag rug contemplating whatever it is he contemplates in this state. She's relieved to see him unhurt.

"You have to sign a form," the cop says.

"Me or him?" she asks.

"You. He's done his paperwork." She steps to the front desk, and the cop places two folders on it. "Here," he says, pointing to a line.

"What am I signing?" Mimi asks, something she learned to ask long ago, she can't remember when, but she's sure it had something to do with a bank.

"That we are releasing your husband into your custody, and that you accept the responsibility."

"I have a choice?" she asks, and at this the cop smiles. He's heard this one before. She signs her name.

"And here," he says, pointing to another line.

"And this is what?" she asks.

"Same. That he is your responsibility."

"But he's an adult."

"You are taking him from us, and you need to accept responsibility for that."

She sighs, signs her name, and returns the pen.

"One more," the cop says. He opens the second folder and points to a line. "Here."

"And what's this one?"

"Your husband has a court date."

"What is he charged with?" She looks at Bobby and notes that he is looking in the opposite direction.

"Trespassing."

"Bobby," she says, with resigned disapproval.

"It's a long story," he says, not looking at her.

She can't imagine what he's done. She had not expected trespassing. She signs the form. The cop tears out copies from all the forms she's signed, folds them carefully, and hands them to her. "Merci, madame."

Mimi takes a sip of her coffee. She puts the papers in her purse. "Thank you," she says. "I'd apologize for my husband, but he's supposed to be an adult."

The cop winks, which she finds at the limits of being appropriate, and she takes Bobby by the arm and leads him outside. They walk toward her car, and when she doesn't let go, Bobby takes his arm from her clutches. "I'm not a criminal, come on."

"Said the man who called his wife in the middle of the night to get him out of jail."

"It was hardly a jail," Bobby says.

"I had to sign you out."

"It was more like a holding cell."

"You were behind bars."

At this he looks to the ground. They reach her car. She takes another sip of her coffee. "What happened?" she asks.

"We went to the golf course."

"What golf course?"

"Valley Meadows."

This was nostalgia. Booze led to nostalgia led to a trip to the golf course. To their youth. She has little patience for this. She never has. Her past is across the ocean. Her parents' past is across half the world. She is not the issue of a family with much patience for nostalgia. Her father had once said they could not afford nostalgia. "For god's sake," she says, pressing the button on her key chain that opens the car doors.

"We just thought we'd go take a look," Bobby says, sheepishly, she can see that. He's embarrassed. By putting himself in this exact situation. She knows he's more embarrassed that she had to come get him out of the police station than of the arrest itself. The arrest is going to become a talking point. This part, not so much. "Phil was in town, his dad's in the hospital, and —"

"What's wrong with his father?" Mimi interrupts.

"They thought it was pneumonia, but it turns out to be nothing."

"This isn't good for Jonathan."

"He knows this."

"What were you thinking?"

"First Phil wanted a poutine, and then we got to talking about the golf course, and hanging out in the valley; I told you about that, that's where we grew up, it was an important place, you know, that valley made me who I am."

"Your parents would love to hear that."

"You know what I mean. Don't you have a place like that? From when you were growing up?"

"No." She doesn't. She might say "Paris," but she doesn't have a specific spot, a singular place that she envisions when she recalls her childhood. There is her father's lap. She remembers his lap, his smell, she remembers specific things, a scene, but there is no place. There is certainly no place that could usurp the memory of her parents.

"We didn't even make it to the valley. They have a gate now. We were just on the other side of it. Then we got caught. We hadn't even done anything wrong."

"You entered private property."

"Please."

"Trespassing!"

"If the golf course presses charges. The cop wasn't sure it's worth it for them."

"And Jonathan's efforts . . ."

"Jonathan is on their side," he says.

She opens her door and gets in the car. She has meetings tomorrow. She has to figure out what to do with her inventory management system. She's hiring two people for shipping. Karim's replacement is still figuring out things. She's thankful for The Butcher's help. But she can't be tired. Bobby gets in. Mimi starts the car and finishes her coffee. "I'll never get to sleep," she says.

"I'm sorry."

"I had just gotten to bed."

"I'm sorry. I mean it, I'm sorry."

They drive home in silence, Mimi keeps her eyes on the road, and Bobby stares out his window at the landscape of his youth. Every street here, every park, every building, a memory, a gateway to something, a place he thought he'd left long ago, though he never had, he'd bought a home deep within the streets that raised him, and for the first time he wonders why he'd done it.

Mimi pulls into the driveway and shuts off the car. "I'm sorry," Bobby says again.

"I heard you the first time," Mimi says, regretting her tone immediately. She's mad at her husband, but she's angrier about tomorrow. She's worried about tomorrow.

"I'll make you breakfast," Bobby says.

Mimi looks at her husband. She tries to smile. She can't. She has too much on her mind. "I need to sleep," she says. Except she just finished a giant cup of coffee, and she can feel it, in her fingers, in her stomach, her eyes. Her mind is racing but not fast enough that she can't make sense of anything.

Bobby opens the passenger door and steps out. "I'm sorry," he says.

Mimi feels on the verge. She thinks she's comported herself well up to this point. She can see the shame on her husband's face, the lips hanging on the verge of a frown, awaiting gravity, the coyote in mid-air before the pull back to earth makes its omniscience known. She knows there is nothing she can say to make him feel worse, that anything she says now might make her feel better but won't do anything for him. He had seen old friends. They wanted to revisit their past. Getting caught by a cop willing to bring them in and charge them was bad luck. Perhaps Bobby's had enough bad luck lately. She doesn't know. They haven't talked about it.

She grabs her purse and gets out of the car. Bobby has gone ahead through the door into the house, his shoulders drooping. She follows him inside. He's already in the living room, pouring himself a Scotch. "Oh, come on," she says.

He looks at her and sits on the shag rug. "Come here," he says. He takes a sip of his drink.

"You get drunk, I come get you out of jail in the middle of the night, then you get home and you pour yourself another drink?"

He pats the carpet. She can feel her blood pressure rise. She's less tired than she was a minute ago. A second ago.

"Sit with me," he says.

"Have you no shame?"

"That's all I have," he says.

She sighs. She puts down her purse and steps out of her shoes. She walks into the living room and sits on the couch. And then he doesn't say anything. Her husband stares into his drink. She can smell his night's activities on him. The dankness of the bar. The booze. The tobacco. The foliage of the golf course. She sits by him and grows angry. Angrier. If she continues to sit here, she's unsure of the outcome. Of what might come out of her.

She misses smoking. She has cigarettes in her purse.

She knows she's been distant. She has work. She has too much of it. But her future is now. She's been repeating this to herself, the investors have been repeating this to her, the cliché has become even more so, thicker, like dead leaves in the corner of the backyard, never raked, becoming mulch. She has realized that the investors don't care about furniture, or design, or Hummels, or retail, they only care about money; they don't care about her or her employees, they care about money; and all the people of the world, the entrepreneurs who think investors care about them, all the self-help books she's read, all the testimonials, all the seminars and podcasts she's listened to, of all of them, not a single one mentions this fact, that no one cares about anyone but themselves, perhaps because it is self-evident, but if she is going to take their money, she's going to have to work, and that means what she is doing now, losing touch with her family, because the rewards are worth it, the rewards will be worth much more than a temporary tear in the fabric of her family.

"I want to talk," Bobby says.

Mimi sighs and eyes the drink tray. Perhaps a Scotch isn't a terrible idea. "I'm so tired," she says.

"That's what I want to talk about. Indirectly."

"Bobby, if you want to talk about how busy I've been, I know." This is what bothers her more. She knows she's ignoring her family. She's aware of what she's doing. It feels like she hasn't seen her son in weeks. She doesn't know what is happening with his show. She's sure he mentioned he was going to have a show. In a gallery. She doesn't know when. Her daughter is going to come work for her, and Mimi hasn't thought about what Dee is going to do. She knows Dee is thinking about what she said at that dinner. Or didn't say. Or hasn't said since. Mimi wonders if she's doing this on purpose, if there is a sinister motive behind this, and she can't think of one. She is busy. Why should she say anything else?

"I don't want to talk about how busy you've been."

Mimi leans over and takes a tumbler and pours herself a Scotch. She takes a sip and closes her eyes and leans back into the couch.

She can feel her heart running caffeine-induced laps around her chest. “What then?” she says.

“I just want to talk.”

“Bobby . . .”

“What about Dee?” he asks.

“Bobby, not now.”

“Mimi, she’s hurt.”

She knows this. “I know,” she says.

“Confused. You hurt her.”

Mimi thinks about why she said what she did. She thinks about her own friends and the ones who experimented with other girls, teenagers finding outlets for the chemicals in their brains, in their bodies, and none of them were lesbians, not that she knows of, all of them are married, at least the ones she keeps in touch with, all of them leading lives approaching normal, and that experimentation was also normal. Dee had pronounced her very self, an identity, she had chosen, and Mimi was in mid-speech, she was talking, Dee had interrupted her with this thing about her identity; if she truly were a lesbian, she would not have said it in such a setting, the context was wrong. How could Mimi have thought otherwise? She heard a young girl announcing she is sexual. Not announcing who she is. “I’m so tired.”

“You can’t ignore her forever.”

She dives deep into her memory. “I grew up, first in Osaka, and then Paris.”

“I know this.”

“In Paris, for the longest time, perhaps the entire time, I was intensely aware of my difference. Of being étranger. No matter how perfect my French, or what I wore, or the clubs I went to, I was always étranger. It was just a fact. My father’s friends were all Japanese. I didn’t want to be just Japanese. I wanted to be me, to be accepted. I didn't want to be exotic. I was worldly. I wanted the world to let me be myself. To see me."

Bobby listens to this confession and wonders why he's never heard it before.

"I had a nightmare all the time. That I was with my parents at a museum. In a grand hall, surrounded by giant vases. Porcelain. Vases larger than me. Set up on pedestals. A beautiful room in an old building. And in the dream, I trip, and I fall into one of the pedestals, and I watch the vase fall off the pedestal, in slow motion almost, and then it tumbles into the next vase and then the next. And I watch the vases fall and shatter, and the expression of horror on my parents' faces. And then the police take me away, and they take me to my room and stand guard outside my door so that I don't leave. And in the morning, all the newspapers are brought to me, and all of the front pages show the grand hall of shattered vases."

Bobby reaches out for her.

She remembers the first sight of Dee, of this beautiful girl, wailing in her bassinet, the *perfectness* of her. That's what she remembers. Dee was perfect when she first saw her. She was everything she imagined her daughter might be. Of how her heart was Dee's, completely, at that first meeting.

"You can't ignore her forever."

"I won't ignore her forever."

"She feels that way."

"She's going to start working for me."

Bobby finishes his Scotch. "What, you're going to take her out for lunch and sort it all out?"

Mimi closes her eyes again. She can't imagine taking Dee out for lunch. If only because she's doing too much at work herself. She's thankful Jean-Marc delivers her lunch to her every day.

And sometimes dinner too. Even The Ayatollah has noticed her hours. He's told her to slow down. "I'm so tired," she says.

"You need to talk to her and resolve this before she starts working for you."

"There's nothing to resolve."

"You know that's not true."

"She's too young to know."

Bobby pours himself another drink. "I don't think you're thinking about this properly."

"She's sixteen."

"I think she has a girlfriend."

"She's sixteen, Bobby, she can't know." Mimi can feel herself drifting off on the couch. Not to sleep, not with the coffee swooshing around inside of her, but drifting off, to a desert island, someplace where she can be free of the pressures that surround her, the pressures she's imposed on herself and the ones the world imposes on her. She realizes her desert island looks Japanese, a rock garden, outside a ryokan, with birdsong hovering above the tranquility. She thinks she's picturing a photo her father once showed her, of his parents' house, outside Kyoto. She's so tired, so parched for something, that she's retreating to a place she's never been, some place ancestral.

"Who is her *girlfriend*?" she asks. The emphasis on the last word is her own skepticism seeping out. She's not even sure she approves. What if her daughter *is* a lesbian? What does that mean? For Dee? Being a lesbian is difficult. Not in the legal sense, but in the societal sense. Mimi doesn't know how this plays itself out now. Is her daughter making her own life more difficult? This is yet another identity for her. Another badge among existing badges. Their family is already . . . odd. They are an odd collection bound by intractable love. By so much of it. What is she doing to them? To their collective? "Being different is difficult," she says.

"Society values individuality but then punishes it. I've seen this everywhere I've lived."

"Don't say that."

"We are already such a bunch."

"Meaning what?"

"We're like every colour under the rainbow."

Bobby is taken aback. Is the family's diversity, the very thing he thinks makes it so special, something that bothers his wife? Is she sensitive to the colour of her children's skin? "Mimi . . ."

"All I mean is, it's difficult being different."

"You don't believe that."

"Look at us."

"What does this have to do with Dee?"

"I don't know." Mimi sighs. She doesn't know what she believes. She's so tired. "I want her to be happy. What am I supposed to say?"

"That you love your daughter."

"I do, don't be silly."

"She has doubts."

"She's only sixteen."

"You keep saying that."

"She doesn't know."

"You keep saying that too."

Mimi did not know who she was when she was sixteen. She didn't know who she was when she met Bobby, when she agreed to move to Montreal, when she first felt the sting of a Canadian winter. She didn't know who she was until she started her business, and now she feels on the cusp of discovery, of something more than achievement. Of purpose. And that is why the floundering she feels, the endlessness of her project, of her work, wears her down; the pressure is like being under water. She's afraid of failure. She feels like failure is around the corner, if she doesn't do it, and doesn't get every bit right, that failure looms before her like a cliff. Like a wall of television sets at an electronics store. Like the tumbler of Scotch she holds in front of her face. "Come work with me," she says.

"Don't change the subject."

She's been thinking this. Ever since the magnitude of Karim's work became evident to her. Ever since she realized not just what he did but how much of it he did. How he held the company together. How her speaking engagements, her long meetings with the investors, her talks with Esme or The Ayatollah, her motherly advice to the workers in the back, how all of that was made possible by the depth of Karim's diligence. "You're a numbers person," she says.

Bobby laughs. He puts down his drink and covers his face. He rubs his eyes. "No. Really," he says.

"You've run an entire department of people."

"Who hated me."

"Don't say that."

"They hated me because I was an asshole."

"You're not an asshole."

"I didn't say I am."

Maybe she's too tired for this. Maybe she shouldn't finish her Scotch. Or is the Scotch making her tired? Maybe she should finish the Scotch in her tumbler, and maybe she should then pour herself another. "You just did."

"At work, yes, I was in an environment that changed me, that turned me into a joke. I was an asshole, and everyone hated me, and when my way became a liability I was fired."

Mimi finishes her Scotch. "I would like you to think about it."

"I would like you to speak to your daughter."

"Karim left, and if I want this business to succeed, I need you."

Bobby sits up. "Are you going to speak to Dee?"

Mimi puts her tumbler on the tray. "What am I supposed to say?"

"That you heard her."

Mimi realizes he might be offended. That she has offended and surprised her entire family. And hurt them. She admits, she was surprised herself. "I'll come around."

"You'll come around?"

"Bobby, please."

"You'll come around?"

"Yes."

"This is your daughter."

"I know."

"All she expects, and deserves, is love. And support. And you'll come around?"

Mimi downs her Scotch. She hasn't downed anything stronger than red wine in a long time. In years. And she feels the Scotch hit her, in a deep place, her insides feel on fire, and finally the coffee is nothing more than a memory, and she knows that if she leans back on the couch again, she might close her eyes and fall asleep. And that wouldn't make Bobby happy. "Let me deal with it in my own way," she says. She can feel herself leaning back, she can feel the sleep coming on, she can feel herself enveloped in fog, surrounded by the immensity of her labour, by the sheer mass of work she has built for herself.

She sees Dee in that bassinet. She will always see her in that bassinet.

"You're going to lose her."

"She's my daughter."

"You're going to lose her for a very long time."

"I still love her."

"So tell her."

"I'll tell her tomorrow." But she's going to work. "I've loved her from the moment we first saw her photo." Perhaps she'll sleep in. Perhaps tomorrow she'll give herself some time. She'll sleep in, she'll speak to Dee, and she'll work late. Or later. Her eyes are closed now. She's drifting. She feels Bobby's hand on her shoulder and opens her eyes. He leans in and kisses her. The smells of his evening. Again. She puts her hand on his back.

"Okay," he says.

She smiles. "I'm not a bad person," she says.

"Neither of us are," Bobby replies.

He kisses her again, and she pushes her face into his. She hums.

"Okay," he says again. He pulls her off the couch. He stumbles backward a step. She reaches for him and rights his balance. "Yesterday I thought I might trim the carpet," he says. "With scissors."

"What?"

"And then I thought you'd kill me. My mind's been going to some strange places." He puts his arm around her.

"Mine, too, maybe," Mimi says, considering, finally, that her reaction to Dee was selfish, realizing she'd said what she'd said because she didn't need a new complication. "I'll talk to Dee. And I'll apologize."

Bobby taps Mimi on the ass. And then he leaves his hand there. And they head for the stairs, then up to the bedroom, to sleep, just as the first hints of dawn enter the house, changing the light inside.

Chapter 33

They eat silently as if at a funeral reception.

Bobby has barbecued hamburgers and chicken breasts and kosher hot dogs. He's made a potato salad, the tangy kind, with vinegar, because Mimi has always liked the tangy potato salad and it's his gesture to her, one that only she might recognize, but a gesture because Bobby hates the tangy potato salad, even though he makes it well.

He's made lemonade. Dee loves his lemonade. Because it's tart and sweet, and she's always felt that her father's lemonade made her mouth sing.

He's tossed a salad and has two dressings out, a basil-infused vinaigrette but also one he found online, a creamy sriracha dressing that he thought might work on greens; Abbie surely understands why such a thing is on the table.

Dee has brought Beth. Because Dee does not understand love, but she knows Beth makes her feel good and that might be the only way she will get through the summer. After their tryst by the tracks, Dee does not want to do anything to lose Beth, and Coco Chanel has already told her that was the wrong strategy, that fear always ends with the thing you fear happening, fear is like gravity to that which you fear; Coco Chanel, wise beyond her years. So Dee is trying not to let her fear of losing Beth translate into actually losing Beth. She's trying to balance her fear with her joy. She feels joy. She is already in love with the idea of belonging to Beth.

And with Beth at the table, the family eats in silence. Bobby does not want to upset anybody. He's more obsessed with an idea of working for his wife, or with his wife, she might have said *with*, he can't remember, but the idea is starting to build inside him. He likes the idea of helping his wife, he feels he owes Mimi, and she had said, this morning, she had suggested that if he started working, it would become a family business, their business, though he's not fooled by this idea; she's built this thing, if it's successful at all now, it is all because of her, if she gets the backing and he helps the business grow, it will be because of her, it is all her, and it will always be that way.

Mimi has spent the day in the garden; she weeded the front yard and she pushed the lawn mower around. She felt if she was going to stay away from work, something Bobby had begged her to do, she was going to work the garden, she was going to get dirty, get mud and grass stains on the knees of her overalls, she was going to crawl around the grass and wiggle her ass at her husband and laugh. She would forget work and she would do things to the lawn and the garden, and her gardener would chastise her, *Why are you doing my job?* he'd ask, and she didn't care, she needed to feel the earth between her fingers. And mucking around while Bobby barbecued the various meats, she flashed back to a scene of the children running around the yard, of the domestic bliss of a garden; she'd grown up in Paris, she'd never had a garden — just patio boxes, just plants in the house — and now she had an entire garden, and after the endlessness of the winter, the rapid melt of the snow and the onset of green was an astonishing sight, it had made her fall in love with Montreal for the first time, that transition, when spring just happens, and the mood of the city lifts, and suddenly the world is a wondrous and just place.

And then Beth arrived, Dee had answered the door, and Beth had come out to the backyard, and Dee had asked if Beth could eat over, and Bobby had been so quick with his yes, but Mimi said nothing, she smiled at Beth and asked about her sports, and then Mimi had returned to the garden, she concentrated on the weeds in the back corner, near the Zederbaums', who had a garden of weeds. Mimi remembers spending years trying to convince Channa to let her *pay* for the weeding, she would pay, and no one would never know, but Channa had said no, always, wondering what the fuss was, weeds were green, too, after all.

But with Beth, Mimi didn't know what to say, because everything she would say would be in context of what she'd said already, because she'd waited so long to speak to Dee about it, and she was aware that the family had waited for that conversation, but surely they could not have it in front of Beth herself.

Abbie wants the conversation. He finds the silence more funny than awkward. His mind might wander over to his own work, to Etienne and his feud with Jacques, the silliness of the whole thing, the augmented nature of Jacques's surliness, the tone Jacques used while employing the same, helpful words, but then he would be brought back, to Beth and Dee, and he would look around the room and want to laugh.

Beth drinks down the lemonade and Dee pours her another glass. And Abbie starts to laugh. He drops his cutlery and tries not to laugh out loud, but that might leave him with a pulled muscle, so his laughter wheezes out, a Snidely Whiplash sound, and soon his father joins him, because Bobby gets it, too, he can feel the absurdity of the silence, and he gets out of his chair and excuses himself, and this makes Abbie laugh harder, and they both stumble into the dining room and then into the living room and then they find themselves on the shag carpet, clutching their stomachs, trying not to laugh out loud. "I'm going to have a heart attack," Bobby says. And Abbie finally lets loose, and tears flow out of his eyes, and he is hugging his father, and his father is hugging him.

"A heart attack," Abbie wheezes, barely.

They roll onto their backs and laugh at the ceiling. Abbie covers his face. Bobby clutches his sides. Their laughter now fills the house, surely people outside can hear this, perhaps even the Zederbaums, who will wonder about the sanity of the Reed family — and not for the first time — and Saul — also not for the first time — will think about the things he is not privy to, the life he cannot lead, because he already knows he doesn't have the courage to change his destiny and he's not even sure he wants to change it.

"I don't know what's so funny," Mimi says, cutting into a piece of chicken.

Beth has known these people for a long time, not well, but she has been in this house before, she's eaten ice cream in this very backyard, and Bobby was at the table, too, making ridiculous faces at the girls, that's how long ago it was.

Mimi gets up and walks out into the living room. "My family is weird," Dee says.

Beth shrugs. She reaches under the table and gives Dee's leg a squeeze and Dee almost collapses from it.

"Boys," Mimi says. She has her hands on her hips. She's trying to be the adult here, she's spent the day doing adult things, she's pushed a lawn mower, she would like nothing better than to be working, to be building, it's what she wants, she needs it, she realizes this now, watching her husband and son rolling around the floor, filling the house with their laughter, she is more at home away from home. She sits on the couch and thinks about this. About what it means, if anything. And tomorrow her daughter is going to start working for her. And she is sitting in the kitchen with her girlfriend. And she looks happier and more at ease and more comfortable than she has looked in a long while.

But if Mimi is going to acknowledge that her work is her home, at least for now, at least while she is building it, then she is going to insist Bobby work with her, that they build this thing together. "Bobby, you have to come work with me," she says, and at this Bobby's laughter ceases, and then it's like he was never laughing at all, his reality has changed, like when a rainstorm passes and the sun comes out quickly and the earth is dry once again and anyone suggesting it has just rained is deemed insane.

Abbie's laugh is reduced to hiccups. He thinks it might be a good idea to return to the kitchen, the safety of his sister and her athletic girlfriend, to the food, he's hungry, he remembers, and the laughing fit has made him hungrier. "Hey," he says, re-entering the kitchen.

"You okay?" Dee asks.

"I'm fine," he says, and he stabs at another hot dog.

"We're not usually like this," Dee tells Beth.

"Show me a normal family," she says.

In the living room Bobby thinks of lifting himself up. And then he doesn't. "Why?" Bobby asks Mimi. "Why is this so important now?"

Mimi plays with a loose thread on the couch. She's going to have to get that checked. It's not a problem yet. But it will be. "I've told you why. I need you — it's as simple as that."

Bobby is unsure, but only when Mimi asks him. Because inside, he's resolved to do it. If he is unsure, it's because he is unsure of everything. And because he doesn't trust himself. Because what if he can't behave? Because what if Mimi is introduced to the reptilian Bobby, from whom terror emanated and which the Leopard Lady duly rendered extinct? Does he want to work? He's become domesticated. He's not as ashamed of his booze-soaked domestication as he thought he'd be. Perhaps later, in the fall, when lazing around the yard loses its appeal on account of the cold, perhaps then. "Mimi," he says. Pleads. "How can I ignore the question when you're going to keep asking it?"

Mimi smiles. She knows he will say yes. Eventually. He needs it. The control. She understands that. She knows him. She feels she always has. That's why she agreed to accompany him home and build a life. That's why she has never left, even in the depths of winter, when February feels like the longest month on the calendar, which is every year, and she thinks of how empty and romantic and grey Paris can be in winter, without the tourists, with just Parisians being Parisians, and not the surly hosts for people they never asked to meet.

Bobby will say yes. She knows it, and he knows she knows it. He knows he's going to say yes. Not because it's easy, but because he wants to help her. He wants to help build her thing. He knows that she knows he's going to say yes. The communication beyond words, beyond telepathy. The knowledge that couples share. The certainty. What a thing it is, he thinks. Until it's not.

"Come on, dinner's getting cold!" Dee yells.

Mimi holds out her hand, and Bobby takes it. "Play nice," he says.

They pull each other until each are standing. "I don't want to upset Dee."

"Just treat Beth as a friend, which she is."

"I'm under a microscope."

"So, imagine how those girls feel."

Mimi would like to believe. She would like to believe in young love, in what her eyes tell her, that Dee is happy, that she has found her first love, that's what Beth is, perhaps, that feeling of first longing, her daughter has it, and she doesn't want to ruin it. "I envy them," she says, surprising herself.

"Silence is the worst thing. Either we fight or we make small talk, but staying silent is the worst possible thing we can do. I'm guilty too."

"That's why you laughed."

He leads Mimi to the kitchen. They take their seats.

"Okay?" Dee asks.

"Okay," Mimi says. And she smiles at her daughter.

And Dee smiles at her mother. And wonders when they will have their argument. About whatever. There's an argument coming. She knows it. But that's for another time. She's going to work for her mother tomorrow. Perhaps they'll argue then. But not now. Not in front of Beth. Not with a pitcher of lemonade before her.

"Tell me how the sports are going," Mimi says, cutting into a spear of grilled zucchini. "You're quite something, I hear."

Chapter 34

Dee walks to the strip mall. Past the squat apartments that pass in these parts for low-income housing, past the fruit markets that look abandoned and dust-covered from the street, past the quaint fire station, past the small neighbourhood of faux-stately homes, past the bank and the donut shop with its eternal jam of cars at the drive-thru, and then there it sits, the strip mall, the expanse of asphalt half empty, always.

She walks across the lot to the entrance to her mother's store. There is no sign, no awning even, nothing that might tell you about its inner life, about the commerce inside, about the things for sale. No invitation, no welcome, no expectation of a visit. No hope. It is sadness, more sadness in a mall of sadness and geriatrics and stale bread. The deliberately awful smell of the past lives here. It's the smell of an end. Of death itself.

Val works two doors down. Dee will meet her after work. She didn't want to leave her mother on her first day of work; she felt that would transgress protocol. Even though, or perhaps because, they have not spoken properly in so long. They have danced around the only thing they are thinking because what they are thinking is volcanic.

Her mother had finally been civil. Had smiled. They'd exchanged smiles, and Dee had felt like something had been attempted, that her mother had tried to scale the wall that had been built between them, and she had treated Beth with kindness, and had asked her questions. Had treated her with a kind of normalcy. After the weirdness of the giggle fits, her mother had taken control of things, and the evening had unfolded with the calm of a cloudless sky.

Dee enters the store. Esme sits on her stool behind the cash reading a book. She barely looks up at Dee, and Dee makes straight for the back door to enter the warehouse. She doesn't remember it being so vast, or so bright, or so busy. The rows of shelving seem to extend forever now, and her understanding of her mother's business shifts, immediately, and somehow things start to make sense, or more sense, and her earlier impressions, which are of the store and not really of this warehouse, vanish.

She waits by the door. She was told to wait by the door, and she doesn't want to add to the wall that has been built up and separates her and her mother, and that grows, at least in her mind, with each moment, with the silence between them, despite the smiles, despite the civility. How can a wall be so menacing and built of silence?

Her mother is late, at least according to the clock on the wall, and now Dee wonders if she's misunderstood, because her mother should be here, she's been here since early this morning, she had insisted Dee be on time last night, more than once.

Dee heads up one of the aisles. On her left, shelves filled with Hummels: puppies and kittens, boys with floppy hats, girls in kerchiefs, sheep, angels, cherubs. Figures of shoddy porcelain to weigh down dusty shelves. Dee looks at these things and feels embarrassed by the display because her mother still sells these things, she won't give them up, and because that money has somehow made it to her dinner plate. She has eaten things because someone has bought a pudgy white cherub floating about in mid-blessing.

Across the aisle, coffee mugs and tea sets adorned with red and blue flowers, glass dogs, brass fish, cheap wicker baskets, silver-framed mirrors, wooden spice racks. This low rent stuff has no place in a store that sells expensive furniture. No one can convince her mother of this.

Kalpani appears from around the corner, holding a clipboard. She shrieks and puts her hand to her chest. "Sorry," Dee says.

"Can I help you?" Kalpani asks.

"I'm looking for my mother."

And Kalpani registers understanding. "You're Dee," she says, and Dee nods. "She's waiting by the back door."

And she points toward the back of the warehouse. Dee didn't even know there was a door there, but it makes sense now that she thinks about it. There must be a loading dock as well. She's never been deep inside the warehouse, her mother's desk, near the front, as far as she's bothered to enter. "Thank you," Dee says, flushed. She starts to make her way toward her mother. She passes by lamps and desks and furniture, entire couches, beautiful and elegant and modern, things she hadn't imagined her mother selling, even though she'd been told she was selling exactly this. She picks up her pace. Her mother had explained, or had tried to explain, once, before a scouting trip to Germany, the nature of her work, the stuff she sold now, but Dee had always remembered the store and had always imagined a warehouse full of knick-knacks, junk, trinkets. It had comforted her to imagine that her mother was a peddler of kitsch.

Her mother sells high-end furniture. And then the pronouncement, the dollar figures, the interest from investors, all of it starts to make sense to Dee, and she feels silly, walking faster and faster toward her mother, she feels silly that she hasn't even visited the website, or prepared at all, it's like she's walked into an exam without opening a textbook.

They haven't even discussed Dee's work here. They have avoided that, like everything else. They have built a wall and have lived their separate lives. Her mother had said something wrong, and then nothing. Her mother had ignored her. *Neglected* her. And now Dee feels those feelings, the raw feelings, bubbling inside her again, and then in front of her stands her mother.

"You're late," she says. Her hands are on her hips.

"I was waiting by the door."

"The door is right here," Mimi says, pointing to a red door.

"Sorry. I was waiting by the front. The store."

"No one uses that door."

"*I* said I'm sorry," Dee says, emphasizing the *I*. This is a mistake, she thinks, already, within a second of speaking to her mother. She should be working behind the cash at a pizza joint. Or selling jeans. Or scooping ice cream.

Mimi decides to start off better than this. She is going to try. She promised Bobby. She owes Dee. She owes her this much. "You're going to help with inventory."

"What's that?"

"You don't know what *inventory* means?"

Dee shrugs. She wants to run somewhere else, perhaps see Val and commiserate and cry on her shoulder, or hide.

"Follow me," Mimi orders, and starts walking down the same aisle Dee has just walked.

“Mom, we should talk,” Dee says as she follows her mother, running to keep pace. She’d forgotten how fast her mother could walk when she wanted to, how keeping pace with her was not always a given, that a walk with Mom was sometimes hard work. They walk past the furniture and the lamps and then cross over into the kitsch, the old stuff, and then Mimi stops, so suddenly that Dee almost walks into her, and Mimi turns and holds out a finger. “You have to come to work on time. This isn’t home.”

“Mom.” Dee eyes the Hummels.

“Do you understand?”

“Yes,” Dee says, lowering her eyes.

“I’m sorry, Dee,” Mimi says. “I love you.”

“Thanks.” Dee is surprised by how small her mother’s apology feels.

“I just want you to be happy.”

“I am.”

Mimi and Dee stare at each other. Mimi smiles. “Are you sure?” she asks.

Dee fixes on a ridiculous figurine of a girl sitting on a fence surrounded by a lamb munching on what look to be daisies. Dee reaches out and grabs it.

“What are you doing?” Mimi asks, and she holds out her hand, and her fingers swim in the air with the expectation that her daughter will hand over the product so she can reshelve it and get on with the task of initiating Dee into this world of work, her world, she will teach her daughter of the world inside this warehouse, the womb of her expanding wealth.

Dee squeezes the Hummel harder. She’s trying to crush it, she realizes, and she takes a step away from her mother. She doesn’t know what she wants to do first: scream or smash the little statue to dust. She feels humiliation. She feels the weight of her mother’s question. Of everything she's said. "When are you going to treat me like an actual person?" she asks, her voice raised.

She's surprised by how that came out, in both subject matter and tone, because she had not until this point thought her mother was not treating her like a person. She had wanted to use the word *respect*. She has felt, ever since the meal, that her mother had decided to stop respecting her. And now Dee has stopped just short of yelling in the warehouse, and the background din is diminished, the centre of gravity of the place is here, surrounding her, surrounding the force with which she holds the Hummel.

"Dee!" Mimi says, with hushed venom. "I said I was sorry."

"You need to respect who I am," Dee says, proud that came out right. And with less volume. "And what I am."

"I do," Mimi says. "It doesn't feel like it, but I do."

Dee laughs. She'd always thought her mother was smart and that everything she did was for a reason, and the reason was well thought out. Planned. And then she realizes that her mother has planned nothing. She's just working. She's busy, and she's not thinking about her family, and she's certainly not thinking of her. She has abandoned Dee. Her mother is just trying to make things work, and that makes Dee angrier. Because now she sees that her mother has failed her. That she has failed at being a mother.

And Dee takes another look at the Hummel. And she throws it to the ground.

It explodes. It becomes nothing. Powder. Kalpani and Sampath and Ximena appear from around the aisle. Dee lunges for the shelves, and Mimi lunges after her. Hummels shatter like ice, bouncing off the shelves and on to the floor where mass-produced glass and porcelain and ceramic meet the cold reality of concrete. Dee continues to attack, she is a mess of hair and flailing arms, and then Kalpani and Ximena are upon her, and Mimi steps back and allows her employees to control her daughter, and she watches as Sampath approaches with a broom and Manuel approaches with an industrial vacuum, and Kalpani and Ximena have control of Dee now, and they start to take her toward the employee sitting area, and Dee allows herself to be taken, she calms down, she's made her point, she has her mother's attention, she's let her see her pain, to visit it, to know what she has done.

Mimi takes the broom from Sampath. She starts the work of cleaning up. She blames herself. She realizes she has ignored everything Bobby has said. The gentle tinkle of cheap broken porcelain echoes through the warehouse.

Dee thinks the sound pretty. She closes her eyes as she's led away. She wants to remember this moment. This sound. The feeling of release that is overwhelming her. Of her life and what it means now. A sense of being older. Perhaps even in control, for once. In charge. Of knowing who she is and what she is capable of doing. She wonders if this is what freedom feels like.

She can't wait to tell Coco Chanel. But mostly she can't wait to tell Beth.

Chapter 35

Everything is a disappointment waiting to happen. Bobby remembers being disappointed by the Eiffel Tower and wondering what was wrong with him. He was underwhelmed by spectacle of all sorts, by the skylines of cities, by the cathedrals of Europe, by a bridge he was told would be breathtaking, by an elephant, by a sunset. The only thing that never disappointed him, for whatever reason, was a mountain; mountains were the definition of grand, and the more mountains, the greater his awe. That and Japanese fried chicken.

And this is why he is taking a detour. He'd read about a new food truck, serving nothing but karaage, and that it was parked at the base of the mountain, on Park Avenue, and he thought, well, I should try it at least. He diverges from their route above Mimi's complaints and parks behind the truck, Mimi imploring him all the while to not get his shirt dirty and to hurry up, being late for Abbie's opening is *irresponsible*, she uses that word. And he walks to the monument and looks up at the cross atop the mountain and, well, this mountain has always been underwhelming, or maybe he is just too used to it, but it isn't a mountain, the thing in the middle of Montreal is a hill, everyone in the city knows it, too, but is too afraid to say something like that out loud, for fear of offence.

The leaves toward the top have turned. Many of the trees are naked. The air hints at a colder season. He bites into the karaage, a crunchy piece of thigh meat, and he closes his eyes and imagines a mountain, a real one, capped with snow. He imagines a cool breeze flowing off the mountain like a current of down pillows, and he takes another bite, and then he's admitting that maybe this chicken isn't the best he's tasted.

"It's food from a truck," Mimi says.

He wipes his fingers and throws the napkin in a trash can. He takes Mimi's hand, and they head for the car. They walk hand in hand, a couple, the centre of a family, having never worn matching running outfits or sweaters, having never taken a dance class together, never being the type of couple to finish each other's sentences. There had been none of that, but plenty of love and difficulty and more love, a love able enough to mask anger and disappointment and crisis and loss. They had met in a dull conference room in Paris, and now here they are, at the base of a hill in the middle of a city an ocean away, holding hands, about to drive off to an event marking the beginning of their son's adult life.

This morning both Mimi and Bobby felt old, though neither admitted this to their partner. But both knew the other was thinking it. This was as much a passage for them as it was for their son. And then they had caught the other's quick glances in their direction, both smiling, both thinking, They still look good, both thinking, Maybe I'm not *that* old. The same things. In parallel. A silent universe shared.

Aware but unaware. Changing and unchanging. Vast. Collapsing at the moment of rebuilding and then collapsing again.

Dee shares the back seat with Beth, who continues to reach over and tickle Dee's hand with her thumb, and Dee squirms because Beth's parents are in the front, driving to her brother's opening, and she wants to take Beth to a private place and do things she's only started imagining doing to her.

Beth had opened up a new part of Dee, as if part of her brain were now exposed to different elements, unburdened by innocence.

After Dee had destroyed an aisle of porcelain figurines, she had run from the warehouse and had texted Beth and they had gone to the train tracks and Dee had cried and Beth had stroked her hair and let her cry and then she had taken Dee to her house and introduced her to her parents as her girlfriend. After some awkward conversation had convinced them to let Dee sleep on the couch in the basement, in the middle of the night Beth had visited Dee, and they had spent the morning hours in a magically intimate exploration of each other.

And then Dee moved in. She had texted her father to let him know she was safe. He had told her he loved her.

And after a week, Dee returned home. Mimi and Dee danced around each other, ignoring each other, playing a game both knew was going to end badly, worse than what had happened at the warehouse, but neither ready to confront or to acknowledge. Or to fully commit to the game.

Abbie watches as the gallery starts to fill. The crowd a commingling of diverse factions. He watches Etienne de Bosch and Andrea

Dankiewicz hover before the artwork, performing last-minute things, the final photo having been hung less than an hour ago. The smaller photos line the stairway and cover the walls upstairs. The placement of everything is careful, precise. Etienne had tried to explain the challenge of a show where the subject matter in every piece is the same. Because, with his work, the composition of every photo is similar, the fruit, the chimney, the sky. Sometimes the sky is blue. Sometimes there is sunshine. Sometimes sunshine bursts forth and interrupts the mass of the chimney. Sometimes the fruit remains in colour while the objects in the background are black and white. Sometimes the fruit are replaced by Ping-Pong balls. Sometimes the chimneys are in colour with everything else in black and white. Sometimes everything is in colour except the chimney.

Etienne tried to explain all of this and created a narrative, somehow, out of nothing, at least Abbie thought it was nothing, but then the themes surrounding his work became about change. Andrea had written an essay about the changing world, about how these photos held up a mirror to changing socio-economic and gender-based realities, about demographics and labour, about class, about the past but also about the future. Abbie learned about perception and expectation and art and commerce from reading an essay that was both about and above his work.

There is nothing written by or about Abbie. Etienne has decided to call the show *Blowing Smoke*: "It's childish and I know it and that's why I'm doing it." Andrea had approved of the title, and Abbie felt at ease, because he trusted her, for reasons he didn't understand. Abbie let the adults lead him because, so far, they had not led him wrong. There was trust and then there was faith, and Abbie was now understanding the difference.

The crowd swells and spills out into the backyard, but Abbie's parents are late. The Ayatollah is here with his wife. The bangles around her wrists make a sound like maracas. She seems genuinely enamoured of the photography, stepping close to the photos to study details, textures. Standing behind them both is The Butcher.

Bobby and Mimi make their way into the gallery. "Wow," Bobby says, about everything — the crowd, the grandeur of the event, the work.

He takes in the work and he feels overwhelmed. And diminished. The guilt of hindsight.

Abbie comes rushing toward his parents. Mimi sees him and hugs him tight. She's hugging her child for the last time, she thinks, and she thinks she may cry, but not until later, when her display won't detract from Abbie's accomplishment, perhaps she will be alone, staring at herself in the mirror, but she will cry, she knows it. Eventually. Then Abbie moves to his father.

Bobby hugs his son, still looking at the gallery, at the people, and then he sees Leopard Lady, and he registers a range of things: shock and despair and nerves and anger. He kisses his son on the head. "This is great," he says, keeping an eye on his old nemesis, and wondering if he should be civil and let it go. Abbie releases his father, and Bobby decides to ignore her, because that's what he should have thought in the first place, that she is the past, his past, and will live there forever, except that she's here.

"I'd like you guys to meet someone," Abbie says, taking his mother by the hand, toward the bar, toward Etienne, who is shooting back a flute of champagne and ready to head out back for a cigarette. "Etienne de Bosch, I'd like you to meet my parents," he says.

Etienne's mouth opens wide with joy. "Well, well," he says, taking Bobby's hand and giving it a vigorous shake. He then turns to Mimi and throws his arms wide open and she falls into him, as if feeling the gravitational pull of this man wearing multiple scarves on an unseasonably warm day, and he hugs her with force, and love, and she feels affection from this person. "It's an honour," Etienne says, letting Mimi free. "I'm so very honoured to meet you both."

"Etienne is the owner of the gallery," Abbie tells his parents.

"Thank you," Mimi says. "For everything you've done."

"Oh, please." Etienne reaches for two glasses of champagne and hands them to Bobby and Mimi. "But I accept your thanks and your eternal gratitude." Then he takes two more and hands one to Abbie. "I want to propose a toast," Etienne says, raising his glass.

Mimi and Bobby and Abbie raise their glasses. "To Abena Reed," Etienne announces, loudly enough that anyone near them stops to watch the proceedings. "And to his parents. They have created a man. And today, we witness the creation of an artist."

There is applause and then a surge toward Abbie, and Etienne sees this and takes his protégé by the hand. "Excuse us," he says, and they are on the stairs and heading up. Strangers approach Mimi and Bobby and congratulate them and light emanates from Mimi, pure light, she could light the world with her pride. And Bobby catches a glimpse of Leopard Lady again and excuses himself and makes his way toward her.

Andrea sees Roberto Reed making his way toward her. "Hello," she says to him, holding out her hand. Bobby tries to calibrate his feelings. He realizes she has no idea that Abbie is his son. It's not as if his son looks anything like him.

"The surprise is all mine," Bobby says.

"I just figured out you're Abbie's father."

"It's like we're an answer to a trick question," he says. Bobby tries not to revert to type, something he knows he's given up, that lizard brain; an image from *The Elephant Man* flashes through his mind, *I'm not an animal!* he hears, because he's not, he needs to relax, Andrea is the past, and he's working with his wife, he's building a life with her, again, a second life. He resists the urge to devolve. To revisit. "How do you know my son?" he asks.

"I'm on the board here," Andrea says. "I kind of found Abbie. I won't say discovered, but I followed him on social media, and then when I moved here I became involved with this gallery and I suggested Etienne take a look at Abbie's work." Bobby feels like he needs to sit down. He's not sure what kind of expression he's projecting, but he's sure it's not friendly. He imagines he looks like he just shit his pants. "And here we are," she says.

"Here we are."

"You don't have to look that surprised," she says.

"I used to call you Leopard Lady," he says.

She laughs. "Really?"

"I barely remembered your name. But your shoes. They stood out. Leopard Lady."

"I didn't fire you," she says.

"You had a hand in it."

"The decision was made before I moved here."

"It's why you came to Montreal."

"You want more champagne?" Andrea asks.

"Don't change the subject."

"It was all Lamontagne," she says. "And HQ."

"Come on."

"They've been purging your level of management all over the company. I was promoted to something like your job. I don't expect I'll be there for long."

"They don't relocate people to fire them. It's too expensive."

"Maybe. But firing you was expensive too. So, the expense part doesn't seem to bother them."

He looks at his champagne glass again. "Okay, I'll have another."

Andrea takes the empty flute from Bobby and walks toward the bar. Bobby is now in the centre of the gallery, surrounded by his son's work, admirers, and friends, by a manifestation of a success, on some level, and Bobby smiles, he lets the past go, because he's happy, he has to admit this now, he's happy, he's working with his wife, and they are closer than ever, and the house has achieved a kind of equilibrium, despite the tension between his wife and daughter, but at least they are not yelling or hissing, and that is going to have to run its course, he's not sure how that is going to end. But it will get resolved. Because in this family, he thinks, we resolve things. Eventually.

Andrea returns with two flutes of champagne, and Bobby accepts one. "Thanks," he says.

She raises her glass. "To Abbie," she offers. "You made an artist."

Their glasses come together. Bobby takes a deep sip of the champagne — he doesn't like champagne much, but that's all there seems to be.

He has travelled, in his own way, to this place. He is drinking a glass of champagne with the woman who fired him, and he realizes he doesn't care. Not anymore. Andrea is a person before him, nothing more. He feels lighter, somehow. An odd sense of relief.

"In about half an hour, Etienne will make a speech, kind of present Abbie to everyone," Andrea says. "We're just waiting for more press to show up."

Bobby had not thought about press. About opening the paper and finding mention of his son inside.

"There's also a bar upstairs," she says. "With booze. And beer. And there's one in the backyard as well." She points toward the door that leads out back. "Though I think that one only offers rosé. And gin and tonics."

"I'm not a huge fan of champagne."

"Me neither. Nor of rosé."

"So I guess we'll meet again upstairs at some point."

"Probably, yes. It was good to see you again. Under better circumstances."

Abbie spots Saul and runs to him and envelops him in a bear hug. "Oh my god, you came."

"There is a bus stop in my neighbourhood. Like just a few blocks away. And it stops in Outremont."

"How are you?

"I miss Montreal."

"How's school?"

"Do you really want to talk about school?" Abbie watches Saul take in the scene. Abbie recalls all the conversations where Saul seemed to believe in this outcome more than he did. Where he saw it as conceivable, and Abbie saw it as silly talk. But perhaps Saul was simply being polite then. Supportive. A friend. He's maybe a bit surprised by this all now.

"You did it."

"I haven't done anything yet," Abbie says. "I'm freaking out, really."

"But look," Saul says. "I told you."

"You did."

"I knew it."

"I have to go to the bathroom," Abbie says, and he hugs Saul again and leaves him and runs to the private bathroom, in the back office, the one that Etienne does not share with anyone, except the artists, not even the board members know of this washroom, it's under the stairs, looks like it's been built for a hobbit, the secret lair of a man who was once a woman and who has travelled the world to construct his own. Abbie closes the door and sits on the toilet, not because he has to use it, but because he has to sit, and he might be sick, he has to sit here away from the crowd outside and take this in, accept what is happening, he has to finally decide whether or not this is what he wants, forever, if this is the start of a long road, to what he doesn't know; it's not that uncertainty is new, it's that this is a different kind of uncertainty, the kind that results from a choice, and every choice, suddenly, feels important, full of direction. Full of purpose.

Maybe I should take a shit, he thinks; he tries to imagine this, and he finds the idea oddly transgressive, as if nature abhors evacuation, which it doesn't, it lives on it — crapping is life, it's life and death, the circle, rejection and the opposite of rejection. And then he stands up and stares at himself in the mirror; he wants to do something dramatic like slap himself and watch his cheek glow with pain, or punch the mirror and maybe cut his knuckles, but both ideas are silly, he realizes this, he's thought this all through. He thinks, life begins now, think of all the people who helped put you here. He feels like a boxer about to get in the ring, he remembers watching *Rocky* with his father, another movie he loved, and his father telling him he travelled to Philadelphia just to run up those steps at the museum, just to do what Rocky did, and then he discovered cheesesteak sandwiches.

Okay, he thinks, okay, let's do this. And then he leans his head on the mirror, and closes his eyes, and worries about the reaction, he worries about the people who won't like his work; *it's not art*, they'll say, *why are they showing this idiot's photos of chimneys and fruit?* Man Ray didn't do what he did just so Abbie Reed could take snapshots of smokestacks and post them online.

He feels as if this is all the result of some kind of odd luck that he doesn't deserve. And what happens when that luck runs out? What if it runs out today? And then he feels sick again, a low-grade nausea. His forehead feels clammy. In the mirror, he realizes he looks pale, a bit faded. Bleached.

The door opens behind him. He opens his eyes and sees Etienne, smiling like a man who has just found out that the Nigerian prince is real and he is about to become a multi-millionaire. "Oh, crippling self-doubt!" he says.

"I don't know," Abbie says.

"You are such an artist, it's not even funny."

"I don't know."

"If you haven't thrown up, you're fine. The comments out there are fantastic. You're good. Let's go."

"I'm thinking of throwing up." Abbie's head remains on the mirror.

"You have done fantastic work. You are being launched into outer space."

"I've thought about it more than once. And shitting too. Puking and shitting."

"That's lovely."

"I don't feel like I'm old enough for this."

"Come on."

"Like I'm a fraud or something."

"We're all frauds. Every single one of us."

"I'm being serious."

"So am I." Etienne reaches for Abbie and turns him around. "What you're feeling is normal. I understand. But when people, complete strangers, tell you your work is good, you have to be smart enough to believe them. Your age doesn't matter. We have a few hundred people out there. And they're drinking all the booze."

Abbie wants to feel better. Or perhaps he doesn't. Perhaps he's just realized he likes not interacting with people. "Let them drink booze," he says.

"You're not old enough to get the joke you just made." Etienne slaps Abbie's bum. "Come on."

"Marie Antoinette."

"Show-off."

"I'm old enough."

"So you are," Etienne says, drawing out each syllable, pushing the symbolism of his response to kindergarten-level understanding. He smiles coyly. Because he needs to get Abbie out there. Etienne pushes Abbie toward the door of the office. He closes the door to the private washroom. "I used to do a lot of coke in there, when I used to do a lot of coke," he says. He opens the door to the gallery. "You won't have to make a speech," he whispers. "Follow me."

And then Bobby appears at the door. He'd followed Abbie's rush to the bathroom and then Etienne and now he's here. "Is everything alright?" he asks.

"He's amazing," Etienne says. "He's realizing things."

"Give us a moment," Bobby says.

"Quickly," Etienne says, pointing to the invisible watch on his wrist. He closes the door behind him.

"Dad."

"Abbie."

Bobby's son feels like he might cry at this moment. He feels alone. Small.

"When we first saw you, your mother cried. She just exploded. She fell in a kind of love with you. I think she had never felt that level of love before. I was sick. I was already sick. We'd had one meal in Ghana, and it was enough. My constitution sucks."

"Dad . . ."

"I just . . ." Bobby does not know why he is in here. He was worried. "I just wanted to say, this thing, this journey, ending up here, in a gallery. I would never have imagined it."

"Me neither."

Etienne knocks on the door. "Gentlemen, please!" he yells.

"And I wanted to —"

Abbie knows his father is going to apologize and he'd rather not hear it. There is nothing to apologize for. "Dad, don't."

"I love you," Bobby says. "And, wow. I'm proud of you."

The door swings open and hits Bobby. Etienne takes Abbie's hand and leads him to the first photo. It's one Saul had objected to, and it is full of sunlight, the timing was just right, Abbie remembers, the sun just behind the smokestack, sunbursts everywhere, the amount of life in this photo, the emptiness of the fields around, and then the oranges — this is the perfect photo, it really is, and Jacques was right to make it the largest and brightest one. That Abbie had shot it overexposed was, in hindsight, kind of genius, even Jacques had said that, he had said it showed something, that Abbie knew, even if he didn't, but he did it, and it turned out, and now he's standing in front of this radiant image, and Etienne says, "Stand here," and then he leaves, he runs into the crowd, and Abbie does not move, because where would he go?

Abbie is disappointed Saul is not beside him.

Mimi watches Etienne make his way through the crowd. And then she watches him stop and speak to the Khalili brothers, and her heart misses something, more than a beat, and she searches for Bobby, but he's disappeared, and she thinks of all the nefarious reasons why both The Ayatollah and The Butcher are here, and she can't think of any. She makes her way toward them, to register her surprise if nothing else.

Etienne sees her approach and smiles broadly. "Mimi Reed!" he exclaims, about to make introductions, and then the Khalili brothers turn and face her, and The Ayatollah smiles so slyly that Mimi thinks perhaps she's being set up.

"We are acquaintances," The Ayatollah says.

"This is such a small city," Etienne says.

"Imagine my surprise," Mimi says.

The Ayatollah takes his wife's hand and presents her. "This is my wife, Shadi."

"A pleasure, Mrs. Khalili," Mimi says.

"Shadi."

"Shadi."

"Your son's work is lovely," she says.

Mimi cannot imagine for a moment that The Ayatollah appreciates art.

"We collect art, to answer your question," he says. "My brother is more orthodox in his tastes. He's not so much into contemporary art and he despises photography."

"*Despise* is a very strong word," The Butcher says.

"I, on the other hand, am very much a collector of contemporary art, regardless of form or media. My wife derives great pleasure. I appreciate the tax implications. However, when Monsieur de Bosch told me about this, and who it was, I thought I should come. I genuinely enjoy supporting local artists who show promise. Your son interests me with his internet and such."

"You have good taste," Etienne says; sincerely, Mimi notes.

"We bought three of them," Shadi whispers, with the glee of a child.

Mimi needs to run screaming through an open field. She needs to perhaps check her pulse and see if it is anywhere close to normal. She wants to check on the colour of the sky. "I'm surprised, as you can tell," she manages.

"Our relationship is limited," The Ayatollah says, and at this The Butcher laughs.

That is fair, she thinks. She also dislikes how much she has underestimated him. How much she could have never imagined this outcome. This moment.

"Abbie doesn't know anything has sold yet," Etienne says, "so please don't tell him."

"Your son is to be congratulated," The Ayatollah says.

"I know," Mimi says. She doesn't even know the price of her son's work, but here are the Khalili brothers, art patrons. Investing in Abbie. Her son has an income. She feels like a failure and a success all at once. She feels like Abbie has allowed her to become something else. To feel a part of something larger. Surrounded by people here to celebrate her son's work. "Excuse me," she says. "And thank you, again." And she leaves them to find Bobby, because she must speak to someone who is not going to surprise her like this, and to tell him what she has seen and heard and who she has seen, and she needs to make sure the world is still the same.

Dee attempts to order gin and tonics, and after much wrangling, she manages it, she's convinced the bartender it's for her brother, and she takes a drink to Beth.

"I'm not a fan," Beth says.

"Of what?"

"Booze."

Andrea opens the door to the yard. "Etienne de Bosch is going to say a few words, if anyone's interested," she announces.

"Should I go in?" Dee asks. She takes another sip of her drink. "It's not like he'll even see me."

But she realizes she should watch her brother become something. Because that's what's happening here. Her brother is becoming something, and in so doing something basic about her family is changing, because Abbie is now no longer just her brother but something else, a photographer, an artist, she doesn't know what to call him. He's another word. She should bear witness.

"Let's go," Beth says, taking Dee by the hand. And Dee lets Beth lead her, she allows herself to follow. She leans into Beth and she releases her hand and puts it behind Beth's back, and they wait by the door as the guests of this thing make their way inside the gallery to watch the consecration.

Bobby notes his daughter as she steps inside the gallery, and they make eye contact, and he smiles, but she does not, she merely acknowledges him, because her eyes are now on her mother, and Bobby is cast aside by history, and so he shrugs, to show her that he doesn't understand and he hopes she finds it endearing, but then a buzz surrounds the room, someone has tapped the mic, and the crowd shifts, and he loses sight of his daughter, and then he hears a voice and his attention is once again directed toward the centre, to the place where Abbie is, the sun of this room.

Etienne stands by the first photo. Behind him, the essay, looming like a monolith, words assembled to introduce and distill and speak truth. A tablet. Abbie stands beside Etienne, his hands in his pockets. He's been thinking of his hands and what to do with them. He wants to stand still, but he realizes he's swaying slightly, back and forth, and the more he wants to stop, the more he realizes he's swaying, a well-engineered building during an earthquake, he knows he won't topple over.

Around the two of them, photographers, writers, and journalists with pens and pads, phones set to record, electronic microphones. A half-dozen or so, lonely looking, haggard. Andrea stands behind the media, with the crowd, and Abbie can't tell if she looks like an expectant mother or father, because she can't be both, and he's leaning toward father. Etienne taps the microphone again, which is universal, that booming tap, and with it a hush settles over the gallery like the ash from a distant volcano, and then there is silence.

"Thank you," Etienne says. "Thank you all for coming. Today, we are very excited to present a brilliant young artist. An artist who has come to us in a thoroughly contemporary way. Via the internet." He pauses to let the idea resonate and for the rumbles of appreciative laughter to subside. "Abena Reed. Abbie. A young Montrealer documenting a changing city."

Etienne pauses, a smirk on his face. Abbie can tell Etienne's as surprised as he is that the gallery is full. More than full.

"I understand that all cities are complicated. Layered. Places that document change. That's why they intrigue us and why we put up with them. Abbie documents this. The layers. Of the built environment. And, quite simply, he comments on these layers in a manner that is transcendent. Because you think it is simple. And then it's not. And we are lucky to have someone like Abbie among us."

He pats Abbie on the back, and then the sound of applause rises throughout the gallery, and Abbie appears genuinely moved, because he is, he's suddenly in the moment, and realizing how his future has just begun, with Etienne's hand on his back, with the applause, the photographers taking photos of a photographer. Etienne hands the mic to Abbie, but Abbie can't think of anything to say. The applause continues to rise, gaining elevation. Abbie seeks out his parents but can't find them, there are too many people. He waves to the crowd. He sees Saul, alone in a corner, his face contorted by a giant smile. He spies his sister near the door to the backyard, leaning into Beth, drinking something, a cocktail for sure, and their eyes meet, and he shrugs, and she blows him a kiss.

Abbie doesn't know how humble he should appear. He's unaware of his persona, of the public's perception of him, now that they've seen his work, and he wonders. He brings the mic up to his face and decides he has nothing to say. He would rather say nothing than say something meaningless. His work is on the walls, surrounding them all, and he decides Etienne has said enough. "Thank you for coming," he says. He returns the mic to Etienne and the applause rises again.

From a far corner near the entrance, Bobby and Mimi take it all in. They can barely see their son. They listen to the sustained applause, and it overwhelms them. Bobby takes Mimi's hand and squeezes. He thinks about things he may have regretted in the past, parental regrets, things he never did and hasn't done, and he senses them as they vanish, as if by magic, gone in a puff of smoke. Bobby and Mimi. Husband and wife. Best friends. Business partners. Parents. They watch as the small pool of photographers surges toward their son like an incoming tide. The Photographer. The Artist. He is surrounded now. By photographers and media and admirers and his work. The pathetic reporters rush in behind the photographers and start crowding recording devices about Abbie's face.

Bobby and Mimi watch the clamour around their son. They watch with pride and affection and love. With a certain level of astonishment. They watch as the world attempts to record the moment their son is transformed. Born and reborn. Remade.

Thank you

The road to publication is necessarily long, and in the case of this book, it was longer still, perhaps unnecessarily so.

Thanks to Sophie, and then Dean and Paige, who tried and tried, and still improved the thing along the way.

Thanks to Matt and Jay and Chef, and the boys competing for the Steinberg Cup, and to Ad, your absence still feels impossible.

Cecil and Miriam: I feel the loss every single day.

Thanks to Jack and Emily and Samantha and Rachel and anyone who touched this thing (the entire crew at ECW) for fighting the good fight in so many ways and for the finished product. And making everything better.

Thanks to Jo, Karine, Jaya, Lily, and Max, who were all much younger when I started this.

Thanks to Ma — I am grateful for the journey we've taken together and I love you.

And thanks to Naomi, who makes me whole and then some, and to Milo, who was awesome when I started writing this book, and who has grown into something even more awesome.

MILO BASU

Arjun Basu is the author of the Giller-longlisted *Waiting for the Man* (ECW Press). He loves bourbon and plays beer league hockey very poorly. A former magazine editor, he owns his own brand and content consultancy and is the host of *The Full-Bleed*, a podcast about the future of magazines. He lives with his wife in Montreal.

arjunbasu.com

@arjunbasu

@arjun.bsky.social

Entertainment. Writing. Culture.

ECW is a proudly independent, Canadian-owned book publisher. We know great writing can improve people's lives, and we're passionate about sharing original, exciting, and insightful writing across genres.

Thanks for reading along!

We want our books not just to sustain our imaginations, but to help construct a healthier, more just world, and so we've become a certified B Corporation, meaning we meet a high standard of social and environmental responsibility — and we're going to keep aiming higher. We believe books can drive change, but the way we make them can too.

Being a B Corp means that the act of publishing this book should be a force for good – for the planet, for our communities, and for the people that worked to make this book. For example, everyone who worked on this book was paid at least a living wage. You can learn more at the Ontario Living Wage Network.

This book is also available as a Global Certified Accessible™ (GCA) ebook. ECW Press's ebooks are screen reader friendly and are built to meet the needs of those who are unable to read standard print due to blindness, low vision, dyslexia, or a physical disability.

The interior of this book is printed on Sustana EnviroPrint, which is made from 100% recycled fibres and processed chlorine-free.

ECW's office is situated on land that was the traditional territory of many nations including the Wendat, the Anishnaabeg, Haudenosaunee, Chippewa, Métis, and current treaty holders the Mississaugas of the Credit. In the 1880s, the land was developed as part of a growing community around St. Matthew's Anglican and other churches. Starting in the 1950s, our neighbourhood was transformed by immigrants fleeing the Vietnam War and Chinese Canadians dispossessed by the building of Nathan Phillips Square and the subsequent rise in real estate value in other Chinatowns. We are grateful to those who cared for the land before us and are proud to be working amidst this mix of cultures.

ecwpress.com